"KEEP THE LIGHT on," Caine said.

Sam could keep the light burning. That he could do. Light.

His heart was a rusty, dying engine, hammering like it would fly apart. His body was scalded iron, hot, stiff, impossible to move.

The pain . . .

It was at him now, a roaring tiger that ripped him with every step, tore at his mind, shredded his self-control. He couldn't live with it. Too terrible.

"Come on, Sam," Duck said in his ear.

"Aahhhh!" Sam cried out.

"So much for sneaking up on it," Caine said.

The Darkness knows we're here, Sam thought. No sneaking. No tricking. It knew. Sam could feel it. Like cold fingers prodding his mind, poking, looking for an opening.

This is hell, Sam thought. This is hell.

HUN

KATHERINE TEGEN BOOKS

An Imprint of HarperCollins Publishers

GER

A GONE Novel

MICHAEL GRANT

OTHER *GONE* BOOKS BY MICHAEL GRANT:

Gone

Lies

Plague

Fear

Light

Katherine Tegen Books is an imprint of HarperCollins Publishers.

Hunger: A Gone Novel

Library of Congress Cataloging-in-Publication Data
Grant, Michael.
    Hunger : a Gone novel / Michael Grant. — 1st ed.
        p.   cm.
    "Katherine Tegen books."
    Summary: Conditions worsen for the remaining young residents of a small Cali-
fornia coastal town isolated by supernatural events when their food supplies dwindle
and the Darkness underground awakens.
    ISBN 978-0-06-144908-6
        [1. Supernatural—Fiction.   2. Good and evil—Fiction.   3. Survival—
Fiction.   4. Horror stories.]   I. Title.
PZ7.G7671Hu 2009   2008036465
[Fic]—dc22   CIP
                                                                    AC

Typography by Joel Tippie
19   20   PC/LSCH   20
❖
Revised paperback edition, 2014

For Katherine, Jake, and Julia

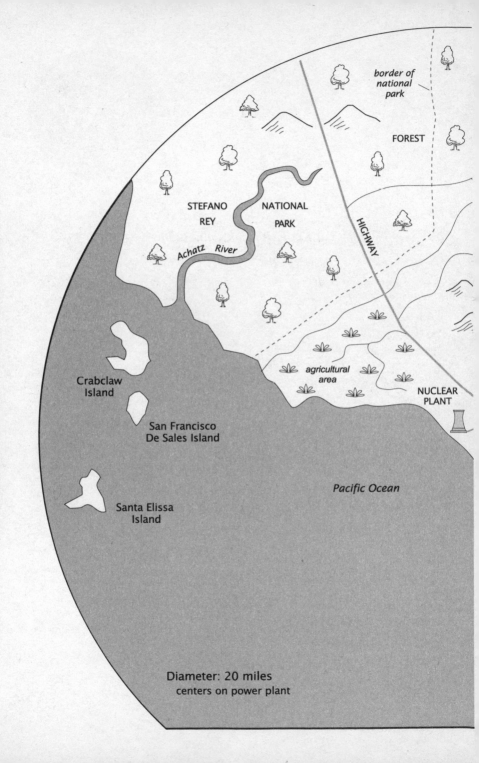

border of national park

FOREST

STEFANO REY NATIONAL PARK

Achatz River

HIGHWAY

Crabclaw Island

San Francisco De Sales Island

Santa Elissa Island

agricultural area

NUCLEAR PLANT

Pacific Ocean

Diameter: 20 miles
centers on power plant

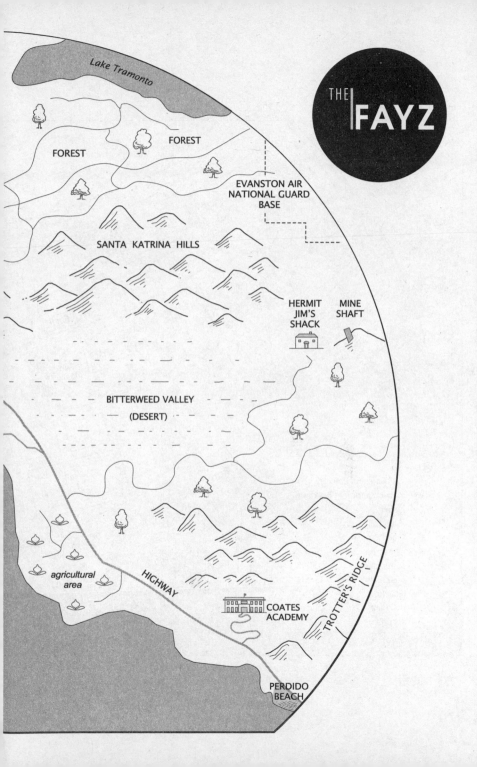

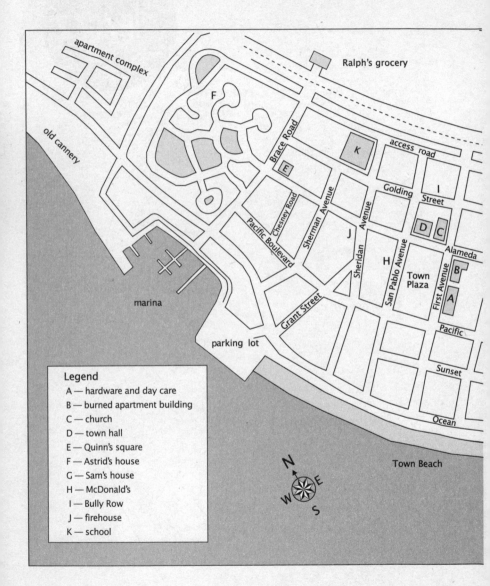

apartment complex

Ralph's grocery

old cannery

F

Brace Road

access road

K

E

Golding

I

Street

Chesney Road

Pacific Boulevard

Sherman Avenue

Sheridan Avenue

D

C

J

Alameda

H

San Pablo Avenue

B

marina

Town Plaza

First Avenue

A

Grant Street

Pacific

parking lot

Sunset

Ocean

Legend
A — hardware and day care
B — burned apartment building
C — church
D — town hall
E — Quinn's square
F — Astrid's house
G — Sam's house
H — McDonald's
I — Bully Row
J — firehouse
K — school

N
E
W
S

Town Beach

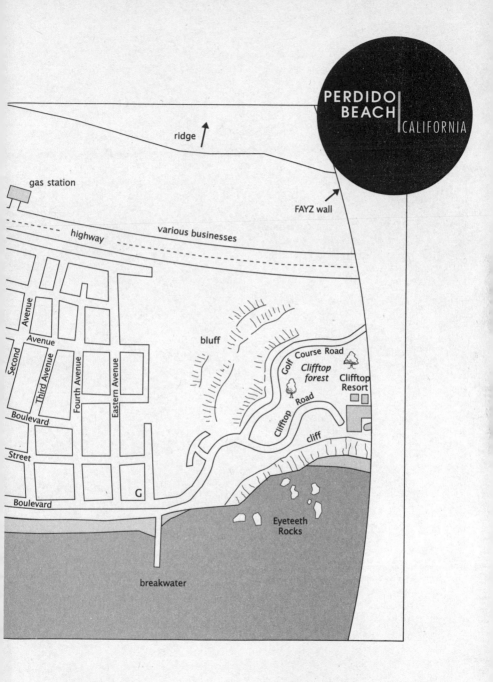

ridge

PERDIDO
BEACH CALIFORNIA

gas station

FAYZ wall

highway   various businesses

Avenue

Second Avenue

Third Avenue

Fourth Avenue

Eastern Avenue

bluff

Golf Course Road

Clifftop
forest

Clifftop
Resort

Boulevard

Clifftop Road

cliff

Street

Boulevard

G

Eyeteeth
Rocks

breakwater

ONE

SAM TEMPLE WAS on his board. And there were waves. Honest-to-God swooping, crashing, churning, salt-smelling, white-foam waves.

And there he was about two hundred feet out, the perfect place to catch a wave, lying facedown, hands and feet in the water, almost numb from cold, while at the same time his wet-suit-encased, sunbaked back was steaming.

Quinn was there, too, lolling beside him, waiting for a good ride, waiting for the wave that would pick them up and hurl them toward the beach.

Sam woke suddenly, choking on dust.

He blinked and looked around at the dry landscape. Instinctively he glanced toward the southwest, toward the ocean. Couldn't see it from here. And there hadn't been a wave in a long time.

Sam believed he'd sell his soul to ride just one more real wave.

He backhanded the sweat from his brow. The sun was like

a blowtorch, way too hot for this early in the day. He'd had too little sleep. Too much stuff to deal with. Stuff. Always stuff.

The heat, the sound of the engine, and the rhythmic jerking of the Jeep as it labored down the dusty road conspired to force his eyelids closed again. He squeezed them shut, hard, then opened them wide, willing himself to stay awake.

The dream stayed with him. The memory taunted him. He could stand it all so much better, he told himself, the constant fear, the even more constant load of trivia and responsibility, if there were still waves. But there had been no waves for three months. No waves at all, nothing but ripples.

Three months after the coming of the FAYZ, Sam had still not learned to drive a car. Learning to drive would have been one more thing, one more hassle, one more pain in the butt. So Edilio Escobar drove the Jeep, and Sam rode shotgun. In the backseat Albert Hillsborough sat stiff and quiet. Beside him was a kid named E.Z., singing along to his iPod.

Sam pushed his fingers through his hair, which was way too long. He hadn't had a haircut in more than three months. His hand came back dirty, clotted with dust. Fortunately the electricity was still on in Perdido Beach, which meant light, and perhaps better still, hot water. If he couldn't go for a cold surf, he could at least look forward to a long, hot shower after they all got back.

A shower. Maybe a few minutes with Astrid, just the two of them. A meal. Well, not a meal, no. A can of something slimy was not a meal. His hurried breakfast had been a can of collard greens.

It was amazing what you could gag down when you got hungry enough. And Sam, like everyone else in the FAYZ, was hungry.

He closed his eyes, not sleepy now, just wanting to see Astrid's face clearly.

It was the one compensation. He'd lost his mother, his favorite pastime, his privacy, his freedom, and the entire world he'd known . . . but he'd gained Astrid.

Before the FAYZ he'd always thought of her as unapproachable. Now, as a couple, they seemed inevitable. But he wondered whether he'd have ever done more than gaze wistfully from afar if the FAYZ hadn't happened.

Edilio applied a little brake. The road ahead was torn up. Someone had gouged the dirt road, drawn rough angled lines across it.

Edilio pointed to a tractor set up to pull a plow. The tractor was overturned in the middle of a field. On the day the FAYZ came the farmer had disappeared, along with the rest of the adults, but the tractor had kept right on going, tearing up the road, running straight into the next field, stopping only when an irrigation ditch had tipped it over.

Edilio took the Jeep over the furrows at a crawl, then picked up speed again.

There wasn't much to the left or right of the road, just bare dirt, fallow fields, and patches of colorless grass broken up by the occasional lonely stand of trees. But up ahead was green, lots of it.

Sam turned in his seat to get Albert's attention. "So what is that up there, again?"

"Cabbage," Albert said. Albert was an eighth grader, narrow-shouldered, self-contained; dressed in pressed khaki pants, a pale blue polo shirt, and brown loafers—what a much older person would call "business casual." He was a kid no one had paid much attention to before, just one of a handful of African-American students at the Perdido Beach School. But no one ignored Albert anymore: he had reopened and run the town's McDonald's. At least he had until the burgers and the fries and the chicken nuggets ran out.

Even the ketchup. That was gone now, too.

The mere memory of hamburgers made Sam's stomach growl. "Cabbage?" he repeated.

Albert nodded toward Edilio. "That's what Edilio says. He's the one who found it yesterday."

"Cabbage?" Sam asked Edilio.

"It makes you fart," Edilio said with a wink. "But we can't be too choosy."

"I guess it wouldn't be so bad if we had coleslaw," Sam said. "Tell you the truth, I could happily eat a cabbage right now."

"You know what I had for breakfast?" Edilio asked. "A can of succotash."

"What exactly is succotash?" Sam asked.

"Lima beans and corn. Mixed together." Edilio braked at the edge of the field. "Not exactly fried eggs and sausage."

"Is that the official Honduran breakfast?" Sam asked.

Edilio snorted. "Man, the official Honduran breakfast when you're poor is a corn tortilla, some leftover beans, and on a good day a banana. On a bad day it's just the tortilla." He killed the engine and set the emergency brake. "This isn't my first time being hungry."

Sam stood up in the Jeep and stretched before jumping to the ground. He was a naturally athletic kid but in no way physically intimidating. He had brown hair with glints of gold, blue eyes, and a tan that reached all the way down to his bones. Maybe he was a little taller than average, maybe in a little better shape, but no one would pick him for a future in the NFL.

Sam Temple was one of the two oldest people in the FAYZ. He was fifteen.

"Hey. That looks like lettuce," E.Z. said, wrapping his earbuds carefully around his iPod.

"If only," Sam said gloomily. "So far we have avocados, that's fine, and cantaloupes, which is excellent news. But we are finding way too much broccoli and artichokes. Lots of artichokes. Now cabbage."

"We may get the oranges back eventually," Edilio said. "The trees looked okay. It was just the fruit was ripe and didn't get picked, so they rotted."

"Astrid says things are ripening at weird times," Sam said. "Not normal."

"As Quinn likes to say, 'We're a long way from normal,'" Edilio said.

"Who's going to pick all these?" Sam wondered aloud. It was what Astrid would have called a rhetorical question.

Albert started to say something, then stopped himself when E.Z. said, "Hey, I'll go grab one of these cabbages right now. I'm starving." He unwound the earbuds and stuck them back in.

The cabbages were a foot or so apart within their rows, and each row was two feet from the next. The soil in between was crumbled and dry. The cabbages looked more like thick-leafed houseplants than like something you might actually eat.

It didn't look much different from a dozen other fields Sam had seen during this farm tour.

No, Sam corrected himself, there *is* something different. He couldn't quite figure out what it was, but there was something different here. Sam frowned and tried to work through the feeling he was having, tried to decide why he felt something was . . . off.

It was quieter, maybe.

Sam took a swig from a water bottle. He heard Albert counting under his breath, shading his eyes with his hand and multiplying. "Totally just a ballpark guess, figuring each cabbage weighs maybe a pound and a half, right? I'm thinking we have ourselves maybe thirty thousand pounds of cabbage."

"I don't even want to think about how many farts this all translates to," E.Z. yelled over his shoulder as he marched purposefully into the field.

E.Z. was a sixth grader but seemed older. He was tall for his age, a little chubby. Thin, dishwater-blond hair hung down to his shoulders. He was wearing a Hard Rock Cafe T-shirt from Cancún. E.Z. was a good name for him: he was easy to get along with, would banter easily, laugh easily, and usually find whatever fun there was to be found. He stopped about two dozen rows into the field and said, "This looks like the cabbage for me."

"How can you tell?" Edilio called back.

E.Z. pulled one earbud out and Edilio repeated the question.

"I'm tired of walking. This must be the right cabbage. How do I pick it?"

Edilio shrugged. "Man, I think you may need a knife."

"Nah." E.Z. replaced the earbud, bent over, and yanked at the plant. He got a handful of leaves for his effort.

"You see what I'm saying," Edilio commented.

"Where are the birds?" Sam asked, finally figuring out what was bothering him.

"What birds?" Edilio said. Then he nodded. "You're right, man, there've been seagulls all over the other fields. Especially in the morning."

Perdido Beach had quite a population of seagulls. In the old days they had lived off bits of bait left by fishermen and food scraps dropped near trash cans. There were no more food scraps in the FAYZ. Not anymore. So the enterprising gulls had gone into the fields to compete with crows and pigeons. One of the reasons so much of the food they'd found was spoiled.

"They must not like cabbage," Albert commented. He sighed. "I don't honestly know anyone who does."

E.Z. squatted down before the cabbage, rubbed his hands

in preparation, worked them down beneath the leaves, down to cradle the cabbage. Then he fell back on his rear end. "Ow!" he yelled.

"Not so easy, is it?" Edilio teased.

"Ah! Ah!" E.Z. jumped to his feet. He was holding his right hand with his left and staring hard at his hand. "No, no, no."

Sam had been only half listening. His mind was elsewhere, scanning for the missing birds, but the terror in E.Z.'s voice snapped his head around. "What's the matter?"

"Something bit me!" E.Z. cried. "Oh, oh, it hurts. It hurts. It—" E.Z. let loose a scream of agony. The scream started low and went higher, higher into hysteria.

Sam saw what looked like a black question mark on E.Z.'s pant leg.

"Snake!" Sam said to Edilio.

E.Z.'s arm went into a spasm. It shook violently. It was as if some invisible giant had hold of it and were yanking his arm as hard and as fast as it could.

E.Z. screamed and screamed and began a lunatic dance. "They're in my feet!" he cried. "They're in my feet!"

Sam stood paralyzed for a few seconds, just a few seconds— but later in memory it would seem so long. Too long.

He leaped forward, rushing toward E.Z. He was brought down hard by a flying tackle from Edilio.

"What are you doing?" Sam demanded, and struggled to free himself.

"Man, look. Look!" Edilio whispered.

Sam's face was mere feet from the first row of cabbages.

The soil was alive. Worms. Worms as big as garter snakes were seething up from beneath the dirt. Dozens. Maybe hundreds. All heading toward E.Z., who screamed again and again in agony mixed with confusion.

Sam rose to his feet but went no closer to the edge of the cabbage field. The worms did not move beyond the first row of turned soil. There might as well have been a wall, the worms all on one side.

E.Z. came staggering wildly toward Sam, walking as if he were being electrocuted, jerking, flailing like some crazy puppet with half its strings cut.

Three, four feet away, a long arm-stretch away, Sam saw the worm erupt from the skin of E.Z.'s throat.

And then another from his jaw, just in front of his ear.

E.Z., no longer screaming, sagged to the ground, just sat there limp, cross-legged.

"Help me," E.Z. whispered. "Sam . . ."

E.Z.'s eyes were on Sam. Pleading. Fading. Then just staring, blank.

The only sounds now came from the worms. Their hundreds of mouths seemed to make a single sound, one big mouth chewing wetly.

A worm spilled from E.Z.'s mouth.

Sam raised his hands, palms out.

"Sam, no!" Albert yelled. Then, in a quieter voice, "He's already dead. He's already dead."

"Albert's right, man. Don't do it, don't burn them, they're staying in the field, don't give them a reason to come after us,"

Edilio hissed. His strong hands still dug into Sam's shoulders, like he was holding Sam back, though Sam wasn't trying to escape any longer.

"And don't touch him," Edilio sobbed. "*Perdóneme*, God forgive me, don't touch him."

The black worms swarmed over and through E.Z.'s body. Like ants swarming a dead beetle.

It felt like a very long time before the worms slithered away and tunneled back into the earth.

What they left behind was no longer recognizable as a human being.

"There's a rope here," Albert said, stepping down at last from the Jeep. He tried to tie a lasso, but his hands were shaking too badly. He handed the rope to Edilio, who formed a loop and after six misses finally snagged what was left of E.Z.'s right foot. Together they dragged the remains from the field.

A single tardy worm crawled from the mess and headed back toward the cabbages. Sam snatched up a rock the size of a softball and smashed it down on the worm's back. The worm stopped moving.

"I'll come back with a shovel," Edilio said. "We can't take E.Z. home, man, he's got two little brothers. They don't need to be seeing this. We'll bury him here.

"If these things spread . . . ," Edilio began.

"If they spread to the other fields, we all starve," Albert said.

Sam fought a powerful urge to throw up. E.Z. was mostly

bones now, picked not quite clean. Sam had seen terrible things since the FAYZ began, but nothing this gruesome.

He wiped his hands on his jeans, wanting to hit back, wishing it made sense to blast the field, burn as much of it as he could reach, keep burning it until the worms shriveled and crisped.

But that was food out there.

Sam knelt beside the mess in the dirt. "You were a good kid, E.Z. Sorry. I . . . sorry." There was music, tinny, but recognizable, still coming from E.Z.'s iPod.

Sam lifted the shiny thing and tapped the pause icon.

Then he stood up and kicked the dead worm out of the way. He held his hands out as though he were a minister about to bless the body.

Albert and Edilio knew better. They both backed away.

Brilliant light shot from Sam's palms.

The body burned, crisped, turned black. Bones made loud snapping noises as they cracked from the heat. After a while Sam stopped. What was left behind was ash, a heap of gray and black ashes that could have been the residue of a backyard barbecue.

"There was nothing you could have done, Sam," Edilio said, knowing that look on his friend's face, knowing that gray, haggard look of guilt. "It's the FAYZ, man. It's just the FAYZ."

TWO

THE ROOF WAS on crooked. The blistering bright sun stabbed a ray straight down into Caine's eye through the gap between crumbled wall and sagging roof.

Caine lay on his back, sweating into a pillow that had no case. A dank sheet wrapped around his bare legs, twisted to cover half his naked torso. He was awake again, or at least he thought he was, believed he was.

Hoped he was.

It wasn't his bed. It belonged to an old man named Mose, the groundskeeper for Coates Academy.

Of course Mose was gone. Gone with all the other adults. And all the older kids. Everyone . . . *almost* everyone . . . over the age of fourteen. Gone.

Gone where?

No one knew.

Just gone. Beyond the barrier. Out of the giant fishbowl called the FAYZ. Maybe dead. Maybe not. But definitely gone.

Diana opened the door with a kick. She was carrying a tray and balanced on the tray was a bottle of water and a can of Goya brand garbanzo beans.

"Are you decent?" Diana asked.

He didn't answer. He didn't understand the question.

"Are you covered?" she asked, putting some irritation into her tone. She set the tray on the side table.

Caine didn't bother to answer. He sat up. His head swam as he did. He reached for the water.

"Why is the roof messed up like that? What if it rains?" He was surprised by the sound of his own voice. He was hoarse. His voice had none of its usual persuasive smoothness.

Diana was pitiless. "What are you, stupid now as well as crazy?"

A phantom memory passed through him, leaving him feeling uneasy. "Did I do something?"

"You lifted the roof up."

He turned his hands around to look at his palms. "Did I?"

"Another nightmare," Diana said.

Caine twisted open the bottle and drank. "I remember now. I thought it was crushing me. I thought something was going to step on the house and crush it, squash me under it. So I pushed back."

"Uh-huh. Eat some beans."

"I don't like beans."

"No one likes beans," Diana said. "But this isn't your neighborhood Applebee's. And I'm not your waitress. Beans are what we have. So eat some beans. You need food."

Caine frowned. "How long have I been like this?"

"Like what?" Diana mocked him. "Like a mental patient who can't tell if he's in reality or in a dream?"

He nodded. The smell of the beans was sickening. But he was suddenly hungry. And he remembered now: food was in short supply. Memory was coming back. The mad delusion was fading. He couldn't quite reach normal, but he could see it.

"Three months, give or take a week," Diana said. "We had the big shoot-out in Perdido Beach. You wandered off into the desert with Pack Leader and were gone for three days. When you came back you were pale, dehydrated, and . . . well, like you are."

"Pack Leader." The words, the creature they represented, made Caine wince. Pack Leader, the dominant coyote, the one who had somehow attained a limited sort of speech. Pack Leader, the faithful, fearful servant of . . . of it. Of it. Of the thing in the mine shaft.

The Darkness, they called it.

Caine swayed and before he rolled off the bed, Diana caught him, grabbed his shoulders, kept him up. But then she saw the warning sign in his eyes and muttered a curse and managed to get the wastebasket in front of him just as he vomited.

He didn't produce much. Just a little yellow liquid.

"Lovely," she said, and curled her lip. "On second thought, don't eat any beans. I don't want to see them come back up."

Caine rinsed his mouth with some of the water. "Why are we here? This is Mose's cottage."

"Because you're too dangerous. No one at Coates wants

you around until you get a grip on yourself."

He blinked at another returning memory. "I hurt someone."

"You thought Chunk was some kind of monster. You were yelling a word. Gaiaphage. Then you smacked Chunk through a wall."

"Is he okay?"

"Caine. In the movies a guy can get knocked through a wall and get up like it's no big deal. This wasn't a movie. The wall was brick. Chunk looked like roadkill. Like when a rac- coon gets run over and over and over and keeps getting run over for a couple of days."

The harshness of her words was too much even for Diana herself. She gritted her teeth and said, "Sorry. It wasn't pretty. I never liked Chunk, but it wasn't something I can just forget, okay?"

"I've been kind of out of my mind," Caine said.

Diana wiped angrily at a tear. "Answer the question: Can you give an example of understatement?"

"I think I'm better now," Caine said. "Not all the way bet- ter. Not all the way. But better."

"Well, happy day," Diana said.

For the first time in weeks Caine focused on her face. She was beautiful, Diana Ladris was, with enormous dark eyes and long brown hair and a mouth that defaulted to smirk.

"You could have ended up like Chunk," Caine said. "But you've been taking care of me, anyway."

She shrugged. "It's a hard new world. I have a choice: stick by you, or take my chances with Drake."

"Drake." The name conjured dark images. Dream or reality? "What's Drake doing?"

"Playing junior Caine. Supposedly representing you. Secretly hoping you'll just die, if you ask me. He raided the grocery store and stole some food a few days ago. It's made him almost popular. Kids don't have a lot of judgment when they're hungry."

"And my brother?"

"Sam?"

"I don't have another long-lost brother, do I?"

"Bug's gone into town a couple of times to see what's going on. He says people still have a little food but they're getting worried about it. Especially since Drake's raid. But Sam is totally in charge there."

"Hand me my pants," Caine said.

Diana did as he asked, then ostentatiously turned away as he pulled them on.

"What defenses do they have up?" Caine asked.

"They keep people all over the grocery store now, that's the main thing. Now Ralph's always has four guys with guns sitting on the roof."

Caine nodded. He bit at his thumbnail, an old habit. "How about freaks?"

"They have Dekka and Brianna and Taylor. They have Jack. They may have some other useful freaks, Bug isn't sure. They have Lana to heal people. And Bug thinks they have a kid who can fire some kind of heat wave."

"Like Sam?"

"No. Sam's like a blowtorch. This kid is like a microwave. You don't see any flames or anything. It's just that suddenly your head is cooking like a breakfast burrito in a Kitchen-Aid."

"People are still developing powers," Caine said. "Any here?"

Diana shrugged. "Who knows for sure? Who's going to be crazy enough to tell Drake? Down in town a new mutant gets some respect. Up here? Maybe they get killed."

"Yeah," Caine said. "That was a mistake. Coming down on the freaks, that was a mistake. We need them."

"Plus, in addition to some possible new moofs, Sam's people still have machine guns. And they still have Sam," Diana said. "So how about if we don't do something stupid like try and fight them again?"

"Moofs?"

"Short for mutant. Mutant freaks. Moofs." Diana shrugged. "Moofs, muties, freaks. We're out of food, but we've got plenty of nicknames."

Caine's shirt was laid over the back of a chair. He reached for it, wobbled, and seemed about to fall over. Diana steadied him. He glared at her hand on his arm. "I can walk."

He glanced up and caught sight of his reflection in a mirror over the dresser. He almost didn't recognize himself. Diana was right: He was pale, his cheeks were concave. His eyes seemed too large for his face.

"I guess you are getting better: you're becoming a prickly jerk again."

"Get Bug in here. Get Bug and Drake. I want to see them both."

Diana made no move. "Are you going to tell me what happened to you out there in the desert with Pack Leader?"

Caine snorted. "You don't want to know."

"Yes," Diana insisted, "I do."

"All that matters is I'm back," Caine said with all the bravado he could manage.

Diana nodded. The movement caused her hair to fall forward, to caress her perfect cheek. Her eyes glittered moistly. But her lush lips still curled into an expression of distaste.

"What's it mean, Caine? What does 'gaiaphage' mean?"

He shrugged. "I don't know. I've never heard the word before."

Why was he lying to her? Why did it seem so dangerous that she should know that word?

"Go get them," Caine said, dismissing her. "Get Drake and Bug."

"Why don't you take it easy? Make sure you're really . . . I was going to say 'sane,' but that might be setting the bar kind of high."

"I'm back," Caine reiterated. "And I have a plan."

She stared at him, head tilted sideways, skeptical. "A plan."

"I have things I have to do," Caine said, and looked down, incapable, for reasons he couldn't quite grasp, of meeting her gaze.

"Caine, don't do this," Diana said. "Sam let you walk away

alive. He won't do that a second time."

"You want me to bargain with him? Work something out?"

"Yes."

"Well then, that's just what I'm going to do, Diana. I'm going to bargain. But first I need something to bargain with. And I know just the thing."

Astrid Ellison was in the overgrown backyard with Little Pete when Sam brought her the news and the worm. Pete was swinging. Or more accurately he was sitting on the swing as Astrid pushed him. He seemed to like it.

It was dull, monotonous work pushing the swing with almost never a word of conversation or a sound of joy from her little brother. Pete was five years old, just barely, and severely autistic. He could talk, but mostly he didn't. He had become, if anything, even more withdrawn since the coming of the FAYZ. Maybe it was her fault: she wasn't keeping up with the therapy, wasn't keeping up with all the futile, pointless exercises that were supposed to help autistics deal with reality.

Of course Little Pete made his own reality. In some very important ways he had made everyone's reality.

The yard was not Astrid's yard, the house not her house. Drake Merwin had burned her house down. But one thing there was no shortage of in Perdido Beach was housing. Most homes were empty. And although many kids stayed in their own homes, some found their old bedrooms, their old family rooms, too full of memories. Astrid had lost track of how many times she'd seen kids break down sobbing, talking about their mom in the kitchen, their dad mowing the lawn, their older brother or sister hogging the remote.

Kids got lonely a lot. Loneliness, fear, and sadness haunted the FAYZ. So, often kids moved in together, into what amounted almost to frat or sorority houses.

This house was shared by Astrid; Mary Terrafino; Mary's little brother, John; and more and more often, Sam. Officially Sam lived in an unused office at town hall, where he slept on a couch, cooked with a microwave, and used what had been a public restroom. But it was a gloomy place, and Astrid had asked him more than once to consider this his home. They were, after all, a family of sorts. And, symbolically at least, they were the first family of the FAYZ, substitute mother and father to the motherless, fatherless kids.

Astrid heard Sam before she saw him. Perdido Beach had always been a sleepy little town, and now it was as quiet as church most of the time. Sam came through the house, letting himself in, calling her name as he went from room to room.

"Sam," she yelled. But he didn't hear her until he opened the back door and stepped out onto the deck.

One glance was all it took to know something terrible had happened. Sam wasn't good at concealing his feelings, at least not from her.

"What is it?" she asked.

He didn't answer, just strode across the weedy, patchy grass and put his arms around her. She hugged him back, patient, knowing he'd tell her when he could.

He buried his face in her hair. She could feel his breath on her neck, tickling her ear. She enjoyed the feel of his body against hers. Enjoyed the fact that he needed to hold her. But there was nothing romantic about this embrace.

At last he let her go. He moved to take over pushing Little Pete, seeming to need something physical to do.

"E.Z.'s dead," he said without preamble. "I was touring the fields with Edilio. Me, Edilio, and Albert, and E.Z. along for entertainment. You know. No good reason for E.Z. to even be there, he just wanted to ride along and I said okay because I feel like all I ever do is say no, no, no to people, and now he's dead."

He pushed the swing harder than she'd been doing. Little Pete almost fell backward.

"Oh, God. How did it happen?"

"Worms," Sam said dully. "Some kind of worm. Or snake. I don't know. I have a dead one in there on the kitchen counter. I was hoping you'd . . . I don't know what I was hoping. I figure you're our expert on mutations. Right?"

He said the expert part with a wry smile. Astrid wasn't an expert on anything. She was just the only person who cared enough to try and make sense in a systematic, scientific way of what was happening in the FAYZ.

"If you keep pushing him, he'll be fine," Astrid said of her brother.

She found the creature in a Baggie on the kitchen counter.

It looked more like a snake than a worm, but not like any normal snake, either.

She pressed gingerly on the bag, hoping it really was dead. She spread waxed paper on the granite counter and dumped the worm out. She rummaged in the junk drawer for a tape measure and did her best to follow the contours of the creature.

"Eleven inches," she noted.

Then she found her camera and took a dozen photos from every angle before using a fork to lift the monstrous thing back into the Baggie.

Astrid loaded the pictures onto her laptop. She dragged them into a folder labeled "Mutations—Photos." There were dozens of pictures. Birds with strange talons or beaks. Snakes with short wings. Subsequent pictures showed larger snakes with larger wings. One, taken at a distance, seemed to show a rattlesnake the size of a small python with leathery wings as wide as a bald eagle's.

She had a blurry photo of a coyote twice the size of any normal coyote. And a close-up of a dead coyote's mouth showing a strangely shortened tongue that looked creepily human. There was a series of grotesque JPEGs of a cat that had fused with a book.

Other photos were of kids, most just looking normal, although the boy called Orc looked like a monster. She had a picture of Sam with green light blazing from his palms. She hated the picture because the expression on his face as he demonstrated his power for her camera was so sad.

Astrid clicked opened the worm pictures and used the zoom function to take a closer look.

Little Pete came in, followed by Sam.

"Look at that mouth," Astrid said, awestruck. The worm had a mouth like a shark. It was impossible to count the hundreds of tiny teeth. The worm seemed to be grinning, even dead, grinning.

"Worms don't have teeth," Astrid said.

"They didn't have teeth. Now they do," Sam said.

"See the things sticking out all around its body?" She squinted and zoomed in closer still. "They're like, I don't know, like minuscule paddles. Like legs, only tiny and thousands of them."

"They got into E.Z. I think they went right through his hands. Right through his shoes. Right through his body."

Astrid shuddered. "Those teeth would bore through anything. The legs push it forward once it's inside its victim."

"Thousands of them in that field," Sam said. "E.Z. goes in, they attack him. But me and Albert and Edilio are outside, we haven't stepped into the field, and they don't come after us."

"Territoriality?" Astrid frowned. "Very unusual in a primitive animal. Territoriality is usually associated with higher life-forms. Dogs or cats are territorial. Not worms."

"You're being very calm about all this," Sam said, almost but not quite accusingly.

Astrid looked at him, reached with her hand to gently turn him away from the horrible image, forcing him to look at her instead. "You didn't come to me so I could scream and run away and you could be brave and comforting."

"No," he admitted. "Sorry. You're right: I didn't come to see Astrid my girlfriend. I came to see Astrid the Genius."

Astrid had never liked that nickname much, but she'd accepted it. It gave her a place in the dazed and frightened community of the FAYZ. She wasn't a Brianna or a Dekka, or a Sam, with great powers. What she had was her brain and her ability to think in a disciplined way when required.

"I'll dissect it, see what I can learn. Are you okay?"

"Sure. Why not? This morning I was responsible for 332 people. Now I'm only responsible for 331. And part of me is almost thinking, okay, one less mouth to feed."

Astrid leaned close and kissed him lightly on the mouth. "Yeah, it sucks to be you," Astrid said. "But you're the only you we have."

That earned her a bleak smile. "So, shut up and deal with it?" he said.

"No, don't ever shut up. Tell me everything. Tell me anything."

Sam looked down, unwilling to make eye contact. "Everything? Okay, how about this: I burned the body. E.Z. I burned the mess they left behind."

"He was dead, Sam. What were you supposed to do? Leave him for the birds and the coyotes?"

He nodded. "Yeah. I know. But that's not the problem. The problem is, when he burned? He smelled like meat cooking, and I . . ." He stopped talking, unable to go on. She waited while he mastered his emotions. "A dead sixth grader was burning, and my mouth started watering."

Astrid could too easily imagine it. Even the thought of burning meat made her mouth water. "It's a normal, physiological reaction, Sam. It's a part of your brain that's on automatic."

"Yeah," he said, unconvinced.

"Look, you can't go around moping because something bad happened. If you start acting hopeless, it will spread to everyone else."

"Kids don't need my help to feel hopeless," he said.

"And you're going to let me cut your hair," Astrid said, pulling him close and ruffling his hair with one hand. She wanted to get his mind off the morning's disaster.

"What?" He looked confused by the sudden change of topic.

"You look like a fugitive from some old 1970s hair band. Besides," she argued, "Edilio let me cut *his* hair."

Sam allowed himself a smile. "Yeah. I saw. Maybe that's why I keep accidentally calling him Bart Simpson."

When she glared at him, he added, "You know, the spiky look?" He tried to kiss her, but she drew back.

"Oh, you're just so clever, aren't you?" she said. "How about I just shave your head? Or hot-wax it? Keep insulting me, people will be calling you Homer Simpson, not Bart. Then see how much Taylor makes goo-goo eyes at you."

"She does not make goo-goo eyes at me."

"Yeah. Right." She pushed him away playfully.

"Anyway, I might look good with just two hairs," Sam said.

He looked at his reflection in the glass front of the microwave.

"Does the word 'narcissist' mean anything to you?" Astrid asked.

Sam laughed. He made a grab for her but then noticed Little Pete eyeing him. "So. Anyway. How's LP doing?"

Astrid looked at her brother, who was perched on a kitchen counter stool and gazing mutely at Sam. Or, anyway, in Sam's direction—she could never be sure what he was really looking at.

She wanted to tell Sam what had been happening with Little Pete, what he had started doing. But Sam had enough to worry about. And for a moment—a rare moment—he wasn't worrying.

There would be time later to tell him that the most powerful person in the FAYZ seemed to be . . . what would the right term be for what Little Pete was doing?

Losing his mind? No, that wasn't quite it.

There was no right term for what was happening to Little Pete. But, anyway, this wasn't the time.

"He's fine," Astrid lied. "You know Petey."

THREE

106 HOURS, 11 MINUTES

LANA ARWEN LAZAR was on her fourth home since coming to Perdido Beach. She'd first stayed in a house she'd liked well enough. But that house was where Drake Merwin had captured her. It felt like a bad place after that.

Then she'd moved in with Astrid for a while. But she quickly discovered that she preferred being alone with just her Labrador retriever, Patrick, for company. So she'd taken a house near the plaza. But that had made her too accessible.

Lana didn't like being accessible. When she was accessible, she had no privacy.

Lana had the power to heal. She'd first discovered this ability the day of the FAYZ, when her grandfather had disappeared. They'd been driving in his pickup truck at the time, and the sudden disappearance of the driver had sent the truck rolling down a very long embankment.

Lana's injuries should have killed her. Almost did kill her. Then she discovered a power that might have lain hidden within her forever, but for her terrible need.

She had healed herself. She'd healed Sam when he was shot; and Cookie, whose shoulder had been split open; and many wounded children after the terrible Thanksgiving Battle.

The kids called her the Healer. She was second only to Sam Temple as a hero in the FAYZ. Everyone looked up to her. Everyone respected her. Some of them, especially the ones whose lives she'd saved, treated her with something like awe. Lana had no doubt that Cookie, for one, would give his life for her. He had been in a living hell until she'd saved him.

But hero worship didn't stop kids from pestering her at all hours, day and night, over every little pain or problem: loose teeth, sunburn, skinned knees, stubbed toes.

So she had moved away from town and now lived in a room in the Clifftop Resort.

The hotel hugged the FAYZ wall, the blank, impenetrable barrier that defined this new world.

"Calm down, Patrick," she said as the dog head-butted her in his eagerness for breakfast. Lana pried the lid off the ALPO can and, blocking Patrick, spooned half of it into a dish on the floor.

"There. Jeez, you'd swear I never feed you."

As she said it she wondered how long she would be able to go on feeding Patrick. There were kids eating dog food now. And there were skin-and-bones dogs in the streets, picking through trash next to kids who were picking through trash to find scraps they'd thrown out weeks earlier.

Lana was alone at Clifftop. Hundreds of rooms, an algae-choked pool, a tennis court truncated by the barrier. She had a balcony that afforded a sweeping view of the beach below and the too-placid ocean.

Sam, Edilio, Astrid, and Dahra Baidoo—who acted as pharmacist and nurse—knew where she was and could find her if they really needed her. But most kids didn't, so she had a degree of control over her life.

She looked longingly at the dog food. Wondering, not for the first time, what it tasted like. Probably better than the burned potato peels with barbecue sauce she'd eaten.

Once, the hotel had been full of food. But on Sam's orders Albert and his crew had collected it all, centralized it all at Ralph's. Where Drake had managed to steal a good portion of the dwindling remainder.

Now there was no food in the hotel. Not even in any of the mini-bars in the rooms, which once had been stocked with delicious candy bars, and chips and nuts. Now all that was left was alcohol. Albert's people had left the booze, not knowing quite what to do with it.

Lana had stayed away from the little brown and white bottles. So far.

Alcohol was how she had managed to get herself exiled from her home in Las Vegas. She'd snuck a bottle of vodka from her parents' house, supposedly for an older boy she knew.

That was the cleaned-up story she'd managed to sell to her parents, anyway. They had still packed her off for some time to "think about what you've done" at her grandfather's isolated ranch.

Now, in the world of the FAYZ, Lana was a sort of saint. But she knew better.

Patrick had finished his food as coffee brewed in the room. Lana poured herself a cup and dumped in a Nutrasweet and some powdered cream, rare luxuries that she'd found by searching the maids' carts.

She stepped out onto the balcony and took a sip.

She had the stereo on, the CD player that had been in the room. Someone, some previous inhabitant of the room, she supposed, had left an ancient Paul Simon CD in there, and she'd found herself playing it.

There was a song about darkness. A welcoming of darkness. Almost an invitation. She had played it over and over again.

Sometimes music helped her to forget. Not this song.

Out of the corner of her eye she spotted someone down on the beach. She went back inside and retrieved a pair of binoculars she'd liberated from some long-gone tourist's luggage.

Two little kids, they couldn't be more than six years old, playing on the rock pier that extended into the ocean. Fortunately there was no surf. But the rocks were like jumbled razor blades in places, sharp and slick. She ought to . . .

Later. Enough responsibility. She was not a responsible person, and she was sick of having it forced on her.

Various adult vices were spreading through the population of the FAYZ. Some as benign as coffee. Others—pot, cigarettes, and alcohol—were not so harmless. Lana knew of six kids who were confirmed drinkers. They had tried to get her to cure their hangovers.

Some others were smoking their way through bags of weed found in their parents' or older siblings' bedrooms. And on just about any day you could see kids as young as eight choking on cigarettes and trying to look cool. She'd once spotted a first grader trying to light a cigar.

Lana couldn't cure any of that.

Sometimes she wished she was back at Hermit Jim's cabin.

It was not the first time she'd had that thought. She had often thought of the strange cabin in the desert with its quirky little lawn—now all brown and dead, most likely.

It's where she had found sanctuary after the crash. And then again, briefly, after escaping from the coyote pack.

The cabin itself had been burned to the ground. It was nothing but ash. And gold, of course. Hermit Jim's stash of gold might have been melted, but it would still be there beneath the floorboards.

The gold. From the mine.

The mine . . .

She took a big gulp from the Styrofoam cup and burned her tongue. The pain helped her focus.

The mine. That day was clear in her memory, but it was the clarity of a well-remembered nightmare.

At the time she hadn't known that the FAYZ meant the disappearance of all adults. She'd gone to the mine in search of the hermit, or hoping at least to find his missing truck and use it to get to town.

She'd found the hermit, dead in the mouth of the mine. Not disappeared, dead. Which meant he'd been killed before the FAYZ.

The coyotes had come after her then and driven her deeper into the mine. And there she'd found . . . it. The thing. The

Darkness, the coyotes called it: the Darkness.

She remembered the way her feet had felt heavy as bricks. The way her heart had slowed down and thudded, each beat like a blow from a sledgehammer. The dread that went deeper than simple fear. The sickly green glow that made her think of pus, disease, a cancer.

The dream state that had overtaken her . . . the heavy-lidded eyes and mind gone blank and the feeling of being invaded, of . . .

Come to me.

"Ah!"

She had crushed the cup. Hot coffee all over her arm.

Lana was sweating. Her breathing was labored. She took a deep breath and it was as if she'd forgotten how until that very moment.

It was in her head still, that monster in the mine shaft. It had its hook in her. Sometimes she was sure she heard its voice. A hallucination, surely. Surely not the Darkness itself. It was miles away. Far beneath the ground. It couldn't . . .

Come to me.

"I can't forget it," she whispered to Patrick. "I can't get away from it."

In the early days after she had come out of the desert and joined this strange community of children, Lana had felt almost at peace. Almost. There had been, from the start, a sense of damage done, an invisible wound with no specific location except that it was inside her.

That unseen, unreal, unhealed wound had reopened. She told herself at first that it would go away. It would heal.

A psychic scab would form. But if that was true, if she was healing, why did it hurt more with each passing day? How had that dreadful voice grown from faint, distant whisper to insistent murmur?

Come to me. I need you.

It had words now, that urgent, demanding voice.

"I'm going crazy, Patrick," Lana told her dog. "It's inside me, and I am going crazy."

Mary Terrafino woke up. She rolled out of bed. Morning. She should go back to sleep: she was exhausted. But she would not fall back to sleep, she knew that. She had things to do.

First things first, she stumbled to her bathroom and used her bare foot to pull the scale across the tile floor. There was a special spot for the scale: aligned with the center of the mirror over the sink, upper-right corner of the scale precisely in line with the tile.

She removed her sleep shirt and stepped onto the scale.

First reading. Step off.

Second reading. Step off.

Three times made it official.

Eighty-one pounds.

She'd been 128 pounds when the FAYZ came.

She still looked fat. There were still pockets of chubbiness here and there. No matter what anyone else said. Mary could see the flab. So no breakfast for her. Which was fine, given that breakfast at the day care would be oatmeal made with powdered milk and sweetened with pink packets of Sweet'n Low. Healthy enough—and much, much better than what most people were getting—but not exactly worth gaining weight over.

Mary popped her Prozac, plus two tiny red Sudafed and a multivitamin. The Prozac kept depression at bay—mostly— and the Sudafed helped keep her from getting hungry. The vitamin would keep her healthy, she hoped.

She dressed quickly, T-shirt, sweatpants, sneakers. Each was roomy. She was determined not to wear anything more body-conscious until she had really lost some weight.

She went to the laundry room and spilled a dryer full of cloth diapers into a plastic bag. There were still a few dis-posable diapers in storage, but they were saving those for emergencies. They had made the switch to cloth a month earlier. It was gross and everyone hated it, but as Mary had pointed out to her grumbling workers, the Pampers factory wasn't exactly delivering anymore.

Down the stairs with the bag bump-bumping along.

Sam was with Astrid and Little Pete in the kitchen. Mary didn't want to interrupt—or be nagged about having breakfast—so she let herself quietly out the front door.

Five minutes later she was at the day care.

The day care had fared badly in the battle. The wall it shared with the hardware store had been blown out. So now the gaping hole was covered by plastic sheeting that had to be retaped just about every day. It was a reminder of how close they had come to disaster. The coyote pack had been in this very room, holding these same children hostage, while Drake Merwin preened and gloated.

Mary's brother, John, was already at the day care waiting for her.

"Hey, Mary," John said. "You shouldn't be here. You should be sleeping."

John was working the morning shift, 5:00 a.m. to noon, breakfast to just before lunch. Mary was supposed to take over at lunch and work straight through until 10:00 p.m. Lunch through dinner through sleep time, with an hour at the end to work out schedules and clean up. Then she'd have time to go home, watch some DVDs while she worked out on the treadmill in the basement. That was the schedule. Eight hours of sleep and a few hours free in the morning.

But in reality she often spent two or three hours exercising at night. Going after those last few pounds. On the treadmill, down in the basement, where Astrid wouldn't hear her and ask her why.

Most days she consumed fewer than seven hundred calories. On a really good day it would be half that.

She hugged John. "What's up, little brother? What's today's crisis?"

John had a list. He read it off his *Warriors* notebook. "Pedro has a loose tooth. He also had an accident last night. Zosia claims Julia punched her, so they're fighting and refusing to play together. I think maybe Collin has a fever . . . anyway, he's kind of, you know, cranky. I caught Brady trying to run away this morning. She was going to look for her mommy."

The list went on and as it did, some of the kids ran over to hug Mary, to get a kiss, to get an appreciation of their hairdo, to earn an approving "good job" for the way they had brushed their teeth.

Mary nodded. The list was about like this every day.

A guy named Francis came in, pushed rudely past Mary. Then he realized whom he had just shouldered aside, turned back to her with a scowl, and said, "Okay, I'm here."

"First time?" Mary asked.

"What, am I supposed to be sorry? I'm not a babysitter."

This scene, too, had been repeated every day since peace had come to Perdido Beach. "Okay, here's the thing, kid," Mary said. "I know you don't want to be here, and I don't care. No one wants to be here, but the littles have to be taken care of. So lose the attitude."

"Why don't you just take care of these kids? At least you're a girl."

"I'm not," John pointed out.

Mary said, "See that easel? There are three lists on there, one list for each of the daily helpers. Pick a list. That's what you do. Whatever is on the list. And you smile while you're doing it."

Francis marched over and checked the list.

John said, "I'll bet you a cookie he doesn't pick diaper duty."

"No bet," Mary said. "Besides, there are no cookies."

"I miss cookies," John said wistfully.

"Hey," Francis yelled. "All these lists suck."

"Yes," Mary agreed. "Yes, they do."

"This all sucks."

"Please stop saying 'sucks.' I don't want to have three-year-olds repeating it all day."

"Man, when my birthday comes, I'm stepping out," Francis sulked.

"Fine. I'll be sure not to schedule you after that. Now, pick a work list and do it. I don't want to have to waste Sam's time calling him over here to motivate you."

Francis stomped back to the easel.

"Stepping out," Mary said to John, and made a face. "How many people have hit the magic fifteen so far? Only two have poofed. People talk about it. But they don't actually do it."

The FAYZ had eliminated everyone over the age of fourteen. No one knew why. At least, Mary didn't, although she had overheard Sam and Astrid whispering in a way that made her think they might know more than they admitted.

A fourteen-year-old who reached his fifteenth birthday would also disappear. Poof. If he let himself. If he decided to "step out."

What happened during what kids called Stepping Out was now known to just about everyone. The way subjective time would slow to a crawl. The appearance of the person you loved and trusted most to beckon you across, to urge you to leave the FAYZ. And the way this person transformed into a monster if you resisted.

You had a choice: stay in the FAYZ, or . . . But no one knew just what the "or" was. Maybe it was escape back into the old world. Maybe it was a trip to some whole new place.

Maybe it was death.

Mary noticed John looking intensely at her. "What?" she said.

"You wouldn't ever . . ."

Mary smiled and ruffled his curly red hair. "Never. I would never leave you. Missing Mom and Dad?"

John nodded. "I keep thinking about how many times I made them mad."

"John . . ."

"I know. I know that doesn't matter. But it's like . . ." He couldn't find the words, so he made the motion of a knife stabbing his heart.

Someone was tugging at Mary's shirt from behind. She looked around and with a sinking heart saw a little boy named . . . named . . . she couldn't remember his name. But the second little boy behind him she remembered was Sean. She knew why they were there. They had both recently had their fifth birthdays. The age limit for the day care was four. At age five you had to move out—hopefully to a house with some responsible older kids.

"Hi, kids. What's up?" Mary asked as she brought her face down to their level.

"Um . . . ," the first one said. And then he burst into tears.

She shouldn't do it, she knew she shouldn't, but she couldn't stop herself from putting her arms around the little boy. And then Sean started crying as well, so the embrace was extended, and John was in there, too, and Mary heard herself saying of course, of course they could come back, just for today, just for a little while.

FOUR

COATES ACADEMY WAS quite a bit the worse for wear. Battles had damaged the façade of the main building. There was a hole in the whitewashed brick so big, you could see an entire second-story classroom, a cross-section of the floor beneath it, and a jagged gap that didn't quite reach to the top of the first-story window below. Most of the glass in the windows was gone. The kids had made an effort to keep the elements out by duct-taping sheets of plastic over the holes, but the tape had loosened and now the plastic and the tape hung limp, stirring with the occasional breeze. The building looked as if it had been through a war. It had been.

The grounds were a mess. Grass that had always been trimmed to obsessive perfection in the old days now grew wild in some areas and had gone yellow as hay in others. And weeds pushed up through the circular gravel driveway where once parents' minivans and SUVs and luxury sedans had lined up.

The plumbing was out in half the building, toilets overflowing and reeking. The smaller buildings, the art classroom, and the dormitories were in better shape, but Drake insisted on staying in the main building. He had occupied the office of the school shrink, a place where in the old days Drake had standing appointments for counseling and testing.

Do you still dream of hurting animals, Drake?

No, Doc, I dream of hurting you.

The office was an armory now. Drake's guns, nine of them, ranging from hunting rifles with scopes to handguns, were laid out on a table. He kept them unloaded, all but two, the guns he carried on him. He'd hidden the ammunition for the other guns: there was no one Drake trusted. The ammunition, never enough of it, to Drake's thinking, rested behind the ceiling tiles and in air-conditioning vents.

Drake sat watching a DVD on the plasma screen he'd stolen. The movie was *Saw II.* The sound effects were so great. Drake had the volume up high enough to rattle one of the few surviving panes of glass. So he didn't at first hear Diana's voice when she said, "He wants you."

Drake turned, sensing her presence. He flicked his tentacle arm, the arm that gave him his nickname, Whip Hand, and turned off the set. "What do you want?" he demanded with a scowl.

"He wants you," Diana repeated.

Drake loved the fear in her eyes. Tough-chick Diana: snarky, sarcastic, superior Diana. Scared Diana. Scared of him and what he could do to her.

"Who wants me?"

"Caine. He's up."

"He's been up before," Drake said.

"He's back. Mostly. He's back and he wants you and Bug."

"Yeah? Well, I'll get there when I get there." He flicked his whip and turned the set back on. "Great, now I missed the best part. Where's the remote? I can't rewind without the remote."

"You want me to tell Caine to wait?" Diana asked innocently. "No problem. I'll just go tell him you're too busy to see him."

Drake took a deep breath and glared at her. Slowly the whip moved toward her, the end twitching with anticipation, wanting to wrap around her neck.

"Go ahead, do it," she challenged him. "Go on, Drake. Go ahead and defy Caine."

His cold eyes flinched, just a little, but he knew she'd seen it and it made him mad.

Not today. Not yet. Not until Caine took care of Sam.

Drake coiled the whip. He had a way of wrapping it sinuously around his waist. But the arm was never entirely still, so it always looked like a pink and gray anaconda squeezing him, always looked like Drake was its prey.

"You'd like that, wouldn't you, Diana? Me fighting Caine. Sorry to disappoint you. I am one hundred percent loyal to Caine. We're like brothers, the two of us. Not like him and Sam, more like blood brothers." He winked at her. "The brotherhood of the Darkness, Diana. Me and him, we've both been there. We've both faced it."

Drake knew Diana was eaten up with curiosity about the thing in the mine shaft, the thing that had given Drake his arm after Sam had burned his old arm off. But Drake wasn't going to give her anything. Let her wonder. Let her worry. "Let's go see the boss."

Caine looked better already. Whatever sickness had been consuming him these last three months, imprisoning him in a world of fevers and nightmares, must have finally run its course.

Too late for Chunk.

The memory made Drake smile. Fat-ass Chunk flying through the air, smacking into a solid wall, hitting it so hard, he actually went through it. Man, that had been something to see.

After that, no one—including Drake—had been crazy enough to be around Caine. Even now Drake was wary. Only Diana was desperate enough to stay and change Caine's soiled sheets and spoon-feed him soup.

"You look good, Caine," Drake said.

"I look like hell," Caine said. "But my head is clear."

Drake thought that probably wasn't true. He'd spent just a few hours with the Darkness himself, and his head still wasn't clear of it, not by a long shot. He heard the voice in his head, sometimes. He heard it. And he was pretty sure Caine did, too.

Once you heard that voice, you never stopped hearing it, Drake thought. He found the idea comforting.

"Bug, are you in here?" Caine asked.

"Right here."

Drake almost jumped. Bug was just three feet away, not quite invisible but not quite visible, either. He had the mutant power of camouflage, like a chameleon. Looking at Bug when he was using his power, the most you might notice was a sort of ripple in the scenery, a bending of light.

"Knock it off," Caine growled.

Bug became visible as the snot-nosed little creep he was. "Sorry," he said. "I just . . . I didn't . . ."

"Don't worry, I'm not in the mood to throw anyone into a wall," Caine said dryly. "I have a job for you, Bug."

"Go into Perdido Beach again?"

"No. No, that's what Sam is expecting," Caine said. "We stay out of Perdido Beach. We don't need the town. They can have the town. For now, anyway."

"Yeah, let them keep what we can't take away. That's very generous," Diana said, mocking them.

"It's not about territory," Caine said. "It's about power. Not *powers*, Drake, power." He put his hand on Bug's shoulder. "Bug, you're the key person on this. I need your skills."

"I don't know what else I can see in Perdido Beach," Bug said.

"Forget Perdido Beach. Like I said, it's about power. *Nuclear* power." Caine winked at Diana and slapped Drake's shoulder, working his old charm, getting them to believe in him again. But Drake wasn't fooled: Caine was weak in his body and disturbed in his mind. The old confidence was subdued:

Caine was a shadow. Although he *was* a shadow who could throw a person through a wall. Drake's whip hand twitched against the small of his back.

"That power plant is the town's lifeline," Caine said. "Control the electricity and Sam will give us whatever we want."

"Don't you think Sam knows this? And probably has guards at the power plant?" Diana said.

"I'm sure there are guards. But I'm sure they won't see Bug. So, fly now, little Bug. Fly away and see what you can see."

Bug and Diana both turned to leave. The one excited, the other seething. Drake stayed behind.

Caine seemed surprised, maybe even a little worried. "What is it, Drake?"

"Diana," Drake said. "I don't trust her."

Caine sighed. "Yeah, I think I get that you don't like Diana."

"It's not about me not liking the . . ." He'd been about to use the "b" word, but Caine's eyes flared and Drake reworded it. "It's not about me not liking her. It's about her and Computer Jack."

That got Caine's full attention. "What are you talking about?"

"Jack. He's got powers now. And I'm not just talking about his tech skills. Bug saw him down in Perdido Beach. That backhoe they have? The wetback was digging a grave, and the backhoe toppled into it. Bug says Jack picked it up. Just pulled it up out of the hole like it was no heavier than a bike."

Caine sat down on the edge of his bed. Drake had the

impression Caine had needed to sit down for a while, that standing for more than a few minutes was still heavy work.

"Sounds like he's at least a two bar. Maybe even a three," Caine said. Diana had invented the system of bars, copying the idea from cell phones. Diana's own power was the ability to gauge power levels.

Drake knew that there were only two known four bars: Sam and Caine. There was speculation about Little Pete, who had demonstrated some major stuff, but how dangerous could a half-brain-dead little five-year-old really be?

"Yeah, so Jack could be a three bar. Only not according to Diana, right? Diana says she read him at zero bars. So maybe the power develops late, okay. But from zero to three?" Drake shrugged, not needing to push the issue, knowing that Caine—even a sick, weakened Caine—was connecting the dots in his head.

"We never did get an explanation for why Jack switched sides and ran to Sam," Caine said softly.

"Maybe someone put him up to it," Drake said.

"Maybe," Caine said, not wanting to admit the possibility. "Get someone to watch her. Not you, she knows you watch her. But get someone to keep an eye on her."

The worst thing about the FAYZ from Duck Zhang's point of view was the food. It had been great at first: candy bars, chips, soda, ice cream. That had all lasted a few weeks. It would probably have lasted longer but people had wasted it—leaving ice cream to melt; gorging on cookies, then leaving the bag out where dogs could get at it; letting bread mold.

By the time they'd burned through all the sweets and snack food it was too late to do anything about the fact that all of the meat and chicken, with the exception of bacon, sausage, and ham, and all the fresh produce except potatoes and onions was expired or rotten. Duck had been forced to help clean all that out of Ralph's. A crew of resentful kids had shoveled rotting lettuce and stinking meat for days. But what could you do when Sam Temple looked right at you, pointed his finger, and said, "You." The boy could fry you. Plus, he was the mayor, after all.

Then had come the canned soup, dry cereal, crackers and cheese period.

Right now Duck would give anything for a can of soup. His breakfast had been canned asparagus. Which tasted like vomit and everyone knew it made your pee stink.

But there were good things about the FAYZ, too. The best thing about the FAYZ, from Duck Zhang's point of view, was the pool. It wasn't exactly his pool, but it might as well be because here he was, floating in it. On a Monday morning in early March when he normally would have been in school.

No school. Nothing but pool. It took some of the sting out of hunger.

He was a sixth grader, small for his age, Asian, although his family had been American since the 1930s. Back in the day his folks had worried he was getting fat. Well, no one was very fat in the FAYZ. Not anymore.

Duck loved the water. But not the ocean. The ocean scared

him. He couldn't get past the idea that a whole world was down there below the waves, invisible to him while he was visible to them. Them being squids, octopi, fish, eels, jellyfish and, above all, sharks.

Pools on the other hand were great. You could see all the way to the bottom.

But he'd never had a pool of his own. There was no public pool in Perdido Beach, so he could only swim when he happened to have a friend with a pool, or when he was on vacation with his parents and they stayed at a hotel with a pool.

Now, however, with kids in Perdido Beach able to live pretty much wherever they liked, and go pretty much wherever they liked, Duck had found a perfect, secluded, private pool. Whom it belonged to, he couldn't say. But whoever they were, they had a great setup. The pool was big, kidney-shaped, with a ten-foot depth at one end so you could dive in headfirst. The whole thing was the prettiest shade of aqua tile with a gold sunburst pattern in the bottom. The water—once he'd figured out how to add chlorine and clean the filters— was as clear as glass.

There was a nice wrought-iron table with an umbrella in the middle and some very comfortable chaise lounges for him to lie out on if he chose. But he didn't choose to lie out. He chose to lie back on a float. A bottle of water bobbed alongside him on its own separate float. He had a cool pair of Ray-Bans on and a light coating of sunblock and he was—in a word—happy. Hungry, but happy.

Sometimes, when Duck felt particularly good, it almost seemed as if he didn't even need the raft to hold him up. Sometimes if he was happy enough he could actually feel the pressure of his back on the plastic lessen. Like he weighed less or something. In fact he'd once awakened suddenly from a happy dream and had fallen a couple of feet into the water. At least, that's what it seemed like, although it was obviously just part of the dream.

Other times, if he became angry for some reason, maybe just remembering some slight, it seemed to him that he grew heavier and the float would actually start to sink into the water.

But Duck was seldom either very happy or very angry. Mostly he was just peaceful.

"Yeee-ahhh!"

The shout was completely unexpected. As was the huge splash that followed it.

Duck sat up on his raft.

Water sloshed over him. Someone was in the water. *His* water.

Two more blurs raced toward the pool's edge and there were two more shouts, followed by two more cannonball splashes.

"Hey!" Duck yelled.

One of the kids was a jerk named Zil. The other two Duck didn't recognize right away.

"Hey!" he yelled again.

"Who are you yelling at?" Zil demanded.

"This is my pool," Duck said. "I found it and I cleaned it. Go get your own pool."

Duck was aware that he was smaller than any of the three. But he was angry enough to feel bold. The float sank beneath him and he wondered if one of the boys had poked a hole in it.

"I'm serious," Duck yelled. "You guys take off."

"He's serious," one of the boys mocked.

Before he knew it Zil was leaping up from beneath the water and had grabbed Duck by the neck. Duck was plunged underwater, gasping, choking, sucking water into his nose.

He surfaced with difficulty, fighting with suddenly leaden arms to stay afloat.

They hit him again, just roughhousing, not really trying to hurt him, but forcing him under once more. This time he touched down on the bottom of the pool and had to kick his way back to the surface to gasp for air. He clutched at the float, but one of the boys yanked it away, giggling loudly.

Duck was filled with sudden rage. He had one good thing in his life, this pool, one good thing, and now it was being ruined.

"Get out!" he shrieked, but the last word glub-glub-glubbed as he sank like a rock.

What was going on? Suddenly he couldn't swim. He was on the bottom of the pool, in the deep end, under ten feet of water. He kicked at the tile bottom, trying to shoot back up, but his foot shattered the tile and sent pieces of it spinning through the water.

Now panic took hold. What were they doing to him?

He kicked again, both feet as hard as he could. But he did not rise to the surface. Instead, both feet punched through the tile. He rose not at all. In fact, he was still sinking. His feet were sinking through the tile, scraping through jagged mortar and crumbled concrete, down into mud beneath.

It was impossible.

Impossible.

Duck Zhang was falling through the bottom of the pool. Through the ground beneath the bottom of the pool. It was as if he were standing in quicksand.

Up to his knees.

Up to his thighs.

Up to his waist.

He thrashed madly but he only fell faster.

Broken tile scraped his flanks. Mud slithered into his bathing suit.

His lungs burned. His vision was blurring now, head pounding, and still he fell through solid earth, as if the ground itself were nothing but water.

As the tile reached his chest he slammed his arms down to block himself falling farther, but his arms plowed through the tile and the concrete beneath and the dirt beneath that, and all of it swirled around his head in a cloud of murk and mud.

The pool water was now rushing down around him, pushing into his mouth and nose. He was a loose plug caught in a drain.

Duck Zhang's world swirled, crazy flashes of feet kicking

above him, sparkling sunlight, then his vision tunneled, narrowed, and darkness crowded out the light.

It had been funny for the first minute or so. Zil Sperry had enjoyed sneaking up on Dork Zhang: he and Hank and Antoine creeping around the side of the house, shoving one another playfully, suppressing giggles.

It was Hank who'd found out about Duck's secret swimming pool. Hank was a born spy. But it was Zil's idea to wait until Duck had it all cleaned up, until he adjusted the chlorine and got the filter working.

"Let him do the work first," Zil had argued. "Then we take it from him."

Antoine and Hank were cool, Zil realized, but if there was serious thinking or planning to be done, it was up to him.

They had achieved total surprise. Duck had probably wet himself. Stupid dork. Big, whiny baby.

But then things had gone wrong. Duck had sunk like a rock. And kept sinking. And suddenly the sun-dappled water had turned into a whirlpool of shocking power. Hank had been standing on the steps and managed to leap up and out of the pool. But Antoine was with Zil in the deep end when Duck pulled the plug.

Zil had managed, just barely, to grab on to the end of the diving board. The water sucked at him, practically pulled his bathing suit off. He barely held on, fingertips scrabbling at the sandpapery surface of the board.

Antoine had been swept away, drawn into the circular

motion. The force of the water had rammed him into the chrome ladder, and Antoine had managed to wedge one fat leg between the ladder, and the side of the pool. He was lucky he hadn't broken his ankle.

Hank hauled Zil to safety. The two of them together helped Antoine clamber awkwardly up where he collapsed like a beached whale on the deck.

"Dude, we almost drowned," Antoine gasped weakly.

"What happened?" Hank asked. "I couldn't see."

"Duck, man," Zil said, his voice shaky. "He, like, sank through the water and just kept going."

"I almost got sucked down," Antoine said, practically in tears.

"More like you almost got flushed," Hank said. "You looked like a big pink turd going down the bowl."

Zil didn't feel like laughing at the joke. He had been humiliated. He'd been made a fool of. He'd been hanging on for dear life, scared to death. He turned his hands palm-up and looked at his scraped, ragged fingertips. They burned.

He could imagine what he must have looked like, dangling from the end of the board, his swimsuit halfway down his butt as the water tugged at him.

There was nothing funny about it.

Zil would not allow there to be anything funny about it.

"What are you two laughing at?" Zil demanded.

"It was kind of—" Antoine began.

Zil cut him off. "He's a freak. Duck Zhang is a mutant freak. Who tried to kill us."

Hank looked sharply at him, hesitating, but only for a moment before he picked up Zil's line. "Yeah. Freak tried to kill us."

"This stuff isn't right, man," Antoine agreed. He sat up and wrapped his hands around his bruised ankle. "How were we supposed to know he was a mutant freak? We were just playing around. It's like anything we do now we have to be worried about whether someone is normal or some kind of freak."

Zil stood and looked down into the empty pool. The hole was ragged with broken tile teeth. A mouth that had opened and swallowed Duck and almost gotten Zil as well. Alive or dead, Duck had made a fool of Zil. And someone was going to have to pay for that.

FIVE

"**BULLETS ARE** FAST. That's why they work," Computer Jack said condescendingly. "If they moved slowly, they wouldn't be worth much."

"I'm fast," Brianna said. "That's why I'm the Breeze." She shaded her eyes from the sun and squinted at the target she had in mind, a real estate sign in front of an empty lot pushed up against the slope of the ridge.

Jack pulled out his handheld. He punched in the numbers. "The slowest bullet goes 330 meters per second. Say 1,100 feet per second in round numbers. I found a book full of useless statistics like that. Man, I miss Google." He seemed to actually choke up with emotion. The word "Google" caught in his throat.

Brianna laughed to herself. Computer Jack was just so *Computer Jack*. Still, he was cute in his own awkward, maladjusted, twelve-year-old and barely into puberty, voice-breaking kind of way.

"Anyway, 3,600 seconds in an hour, right? So about four million feet per hour, divided by 5,280 feet in a mile. So call it 750 miles an hour. Just one side or the other of the speed of sound. Other bullets are faster."

"I bet I can do that," Brianna said. "Sure, I can."

"I do not want to shoot that gun," Jack said, looking dubiously at the gun in her hand.

"Oh, come on, Jack. We're across the highway, we're aiming toward the ridge. What's the worst that happens? You shoot a horned toad?"

"I've never shot a gun," Jack said.

"Any idiot can do it," Brianna assured him, although she had never fired a weapon, either. "But I guess it kicks a little, so you have to grip it firmly."

"Don't worry about that. I have a strong grip."

It took Brianna a few seconds to figure out his ironic tone. She remembered hearing someone say that Jack had powers. That he was extremely strong.

He didn't look strong. He looked like a dweeb. He had messy blond hair and crooked glasses. And it always seemed like he wasn't really looking through those glasses but was seeing his own reflection in the lenses.

"Okay. Get ready," Brianna instructed. "Hold the gun firmly. Aim it at the sign. Let's do a—"

The gun exploded before she could finish. An impossibly loud bang, a cloud of bluish smoke, and a strangely satisfying smell.

"I was going to say let's do a test shot," Brianna said.

"Sorry. I kind of squeezed the trigger."

"Yeah. Kind of. This time just aim it. At the sign over there, not at me."

Jack leveled the gun. "Should I count down?"

"Yes."

"On zero?"

"On zero."

"Ready?"

Brianna dug her sneakers into the dirt, bent down, cocked one arm forward, the other back, like she was frozen in midrun.

"Ready."

"Three. Two. One."

Brianna leaped, just a split second ahead of Jack pulling the trigger. Instantly she realized her mistake: the bullet was behind her, coming after her.

Much better to be chasing the bullet rather than have it chasing you.

Brianna flew. Almost literally flew. If she spread her arms and caught some wind she'd go airborne for fifty feet because she was moving faster, quite a bit faster, than a jet racing down the runway toward take-off.

She ran in an odd way, pumping her arms like any runner, but turning her palms back with each stroke. For almost all the mutants of the FAYZ, the hands were the focus of their powers.

The air screamed past her ears. Her short hair blew straight back. Her cheeks vibrated, her eyes stung. Breathing was a struggle as she gasped at hurricane winds.

The world around her became a smear of color, objects flying past at speeds her brain could not process. Streaks of light
without definite form.

She knew from experience that her feet would need to
be iced down afterward to stop the swelling. She'd already
popped two Advil in anticipation.

She was fast. Impossibly fast.

But she was not faster than a speeding bullet.

She risked a glance back.

The bullet was gaining. She could see it, a blur, a small
gray blur spiraling after her.

Brianna dodged right, just half a step.

The bullet zoomed languidly by.

Brianna chased it, but it hit the dirt—not really anywhere
near the target—while Brianna was still a dozen feet back.

She dropped speed quickly, used the upward slope to slow
herself gently, and came to a stop.

Jack was three hundred yards away. The whole race had
lasted just over a second, though it had felt longer in Brianna's
subjective experience.

"Did you do it?" Jack shouted.

She trotted back to him at a pace she now thought of as
pokey—probably no more than eighty or ninety miles an
hour—and laughed.

"Totally," she said.

"I couldn't even see you. You were here. And then you were
there."

"That's why they call me the Breeze," Brianna said, giving him a jaunty wink. But then her stomach reminded her that she had just burned up the day's calories. It rumbled so loudly, she was sure Jack must hear it.

"You know, of course, that a breeze is actually a slow, meandering sort of wind," Jack said pedantically.

"And you know, of course, that I can slap you eight times before you can blink, right?"

Jack blinked.

Brianna smiled.

"Here," Jack said cautiously. He handed the gun to her, butt first. "Take this."

She stuffed it into the backpack at her feet. She drew out a can opener and the can of pizza sauce she'd saved up. She cut the lid from the can and drank the spicy slop inside.

"Here," she handed the can to Jack. "There's a little left."

He didn't argue but tilted the can up and patiently waited as no more than an ounce of red paste slid into his mouth. Then he licked the inside of the can and used his forefinger to spoon out whatever he hadn't been able to reach with his tongue.

"So, Jack. Whatever happened to you getting the phones working again?"

Jack hesitated, like he wasn't sure he should tell her anything. "They're up and running. Or will be as soon as I get the word from Sam."

Brianna stared at him. "What?"

"It was a pretty simple problem, really. We have three

towers, one here in Perdido Beach, one more up the highway, and one on top of the ridge. There's a program that checks numbers to make sure the bill has been paid and so on, so that the number is authorized. The program isn't in the tower, obviously, it's outside the FAYZ. So I fixed it so that all phones are authorized."

"Can I call my mom?" Brianna asked. She knew the answer, but she couldn't quash the bounce of hope in time to stop herself from asking.

Jack stared in confusion. "Of course not. That would mean penetrating the FAYZ barrier."

"Oh." The disappointment was like a sharp pain. Brianna, like most of the kids in the FAYZ, had learned to deal with the loss of parents, grandparents, older siblings. But the hope of actually speaking with them . . .

It was her mother Brianna missed most. There was a big age gap between Brianna and her little sisters. Brianna's father had been out of her life since the divorce. Her mother had remarried—a jerk—and then had had twins with him. Brianna liked the twins okay, but they were eight years younger than she was, so it wasn't like they hung out together.

It was Brianna's stepfather who had insisted on sending her to Coates. His reason was that her grades were falling. Which was a lame excuse. Lots of kids had trouble with math and didn't end up getting shipped off to a place like Coates.

Brianna had talked her mother into standing up to her stepfather. This was going to be her last year at Coates. Next year she was going to be back at Nicolet Middle School, in

Banning. Back where she belonged. Not that there weren't some tough kids at Nicolet, but there were no Caines, no Bennos, no Dianas, and definitely no Drakes.

No one at Nicolet had ever encased her hands in a block of cement and then left her to starve.

Besides, it would be so cool to blow all her old friends away with her new power. Their heads would explode. Their brains would melt. She could be a whole track team all by herself.

"There are no satellites to link to," Jack was going on in his pedantic way. He was definitely kind of cute. And she thought he was kind of interesting. Kind of cute mostly because he was so clueless while at the same time being scary smart. She had noticed him even before, back when Coates was just a miserable hellhole and Jack was only on the periphery of the Caine clique.

"Why hasn't Sam told anyone?" Brianna asked. "Why hasn't he turned the system back on?"

"There's no way to stop the Coates kids from using it, too, unless we disable the tower up on the ridge. Or unless I figure out a way to replace the entire authorization protocol and then authorize only certain numbers. Which would be a big programming job since I would be starting from scratch."

"Oh." Brianna peered closely at him. "Well, we don't want to do anything that will help Caine and Drake and that witch, Diana. Do we?"

Jack shrugged. "Well, I was scared of Drake. I mean, everyone is scared of Drake. But Caine and Diana, they were okay to me."

Brianna didn't like that answer. The "interested" smile

she'd worn for him evaporated. She held up her hands. The scars from Drake's cruel "plastering" were gone. But the memory of that abuse, and the horror of starvation, especially now that it was back, were still fresh. "They weren't so nice to me."

"No," Jack admitted. He looked down at the ground. "But still. I mean, they all—Sam and Astrid and all—they asked me to figure it out, the phones I mean, and I did. I want . . . I mean . . . I mean, I did it. I *did it*. It works. So we should turn it back on."

Brianna's expression hardened. "No. If it helps the Coates people in any way, then no. I don't want their lives to be any easier. I want them to suffer. I want them to suffer in every way they can suffer. And then I want them to die."

She saw shock register behind those askew glasses. Jack was no different from most people, Brianna admitted to herself with some bitterness: he didn't take her seriously. Of course she maintained an aura of cool and everything—after all, she was the Breeze. She was a superhero, so she had some obligation to carry off a certain style. But she was also Brianna. Regular girl.

"Oh, did that sound too harsh?" she asked, letting annoyance resonate in her tone of voice.

"A little bit," Jack said.

"Yeah? Well, thanks for helping. Later," Brianna said. And she was gone before he could say something else stupid.

Duck woke up.

He was completely disoriented. He was flat on his back. Wet. Wearing nothing but a bathing suit. In the dark.

He was cold. His fingertips were numb. He was shivering.

He felt something hard and sharp beneath his shoulder blades and he shifted to lessen the pain. He looked around, bewildered. There was a faint light from above. Sunlight bouncing weakly down a long dirt shaft.

Duck tried to make sense of it. He remembered everything: sinking to the bottom of the pool, then sinking through the bottom of the pool. He remembered choking on water and his lungs burning. There were scrapes down his sides, and along the underside of his arms.

And now, here he was, in a hole. A deep hole. At the bottom of a mud-sided shaft that he had somehow caused by falling into the earth.

Falling into the earth?

It was impossible to be sure how far down underground he was. But from the faraway look of the light, he had to be at least twenty feet down. Twenty feet. Underground.

Fear stabbed at his heart. He was buried alive. There was no way he'd be able to clamber back up through that narrow muddy shaft to the surface.

No way.

"Help!" he yelled. The sound echoed faintly.

Duck realized that he was not in a confined space. There was air. And the surface beneath him was too hard and too rough to be dirt. He got to his knees. Then, slowly, stood up. There was a ceiling just inches above his head. He stretched his arms to either side and touched a wall to his left, nothing to his right.

"It's a pipe," Duck said to the darkness. "Or a tunnel."

It was also pitch black in both directions.

"Or a cave."

"How did this happen?" Duck demanded of the cave. His teeth chattered from cold. From fear as well. There was a faint echo, but no answer.

He looked up toward the light and yelled, "Help! Help!" a couple more times. But there was zero chance of anyone hearing. Unless of course Zil and the boys who'd been harassing him had gone for help. That was possible, wasn't it? They might be jerks, but surely they would go for help. They wouldn't just leave him down here.

And yet, there were no anxious faces peering down at him from above.

"Come on, Duck: Think."

He was in a tunnel, or whatever, far underground. The tunnel floor was muddy and wet. Despite this, the tunnel did not feel particularly damp, not like it was a sewer. And he himself was far less muddy than he should have been.

"I fell down through the ground. Then I practically drowned and passed out and stopped. The water kept flowing past me and mostly cleaned me off."

He was pleased to have even figured that out.

Gingerly he took steps down the tunnel, holding his hands out ahead of him. He was scared. More scared than he had been in his life. More scared even than the day the FAYZ had happened, or the day of the big battle, when he had hidden in a closet with a flashlight and some comic books.

He was down here now, alone. No Iron Man. No Sandman. No Dark Knight.

And it was cold.

Duck noticed the sound of his own sobbing, and was dismayed to realize he was crying. He tried to stop. It wasn't easy. He wanted to cry. He wanted to cry for his mother and father and grandmother and aunts and uncles and even his obnoxious big brother and the whole, whole, whole world that was gone and had abandoned him to this grave.

"Help! Help!" he cried, and again there was no answer.

Before him were two equally dark choices: The dark tunnel extending to his left. The dark tunnel extending to his right. He felt a slight, almost imperceptible whisper of breeze on his face. It seemed to come from his left.

Toward air. Not away.

Carefully, Duck made his way down the tunnel, hands outstretched like a blind person, down the tunnel.

It was so dark, he could not see his hand in front of his face. No light. None.

He soon found that it was easier if he kept one hand on the wall. It was rock, pitted and rough, but with bumps and protrusions that felt worn down. The ground below him was uneven but not wildly so.

"Cave has to lead somewhere," Duck told himself. He found the sound of his own voice reassuring. It was real. It was familiar.

"I wish it was a tunnel. People don't build a tunnel for no reason." Then, after a while, "At least a tunnel has to go somewhere."

He tried to make sense of the direction. Was he going north, south, east, west? Well, hopefully not too far west, because that would lead him to the ocean.

He walked and occasionally started crying and walked some more. It was impossible to guess how long he'd been down there. He had no idea what time of day it might be. But he soon realized that the place where he'd fallen in was seeming more and more homey by comparison. There wasn't much light back there, but at least there had been some. And here there was none.

"I don't want to die down here," he said. He was instantly sorry that he had voiced that thought. Saying it made it real.

At that moment he banged his head on something that shouldn't have been there, banged it hard.

Duck cursed angrily and put his hand to his forehead, feeling for blood, and realized his feet were sinking into the ground. "No!" he yelped.

The sinking stopped. He'd gone up to his knees. But then he had stopped. He had stopped sinking. Carefully, cautiously, he pulled his legs up out of the hard-packed dirt.

"What is happening to me?" he demanded. "Why . . ." But then he knew the answer. He knew it and couldn't believe it hadn't occurred to him earlier.

"Oh, my God: I'm a freak."

"I'm a moof!"

"I'm a moof with a really sucky power."

What exactly the mutant ability was, he wasn't sure. It seemed to be the power to sink right down through the earth. Which was crazy. And, besides, he hadn't intended to do any such thing. He sure hadn't said, "Sink!"

He started walking again, careful of his head, trying to work through what had happened. Both times he had sunk he'd been angry, that was the first thing. He'd heard the stories of how Sam had discovered his abilities only when he was really scared or really mad.

But Duck had been scared now for quite a while. He'd been scared since the FAYZ. It was only when he got angry that the thing happened.

The thing. Whatever it was.

"If I got mad enough maybe I'd sink clear through the earth. Come out in China. See my great-great grandparents."

He crept along a bit farther, toward a dim glow.

"Light?" he said. "Is that really light?"

It wasn't bright, that was for sure. It wasn't a lightbulb. It wasn't a flashlight. It wasn't even a star. It was more like a less dark darkness. Hazy. At a distance that was impossible to guess.

Duck was sure it was a hallucination. He wanted it to be real, but he feared it wasn't. He feared it was imagination.

But he kept moving and the closer he got the less likely it seemed that it was a mirage. There was definitely a glow. Like a glow-in-the-dark clock face, a sickly, cold, unhealthy-looking light.

Even close up it didn't glow enough to make out many features, just a few faint outlines of rock. He had to stand and stare hard, straining his eyes for quite some time before he could figure out that the glow was mostly along the ground. And that it came from a side tunnel of the main cave. This second shaft was narrow, far smaller than the main cave, which, it seemed to Duck, had gradually broadened out.

He could follow this new shaft and at least see something. Not much, but something. Some proof that he wasn't actually blind.

But some little voice in his brain was screaming, "No!" His instincts were telling him to run.

"There's light down there. It must lead to somewhere," Duck argued with himself.

But although Duck had never been the most attentive student, and had very little information of a scientific nature in his brain, he was an avid fan of *The Simpsons*. He'd seen this glow, in cartoon form. And it featured in any number of comics.

"It's radiation," he said.

This was wrong, he realized, filled with righteous indignation. Everyone said there was no radiation left from the big accident at the power plant thirteen years ago, when the meteorite hit. But where else would this glow have come from? It must have seeped along underground seams and crevices.

They had lied. Or maybe they just hadn't realized.

"Not a good idea to go that way," he told himself.

"But it's the only light," he cried, and began to weep with frustration because it seemed he had no choice but to plunge back into absolute darkness.

And then, Duck heard something.

He froze. He strained his senses to listen.

A soft, swishing sound. Very faint.

A long silence. And then, there it was again. Swish. Swish.

He'd missed the sound because he'd been focusing on the glow. It was a sound he knew. Water. And it did not, thank God, come from the radioactive shaft.

Duck hated the ocean. But all things considered, he hated it a bit less than he hated this cave.

Leaving the glow behind, and feeling carefully ahead, cautious about his bruised forehead, he crept on through pitch blackness.

"LOOK, ALBERT, DON'T tell me we have a problem and I can't do anything about it," Sam said, practically snarling. He marched along at a quick walk from the town hall to the church next door. Albert and Astrid were with him, struggling to keep up.

The sun was setting out over the ocean. The dying light laid down a long red exclamation point on the water. A boat was out there, one of the small motorboats. Sam sighed. Some kid who'd probably end up falling in.

Sam stopped suddenly, causing Albert and Astrid to bump into each other. "Sorry. I didn't mean to sound mad. Although I am mad, but not at you, Albert. It's just I have to go in there and lay down the law, and I'm sorry, but killer worms aren't making it any easier."

"Then hold off for a few days," Albert said calmly.

"Hold off? Albert, you were the one who was saying weeks ago, months ago, we had to make everyone get to work."

"I never said we should *make* them work," Albert countered.

"I said we should figure out a way to pay them to work."

Sam was not in the mood. Not in the mood at all. Losing a kid was a tragedy to everyone, but to him it was a personal failure. He'd been handed the job of being in charge, which meant everything that went wrong was on him. E.Z. had been under his care and protection. And now E.Z. was a pile of ash.

Sam sucked in a gulp of air. He shot a baleful look at the cemetery in the square. Three more graves in just the last three months since Sam had been officially elected mayor. E.Z. wouldn't get a grave, just a marker. At the rate things were going, they'd run out of room in the square.

The front door of the church stood open. Always open. That was because it, and much of the church roof, had been damaged in the big Thanksgiving Battle. The wide wooden doors had been blown off. The sides of the opening were shaky, held up by a slab of stone across the top that made the wreckage look like a lopsided Stonehenge monolith.

Caine had come close to collapsing the entire church, but it was built strong, so three quarters of it still stood. Some of the rubble had been cleared, but not much, and even that had only been pushed into the side street. Like so many ambitious undertakings that had fallen apart as kids quit working and could not be convinced to come back.

Sam walked straight to the front of the church and mounted the three low steps to what he thought of as the stage, although Astrid had patiently explained that it was called a chancel. The great cross had not been replaced in its rightful spot, but stood leaning in a corner. A close examination would reveal bloodstains where it had once crushed Cookie's shoulder.

Not until he turned around did Sam notice how little of the church was filled. There should have been close to 250 kids, leaving aside the day care and the people on guard in various locations. There were closer to eighty present, half of those so young, Sam knew they'd been dumped there by big brothers or sisters looking for a bit of free babysitting.

Astrid and Albert took seats in the first pew. Little Pete was at the day care. Now that Mother Mary had more help at the day care, Astrid could occasionally leave Pete there, although never for very long. As long as Pete stayed lost in his video game, anyone could care for him. But if Pete got upset . . .

Mother Mary Terrafino herself was two rows back, too humble to insert herself in the leadership area of the church. Sam was struck by how good Mary looked. Weight loss. Probably from overwork. Or maybe she didn't enjoy living on the kinds of canned food that, in the old pre-FAYZ days, people had donated to food drives. But she was quite thin, which was not an adjective normally applied to Mary. Model thin.

Lana Arwen Lazar slumped in a back row. She looked tired and a little resentful. Lana often looked resentful. But at least she had come, which was more than could be said for most kids.

Sam gritted his teeth, angry that so many had skipped this town meeting. Just what exactly did they have to do that was more important?

"First off," he said, "I want to say I'm sorry about E.Z. He was a good kid. He didn't deserve . . ." For a moment he almost lost it as a surge of emotion welled up from nowhere. "I'm sorry he died."

Someone sobbed loudly.

"Look, I'm going to get right to it: we have three hundred and thirty-two . . . I'm sorry, three hundred and thirty-one mouths to feed," Sam said. He placed his hands on his hips and planted his feet wide apart. "We were already pretty bad off for food supplies. But after the attack by the Coates kids . . . well, it's not pretty bad off, anymore, it's desperate."

He let that sink in. But how much were six- and eight-year-olds really grasping? Even the older kids looked more glazed than alarmed.

"Three hundred and thirty-one kids," Sam reiterated, "And food for maybe a week. That's not a long time. It's not a lot of food. And as you all know, the food we have is awful."

That got a response from the audience. The younger kids produced a chorus of gagging and retching sounds.

"All right," Sam snapped. "Knock it off. The point is, things are really desperate."

"How about the food in everyone's house?" someone yelled.

The light of the setting sun streamed through the damaged façade of the church and stabbed Sam in the eyes. He had to take two steps to the left to escape it. "Hunter? Is that you?"

Hunter Lefkowitz was a year younger than Sam, long-haired like just about everyone except the few who had taken the initiative of cutting his or her own hair. He was not someone who had ever been popular in school before the FAYZ. But then, Sam reflected, the things that had made kids popular in the old days didn't mean much anymore.

Hunter had begun developing powers. Sam was trying to keep that fact secret—he suspected that Caine was sending spies into Perdido Beach. He wanted to be able to use Hunter as a secret weapon if it came to another fight with Caine's people. But secrets were tough to keep in a place where everyone knew everyone else.

"Hunter, we've searched all of the homes and carried the food to Ralph's," Sam continued. "The problem is that all the fruit and veggies spoiled while we were all filling up on chips and cookies. The meat all rotted. People were stupid and careless, and there's nothing we can do about that now." Sam swallowed the bitterness he felt, the anger he felt at his own foolishness. "But we have food sitting out in the fields. Maybe not the food we'd like, but enough to carry us for months— many months—if we bring it in before it rots and the birds eat it."

"Maybe we'll get rescued, and we won't have to worry," another voice said.

"Maybe we'll learn to live on air," Astrid muttered under her breath but loudly enough to be heard by at least a few.

"Why don't you go get our food back from Drake and the chuds up there?"

It was Zil. He accepted a congratulatory slap on the back from a creepy kid named Antoine, part of Zil's little posse.

"Because it would mean getting some kids killed," Sam said bluntly. "We'd be lucky to rescue any of the food, and we'd end up digging more graves in the plaza. And it wouldn't solve our problem, anyway."

"Get your moofs to go fight their moofs," Zil said.

Sam had heard the term "moof" more and more lately. "Chud" was a newer term. Each new term seemed just a little more derogatory than the one it replaced.

"Sit down, Zil," Sam went on. "We have twenty-six kids who are in the . . . have we decided? Are we calling it the army?" he asked Edilio.

Edilio was in the first pew. He leaned forward, hung his head, and looked uncomfortable. "Some kids are calling it that, but man, I don't know what to call it. Like a militia or something? I guess it doesn't matter."

"Mother Mary has fourteen kids working for her, including one-day draftees," Sam said, ticking off the list. "Fire Chief Ellen has six kids at the firehouse, dealing with emergencies. Dahra handles the pharmacy herself, Astrid is my adviser. Jack is in charge of technology. Albert has twenty-four kids working with him now, guarding Ralph's and distributing food supplies. Counting me, that's seventy-eight kids who do various jobs."

"When they bother to show up," Mary Terrafino said loudly. That earned a nervous laugh, but Mary wasn't smiling.

"Right," Sam agreed. "When they bother to show up. The thing is, we need more people working. We need people bringing in that food."

"We're just kids," a fifth grader said, and giggled at his own joke.

"You're going to be hungry kids," Sam snapped. "You're

going to be starving kids. Listen to me: people are going to starve. To death.

"To. Death." He repeated it with all the emphasis he could bring to bear on the word.

He caught a warning look from Astrid and took a deep breath. "Sorry. I didn't mean to yell. It's just that the situation is really bad."

A second-grade girl held up her hand. Sam sighed, knowing what to expect, but called on her, anyway.

"I just want my mom."

"We all do," Sam said impatiently. "We all want the old world back. But we don't seem to be able to make that happen. So we have to try to make this world work out. Which means we need food. Which means we need kids to harvest the food, and load it into trucks, and preserve it, and cook it, and . . ." He threw up his hands as he realized he was staring at rows and rows of blank expressions.

"You crazy with that stuff about picking vegetables?" It was Howard Bassem, leaning against the back wall. Sam hadn't seen him come in. Sam glanced around for Orc, but didn't see him. And Orc wasn't something . . . no, someone, still some *one* despite everything . . . you overlooked.

"You have another way to get food?" Sam asked.

"Man, you think people don't know about what happened to E.Z.?"

Sam stiffened. "Of course we all know what happened to E.Z. No one is trying to hide what happened to E.Z. But as far as we know, the worms are just in that one cabbage field."

"What worms?" Hunter demanded.

Obviously not everyone had heard. Sam would have liked to smack Howard right at that moment. The last thing they needed was a retelling of E.Z.'s gruesome fate.

"I've taken a look at one of the worms," Astrid said, sensing that Sam was reaching the limit of his patience. She didn't come up onto the chancel but stood by her pew and faced the audience, which was now paying very close attention. Except for two little kids who were having a shoving match.

"The worms that killed E.Z. are mutations," Astrid said. "They have hundreds of teeth. Their bodies are designed for boring through flesh rather than tunneling through the dirt."

"But as far as we know, they're just in that one cabbage field," Sam reiterated.

"I dissected the worm Sam brought me," Astrid said. "I found something very strange. The worms have very large brains. I mean, a normal earthworm's brain is so primitive that if you cut it out, the worm still keeps doing what it normally does."

"Kind of like my sister," a kid piped up, and was poked by his sister in retaliation.

Howard drifted closer to the front of the room. "So these E.Z. killer worms are smart."

"I'm not implying that they can read or do quadratic equations," Astrid said. "But they've gone from brains that were a bundle of cells that did nothing more than manage the organism's negative phototropism to a brain with differentiated hemispheres and distinct, presumably specialized, regions."

Sam hid a smile by looking down. Astrid was perfectly capable of simplifying the way she explained things. But when someone was irritating her—as Howard was doing now—she would crank up the polysyllables and make them feel stupid.

Howard came to a stop, perhaps paralyzed by the word "phototropism." But he recovered quickly. "Look, bottom line, you step into a field full of these E.Z. killers, these zekes, and you're dead. Right?"

"The large brains confirm the possibility that these creatures are capable of territoriality. My point is, judging by what Sam, Edilio, and Albert observed, the worms may stay perfectly within their territory. In this case, the cabbage field."

"Yeah?" Howard said. "Well, I know someone who could walk right through that field and not be bothered."

So that was it, Sam thought. Inevitably with Howard, it all came back to Orc.

"You may be right that Orc would be invulnerable," Sam said. "So?"

"So?" Howard echoed. He smirked. "So, Sam, Orc can pick those cabbages for you. Of course he's going to need something in exchange."

"Beer?"

Howard nodded, maybe a little embarrassed, but not much. "He has a taste for the stuff. Me, I can't stand it. But as Orc's manager I'll need to be taken care of, too."

Sam gritted his teeth. But the truth was it might be a solution to the problem. They had quite a bit of beer still at Ralph's grocery.

"If Orc wants to try it, fine with me," Sam said. "Work something out with Albert."

It was not fine with Astrid. "Sam, Orc has become an alcoholic. You want to give him beer?"

"A can of beer for a day's work," Sam said. "Orc can't get very drunk on—"

"No way," Howard said. "Orc needs a case a day. Four six-packs. After all, it's hot work out there in the field picking cabbage."

Sam shot a glance at Astrid. Her face was set. But Sam had the responsibility for feeding 331 kids. Orc was probably invulnerable to the zekes. And he was so strong, he could yank up thirty thousand pounds of cabbage in a week's work. "Talk to Albert after the meeting," Sam said to Howard.

Astrid fumed but sat down. Howard did a jaunty little finger-pointing thing at Sam, signifying agreement.

Sam sighed. The meeting wasn't going the way he'd planned. They never did. He understood that kids were kids, so he was used to the inevitable disruptions and general silliness of the younger ones. But that even so many of the older kids, kids in seventh, eighth grade, hadn't bothered to show up was depressing.

To make things worse, all this talk of food was making him hungry. Lunch had been grim. The hunger was almost always present now. It made him feel hollow. It occupied his brain, when he needed to be thinking of other things.

"Look, people, I'm announcing a new rule. It's going to seem harsh. But it's necessary."

The word "harsh" got almost everyone's attention.

"We can't have people sitting around all day playing Wii and watching DVDs. We need people to start working in the fields. So, here's the thing: everyone age seven or older has to put in three days per week picking fruit or veggies. Then Albert's going to work with the whole question of freezing stuff that can be frozen, or otherwise preserving stuff."

There was dead silence. And blank stares.

"What I'm saying is, tomorrow we'll have two school buses ready to go. They hold about fifty kids each and we need to have them mostly full because we're going to pick some melons and it's a lot of work."

More blank stares.

"Okay, let me make this simple: get your brothers and sisters and friends and anyone over age seven and be in the square tomorrow morning at eight o'clock."

"But how about—?"

"Just be there," Sam said with less firmness than he'd intended. His frustration was draining away now, replaced by weariness and depression.

"Just be there," someone mimicked in a singsong voice.

Sam closed his eyes, and for a moment he almost seemed to be asleep. Then he opened them again and managed a bleak smile. "Please. Be there," he said quietly.

He walked down the three steps and out of the church, knowing in his heart that few would answer his call.

SEVEN

"PULL OVER HERE, Panda," Drake said.

"Why?" Panda was behind the wheel of the SUV. He was getting more and more confident as a driver, but being Panda, he still wouldn't go more than thirty miles an hour.

"Because that's what I said to do, that's why," Drake said irritably.

Bug knew why they were stopping. And Bug knew why it bothered Drake. They couldn't risk driving down the highway to the power plant. In the three months Caine had spent hallucinating and yelling crazy stuff, the Coates side had grown steadily weaker while the Perdido Beach side cruised right along. Drake had pulled off his raid at Ralph's, but he didn't dare do anything more.

Bug knew. He'd been in and out of Perdido Beach many times. They might be running low on food in town but they still had more than Coates. It was frustrating for Bug because he should have been able to steal more of that food, but his chameleon powers didn't work that well on things he was carrying. The best he could do was slip a package of dried soup or a rare PowerBar inside his shirt. Not that there were PowerBars to be found nowadays. Or dried soup.

"Okay, Bug, we hike from here," Drake said. He swung his door open and stepped out onto the road. Bug slid across the seat and stood beside Drake.

Bug's real name was Tyler. His fellow Coates kids assumed he had earned his nickname from his willingness to accept crazy dares—specifically, eating insects. Kids would dare him and he'd say, "What do I get if I do it?" Mostly, in the old days, he'd gotten kids to give him money or candy.

He didn't mind most bugs. He kind of liked the way they would squirm before he would bite down on them, ending their little insect lives.

But Bug had been called that before ever coming to Coates, before he'd gotten a reputation as the kid who would try anything. The nickname Bug had stuck to him after he was caught recording parent-teacher conferences at his old school. He'd posted the conversations on Facebook, embarrassing any kid with a psychological issue, a learning disability, a bedwetting problem—about half his class.

Bug hadn't just been sent to Coates as punishment; he'd been sent for his own safety.

Bug edged nervously away as Drake unlimbered his tentacle, stretched it out, and rewrapped it around himself. Bug didn't like Drake. No one did. But if he was going to get caught out in the open sneaking toward the power plant, he figured Drake would do all the fighting while he himself just disappeared. At night he was completely invisible.

They left Panda behind with firm instructions to stay where he was until they got back. Which was on a back road that went from tarmac to gravel, back and forth, as though the guys who'd built it couldn't make up their minds.

"We have a good two miles to cover to get to the main road," Drake said. "So keep up."

"I'm hungry," Bug complained.

"Everybody's hungry," Drake snapped. "Shut up about it."

They plunged off the road into some kind of farmland. It was tough walking because the field was plowed into furrows, so it was hard not to trip. Something was growing there, but Bug had no idea what, just that it was some kind of plant. He wondered if he could eat it: he was that hungry.

Maybe there would be some food at the plant. Maybe he could find something while he was scoping the place out.

They walked in silence. Drake was not one for small talk, and neither was Bug.

The highway's lights were visible from far off. It was impossible, even now, to see those bright lights and not think of busy gas stations, bright Wendy's and Burger Kings, bustling stores, cars, and trucks. Just south of Perdido Beach had been a long strip of such restaurants, plus a Super Target where they sold groceries, and a See's candy store where . . .

Bug couldn't stand it that it was all there, just outside the FAYZ wall. If there was an outside anymore.

See's candy. Bug would have just about cut off his ear to have five minutes inside that store. He liked the ones with nuts in them, especially. Oh, and the ones with raspberry cream. And the kind of brown sugar ones. The ones with caramel, those were good, too.

All out of reach now. His mouth watered. His stomach ached.

It was so quiet in the FAYZ, Bug thought. Quiet and empty. And, if Caine succeeded in his plan, it would soon be dark as well.

Only some portions of the highway were lit up. The part that went through town, and here, at the turn-off to the power plant. Bug and Drake stayed well away from the pool of light.

Bug looked left, toward town. No sign of movement coming down the road. Nothing to the right, either. Across the highway and a little distance down the access road Bug knew there was a guardhouse. But that shouldn't be any problem.

"You have to stay off the road and go cross-country," Drake told him.

"What? Why? No one can see me."

"There might be infrared security cameras at the plant, moron, that's why. We don't know if you're invisible to infrared cameras."

Bug acknowledged that could be a problem. But the prospect of covering another couple of miles going uphill and down, through tall grass and across unseen ditches, wasn't very exciting. He would probably get lost. Then he would never get back in time for breakfast.

"Okay," he said, having no intention of obeying.

Suddenly Drake's creepy tentacle wrapped around him. Drake squeezed hard enough that Bug had to struggle to breathe.

"This is important, Bug. Don't screw it up." Drake's eyes were cold. "If you do? I'll whip the skin off you."

Bug nodded. Drake released him.

Bug shuddered as the tentacle slithered away. It was like a snake. Just like a snake. And Bug hated snakes.

It was easy for Bug to turn the camouflage on. He just thought about disappearing and passed his hands down his front like he was smoothing his shirt. He saw Drake's confused stare, his mean eyes not quite able to focus on Bug's true location. He knew he was all but invisible. He raised a middle finger to Drake.

"Later," Bug said, and crossed the highway.

Bug hiked cross-country until he was well away from Drake. The moon was up but it was only a sliver and touched only the occasional rock, the odd stalk of weed. He walked straight into a low-hanging tree branch and fell on his butt, mouth bleeding and bruised.

After that he cut back to the road. The road curved high above the glittering ocean, affording a pretty, if disquieting view. Something about the ocean always felt ominous to Bug.

Bug figured if he was visible on infrared, well, too bad. He could always switch sides like Computer Jack had done. Of course then he'd be in trouble if Drake ever got hold of him.

He took Drake's threats seriously. Very seriously.

Bug had been beaten many times. His father had been quick with a slap or, when he was good and drunk, a punch. But his father had some limits on his behavior: he was always worried that Bug's mother would be able to take custody away from him. Not that his father loved him so much—it was that he hated Bug's mother and wouldn't do anything that would allow her to win.

At the worst of times, when his father had been out drinking with his girlfriend and they'd had a fight, Bug had learned to hide. His favorite place was in the attic because it was stuffed with boxes, and behind the boxes there was a spot where Bug could crawl under the eaves and lie flat on the insulation between cross-beams. His father had never found him there.

It seemed like forever before Bug began to catch sight of the brightly lit power plant. A glimpse through a crease in the hill, a glow coming from beyond a bend in the road. It felt like another forever before he came upon the second guardhouse, the one that squatted across the road with a chain-link and barbed-wire fence extending out in both directions.

Caine had speculated that the fence, which only one Coates kid had ever seen, might be electrified. Bug wasn't going to take any chances. He walked along the fence, uphill, into the rough, away from the guardhouse for a hundred yards. He found a stick and began to scoop out the dirt below the fence. It wouldn't take much, he wasn't very big.

Bug felt very exposed. As long as he was digging with the stick, he was visible: sticks did not have the power of camouflage. The moon that before had seemed to cast no light at all now felt like a searchlight focused right on him. And the power plant itself was like some vast, terrifying beast crouched beside the water, blazingly bright in the blackness.

Bug crawled under the fence on his back. Dirt found its

way inside his shirt, but he did not get electrocuted. Not that he really thought the fence was electrified. Still, better to be careful.

Bug stood up, brushed himself off, and began marching down the hill toward the power plant.

He was hungry. He would spy and do all the things Drake had told him to do. But first, he would look for food.

Sam tried to sleep. Wanted desperately to sleep.

He was in the spare bedroom at Astrid and Mary and John's house. In the dark. On his back. Staring up at the ceiling.

Downstairs, in the kitchen, there were a half dozen cans of food. He was hungry. But he had had his ration for the day. He had to set the example.

Still, he was hungry, and the hunger didn't care about setting an example.

Food downstairs. And Astrid down the hall.

A different kind of hunger, that. And there, too, he had to set a good example.

I am nothing but good examples, he told himself gloomily.

Not that Astrid would . . . although, how could he know for sure?

His head buzzed with a crazy list of things he had to do. Had to get people working on picking crops. Had to get people to start carrying their trash to one central location: rats were taking over the nighttime streets, scurrying from trash pile to trash pile.

Had to get a whole list of younger kids set up in houses with older kids. There were five- and six-year-olds living alone. That was crazy. And dangerous. One of them had thrown a hair dryer into a bathtub last week and blown out power in their home. It was just sheer luck no one had been electrocuted. Two weeks before that a second-grade boy, living by himself, had set his house on fire. Deliberately, it seemed. As a way to get someone, anyone, to pay attention. The blaze had consumed three homes, half a block, before anyone got around to telling the fire department. By the time Ellen had driven the huge old fire truck to the scene, the fire had almost burned itself out.

The kid had survived with painful burns that Lana had healed. But only after the little boy had writhed and cried in unbearable agony for hours.

Was Astrid still awake? Was she lying there in the dark? Same as him? Thinking the same thoughts?

No. She was thinking he was a jerk for authorizing Albert to bribe Orc with beer. Thinking he had no morals. Thinking he was losing it.

Maybe she was right.

Not helpful. Not helpful when what you needed was sleep. Not helpful to go over the list of things you needed to do, and the list of things you couldn't do.

How crazy was it that he was reduced to fantasizing about a can of chili, the last slightly tasty thing he'd eaten? How long ago? A week? Fantasizing about canned chili. Hamburgers. Ice cream. Pizza. And Astrid, in her own bed.

He wondered what it would be like to be drunk. Did it make you forget all of that? There was still plenty of alcohol in the FAYZ, even though some kids had started drinking it.

Could he stop them? Should he bother? If they were going to starve to death, why not let them drink?

Little kids, drinking rum. He'd seen it. Drinking vodka. They'd make faces at the horrible taste and the burn of it, then they'd take another sip.

Food poisoning last week, two kids sharing something they had dug out of the garbage. They'd staggered into Dahra's so-called hospital with fevers. A hundred and four degrees. Vomiting. Vomiting the water and the Tylenol she'd tried to get down them. Thank God for Lana, she'd saved them, but it was a close call. Lana's power worked better on wounds, things that were broken.

There would be more electrocutions. More fires. More poisonings. More accidents. Like the boy who had fallen off the roof. He'd fallen two stories, and no one had seen him fall. His sister had found the body.

He was buried in the town square now, next to the victims of the battle.

Caine was still out there. Drake. Pack Leader. All of them still out there, somewhere. Sam had fooled himself into believing he was done with them, until Drake and his crew hit Ralph's.

In the old days if you had just a little money you could make a phone call and, thirty minutes later, there would be Papa John's bringing you a giant pizza.

Melted, bubbly, brown cheese. Greasy pepperoni. Just like that. Just like it was no big deal. He would sell his soul for a pizza.

Astrid was religious, so probably no, she was not lying in her bed thinking of him. Almost certainly not. Although when they kissed she didn't seem like she was pulling away. She loved him, he knew that for sure. And he loved her. With all his heart.

But there were other feelings, in addition to love. Kind of attached to the love feeling, but different, too.

And Chinese. Oh, man, the little white cardboard boxes full of sweet-and-sour chicken and lemon chicken and Szechuan prawns. He'd never cared much for Chinese food. But it beat cans of butter beans and half-cooked pinto beans and what passed for tortillas made out of flour and oil and water and burned on a stove.

Someone would probably come and wake him up, soon, only he wouldn't be asleep. They came almost every night. *Sam, something's burning. Sam, someone's hurt. Sam, a kid crashed a car. Sam, we caught Orc all drunk and breaking windows for no reason.*

It wouldn't be *Sam, the pizza's here.*

It wouldn't be Astrid saying *Sam, I'm here.*

Sam drifted off to sleep. Astrid came in. She stood in the doorway, beautiful in her gauzy nightgown, and said, *Sam, it's okay, E.Z.'s alive.*

Even asleep, Sam knew that was a dream.

An hour later Taylor simply appeared, teleported into his room—she called it "bouncing"—and said, "Sam, wake up."

No dream, this time. It was often Taylor who brought the bad news. She or Brianna, if either was available. They were the fastest means of communication.

"What is it, Taylor?"

"You know Tom? Tom O'Dell?"

Sam didn't think he did. His brain was not focusing. He couldn't seem to quite wake up.

"Anyway, there was a fight between Tom and the girls who live next door—Sandy and . . . and I forget the other girl. Tom got hurt pretty bad from Sandy hitting him with a bowling ball."

Sam swung his legs over the side of the bed, but could not keep his eyes open. "What? Why did she hit him with a bowling ball?"

"She says Tom killed her cat," Taylor said. "And then he was cooking it on the barbecue in his backyard."

That at last penetrated Sam's bleary brain. "Okay. Okay." He stood up and fumbled around for his jeans. He had gotten over the embarrassment of being seen in his underwear.

Taylor handed him his pants. "Here."

"Bounce back. Tell them I'm coming."

Taylor disappeared, and for a moment Sam tried to tell himself that this was just another dream. There was nothing, after all, that he could do about a dead cat.

But it was his duty to show up. If he started blowing off his duties, it would look bad.

"Set a good example," he muttered under his breath as he crept silently past Astrid's door.

EIGHT

ORSAY PETTIJOHN STOOD transfixed. Two kids, the first human beings she had seen in three months, and both were bizarre, creepy. In the one boy's case, monstrous.

One was some sort of a demon with a thick tentacle where his right arm should have been.

The other . . . she wasn't even sure the other was there for a moment. He appeared, then he disappeared.

The boy with the frightening tentacle stared after the invisible one. Not quite invisible, Orsay realized when the boy stepped into a pool of light, but close enough. Then the boy with the python arm sighed, cursed under his breath, and opened the creaking door of a Toyota that had unaccountably run fifty feet off the road.

The boy evidently wanted the window open, but the battery was dead. So he drew a gun, aimed it at the driver's side window, and fired. The bang was so loud that Orsay gasped. She would have given away her position, but the sound of the explosion also camouflaged the sound of her cry.

Orsay squatted in the dark, in the dirt, and waited. The boy with the python arm would almost certainly go to sleep.

And then it would begin again.

Orsay had been living at the ranger station in the Stefano Rey National Park on the day everyone disappeared.

She had been mystified. She had been frightened.

She had also been relieved.

Just about three months earlier, she had been begging her father for help.

"What do you mean?" he had asked. He'd been busy poring over paperwork. There was a lot of paperwork involved in being a ranger. It wasn't just about helping find lost hikers and making sure campers didn't set the woods on fire while they were toasting marshmallows.

She had wanted to make him pay attention to her. Just to her. Not phony attention where he was really focused on his work. "Dad, I'm going nuts or something."

That declaration had earned her a dubious glance. "Is this about going to see your mom? Because I told you, she's still not ready. She loves you very much, but she's not ready for the responsibility."

That was a lie, but a well-intentioned one. Orsay knew about her mother's drug addiction. She knew about her mother's trips to rehab, each of which was followed by a period of normalcy where she would take Orsay, and put her in school, and arrange tidy little family dinners. Always just enough normal time for Orsay to think, maybe this time, before she would once again find her mother's "works" stashed in the back of a cupboard, or find her mother barely conscious and sprawled across the couch.

Her mother was a heroin addict. She'd been a secret heroin addict for a long time, faking it well during the early years when she'd still been married to Orsay's father and they'd lived in Oakland. Orsay's father had worked out of the park service regional headquarters.

But Orsay's mother's addiction grew ever worse, and soon there was no hiding it. There was a divorce. Orsay's mother did not fight for custody. Her father took a job at Stefano Rey, wanting to get far away from the city and far away from his ex-wife.

Orsay had lived a lonely life since then. School was a once-a-day video link with a classroom all the way off in Sunnyvale.

Occasionally she'd make a short-term friend with one of the kids who came with their parents to camp. Maybe a nice couple of days of swimming and fishing and hiking. But never more than a day here and a day there.

"Dad. I'm trying to tell you something important here. It's not about Mom. It's about me. There's something wrong with me. There's something very, very weird in my head."

"Sweetheart, you're a teenager. Of course there's something wrong in your head. If there wasn't, you wouldn't be a teenager. It's normal for you to start thinking about . . . well, diff—"

And that's when her father had simply disappeared.

There.

Not there.

She'd thought she was hallucinating. She had thought the craziness had suddenly overtaken her.

But her father was really gone. So were Ranger Assante and Ranger Cruz and Ranger Swallow.

So was everyone in the Main West campground.

The satellite uplink was dead. The cell phones were dead.

All that first day she had searched, but there was no one. Not in any of the campgrounds she could reach easily, anyway.

She had been terrified.

But that night she had felt silence descend on her battered mind. For the first time in weeks.

The creepy, lurid, crazy-quilt visions of people and places she didn't know were gone. In its place . . . not peace, exactly. But quiet. Her mind and dreams were her own again.

Despite her fear, Orsay slept. Reality had become a nightmare, but at least now it was her own nightmare.

On the second day, Orsay had hiked until she'd encountered the barrier. And then she knew that whatever was happening to her, it was real.

The barrier was impassable. It hurt to touch it.

There was no going north. The only way open was to the south, toward the distant town of Perdido Beach, almost twenty miles away.

Orsay had resisted. She was desperately lonely, but then she had been for a long time. And the compensation for feeling sane again was almost enough to make up for the utter isolation.

She found enough food in the storehouse and, when that was used up, in the campgrounds.

For a while she thought she might be the only person left alive. But then she had chanced upon a group of kids hiking through the forest. There were five of them. Four boys and a girl, all about Orsay's age, except for one younger boy, maybe four or five years old.

She followed them a while, keeping out of sight. They were noisy enough to hear from a distance. They lacked Orsay's well-developed woodsman's skills.

That night, as they began to sleep, Orsay crept closer, wondering, hoping . . .

And then it started.

The first dream was from a boy named Edilio. Flashes of a day filled with insane action: a huge boat that flew through the air and crashed down on his head; a hotel atop a cliff; a race around a marina.

Crowding behind Edilio's dream came visions from a boy named Quinn. These were sad dreams, dark and gloomy and full of emotion, with only a few dark shapes to give them life.

But then the little boy, the four-year-old, fell into an REM state, and his dreams had blown away the others. It was as if the others' dreams were on small TVs while the little boy's dream was on an IMAX movie screen with surround sound.

Images of terrible menace.

Images of staggering beauty.

Things that were somehow both beautiful and terrifying.

None of it was logical. None of it made sense. But there

was no looking away, no chance of hiding from the cascade of pictures, sounds, feelings. It was as if Orsay had tried to stand in front of a tornado.

The boy, Little Pete, had seen her. Dreamers often did, although they usually weren't sure who she was or why she was there. They usually ignored her as just another nonsensical element of a random dream.

But Little Pete had stepped into his own dream and he had come to her. He had stared right at her.

"Be careful," Little Pete said. "There's a monster."

And that was when Orsay had sensed a dark presence, looming up behind her. A presence that was like a black hole, eating the light of Little Pete's dream.

There was a name for the dark thing. A word Orsay couldn't make sense of. A word she had never heard. In the dream she had turned away from Little Pete to face the darkness, to ask it its name. To ask it what "gaiaphage" meant.

But Little Pete had smiled, just a little. He shook his head no, as if chiding a foolish child who'd been about to touch a hot stove.

And she had awakened, expelled from the dream like an unwelcomed guest at a party.

Now, months later, she still winced at the memory. But she also craved it. She had spent every night since wishing that she could touch Little Pete's sleeping mind once more. She savored the fragments she could recall, tried to get that same rush but always failed.

She was almost out of food, down to MREs—meals ready

to eat, the overly salted meals in a pouch that soldiers and some campers ate. She told herself that she was coming down from the forest at long last for food. Just for food.

Now Orsay watched from a safe distance, concealed by darkness, as a real-life monster, a boy with a thick, powerful tentacle in place of one arm, said good-bye to a boy who simply disappeared.

She waited as he lost the fight with sleep.

And then, ah yes, such strange visions.

Drake. That was his name. She could hear the echo of that sound in her head.

Drake Merwin.

Whip Hand.

For what felt like a very long time she wandered through dreams of pain and rage. She had to shield herself from the physical agony, memories of which kept flooding the boy's dreams.

In Drake's dream Orsay saw a different boy, a boy with piercing eyes, a boy who made things fly through the air.

And she saw a boy with fire coming from his hands.

Then she saw the girl, the dark-haired, dark-eyed beauty. And the angry, resentful visions took a turn to something worse still.

Far worse.

For weeks before the great disappearance Orsay had been tortured by dreams she couldn't shut out, many of them the dreams of adults filled with disturbingly adult imagery.

But she had never entered a dream like this.

She was shaking. Feeling as if she couldn't breathe.

She wanted to look away, spare herself from witnessing the sick boy's vile nightmares. But it was the curse of her condition: She had no power to block the dreams out. It was like she was strapped into a chair, eyes pried open, forced to look at images that made her sick.

Only distance would protect her. Sobbing, Orsay crawled away, crawled toward the desert, indifferent to the stones that cut her knees and palms.

The dreams faded. Gradually, Orsay steadied her breathing. This had been a mistake, coming down from the forest, a terrible mistake.

She had told herself she was going in search of food. But in her heart she knew there was a deeper reason for leaving the forest. She missed the sound of a human voice.

No, that wasn't the whole truth, either.

She missed the dreams. The good ones, the bad ones. She found herself longing for them. Needing them. Addicted.

But not this. Not this.

She sat with eyes closed tight, rocking slowly back and forth in the sand, trying to—

The tentacle was around her, squeezing her tight, squeezing the air out of her lungs before she could even scream.

He was behind her. Her movement had awakened him, and he'd found her and now, now . . . Oh, God . . .

He lifted her up and turned her around to face him. His face would have been handsome if she had not known what lurked behind those icy eyes.

"You," he whispered, his breath in her face. "You were in my head."

Duck had found the cause of the ocean sounds. It was, in fact, the ocean.

At least that's what it seemed like. He couldn't see it. It was as black as everything else. But it smelled of salt. And it moved like a heaving body of water should, rolling up to his toes and receding. But he could see nothing.

He told himself it was dark outside, out beyond the mouth of the cave. That's why he couldn't see anything. It was obvious now that this had to be a sea cave, a cave cut into the land by the constant motion of water over a long, long period of time. Which meant there had to be a way out.

In his mind he pictured it opening onto the beach below Clifftop. Or somewhere near there. Anyway, the important word was: opening.

Had to be.

"You keep saying 'had to be' like that makes it so," he said.

"No, I don't," he argued. "I was thinking it, I didn't say it out loud."

"Great. Now I'm arguing with myself."

"Not really, I'm just thinking out loud."

"Well, try thinking more and arguing less."

"Hey, I've been down here for, like, a hundred hours! I don't even know what time it is. It could be three days from now!"

He bent down and touched wet sand. Water surged over his fingers. It was cold. But then, everything was cold. Duck had been cold for a long time now. It was slow work walking when you couldn't see where you were going.

He raised wet fingers to his tongue. Definitely salt. So yes, it was the ocean. Which meant that yes, this cave opened onto the ocean. Which meant there was a pretty good mystery as to why he couldn't see any light at all.

He shivered. He was so cold. He was so hungry. He was so thirsty. He was so scared.

And suddenly, he realized, he was not alone.

The rustling sound was different from the water-sloshing sound. Very different. It was a distinctly dry sound. Like someone rubbing crinkly leaves together.

"Hello?" he called.

"No answer," he whispered.

"I know: I heard. I mean, I didn't hear," he said. "Is someone there?"

The rustling sound again. It was coming from overhead. Then a chitter-chitter-chitter noise, soft but definite. He didn't miss many sounds now, not with his eyes useless. Hearing was all he had. If something made a sound, he heard it. And something had made a sound.

"Are you bats?" he asked.

"Because if they were bats, they would totally answer."

"Bats. Bats are not a problem." He chattered.

"Bats have to have a way out, right? They can't live in a cave all the time. They have to be able to fly out and . . . and drink blood."

Duck stood frozen, awaiting the bat attack. He would never see it coming. If they came after him, he would jump into the water. Yes. Or . . . or he could get mad and maybe sink through the ground and be safe in the dirt.

"Yeah, that's a great plan: bury yourself alive."

The bats—if that's what they were—demonstrated no interest in attacking him and drinking his blood. So Duck returned to the question of what exactly he should do next. In theory he could jump into the water and swim out into the ocean.

In theory. In reality he could not see his own hand in front of his face.

He squatted in a dry corner of the cave, well away from the water. And in an area that seemed somewhat less populated by weird rustling sounds.

He hugged himself and shivered.

How had he ended up here? He'd never hurt anyone. He wasn't some evil guy, he was just a kid. Like any other kid. He just wanted to go online and play games and watch TV and listen to music. He wanted to read his comics. He didn't want to be able to sink through the ground.

What kind of a stupid power was that, anyway?

"The Sinker," he muttered.

"Weightman," he countered.

"The Human Drill."

There was no chance he would ever be able to sleep. But he did. Through the worst night of his life, Duck Zhang drifted into and out of a weird nightmare, asleep, awake, and something in between that made him wonder if he was going slowly crazy. He dreamed of food. At one point he dreamed of a pizza chasing him, trying to eat him. And him wishing the pizza just would.

Then at last he woke up and saw . . .

Saw!

The light was dim, but it was bright enough.

"Hey! I can see!" he cried.

The first thing he could see was that the cave did not open onto the outside. The mouth of the cave was underwater. That was the source of the light, it filtered up through the blue-green water itself. The open air couldn't be too terribly far away, no more than a hundred feet maybe, but he would have to swim underwater to get there.

The second thing he saw was that the cave was bigger than he'd imagined. It had widened out and was large enough that you could park five or six school buses and have space left over.

The third thing he saw were the bats.

They hung from the cave ceiling. They had leathery wings and big blinking yellow eyes. There were thousands packed close together.

They stared at him.

That's when it occurred to him: bats didn't stay in caves at night, they went out at night and hid during the day.

Plus, normally, bats weren't blue.

And suddenly they began dropping, opening their wings. He was enveloped in a leathery tornado.

He dove for the water. Freezing cold. He powered down

and forward, aiming for the light. Much safer underwater, even with sharks or jellyfish or—

The water around him churned and boiled.

He screamed into bubbles.

Thousands of bats swam around and past him, spun him around in a waterspout, slapped wetly at him with wings that suddenly seemed far more like flippers.

He gagged on salt water, kicked and motored his arms in a panic crawl.

He ran out of air after fifteen seconds. But he still did not see a way out. Should he turn back?

He stopped. Froze in place. Enough air to make it back? And then what? Learn to live in a cave?

Duck kicked his feet and plowed ahead, no longer sure which way he was going. Forward or back?

Or just swimming in circles?

At last he came up. His head broke the surface as ten thousand bats erupted from the water all around him, wheeled overhead, then dove straight back into the sea a hundred yards off.

It wasn't far to the beach. He just had to swim there. Before the water bats came back.

"Just don't get mad," Duck chattered. "This would be a bad time to sink."

NINE

IT WAS MORNING. The buses were in the square. Edilio behind the wheel of one, yawning hugely. And Ellen, the fire marshal, behind the wheel of the other. Ellen was a small, dark, very serious girl. Sam had never seen her smile. She seemed to be a very capable girl, but she hadn't really been put to the test much yet. But she was a good driver.

Unfortunately, neither Ellen nor Edilio had many kids to drive.

Astrid was standing there with Little Pete, offering moral support, Sam supposed.

"I guess we don't really need two buses," Sam said.

"You could just about go with a minivan," Astrid agreed.

"What is the matter with people?" Sam fumed. "I said we needed a hundred kids and we get thirteen? Fifteen, maybe?"

"They're just kids," Astrid said.

"We're all just kids. We're all going to be very hungry kids."

"They're used to being told what to do by their parents or teachers. You need to be more direct. As in, *Hey, kid, get to work. Now.*" She thought for a moment then added, "*Or else.*"

"Or else what?" Sam asked.

"Or else . . . I don't know. We're not going to let anyone starve. If we can help it. I don't know the 'or else.' All I know is you can't expect kids to just automatically behave the right way. I mean, when I was little my mom would give me a gold star when I was good and take away a privilege when I wasn't."

"What am I supposed to do? Tell three hundred kids spread out in seventy or eighty different homes that they can't watch DVDs? Confiscate iPods?"

"It's not easy playing daddy to three hundred kids," Astrid admitted.

"I'm not anyone's daddy," Sam practically snarled. Another sleepless night, in a long string of them, had left him in a foul mood. "I'm supposed to be the mayor, not the father."

"These kids don't know the difference," Astrid pointed out. "They need parents. So they look to you. And Mother Mary. Me, even, to some extent."

Little Pete chose that moment to begin floating in the air. Just lifted off a foot, eighteen inches, hovered there, his arms floating, toes pointed downward.

Sam noticed immediately. Astrid didn't.

"What the—"

Sam stared, forgetting all about the empty school buses.

Little Pete floated. His omnipresent Game Boy had fallen to the ground. In front of him, just a few feet away, something began to materialize.

It was no bigger than Little Pete himself. Shiny red, laced with gold, a doll's dead-eyed face atop a bowling pin body.

"Nestor," Little Pete said, almost happy.

Sam recognized it. It was the nesting doll that sat on Little Pete's dresser. Identical Russian dolls, shells, really, that nested one inside the other. Sam didn't know how many there were. He had asked Astrid about it once. She'd said it was a souvenir from Moscow sent by some traveling uncle.

It was supposed to be for Astrid, but Little Pete had taken to it immediately. He'd even given it the name: Nestor. And because Little Pete never identified much with toys, Astrid had let him keep it.

"Nestor," Little Pete repeated, but troubled now, uncertain.

As Sam stared, transfixed, the nesting doll began to change. Its smooth, lacquered surface rippled. The colors ran together and formed new patterns. The eerie painted face grew sinister.

Arms grew from its side, like twigs. The twigs thickened, grew flesh, grew talons.

And the doll's painted smile split open, revealing dagger-sharp teeth.

Little Pete reached for the image, but the floating creature seemed to be made of Teflon: Little Pete's hands slid over it, pushed it aside like someone trying to poke a globule of mercury, but never quite touched it.

"No arms," Little Pete said.

The doll's arms withered, shriveled, and turned to smoke.

"Petey. Stop it," Astrid hissed.

"What is it?" Sam asked urgently. "What is that thing?"

Astrid didn't answer. "Petey. Window seat. Window seat."
It was a trigger phrase Astrid used to calm Little Pete down.
Sometimes it worked. Other times not. But in this case, Sam
didn't think Little Pete seemed upset, he seemed fascinated.
It was a weird thing to see that kind of alert, even intelligent,
involvement on Little Pete's usually blank face.

The doll's mouth opened. As if it would speak. Its eyes
focused on Little Pete. Malevolent, hate-filled eyes.

"No," Little Pete said.

The mouth snapped shut. It was a painted line once again.
And the furious eyes dimmed. Painted dots once more.

Astrid made a sound like a sob, quickly stifled. She stepped
in, whispered, "Sorry," and slapped Pete's shoulder, hard.

The effect was immediate. The creature disappeared. Pete
fell in a heap, sprawled out on the brown grass.

"Are you sure you should—" Sam began.

Little Pete was capable of . . . well, no one was quite sure
what he was capable of. All that Sam and Astrid knew was
that Little Pete was far and away the most powerful mutant
in the FAYZ.

"I had to stop him," Astrid said grimly. "It gets worse. It
starts with Nestor. Then the arms. Then the mouth and the
eyes. Like it's trying to come alive. Like . . ." She knelt beside

Little Pete and hugged him to her.

Sam looked sharply toward the buses. The question in his mind—had Pete been observed?—was answered by the slack-jawed stares of the kids with their noses pressed against the dusty windows.

Edilio was definitely wide awake now, and coming their way fast.

Sam cursed under his breath. "This has happened before, Astrid?"

She stuck out her chin defiantly. "A couple of times."

"You might have warned me."

"What the—I mean, what was that, man?" Edilio demanded.

"Ask Astrid," Sam snapped.

Astrid handed Little Pete his Game Boy and pulled him gently to his feet. She kept her eyes down, unwilling to meet Sam's accusing glare. "I don't know what it is. It's some kind of waking nightmare, maybe." There was a distinct note of desperation to her voice.

"The doll, the thing, whatever it was," Sam said. "It was fighting Pete, and Pete was fighting back. Like it was trying to come to life."

"Yes," Astrid whispered.

Edilio was the only other person who knew Little Pete's history. It had been Edilio who had retrieved the videotape from the power plant that showed the moment of the nuclear meltdown when a panicked, uncomprehending Little Pete, there with his father, had reacted by creating the FAYZ.

Edilio asked the question that was on Sam's mind. "Something was fighting Little Pete?" Edilio asked, "Man, who or what has the power to take on Little Pete?"

"We don't talk about this with anyone else," Sam said firmly. "Someone asks you about it, you just say it must have been some kind of . . ."

"Some kind of what?" Edilio asked.

"Optical illusion," Astrid supplied.

"Yeah, that'll work," Edilio said sarcastically. Then he shrugged. "Kids got other things to worry about. Hungry people don't waste much time on questions."

If others learned of Little Pete's guilt . . . and his power . . . he would never be safe. Caine would do anything it took to capture if not kill the strange little boy.

"Edilio, put everyone on one bus. Take a couple of your guys and start driving down residential streets. Go door to door. Round up as many kids as you can. Pack the bus, then take them to pick some melons or whatever."

Edilio looked dubious but said, "Okay, Mr. Mayor."

"Astrid. You come with me." Sam stalked off with Astrid and Little Pete trailing.

"Hey, don't start getting all high and mighty with me," Astrid yelled at his back.

"I'd just appreciate it if you'd let me know when some new weirdness breaks out. That's all." Sam kept moving, but Astrid grabbed his arm. He stopped, glancing around guiltily to make sure no one was in eavesdropping distance.

"What was I supposed to tell you?" Astrid demanded in

a terse whisper. "Little Pete's hallucinating? He's floating off the ground? What were you going to do about it?"

He held up his hands in a placating gesture. But his voice was no less angry. "I'm just trying to keep up, you know? It's like I'm playing a game where the rules keep changing. So today's rules are, hey, killer worms and hallucinating five-year-olds. I can't do anything about it, but it's nice to get a heads up."

Astrid started to say something, but stopped herself. She took a couple of calming breaths. Then, in a more measured tone, she said, "Sam, I figured you had enough on your shoulders. I'm worried about you."

He dropped his hands to his sides. His voice dropped as well. "I'm fine."

"No, you're not," Astrid said. "You don't sleep. You never have a minute to yourself. You act like everything that goes wrong is your fault. You're worried."

"Yeah, I'm worried," he said. "Last night we had a kid who killed and ate a cat. The whole time he's telling me about it he's weeping. He's sobbing. He used to have a cat himself. He likes cats. But he was so hungry, he grabbed it and . . ."

Sam had to stop. He bit his lip and tried to shake off the despair that swept over him. "Astrid, we're losing. We're losing. Everyone is . . ." He looked at her and felt tears threaten. "How long before we have kids doing worse than killing cats?"

When Astrid didn't answer, Sam said, "Yeah, so I'm worried. You look around the plaza here. Two weeks from now?

Two weeks from now it's Darfur, or whatever, if we don't figure something out. Three weeks from now? I don't want to
think about it."

He started toward his office but plowed into two kids
absorbed in yelling at each other. They were brothers, Alton
and Dalton. It was clear they'd been fighting for a while.

Under normal circumstances it might not have been a big
deal—fights were breaking out all the time—but both boys
had submachine guns hanging from their shoulders. Sam
lived in fear of one of Edilio's soldiers doing something stupid with the guns they carried. Ten-, eleven-, twelve-year-old
kids with guns weren't exactly the U.S. Army.

"What now?" Sam snapped at them.

Dalton stabbed an accusing finger at his brother. "He stole
my Junior Mints."

The mere mention of Junior Mints made Sam's stomach
rumble.

"You had . . ." He had to stop himself from focusing on
the candy. Candy! How had Dalton managed to hoard actual
candy? "Deal with it," Sam said and kept moving. Then he
stopped. "Wait a minute. Aren't you two supposed to be out
at the power plant?"

Alton answered. "No, our shift was last night. We came
back this morning in the van. And I did not steal his stupid
Junior Mints. I didn't even know he had Junior Mints."

"Then who stole them?" his brother demanded hotly. "I ate
two each shift. One at the beginning, one at the end. I ate one
when I got there last night and I counted them all. I had seven

left. And then this morning when I went to have another one, the box was empty."

Sam said, "Did it ever occur to you it might be one of the other kids standing guard?"

"No," Dalton said. "Heather B and Mike J were at the guardhouse. And Josh was asleep the whole time."

"What do you mean Josh was asleep?" Sam said.

The brothers exchanged nearly identical guilty looks. Dalton shrugged. "Sometimes Josh sleeps. It's no big deal—he'll wake up if anything happens."

"Doesn't Josh watch the security cameras?"

"He says he can't see anything. Nothing ever happens. It's just like pictures of the road and the hills and the parking lot and all."

"We stayed up. Mostly," Alton said.

"Mostly. How much is 'mostly'?" Sam got no answer. "Get going. Go ahead. And stop fighting. You weren't supposed to be hoarding food, anyway, Dalton. Serves you right." He wanted badly to ask where the kid had found candy, and ask if there was more, but that would have been the wrong message. Bad example.

Still, Sam thought, what if there was still candy? Somewhere? Somewhere in the FAYZ?

Edilio's bus began to pull away. Ellen was onboard and Sam figured Edilio would stop off and grab a couple of his soldiers to help with the drafting of workers for the fields.

Sam could imagine the scenes that would be played out house by house. The whining. The complaining. The running away. Followed by a lazy, mostly wasted effort to pick fruit by kids who didn't want to work in the hot sun for hours.

He thought briefly of E.Z. Of the worms. Albert was taking Orc to the cabbage field this morning, to test Howard's suggestion that he would be invulnerable. Hopefully, that would work.

For a brief moment he worried that the worms might have spread. But even if they had, surely not to the melon field. It was a mile from the cabbages.

A mile was a long distance to cover if you were a worm.

"Beer me," Orc bellowed.

Albert handed Howard a red and blue can of beer. A Budweiser. That's what Albert had the most of, and Orc didn't seem to have any particular brand loyalty.

Howard popped the tab and extended it out of the driver's side window, reaching back. Orc snatched it as they drove down the pitted dirt road.

Orc sat in the bed of the pickup truck. He was too big to fit in anything smaller, too big to fit inside the truck's cab. Howard was driving. Albert was in the front seat, squeezed in beside a large polystyrene cooler. The cooler had the logo of the University of California, Santa Barbara. It was full of beer.

"You know, we should have hung out more, back in the old days," Howard said to Albert.

"You didn't know I existed, back in the old days," Albert said.

"What? Come on, man. There's, like, a dozen brothers in the whole school and I didn't notice one?"

"We're the same shade, Howard. That doesn't make us friends," Albert said coolly.

Howard laughed. "Yeah, you were always a grind. Reading too much. Thinking too much. Not having much fun. Good little family boy, make your momma proud. Now look at you: you're a big man in the FAYZ."

Albert ignored that. He wasn't interested in reminiscing. Not with Howard, for sure, not really with anyone. The old world was dead and gone. Albert was all about the future.

As if reading his mind, Howard said, "You're always planning, aren't you? You know it's true. You are all business."

"I'm just like everyone else: trying to figure out how to make it," Albert said.

Howard didn't respond directly. "The way I see it? It's Sam, top dog. No question. Astrid and Edilio? They're only something because they're in Sam's crew. But you, man, you are your own thing."

"What thing is that?" Albert asked, keeping his tone neutral.

"You got two dozen kids working under you, man. You're in charge of the food. Between you and me? I know you have a food stash somewhere."

Albert did not so much as blink. "If I have a secret food stash, why am I so hungry?"

Howard laughed. "Because you are a smart little uptight dude, that's why. I'm smart, too. In my own way."

Albert said nothing. He knew where the conversation was going. He wasn't going to help Howard lay it out.

"Both of us are smart. Both of us are brothers in a very white town. You with the food. Me with Orc." He jerked a thumb back toward the monster. "Time may come you need some muscle to go along with all that planning and ambition of yours."

Albert turned to face Howard, wanting to send the signal clearly, unambiguously. "Howard?"

"Yeah?"

"I am loyal to Sam."

Howard threw back his head and laughed. "Oh, man, I'm just messing with you. We are all of us loyal to Sam. Sam, Sam the laser-shooting surfer man."

They had reached the deadly cabbage field. Howard pulled over and turned off the engine.

"Beer me," Orc yelled.

Albert dug in the cooler, hand plunged into ice water. He handed the can to Howard. "Last one till he does some work."

Howard handed it back to Orc.

Orc yelled, "Open it, moron, you know I can't pop the tab."

Howard took the beer back and popped the tab. It made a sound just like a soda, but the smell was sour. "Sorry, Orc," Howard said.

Orc took the beer in a fist the size of a bowling ball and drained it down his throat.

Orc's fingers were too big to handle anything delicate. Each finger was the size of a kosher salami. Each joint was made of what looked, and felt, a lot like wet gravel. Gray stones that fitted loosely together

His entire body, except for a last few square inches of his sullen mouth and the left side of his face, and a little bit of his cheek and neck, were covered—or made of—the same slimy gray gravel. He had always been a big kid, but now he was a foot taller and several feet wider.

The tiny human portion of him seemed like the creepier part. Like someone had cut the flesh off a living person and glued it onto a stone statue.

"Another," Orc growled.

"No," Albert answered firmly. "First we see if you can really do this."

Orc rolled himself over the side of the truck and stood up. Albert felt the entire truck rock back and forth. Orc came around to the door and stuck his hideous face in the window, forcing Albert to shrink back and to clutch the cooler.

"I can take the beer," Orc said. "You can't stop me."

"Yes, you can take it," Albert agreed. "But you made a promise to Sam."

Orc digested that. He was slow and stupid, but not so stupid he didn't understand the implied threat. Orc did not want to tangle with Sam.

"All right. I'll see about them worms." Orc belched and lurched toward the field. He was wearing what he usually wore, a pair of very rough-sewn canvas shorts. Albert assumed Howard had made them for his friend. There was no such thing as pants or shirts in Orc's size.

Howard held his breath as Orc stomped into the field. So, for that matter, did Albert. Every hideous detail of the memory of E.Z.'s death was permanently imprinted on Albert's brain.

The attack was immediate.

The worms seethed from the dirt, slithered with impossible speed toward Orc's stone feet and threw themselves against his unnatural flesh.

Orc stopped. He gaped down at the creatures.

He turned with creaky slowness back toward Albert and Howard and said, "Kinda tickles."

"Pick a cabbage," Howard called out encouragingly.

Orc bent down and dug his stone fingers into the dirt and scooped up a cabbage. He looked at it for a minute, then tossed it toward the truck.

Albert opened the door of the truck and bent cautiously down toward the cabbage. He refused to step down. Not yet. Not until they were sure.

"Howard, I need a stick or something," Albert said.

"What for?"

"I want to poke that cabbage, make sure there's no worm in it."

In the field the worms continued their assault on the creature whose rock flesh broke their teeth. Orc scooped up three more cabbages. Then he came stomping back.

The worms did not follow. At the edge of the field they slithered off Orc and retreated into the ground.

"Beer me," Orc demanded.

Albert did.

He wondered how Sam was doing with lining up kids to work in the field. "Not very well, I'd guess," he muttered to himself.

The answer to the problem of food was so simple, really: farms needed farmers. Then the farmers needed motivation. They needed to get paid. Like anyone. People didn't do things just because it was right: people did things for money, for profit. But Sam and Astrid were too foolish to see it.

No, not foolish, Albert told himself. Sam was the main reason they weren't all under Caine's control. Sam was great. And Astrid was probably the smartest person in the FAYZ.

But Albert was smart, too, about some things. And he had gone to the trouble of educating himself, sitting in the dusty, dark town library reading books that made his eyelids droop.

"My boy's going to need another beer pretty soon," Howard said, yawning behind his hand.

"Your boy gets a beer for every one hundred cabbages he picks," Albert said.

Howard gave him a dirty look. "Man, you act like you paid for those cans with your own money."

"Nope," Albert said. "They are community property. For now. But the rate is still one per hundred."

For the next two hours Orc picked cabbages. And drank beer. Howard played some game on a handheld. Albert thought.

Howard was right about that: Albert had thought a lot since the day he walked into the abandoned McDonald's and began grilling hamburgers. He had a lot of standing in the community because of that. And the Thanksgiving feast he'd organized, and pulled off without a hitch, had made him a minor hero. He wasn't Sam, of course; there was only one Sam. He wasn't even Edilio or Brianna or anything like the big heroes of that terrible battle between Caine's people and the Perdido Beach kids.

But at that moment Albert wasn't thinking about any of that. He was thinking about toilet paper and batteries.

Then Orc screamed.

Howard sat up. He jumped from the car.

Albert froze.

Orc was shrieking, slapping at his face, at the still-human part of his face.

Howard ran toward him.

"Howard, no!" Albert yelled.

"They got him, they got him," Howard cried, anguished.

Orc was struggling, staggering, then running toward the truck, his great stone feet pounding six-inch-deep impressions into the dirt.

One of the worms was on his face.

In his face.

He tripped at the edge of the field and fell hard onto neutral territory.

"Help me. Howard, man, help me!" Orc cried.

Albert broke his trance and ran. Up close he could see the

worm, just one, but its black snake's head was buried in pink flesh, boring through Orc's cheek.

Up close Albert could see the blur of the tiny paddle feet driving the worm into strained flesh.

Orc had the tail of the thing in his fist and was pulling hard. But the worm wasn't letting go. Orc was pulling so hard, it seemed he might pull the last of his living flesh away from the rock skin surrounding it.

Howard grabbed on, too, and he was pulling. Weeping and cursing and pulling, despite the danger to himself if the worm should release its grip on Orc and turn against Howard.

"Bite it!" Albert shouted.

"My tongue!" Orc wailed, his speech garbled as the worm slid another inch through his cheek.

"Bite it, Orc," Albert yelled. Then he knelt, and with all his might delivered an uppercut under Orc's chin.

It was like punching a brick wall.

Albert yelled and fell back on his behind in the dirt. He was sure his hand was broken.

Orc had stopped screaming. He opened his mouth and spit out the worm's head, along with a gob of blood and saliva.

The rest of the worm came free. Orc smashed it onto the ground.

There was a one-inch hole in Orc's face.

Blood spread down his neck and disappeared like rain on parched soil as it hit the rock flesh.

"You hit me," Orc said dully, staring at Albert.

"Brother saved your life, Orc," Howard said. "The brother just saved your life."

"I think I broke my hand," Albert said.

"Beer me," Orc said.

Howard raced to comply.

Orc tilted his head back and squeezed the can until the tab burst. Yellow liquid shot from the can and gushed into his mouth.

At least half of it ran, foaming pink, from the bloody hole in his cheek.

TEN

"SHE WAS IN my dreams, in my head. I saw her," Drake said.

"You've lost what little mind you had left," Diana said.

They were in the dining hall. No one was dining. Meals at Coates amounted to a few cans put out for kids to fight over. There were kids who had eaten boiled grass to ease the hunger pangs.

In the echoing, abandoned, damaged dining hall it was Caine, Drake, Bug, Diana, and the girl who said her name was Orsay.

The girl was maybe twelve, Diana figured.

Diana had noticed a look in the girl's eyes. Fear, of course, she'd been hauled in by Drake once Bug got back from the power plant. But that wasn't all of it: the girl, Orsay, looked at Diana like she recognized her.

It was not a good look. Her expression made the hairs on the back of Diana's neck tingle.

"I never saw her before in my life, but I saw her in this dream I was having." Drake glared hatred at the girl. "Then I woke up and found her skulking around, hiding."

It was an unusual feeling for Diana, being in a room with Drake where she was not the main object of his hatred.

Caine said, "Okay, Drake, we get it. Back before all this started I'd have said you were nuts. Now?" He waved a languid hand at Diana. "Diana, read her. Let's see."

Diana went and stood beside the girl, who looked up at her with frightened, protruding eyes.

"Don't be scared. Of me," Diana said. "I just need to hold your hand."

"What's happened? Why won't anybody tell me anything? Where are all the adults? Where are your teachers?" Orsay had a voice with a built-in tremble to it, like she'd always been nervous and always would be.

"We call it the FAYZ. Fallout Alley Youth Zone," Diana said. "You know about the accident at the power plant back in the day, right? Fallout Alley?"

"Hey, Caine told you to read her, not give her a history lesson," Drake snapped.

Diana wanted to argue, but Orsay's expression, her look of terror mixed with pity for Diana, was weirding her out. It was as if Orsay knew something about Diana, like she was a doctor with a fatal diagnosis she hadn't quite nerved herself up to deliver yet. Diana took Orsay's hand.

As soon as she took Orsay's hand she knew her power level. The question was whether she should tell Caine the truth. In

Caine's universe there were only two possible categories of mutants: those who were unquestioningly loyal to Caine, and those who needed to be disposed of.

At least Orsay wasn't a four bar. If she had been, there was little doubt in Diana's mind that Caine would have turned her over to Drake.

"Quit stalling," Drake growled.

Diana released the girl's hand. She ignored Drake and spoke to Caine. "She's a three bar."

Caine sucked air and sat back in his chair. He considered the terrified girl. "Tell me about your power. Tell me the truth, all of it, and you'll be fine. If you lie to me, I'll know I can never trust you."

Orsay looked up at Diana as though she might be a friend. "Do what he says," Diana said.

Orsay twined her fingers together. She sat with her knees knocked, her shoulders pressed in as though she were trying to get them to meet.

"It started happening, like, maybe five months ago. Mostly at night. I thought I was crazy. I didn't know where it was coming from. My head would be filled up with these pictures and sometimes sounds, people talking, flashes of faces or places. Sometimes they were really short, just a few seconds. But sometimes they went on for a half hour, one thing after another, craziness, people being chased, people falling, people having . . . you know, like, sex and all."

She looked down at her twisting fingers, embarrassed.

"Yeah, we get it, you're all sweet and innocent," Drake sneered.

Diana asked, "How did you figure out you were seeing people's dreams?"

"It usually only happened at night," Orsay said. "And then, one night I had this really vivid dream of this woman's face, this kind of nice, red-haired woman, right? But she wasn't even around, yet. She arrived the next morning. I hadn't seen her before, not in reality, just in her husband's dream. That's when I figured it out."

"So you've been up in the forest this whole time? You must have been lonely." Caine was applying a bit of his smile, a fraction of his charm, putting her at ease.

Orsay nodded. "I'm used to being lonely."

"How are you at keeping secrets?" Diana asked. She made her voice casual, but she stared hard into Orsay's eyes, hoping she would get the message, hoping she knew how great a danger she was in.

Orsay blinked. She was about to say something, then blinked again. "I never told anyone anything I saw," Orsay said.

Caine said, "Interesting question, Diana."

Diana shrugged. "A good spy needs to be discreet."

When Caine looked blank, Diana added quickly, "I mean, I assume that's what you're thinking. We have Bug, who can sneak into a place, maybe overhear some conversation. But Orsay could actually get into people's dreams." When Caine's expression remained skeptical, Diana added, "I wonder what Sam dreams about."

"No way," Drake said. "No way. You heard her, she gets anyone's dreams who happens to be nearby. That means she's in our heads, too. No way."

"I doubt she wants any part of your dreams, Drake," Diana said.

Drake uncoiled his arm and lightning quick wrapped it around Orsay, who yelped and froze stiff. "I brought her in. She's mine. I say what happens to her."

"Just what is it you want to do with her?" Diana asked.

Drake grinned. "I don't know. Maybe I'll cook her and eat her. Meat is meat, right?"

Diana glanced at Caine, hoping to see some sign of revulsion, some acknowledgment that Drake was going too far. But Caine just nodded as if he was considering Drake's claim. "Lets find out what her range is first, huh? Orsay: How far away can you be and still get someone's dream?"

Orsay chattered her answer, shaking with fear. "Only like . . . like . . . like from the ranger station and the nearest part of the campground."

"How much distance is that?"

She tried to shrug, but Drake was squeezing her, like a python, taking advantage of every exhalation to tighten his coils. "Maybe two hundred feet," Orsay said.

"Mose's cabin," Diana said. "It's twice that far from the campus."

"I said no," Drake threatened. "She was in my head."

"We already know it's a cesspool in there," Diana said.

"This is uncool, Caine," Drake said. "You owe me. You need me. Don't mess with me on this."

"Don't mess with me?" Caine echoed. That was the step too far.

Caine jumped up, knocking his chair over backward. He raised both hands, palms out. "You really want to challenge me, Drake? I can blow you through the wall into the next room before you can unwrap yourself from that girl."

Drake flinched. Started to answer, but he never had a chance. Caine had gone from calm and contained to crazy in a heartbeat.

"You stupid thug," Caine raged. "You think you can replace me? You think if I was out of the way you'd be able to go down the hill and take out Sam and the rest? You couldn't even beat Orc! You nobody!" Caine screamed, spit flying from a mouth moving as fast as it could but still not fast enough for the fury within.

The blood had drained from Drake's hard face. His eyes burned furiously, his arm twitched, almost out of control. He looked like he might choke on his own bottled rage.

"I'm the brains!" Caine shrieked. "I'm the brains! I'm the brains and the power, the true power, the four bar, the one. I am the one. Me! Why do you think the Darkness kept me for three days? Why do you think . . . Why do you think it's still in my . . . in my . . ."

There was an abrupt change in Caine's voice. For a second it was as if he was sobbing, not raging. He caught himself and righted his voice, swallowed hard. He looked unsteady and reached for a chairback to hold himself up.

Then he saw the not-quite-pitying look in Diana's eyes, and no doubt the shark's cold gleam of triumph on Drake's face as well.

Caine roared, an incoherent, lunatic howl. He extended his hands, aiming down and to either side of Drake.

There was an earsplitting sound, stones ripped apart, as the floor exploded upward in a geyser of shattered floor tile and dirt.

The pillar of rock and debris shot up, slammed into the already-scarred and damaged cathedral ceiling and tumbled back down again, a rain of gravel, as Caine's howl fell silent.

The only sound was the off-key, musical patter of falling debris.

Caine stared, blank. Blank.

It went on for too long. But no one dared speak. Then, as if someone had thrown a switch, Caine's expression became human once more. He smiled a shaky smile.

"We can use this girl, Drake," Caine said calmly. Then, to Orsay directly, "We can, can't we? We can use you? You'll do whatever I tell you to do? And you will obey only me?"

Orsay tried to find her voice but couldn't even manage a whisper. She nodded vigorously.

"Good. Because if I ever doubt you, Orsay, I'll give you to Drake. You don't want that."

Caine slumped, used up. Without another word he weaved his way to the door.

Lana patted her dog, Patrick, on his thick ruff. "Ready?"

Patrick made his little whimpering sound, the one that meant, "Come on, let's get going."

Lana stood up and checked the Velcro strap that held her

iPod in place on her arm. She made sure the bright yellow headphones were in place—her ears were too small for the standard earbuds.

She dialed up her "running" play list. But, of course, she didn't really run now. Running made hunger unbearable. Now she just walked. And not as far as she had run.

Back in the old days, before the FAYZ, she'd done neither. But that, like so much, had changed. There was nothing like dragging through the desert without water or a clue, and then being made a captive of a swift-moving coyote pack, to make you think you should get in shape.

She liked to begin in silence. She liked to hear the sound of her sneaker treads, almost silent on the carpeted hotel floor. Then satisfyingly loud on the blacktop.

Her route began at the front door of Clifftop. It was an automatic door, and it still worked. It was weird, still weird after all this time, that the door's sensor should be patiently awaiting the signal to open wide the doors to the outside world.

From Clifftop she would walk down toward Town Beach. Then she would cut through town, but away from the plaza, join the highway, and complete the circle back to Clifftop. Unless she was too weak from hunger. Then she would cut that short.

She knew she should probably not burn unnecessary calories. But she couldn't bring herself to stop. To stop, to spend a day lying on the bed, was to surrender. Lana didn't like the idea of surrender. She hadn't surrendered to pain, or to Pack

Leader, or to the Darkness.

I don't surrender, she told herself.

Come to me. I have need of you.

As she got beyond the Clifftop approach road and headed down the slope, Lana punched the iPod's touchscreen and her ears were filled with a Death Cab for Cutie song.

But it was the other lyrics she heard, like a whisper, like a second track beneath this song.

She'd gone no more than a hundred yards along when two little kids intercepted her, waving their hands to get her attention.

They looked healthy enough to her. She gave them a short wave and hoped that would be enough.

But the two littles moved to block her way. She stopped, panting a little, even though she shouldn't be, and ripped off her headphones.

"What?" she snapped.

There was some hemming and hawing before the kids could blurt it out.

"Joey's got a loose tooth."

"So what? He's supposed to be getting new teeth."

"But it hurts. You're supposed to fix things that hurt."

"Supposed to?" Lana echoed. "Look, kids, if you're bleeding from some big gaping wound you can bug me. I'm not here for every little headache or skinned knee or loose tooth."

"You're mean," the kid said.

"Yeah. I'm mean." Lana settled her headphones back in place and started off, feeling angry at the kids and angrier at herself for yelling at them. But kids came after her wherever she was. They interrupted her while she was eating. They harassed her when she was sitting on her balcony reading a book. They banged on her door while she was pooping.

It was almost never something that needed a miracle. And increasingly that's what Lana was starting to think about her powers, that they were something miraculous. No one had any better explanation.

And miracles shouldn't be wasted.

Anyway, she had a right to have a life of her own. She wasn't everyone's servant. She belonged to herself.

Come to me.

Lana bit her lip. She was ignoring it, the voice, the hallucination, whatever it was.

Just going to ignore it.

She cranked up the volume on the music.

She veered away from the beach as she approached town. Maybe if she went along the back streets more. Maybe she could vary her route more and make it harder for people to track her down.

So long as she ended the same way: back up the hill to Clifftop. Up to the FAYZ wall. Not to touch it, but to get very close to it as she panted and sweated and nursed the inevitable stitch in her side.

She felt she needed to see that barrier up close every day. It was a devotion, somehow. A touchstone. A reminder that she was here, and this was now. Whatever she had been before, she wasn't that person anymore. She was trapped in this place and in this life. Not her choice: the wall's choice.

Come to me. I have need of you.

"It's not real," Lana shouted.

But it *was* real. She knew it was real. She knew the voice. Where it came from.

She knew she could not shut the voice out of her mind. The only way to silence the voice was to silence it forever. She could be its victim, or she could make it her victim.

Madness. Suicidal madness. She skipped a slow song and went to something manic. Something loud enough to banish crazy thoughts.

She walked harder, faster, almost running, pumping her arms and forcing Patrick into a long lope to keep up. But she wasn't fast enough to outrun a truck that zoomed crazily up to her honking its horn.

Again she tore off her headphones and yelled, "What?"

But this was no loose tooth or skinned knee.

Albert and Howard piled out. Howard helped pull Orc from the back. The boy . . . the creature . . . staggered as if drunk. He probably was, Lana thought. Then again, maybe he had a pretty good excuse.

There was a hole in one of the last human parts of him, his cheek. Dried blood crusted his cheek and neck. Fresher, redder blood still oozed down his cheek and neck.

"What happened?" Lana asked.

"Zekes got him," Howard answered. He was torn between a kind of low-level panic and relief that he had finally reached the Healer. He held Orc's elbow as if Orc needed Howard's frail strength to support him.

"Has he got a worm in him?" Lana asked, cautious.

"No, we got the worm," Albert reassured her. "We were just hoping you could help him."

"I don't want no more rock on me," Orc said.

Lana understood. Orc had been a garden variety thug, unaware of any special power, until the coyotes had gotten to him in the desert. They had chewed him up badly. Very badly. Worse than anything that had happened to Lana, even. Everywhere they had chewed him had filled in with the gravel covering that made Orc nearly indestructible.

He didn't want to lose the last of his human body, the patch of pink skin that included his mouth and part of his neck.

Lana nodded.

"You need to stop weaving back and forth, Orc. I don't want you falling on me," she said. "Sit down on the ground."

He sat down too suddenly and giggled a little at it.

Lana lay her hand against the gruesome hole.

"Don't want no more rock," Orc repeated.

The bleeding stopped almost immediately.

"Does it hurt?" Lana asked. "I mean the rock. I know the hole hurts."

"No. It don't hurt." Orc slammed his fist against his opposite arm, hard enough that any human arm would have been shattered. "I barely feel it. Even Drake's whip, when we was fighting, I barely felt it."

Suddenly he was weeping. Tears rolled from human eyes onto cheeks of flesh and pebbles.

"I don't feel nothing except . . ." He pointed a thick stone finger at the flesh of his face.

"Yeah," Lana said. Her irritation was gone. Her burden was smaller, maybe, than Orc's.

Lana pulled her hand away to see the progress. The hole was smaller. Still crusted with blood, but no longer actively bleeding.

She put her hand back in place. "Just a couple minutes more, Orc."

"My name's Charles," Orc said.

"Is it?"

"It is," Howard confirmed.

"What were you guys doing going into the worm field?" Lana asked.

Howard shot a resentful look at Albert, who answered, "Orc was picking cabbage."

"My name's Charles Merriman," Orc repeated. "People should call me by my real name sometimes."

Lana's gaze met Howard's.

Now, Lana thought, now he wants his old name back. The bully who reveled in a monster's name was now a monster in fact, and wanted to be called Charles.

"You're all better," Lana announced.

"Is it still skin?" Orc asked.

"It is," Lana reassured him. "It's still human."

Lana took Albert's arm and drew him away. "What are you doing sending him into the worm field like that?"

Albert's face went blank. He was surprised at being

reproached. For a moment Lana thought he would tell her to take a jump. But that moment passed, and Albert slumped a little, as if the air had gone out of him.

"I'm trying to help," Albert said.

"By paying him with beer?"

"I paid him what he wanted, and Sam was okay with it. You were at the meeting," Albert said. "Look, how else do you think you get someone like Orc to spend hours in the hot sun working? Astrid seems to think people will work just because we ask them to. Maybe some will. But Orc?"

Lana could see his point. "Okay. I shouldn't have jumped all over you."

"It's okay. I'm getting used to it," Albert said. "Suddenly I'm the bad guy. But you know what? I didn't make people the way they are. If kids are going to work, they're going to want something back."

"If they don't work, we all starve."

"Yeah. I get that," Albert said with more than a tinge of sarcasm. "Only, here's the thing: Kids know we won't let them starve as long as there's any food left, right? So they figure, hey, let someone else do the work. Let someone else pick cabbages and artichokes."

Lana wanted to get back to her run. She needed to finish, to run to the FAYZ wall. But there was something fascinating about Albert. "Okay. So how do you get people to work?"

He shrugged. "Pay them."

"You mean, money?"

"Yeah. Except guess who had most of the money in their

wallets and purses when they disappeared? Then a few kids stole what was left in cash registers and all. So if we start back using the old money we just make a few thieves powerful. It's kind of a problem."

"Why is a kid going to work for money if they know we'll share the food, anyway?" Lana asked.

"Because some will do different stuff for money. I mean, look, some kids have no skills, right? So they pick the food for money. Then they take the money and spend it with some kid who can maybe cook the food for them, right? And that kid maybe needs a pair of sneakers and some other kid has rounded up all the sneakers and he has a store."

Lana realized her mouth was open. She laughed. The first time in a while.

"Fine. Laugh," Albert said, and turned away.

"No, no, no," Lana hastened to say. "No, I wasn't making fun of you. It's just that, I mean, you're the only kid that has any kind of a plan for anything."

Albert actually looked embarrassed. "Well, you know, Sam and Astrid are working their butts off."

"Yeah. But you're looking ahead. You're actually thinking about how we put it all together."

Albert nodded. "I guess."

"Good for you, man," Lana said. "I gotta go. Orc will be okay. As okay as he can be, anyway."

"Thanks," Albert said, and seemed genuinely grateful.

"Hey, let me see that hand," Lana said.

Albert seemed puzzled. He looked at his own hand, swollen and discolored from punching Orc's stone face.

"Oh, yeah," Albert said as Lana briefly took his hand in hers. "Thanks again."

Lana put her headphones back on and trotted a few steps. Then she stopped. She turned and took them off. "Hey. Albert. The money thing."

"Yes?"

She hesitated, knowing that in this moment she was perhaps starting a chain reaction. Knowing that it was dangerous to the point of madness. It was eerie, as if fate had intervened in the person of Albert, showing her the way to her half-formed goal. "Wouldn't gold work? I mean, as money?"

Albert's sharp eyes found hers. "Should we get together and talk?"

"Yeah," Lana said.

"Stop by the club tonight."

"The what?"

Albert grinned. He fished a half sheet of paper from his pocket and handed it to her.

Lana glanced at it. Then at him. She laughed and handed it back. "I'll be there."

She started running again. But her thoughts were taking a different tack than before. Albert was planning for the future, not just letting it happen to him. That was the thing to do. To plan. To act. Not just to let things happen.

She was right to plan.

Come to me.

Maybe I will, Lana thought. And maybe you won't like it much when I do.

ELEVEN

"**MOTHER MARY WANTS** to draft two more kids," Astrid told Sam.

"Okay. Approved."

"Dahra says we're running low on kids' Tylenol and kids' Advil, she wants to make sure it's okay to start giving them split adult pills."

Sam spread his hands in a helpless gesture. "What?"

"We're running low on kid pills, Dahra wants to split adult pills."

Sam rocked back in the leather chair designed for a grown man. "Okay. Whatever. Approved." He took a sip of water from a bottle. The wrapper on the bottle said "Dasani" but it was tap water. The dishes from dinner—horrible homemade split-pea soup that smelled burned, and a quarter cabbage each—had been pushed aside onto the sideboard where in the old days the mayor of Perdido Beach had kept framed pictures of his family. It was one of the better meals Sam had

had lately. The fresh cabbage tasted surprisingly good.

There was little more than smears on the plates: the era of kids not eating everything was over.

Astrid puffed out her cheeks and sighed. "Kids are asking why Lana isn't around when they need her."

"I can only ask Lana to heal big things. I can't demand she be around 24/7 to handle every boo-boo."

Astrid looked at the list she had compiled on her laptop. "Actually, I think this involved a stubbed toe that 'hurted.'"

"How much more is on the list?" Sam asked.

"Three hundred and five items," Astrid said. When Sam's face went pale, she relented. "Okay, it's actually just thirty-two. Now, don't you feel relieved it's not really three hundred?"

"This is crazy," Sam said.

"Next up: the Judsons and the McHanrahans are fighting because they share a dog, so both families are feeding her— they still have a big bag of dry dog food—but the Judsons are calling her Sweetie and the McHanrahans are calling her BooBoo."

"You're kidding."

"I'm not kidding," Astrid said.

"What is that noise?" Sam demanded.

Astrid shrugged. "I guess someone has their stereo cranked up."

"This is not going to work, Astrid."

"The music?"

"This. This thing where every day I have a hundred stupid questions I have to decide. Like I'm everyone's parent now.

I'm sitting here listening to how little kids are complaining because their older sisters make them take a bath, and stepping into fights over who owns which Build-A-Bear outfit, and now over dog names. Dog names?"

"They're all still just little kids," Astrid said.

"Some of these kids are developing powers that scare me," Sam grumbled. "But they can't decide who gets to have which special towel? Or whether to watch *The Little Mermaid* or *Shrek Three*?"

"No," Astrid said. "They can't. They need a parent. That's you."

Sam usually handled the daily dose of nonsense with equanimity, or at least with nothing worse than grouchy humor. But today he was feeling it was finally too much. Yesterday he'd lost E.Z. This morning he'd seen almost no one show up for work. And Edilio had been forced to track kids down for two hours. Even then they had come back with a pitiful amount of cantaloupes, barely enough to feed the day care. All of that followed by Duck Zhang and some crazy story about falling through the ground into a radioactive tunnel full of water bats.

The only person who'd been productive was Orc. He had picked several hundred cabbages before the worms had nearly killed him.

"What is that music?" he demanded, angry and needing to yell at someone or something. Sam stomped to the window and threw it open. Immediately the volume of the music, most of it vibrating bass, increased dramatically.

Down in the square things were dark but for the street-lights and a strobe light blinking through the front window of McDonald's.

"What in the . . ."

Astrid came and stood beside him. "What is that? Is Albert throwing a party?"

Sam didn't answer. He left without a word, annoyed, angry, and secretly glad of any excuse to get out of answering kids' stupid questions and handling their stupid problems.

He took the steps two at a time. Down to the ground floor, out through the big front door, ignoring a "Hello" from the kid Edilio had guarding the town hall, and down the big marble steps to the street.

Quinn was passing by, clearly heading toward McDonald's.

"Hey, brah," Quinn said.

"What is going on, do you know?" Sam asked.

"It's a club." Quinn grinned. "Man, you must be working too hard. Everyone knows about it."

Sam stared at him. "It's a what?"

"McClub, brah. All you need is some batteries or some toilet paper."

This announcement left Sam baffled. He considered asking Quinn for clarification, but then Albert appeared, formally dressed, like he thought it was graduation or something. He actually had on a dark sports coat and slacks in a lighter shade. His shirt was pale blue, collared, and ironed. Spotting Sam, he extended his hand.

Sam ignored the hand. "Albert, what is going on here?"

"Dancing, mostly," Albert said.

"Excuse me?"

"Kids are dancing."

Quinn caught up then and stepped in front of Sam to shake Albert's still-extended hand. "Hey, dude. I have batteries."

"Good to see you, Quinn. The price is four D cells, or eight double As, or ten triple As, or a dozen Cs. If you have a mix, I can work it out."

Quinn dug in his pocket and produced four triple A batteries and three D cells. He handed them to Albert, who agreed to the price and dropped the batteries into a plastic bag at his feet.

"Okay, the rules are no food, no alcohol, no attitude, no fights, and when I call 'time,' there's no arguing about it. Do you agree to these rules?"

"Dude, if I had any food, would I be here? I'd be home eating it." Quinn put his hand over his heart like he was pledging allegiance to the flag and said, "I do." He jerked a thumb back at Sam. "Don't bother with him: Sam doesn't dance."

"Have a good time, Quinn," Albert said, and swung open the door to admit him.

Sam stared in absolute amazement. He was torn between outrage and an urge to laugh in admiration.

"Who told you you could do this?" Sam asked.

Albert shrugged. "Same person who told me I could run the McDonald's until we ran out of food: no one. I just did it."

"Fine, but you gave away the food. Now you're charging people. That's not cool, Albert."

"You're trying to profit?" This from Astrid, who had followed Sam, Little Pete in tow.

Inside, the music had shifted from hip-hop to a song Sam happened to love: the ridiculously hooky Tim Armstrong tune "Into Action." If he ever were to dance, this might be the tune that did it.

Albert considered Astrid and Sam. "Yes. I'm trying to make a profit. I'm using batteries, toilet paper, and paper towels as currency. Each is something that will eventually be in short supply."

"You're trying to get all the toilet paper in town?" Astrid shrilled. "Are you kidding?"

"No, Astrid, I'm not kidding," Albert said. "Look, right now, kids are playing with the stuff. I saw little kids throwing rolls of it around on their lawns like it was a toy. So—"

"So your solution is to try and take it all away from people?"

"You'd rather see it wasted?"

"Yeah, actually," Astrid huffed. "Rather than you getting it all for yourself. You're acting like a jerk."

Albert's eyes flared. "Look, Astrid, now kids know they can buy their way into the club with it. So they're not going to waste it anymore."

"No, they're going to give it all to you," she shot back. "And what happens when they need some?"

"Then there will still be some left because I made it valuable."

"Valuable to you."

"Valuable to everyone, Astrid."

"It's you taking advantage of kids dumb enough not to know any better. Sam, you have to put a stop to this."

Sam had drifted away from the conversation, his head full of the music. He snapped back. "She's right, Albert, this isn't okay. You didn't get permission—"

"I didn't think I needed permission to give kids what they want. I mean, I'm not threatening anyone, saying, 'Give me your toilet paper, give me your batteries.' I'm just playing some music and saying, 'If you want to come in and dance, then it'll cost you.'"

"Dude, I respect you being ambitious and all," Sam said. "But I have to shut this down. You never got permission, even, let alone asked us if it was okay to charge people."

Albert said, "Sam, I respect you more than I can even say. And Astrid, you are way smarter than me. But I don't see how you have the right to shut me down."

That was it for Sam. "Okay, I tried to be nice. But I am the mayor. I was elected, as you probably remember, since I think you voted for me."

"I did. I'd do it again, man. But Sam, Astrid, you guys are wrong here. This club is about all these kids have that can get them together for a good time. They're sitting in their homes starving and feeling sad and scared. When they're dancing, they forget how hungry and sad they are. This is a good thing I'm doing."

Sam stared hard at Albert, a stare that kids in Perdido Beach took seriously. But Albert did not back down.

"Sam, how many cantaloupes did Edilio manage to bring back with kids who were rounded up and forced to work?" Albert asked.

"Not many," Sam admitted.

"Orc picked a whole truckload of cabbage. Before the zekes figured out how to get at him. Because we paid Orc to work."

"He did it because he's the world's youngest alcoholic and you paid him with beer," Astrid snapped. "I know what you want, Albert. You want to get everything for yourself and be this big, important guy. But you know what? This is a whole new world. We have a chance to make it a better world. It doesn't have to be about some people getting over on everyone else. It can be fair to everyone."

Albert laughed. "Everyone can be equally hungry. In a week or so, everyone can starve."

A group of kids were leaving, pushing open the door. Sam recognized them, of course. He knew everyone in town now, at least by sight if not by name.

They came out laughing, giggling, happy.

"Hey, Big Sam," one of them said.

Another said, "You should go in, dude, it's great."

Sam just nodded in acknowledgment.

The decision could no longer be put off. Close down the club or let it go. If he didn't close it down he was giving ground to Albert and would probably have another stupid fight with Astrid, who would feel as if he'd ignored her.

Not for the first time, or even the hundredth time, Sam

wished he had never, ever agreed to become anyone's leader.

Sam stole a glance at the watch on Albert's wrist. It was almost nine P.M.

"Close it down," Sam said firmly. "Close it. At ten thirty. Kids need sleep."

Inside the club Quinn relaxed into the beat. Some ska-punk, sure. Maybe later some hip-hop. Some classic old tunes, maybe.

Give it up for Albert: the guy had turned the Mac's into a decent dance club. The main lights were all off, just the menu boards were illuminated. But they didn't show Happy Meals and combos. Albert had covered them with pink tissue paper so they gave off a mellow glow, just enough to light the whites of people's eyes and their teeth when they smiled.

Hunter, what was he, seventh grade? He was the one spinning the CDs and scratching the turntable. He wasn't exactly a professional, but he was good enough. Cool enough kid, Quinn thought, even though the rumor was he was developing some killer powers. Time would tell if he would stay cool, or turn as arrogant as some of the freaks. Like Brianna, who was suddenly calling herself "the Breeze" and demanding everyone else play along. Like she was a comic book superhero. The Breeze. And he'd kind of liked her, once.

Speaking of which, there she was, dancing like a crazy person, speeding herself up, feet flying, bouncing up and down so fast, she looked like she might start flying around the room.

She'd been telling everyone who would listen how she beat a bullet. "I'm now officially faster than a speeding bullet. Me and Superman."

In another corner the weird little kid named Duck was peddling some crazy story involving fish-bats and an underground city or whatever.

And then there was Dekka, sitting by herself, nodding almost imperceptibly to the beat, eyes on Brianna. No one really knew much about Dekka. She was one of the Coates kids, one of the ones who had been rescued from Caine and Drake's cruel cinderblock torture.

She had a vibe to her, Dekka, a feeling she gave off that she was strong and a little dangerous. There was some history there, Quinn thought, something in her past, like with almost all the Coates kids. Coates was known as a school for troubled rich kids. They weren't all rich, they weren't all troubled, but the majority had some serious issues.

Quinn slid between two fourth graders, a guy and a girl, dancing. Together. When Quinn was that age he would never have danced with a girl like they were on a date. In fact, he still didn't. But things were different now, he supposed. Fourth grade was like . . . like middle-aged or something. He himself was old. Old, old, old at almost fifteen.

Birthday coming up. The question was, what would he do? Stay or step outside?

Mostly, ever since Sam had survived, kids who had hit the Fatal Fifteen had survived. Sam had told them how to do it.

Computer Jack, who back in those days was with Caine,

had used high-speed photography to record a captive kid up at Coates hitting the moment, the AoD, the Age of Destruction. Jack had come to Perdido Beach with the tale of the tape, the great revelation that in that fateful moment your world would slow down, slow down to a crawl as you approached infinity. And there, in that moment, would come a tempter to beckon to you, call to you, ask you to cross over.

But the tempter was a fraud. A liar. Like a devil, Quinn thought, like a devil. He backed into someone and turned to apologize.

"Hey, Quinn." It was Lana, shouting over the music so that it was halfway to lip-reading for Quinn. The Healer actually speaking to him.

"Oh. Hi, Lana. This is cool, huh?" He indicated the room with an awkward motion.

Lana nodded. She looked a little bleak, a little forlorn. Which seemed impossible to Quinn. Lana was second only to Sam in hero status. And the difference was that some people really kind of hated Sam, while no one hated Lana. Sam might make you do something—pick up garbage, take care of the prees at the day care, shoot someone with a machine gun—but all Lana ever did was heal people.

"Yeah. It's kind of cool," Lana said. "But I don't really know anyone."

"No way. You know everyone."

Lana shook her head ruefully. "No. Everyone knows me. Or at least they think they do."

"Well, you know me," Quinn said, and made a kind of slanted grin so she'd know he wasn't trying to get above himself and act like her equal.

But that wasn't how she took it. She nodded, so serious that she looked like she might cry. "I miss my parents."

Quinn felt the sudden, sharp pang he'd felt about every hour back when all this started, and now felt only a couple of times a day. "Yeah. Me too."

Lana held out her hand, and Quinn, after a moment's amazed hesitation, took it.

Lana smiled. "Is it okay if I just hold your hand and don't, you know, heal you of anything?"

Quinn laughed. "Whatever's wrong with me, it isn't something even you can heal." Then, "You want to dance?"

"I've been waiting to talk to Albert, standing around here for like, an hour, and you are the first person to ask me," she said. "Yeah. I would kind of like to dance."

The song had just changed to a hip-hop tune, a raucous, flatly obscene rap. It was a few years old, but still catchy, and had the added attraction of being a song no one in the room had been allowed to listen to three months earlier.

Quinn and Lana danced, even bumped hips a couple of times. Then Hunter changed the mood to a moderately slow, dreamy song by Lucinda Williams. "I love this song," Lana said.

"I . . . I don't know how to dance slow," Quinn said.

"Me neither. Let's try it, though."

So they held each other awkwardly and just swayed back

and forth. After a while Lana laid her face against Quinn's shoulder. He could feel her tears on his neck.

"This is kind of a sad song," Quinn said.

"Do you dream, Quinn?" Lana asked.

The question took him aback. She must have felt him flinch because she looked at his face, looking for the explanation in his eyes.

"I have nightmares," he said. "The battle. You know. The big battle."

"You were really brave. You saved those kids in the day care."

"Not all of them," Quinn said shortly. He fell silent for a moment, back in the dream. "There was this coyote. And this kid, right? And . . . and . . . Okay, so I could have shot him, maybe, a little sooner, right? But I was scared of hitting the kid. I was so scared I'd hit that little kid, so I didn't shoot. And then it was, like, too late. You know?"

Lana nodded. She didn't show any sympathy, and strangely Quinn thought that was a good thing because if it wasn't you, and *you* hadn't been there, and *you* hadn't been holding a machine gun with your finger frozen on the trigger, and *you* hadn't heard your voice coming out of your throat in a scream like an open artery, and *you* hadn't seen what he had seen, then you didn't have a right to be sympathetic because you didn't understand anything. You didn't understand anything.

Anything.

Lana just nodded and put her palm against his heart and

said, "I can't heal that."

He nodded, fighting back the tears that had come . . . how many times since that horrible night? Let's see, three months, thirty days in a month, that would make it about a thousand times. Maybe more. Not less, not if you counted the times he had wanted to cry but had plastered on his happy-go-lucky Quinn smile because the alternative was falling down on the ground and sobbing.

"That's my sad stuff," he said after a while. "What's yours?"

She cocked her head sideways as if sizing him up, asking herself if she wanted to share with him. Him of all people. Unsteady Quinn. Unreliable Quinn. Quinn, who had sold Sam out to end up being tortured by Caine and Drake. Quinn, who had almost gotten Astrid killed. Quinn, who was only tolerated now because when it had all hit the fan in the big battle he had finally stepped up and pulled that trigger and . . .

"You ever meet someone you can't quite forget?" Lana asked him. "Someone who you meet them and forever after it's like they own a piece of you?"

"No," Quinn said. He felt a little disappointed. "I guess he's a lucky dude."

Lana was so startled, she laughed. "No. Not that kind of guy. Maybe not a guy at all. Maybe not . . . well, not a dude the way you mean. More like someone took a fishing hook, right? Like they took that hook and stuck it in me like I was a worm. You know how on the end of a fishhook there's this barb? So you can't pull it out without ripping a big hole in yourself?"

Quinn nodded without really understanding.

"And then, maybe, here's what's weird, right: You almost want the fisherman to reel you in. It's like, okay, you have that hook in me, and it hurts, but I can't get it out, I'm stuck. So just reel me in. Just get it over with and stay out of my dreams because they're all nightmares."

Quinn still didn't understand what she meant, but the image of a fish, reeled in, helpless, stuck with him. Quinn knew hopelessness when he heard it. He'd just never expected to hear it from the most beloved person in the FAYZ.

The musical tempo changed again. Enough with the slow music, kids wanted to rock out, so Hunter dialed up some techno that Quinn didn't recognize. He started to move to the rhythm, but Lana wasn't into it.

She put her hand on his shoulder and said, "I see Albert's free, and I have to talk to him."

She turned away without a further word. Quinn was left with the feeling that however bad his nightmares were, the Healer's were worse.

TWELVE

61 HOURS, 3 MINUTES

THE ARGUMENT WITH Astrid about Albert's club had not been pretty.

Most nights Sam slept at the house Astrid shared with Mary. Not this night.

It wasn't their first argument. It probably wouldn't be their last.

Sam hated arguing. When he added up the total number of people he could really talk to, the number came to two: Edilio and Astrid. His conversations with Edilio were mostly about official business. His conversations with Astrid used to be about deeper stuff, and lighter stuff, too. Now they seemed to be always talking about work. And arguing about it.

He was in love with Astrid. He wanted to talk to her about all the stuff she knew, the history, the math even, the big cosmic issues that she would explain and he would kind of almost understand.

And he wanted to make out with her, to tell the truth.

Kissing Astrid, stroking her hair, having her nuzzle close to him, that was all that kept him from going crazy sometimes.

But instead of making out and talking about the stars or whatever, they argued. It reminded him of his mother and stepfather. Not happy memories.

He spent the night on the lumpy cot in his office and woke early, before the sun was even up. He dressed and crept out before kids could start arriving to bug him with more problems.

The streets were quiet. They usually were nowadays. Some kids had been given permission to drive, but only on official business. So there was no traffic. On the rare occasions there was a car or a truck, you'd hear it long before you saw it.

Now Sam heard a motor. Far off. But it didn't sound like a car.

He reached the low concrete wall that defined the edge of the beach. He jumped atop it and immediately spotted the source of the sound. A low-slung motorboat, a bass boat they were often called, was putt-putting along at no more than walking speed. With dawn just graying the night sky Sam could make out a silhouette. He was pretty sure he recognized the person.

Sam walked down to the water's edge, cupped his hands around his mouth to form a megaphone, and yelled, "Quinn."

Quinn seemed to be fiddling with something Sam couldn't see. He yelled back, "Is that you, brah?"

"Yeah, man. What are you doing out there?"

"Wait a second." Quinn stooped down, dealing with something. Then he turned the boat toward shore. He beached the shallow craft and killed the engine. He hopped out onto the sand.

"What are you doing, man?" Sam asked again.

"Fishing, brother. Fishing."

"Fishing?"

"People are looking for food, right?" Quinn said.

"Dude, you can't just decide to take a boat and go off fishing," Sam said.

Quinn seemed surprised. "Why not?"

"Why not?"

"Why not? No one's using the boat. I found the fishing gear. And I'm still putting in my guard-duty hours with Edilio."

Sam was at a loss for words. "Did you catch anything?"

Quinn's teeth showed white in the darkness. "I found a book on fishing. Just did what they said in there." He reached down into the boat and lifted something heavy. "Here. You can't see it in the dark. But I'll bet it weighs twenty pounds. It's huge."

"No way." Despite his foul mood, Sam grinned. "What is it?"

"I think it's a halibut. I'm not sure. It doesn't look exactly like the fish in the book I got."

"What do you plan to do with it?"

"Well," Quinn said thoughtfully. "I guess I'm going to try and catch some more, and then I'm going to eat a bunch of it, and then maybe see if Albert will trade me something for whatever I don't eat. You know Albert: he'll figure out some way to fry them up at Mickey D's and do fish sticks or whatever. I wonder if he still has any ketchup."

"I'm not sure that's the best idea," Sam said.

"Why?"

"Because Albert doesn't just give stuff away. Not any more."

Quinn laughed nervously. "Look, brah, don't tell me I can't do this, okay? I'm not hurting anyone."

"I never said you were hurting anyone," Sam said. "But look, Albert's going to sell this fish to whoever will give him whatever he wants: batteries and toilet paper, whatever else he figures out he can control."

"Sam. I got, like, twenty pounds of good protein here."

"Yeah. And it ought to go to the people who aren't getting enough, right? Mother Mary could serve some to the prees. They're not eating much better than the rest of us, and they need it more."

Quinn dug his toe in the wet sand. "Look, if you don't want me to sell or trade the fish to Albert, okay. But look, I have this fish, right? What am I supposed to do with it? Someone needs to put it on ice before long. I can't just walk around town handing out pieces of fish, right?"

Once again Sam felt the wave of unanswerable questions rising around him like a tide. Now he had to decide what Quinn did with a fish?

Quinn continued. "Look, I'm just saying I can haul this fish and any others I get up to Albert and he has a refrigerator big enough to keep it in good shape. Plus, you know how he is: he'll figure out how to clean it and cook it and—"

"All right," Sam interrupted. "Fine. Whatever. Give it to Albert this time. Till I figure out some kind of, I don't know, some kind of rule."

"Thanks, man," Quinn said.

Sam turned and headed back toward town.

"You should have come in and danced last night, brah," Quinn yelled after him.

"You know I don't dance."

"Sam, if anyone ever needed to cut loose, it's you."

Sam tried to ignore his words, but their pitying, concerned tone bothered him. It meant that he wasn't keeping his mind secret. It meant he was broadcasting his foul, self-pitying mood, and that wasn't good. Bad example.

"Hey, brah?" Quinn called.

"Yeah, man."

"You know that crazy story Duck Zhang's talking about? Not the cave thing, but the part about, like, flying fish-bats or whatever?"

"What about them?"

"I think I saw some. Came shooting up out of the water. Of course, it was dark."

"Okay," Sam said. "Later, dude."

As he walked across the beach he muttered, "My life is fish stories and Junior Mints."

Something was nagging at him. And not just Astrid. Something. Something about Junior Mints.

But weariness swept over him and dissolved the half-formed thought. He was due at town hall before long. More stupidity to deal with.

He heard Quinn singing Bob Marley's "Three Little Birds" to himself. Or maybe to Sam.

Then the sound of the putt-putt outboard motor starting again.

Sam felt an intense stab of jealousy.

"You don't worry," Quinn said, echoing the song.

"I do."

"Caine?"

No answer. Diana tapped at the door again.

"Hungry in the dark," Caine cried in an eerie, warbling voice. "Hungry in the dark, hungry in the dark, hungry, hungry."

"Oh, God, are we back to this?" Diana asked herself.

During his three-month-long funk Caine had screamed or cried or raged in various different ways. But this phrase had been the one most often repeated. *Hungry in the dark.*

She pushed open the door. Caine was thrashing in his bed, sheet twisted around his body, arms batting at something invisible.

Caine had moved out of Mose's cabin into the bungalow once occupied by the headmistress of Coates Academy and her husband. It was one of the few still-undamaged, un-trashed spaces at Coates. The room had a big, comfortable bed with satin-soft sheets. There were prints of the kind baby boomers bought at Z Gallerie on the walls.

Diana moved quickly to the window as Caine cut loose again, wailing like a lost soul about hunger in the darkness. She raised the room-darkening blinds, and pale early sunlight lit the room.

Caine sat up suddenly. "What?" he said. He blinked hard several times and shivered. "Why are you here?"

"You were doing it again," Diana said.

"Doing what?"

"'Hungry in the dark.' It's one of your greatest hits. Sometimes you change it to 'hungry in the darkness.' You muttered it, moaned it, shouted it for weeks on end, Caine. Darkness, hunger, and that word: 'gaiaphage.'" She sat down on the edge of his bed. "What's it all mean?"

Caine shrugged. "I don't know."

"The Darkness. Drake talks about it, too. The thing out in the desert. The thing that gave him his arm. The thing that messed up your head."

Caine didn't say anything.

"It's a monster of some kind, isn't it?" Diana asked.

"Of some kind," Caine muttered.

"Is it some mutant kid or whatever? Or like the coyotes, some kind of mutant animal?"

"It is what it is," Caine said shortly.

"What does it want?"

Caine looked suspiciously at her. "What do you care?"

"I live here, remember? I have to live in the FAYZ along with everyone else. So I kind of have an interest in whether some evil creature is using all of us for some—"

"No one uses me," Caine snapped.

Diana fell silent, letting his anger ebb. Then, "It messed you up, Caine. You're not you anymore."

"Did you send Jack to warn Sam? Did you send him to tell Sam how to survive the poof?"

The question caught Diana unprepared. It took all her self-control to keep fear from her face. "That's what you think?" Diana managed a wry smile. "So that's why I'm being followed everywhere I go."

Caine didn't deny it. "I'm in love with you, Diana. You took care of me these last three months. I don't want you to be hurt."

"Why are you threatening me?"

"Because I have plans. I have things I have to do. I need to know whose side you're on."

"I'm on my side," Diana said. It was the honest answer. She didn't trust herself to convince him of a lie. If he thought she was lying . . .

Caine nodded. "Yeah. Fine. Be on your own side, I respect that. But if I find out you're helping Sam . . ."

Diana decided it was time for a show of anger. "Listen, you sad excuse for a human being, I had a choice. Sam offered me that choice after he kicked your butt. I could have gone with him. It would have been the smart move. I would have been safe from Drake. And I wouldn't have had to put up with you trying to paw me every time you felt lonely. And I would definitely be eating better. I chose to go with you."

Caine sat up straighter. He leaned toward her. His eyes made his intentions clear.

"Oh, here we go." Diana rolled her eyes.

But when he kissed her, she let him. And after a few seconds of stony indifference she kissed him back.

Then she put her palm on his bare chest and shoved him back onto his pillow. "That's enough."

"Not nearly enough, but I guess it will have to do," Caine said.

"I'm out of here," Diana said. She started for the door.

"Diana?"

"What?"

"I need Computer Jack."

She froze with her hand on the doorknob. "I don't have him hidden in my room."

"Listen to me, Diana, and don't say anything. Okay? I'm telling you: don't say anything. This is a one-time offer. Amnesty. Whatever happened with you and Jack and Sam, it's forgotten, if . . . if you get me Jack. Bygones will be bygones. But I need Jack. I need him soon."

"Caine—"

"Shut up," he hissed. "Do yourself a favor, Diana. Don't. Say. Anything."

She bit back the angry retort. There was no mistaking the menace in his voice. He meant it. This time, he meant it.

"Get me Jack. Use any resource you want. Use Bug. Use Drake, even. Use Pack Leader, if that'll help. I don't care how it gets done, but I want Jack in two days. Starting now."

Diana struggled for her next breath.

"Two days, Diana. You know the 'or else.'"

Albert was supervising the sweeping of his club by one of his crew, and reading about the melting points of various metals—lead and gold, especially gold—when Quinn pushed a wheelbarrow into the McDonald's.

In the wheelbarrow were three fish. One was very big for a fish. The other two looked more average.

Albert's *second* thought was that this was an opportunity.

His *first* thought was that he was hungry and would definitely enjoy a nice piece of fried fish. Even raw fish. The strength of the hunger pangs caught him off-guard. He tried to ignore the hunger, eating very little himself and making sure that his crew were as well fed as possible, but when a guy walked in with actual, honest-to-God fish . . .

"Whoa," Albert said.

"Yeah. Cool, huh?" Quinn said, smiling down at his fish like a proud parent.

"Are they for sale?" Albert asked.

"Yeah. Except for whatever I can eat. Plus, we got to send some to Mary for the prees."

"Of course," Albert agreed. He considered. "I don't have anything I can use to make a batter. But I could probably dip them in a little flour to give them a little crunchiness."

"Man, I'll eat 'em raw," Quinn said. "I barely got them here without chomping on them."

"What do you want for all three?" Albert asked.

Quinn was obviously baffled. "Dude, I don't know."

"Okay," Albert said. "How about this: You get a free pass to the club. Plus, you get all the fish you can eat. And, I owe you a major favor in the future."

"A major favor?"

"Major," Albert confirmed. "Look, I'm doing some things. I have some plans. As a matter of fact, they're plans I would like you to help me with."

"Uh-huh," Quinn said skeptically.

"I'm asking you to trust me, Quinn. You trust me, and I'll trust you."

Albert knew that would hit home with Quinn. Trust was the last thing anyone offered Quinn.

Albert changed the subject, just a little. "How did you catch these fish, Quinn?"

"Um, well, it's not that hard to figure out. I used a net to scoop up some little fish, you know, not like fish you could eat. Then I used them as bait. You get the little fish in tide pools and shallow water. There's plenty of gear and boats. Then you just need to be really, really patient."

"This could be major," Albert said thoughtfully. Then, "Okay, I have a proposition for you."

Quinn grinned. "I'm listening."

"I have twenty-four guys on my crew. Mostly they guard Ralph's and move food around. But the truth is, there isn't much left to guard or to move around. So."

"So?"

"So, I give you six of my best people. The most reliable six guys I can come up with. You take them and train them to fish."

"Yeah?" Quinn frowned, still not getting it.

"And you and me, we're partners in the fish business. Seventy-thirty. I give you workers, I haul the fish, preserve it, prepare it, distribute it. And whatever we bring in, I take seventy percent and you take thirty."

Quinn arched a brow. "Excuse me? How come you get seventy percent?"

"I pay everyone under me," Albert explained. "Your thirty percent is just for you."

"It's thirty percent of nothing," Quinn said.

"Maybe. But not for long." Albert grinned and slapped Quinn on the shoulder. "You have to stay hopeful, man. Things are looking up. We have fish."

Mother Mary smelled it before she saw it.

Fish. Fried fish.

The kids smelled it, too. "What is that smell?" Julia cried, and ran forward, black ponytail flying behind her.

There followed a near riot. Preschoolers surged around Quinn, who was carrying the fried fish piled on a napkin-covered McDonald's tray.

"Okay, okay, okay, everyone gets some," Quinn yelped.

Mary could not move. She knew she should, she knew she had to step in and impose order, but the smell had paralyzed her.

Fortunately, Francis—who had made such a scene over

hating to work at the preschool—had decided after the first day that he wouldn't mind working a second day. Then a third. He was on his way to becoming a regular. Once he'd gotten over his attitude, he had proved to be really good with the children.

"Okay, little creatures," Francis yelled, "back away. Back slowly away from the food."

"Sorry, I probably should have warned you I was coming," Quinn said sheepishly as he waded through a sea of kids and held the fish high above dozens of grabbing hands.

Mary twisted her fingers together as she watched Francis and the other helpers get the kids into line. The smell of the fish was unbelievable. It made her stomach grumble. It made her mouth water.

It made her sick.

"Okay, guys, we have thirty-two pieces," Quinn said. "How do you want to do this?"

Francis glanced at Mary, but she could not respond. It was as if she were frozen in place.

"Everyone starts with half a piece," Francis decided. Then he warned, "And anyone who gets grabby gets nothing."

"Mary, there's enough for you and your workers to have some, too," Quinn said.

Mary nodded. She couldn't. Not for herself. For the others, yes. Of course.

"You okay?" Quinn asked her.

Mary gritted her teeth and forced a shaky smile. "Of course. Thanks for bringing this. The children haven't had . . . they need the protein . . . they . . ."

"Okay," Quinn said, obviously nonplussed.

"Save some for the babies," Mary urged Francis. "We'll purée it in the blender."

The sounds of gobbling filled the room. Many of these kids probably hated fish. Back in the old days. Even two weeks ago they would have turned up their noses. But now? No one would turn away protein. They felt the need way down inside. Their bodies were ordering them to eat.

But Mary's body was ordering her not to.

It would be a sin, she told herself. A sin to consume the fish only to vomit it back up later. She couldn't do that to the littles.

Mary knew there was something wrong with the way she was behaving. She was surrounded by hunger that kids couldn't avoid, and she alone was the cause of her own hunger. A warning sounded, but distant, barely audible. Like someone shouting to her from two blocks away.

"Come on, Mary, you have to try this," Francis urged. "It's amazing."

Unable to manage a reply, Mary turned away, silent, and headed for the bathroom pursued by the slavering sounds of hungry children.

THIRTEEN

SAM KNOCKED AT the front door. He didn't usually do that. Astrid had told him many times he could just walk in.

But he knocked, anyway.

It took her a while to answer.

She must have just come from the shower. Astrid worked out after dinner, when Little Pete usually liked to watch DVDs. Her blond hair was plastered down her neck, strands of it swooping down across one eye to give her a vaguely piratical look. She was wearing a bathrobe and carrying a towel.

"So. You came crawling back, eh?" Astrid said.

"Would it help if I were on hands and knees?" Sam asked.

Astrid considered that for a moment. "No, the abject look is enough."

"I didn't see you all day."

"It would have been surprising if you had. I wasn't interested in being seen."

"Can I come in?"

"Are you asking if you *may* come in? 'Can' is meant to suggest ability. 'May' is proper when the question is one of permission."

Sam smiled. "You know you just get me hot when you do that."

"Oh? Then maybe I should go on to point out that both 'can' and 'may' are considered 'modal verbs.' There are nine modal verbs. Would you like me to tell you what they are?"

"You'd better not," he said. "I can't take too much excitement."

Sam put his arm around her, drew her close, and kissed her on her lips.

"Wimp," she teased when he drew back. "Well, come on in. I have some delicious canned okra, a burned home-made graham-flour tortilla, and half a head of Orc's cabbage left over from dinner if you're hungry. If you wrap the tortilla around some shredded cabbage and a bit of okra and microwave it for thirty seconds you have something really disgusting but kind of healthy."

Sam stepped inside and closed the door behind him. Little Pete was camped out in front of the TV watching a DVD of *How the Grinch Stole Christmas*. Jim Carrey, completely obscured by makeup, was rubbing his hands gleefully.

"It was one of his Christmas presents," Astrid explained.

"I remember," Sam said.

Christmas had not been a great time for anyone. Christmas without parents. Without older siblings. Or grandparents. Without all the weird relatives you saw only at holiday time.

Astrid's parents had an artificial tree that Sam had found in the attic and hauled downstairs to set up. It was still set up, although they'd taken the ornaments off and put them back in boxes.

Everyone had done what they could. Albert had put on a feast, though nothing to rival his great Thanksgiving production. By Christmas there were no pies to be had, no cookies, and fresh fruit or vegetables were all in the half-forgotten past.

"We can't fight over . . . you know . . . politics," Sam said.

"You mean you want me to just agree with you on everything?" Astrid asked, her voice signaling readiness to start it all over again.

"No. I want you to tell me what you think. I need you," Sam admitted. "But that's kind of the point: I need you. So when we disagree, we can't get mad at each other. As people, you know?"

Astrid seemed ready to argue. Instead she exhaled a long, weary breath. "No, you're right. We have enough to deal with."

"Cool," he said.

"Did you get any sleep last night? You look tired."

"I guess I am," he said. "Long day. Hey, did you know Quinn is fishing? He caught something big this morning."

"I didn't know. That's good." She looked troubled. "We should have thought of that. Fishing, I mean."

"We're not going to think of everything, I guess," Sam said wearily. That was the problem with having one person in charge. People expected you to come up with all the answers. They stopped coming up with answers for themselves. Quinn had opened up a new possibility all by himself. And now he was turning to Albert for help, not to Sam.

"What's he doing with the fish?"

"We sent a lot of it over to the day care this morning. We got some protein to the littles, at least."

"A lot of it?" She raised an eyebrow. "What's Quinn doing with the rest? He's not hoarding it, I hope."

"He's . . ." Sam stopped himself. The last thing he wanted was to argue about Quinn and Albert and fish. "Actually, can we talk about that tomorrow? The important thing is that the littles got some protein today. Can we just be happy about that?"

Astrid laid her hand against his cheek. "Go to bed."

"Yes, ma'am."

He trudged upstairs, feeling better than he had all day. He passed Mary coming down. "Hey, Mary. Back to work?"

"What else would I be doing?" she said. "Sorry, that sounded cranky."

"If you can't be cranky, who can?" Sam said. "But hey, are you getting enough to eat?"

Mary seemed startled. "What?"

"I was wondering if you were getting enough food. You've lost some weight. I mean, don't get me wrong, you look good."

"Thanks," Mary managed to say. "I'm um . . . Yes, I'm getting plenty to eat."

"Did you get some of the fish this morning?"

Mary nodded. "Yes. It was really great."

"Okay. Later."

Sam had the use of what had once been a guest room. It was nicely made up, had its own bathroom, with very soft matching towels. He kept the room very neat and clean because it was still somehow not his room. He couldn't imagine it ever being his room. This house belonged to . . . well, that was a good question. But it sure wasn't his.

Which did not stop him from sliding between the sheets and passing almost instantly from hectic consciousness to sleep.

But there was no peace in his dreams. He had a dream of his mother. Only she wasn't really his mother in the dream, not the real person. She was the creature who had called for him in the midst of what would have been the poof.

Happy fifteenth birthday, Sam, now step out of the FAYZ into . . . into no one knew what.

Some kind of illusion. Seeing what you wanted to see. And yet, it had seemed so real at the time. In his dream, Sam relived that moment.

He saw Caine, his fraternal twin, within a circle of blistering light. He saw their mother. And he saw a girl, maybe twelve, thin, with a lot of thick ponytail. He wondered in a vague sort of way about the girl. There had been no girl there during the poof. Not inside the distortion. No girl.

But now that dream was dissolving into another. Sam was standing at the bottom of the town hall front steps and there were cans as big as trash barrels rolling down the steps. It started with a can of beans. And then another. And then a can of ravioli. The cans started coming faster and now Sam was trying to climb the steps but he couldn't because every time he lifted a foot to set it down on a step, he found another can hurtling toward him.

Now a cascade of little cans, almost like insects scurrying around under his feet. He was tripping, slipping and sliding in a cascade of cans, unable to rise.

In his dream he looked up and saw a girl, the same girl again. Lots of brown hair drawn back in a long ponytail. The girl. She was at the top of the stairs. But she wasn't throwing the cans.

The cans became Junior Mints. In cans, oddly, but with the familiar green Junior Mints label. Cans of them rolling and tumbling and tripping Sam, who now was buried under them.

Sam was aware of someone standing beside him. Not a person, an insect, a bug of indistinct shape.

The giant bug picked up a Junior Mint, which now was not a can but a big, novelty-sized box.

Sam woke suddenly.

Astrid was shaking him, yelling right in is face, scared. "Wake up!"

He was up in a flash, almost knocking Astrid over.

"What?"

"Petey," Astrid cried. Her eyes were wild with fear.

Sam ran for Pete's room. He stopped dead in the hallway

outside it. The door was open.

Pete was in his bed. He wasn't moving. His eyes were shut. His face was peaceful. He was asleep. But how he could sleep was beyond Sam, because the room around Pete was filled with monsters.

Literally filled. Wall to wall. Up to the ceiling.

Monsters. A hundred nightmares' worth of monsters. They slithered from under his bed. They crawled from his closet. They floated like they were helium balloons. Like an entire Macy's Thanksgiving parade in miniature had floated into Little Pete's room. But instead of cartoon Shrek and the Cat in the Hat there were things much more sinister in their place.

One of the smaller ones had purple wings in three pairs, grasping tendrils hanging from its belly, a head like the end of a syringe with bloodred eyeballs perched on top.

The largest was a shaggy monstrosity like a grizzly bear with eighteen-inch spikes at the ends of its paws.

There were creatures that were all sharp edges, as if they'd been assembled out of razor blades and kitchen knives. There were creatures of glowing magma. There were creatures who flew and others who slithered.

"Like the other day? In the plaza?" Sam asked in a shaky whisper.

"No. Look: they cast shadows," Astrid said urgently. "They're making sounds. They smell."

The big shaggy monster shifted shape as they watched. The brown fur lightened toward white, then veered suddenly to green.

Its mouth moved.

Opened.

A sound came from it, like a strangling cat. An eerie mewling.

Then the mouth snapped shut with an audible click. The mouth melted and disappeared beneath new-grown fur.

"It was trying to speak," Astrid whispered.

A mustard-colored creature with a vaguely canine shape, pickax head, antennae, and twin tubes mounted on its eyeless head was changing shape as it floated. Its feet were shifting, from mere pads to sharp-ended, fishhook-barbed spears. The barbs clicked in and out. Like the creature was practicing with them, discovering their use.

And then, with its shape determined at last, it too attempted to speak. This time the sound was even less coherent, a chittering, insect sound that died out suddenly when a fleshy membrane grew over its mouth.

"Do they see us?" Sam wondered aloud.

"I don't know. See how they're staring at Petey?"

It was absurd to think about reading the faces of the monsters—some had five eyes; some had a single eye; some had gnashing, razor teeth and no eyes at all. But to Sam they seemed to be gazing with something like awe at Little Pete, who snored softly, oblivious.

A snake as long as a python slithered by, twisting in midair. Tiny centipede legs grew from it, reminiscent almost of the zekes, though these legs looked like they were made for sticking like Velcro.

The snake's mouth hissed. The hissing grew in volume, then stopped abruptly: the snake's entire head had simply disappeared.

"They're trying to communicate," Astrid said. "Something is stopping them. Something won't let them speak."

"Or someone," Sam said. "If they attack us . . ." He raised his hands, palms out.

Instantly Astrid pressed his hands down. "No, Sam. You might hit Petey."

"What happens if he wakes up?"

"The other times the visions just disappeared. But this is different. Look. Look at the curtains, they're singed where that . . . that lava thing got near them."

Sam made up his mind. "Wake him up."

"What if—" she began.

"Look, maybe they're not a threat. But maybe they are. If they are, I'm not just going to let them hurt you, I'm going to burn them."

Then he added, "If I can."

"Pete," Astrid called in a quavering voice.

Until that moment none of the creatures had taken any notice of the two frail-looking humans standing there gawking. But now every eye, every set of eyes, every quivering antenna, turned toward them. It was so sudden, Sam imagined he heard their eyeballs click.

Red eyes, black eyes, yellow-slitted eyes, globular blue eyes, maybe fifty eyes in all, stared straight at Sam and Astrid.

"Try again," Sam whispered. He stretched out his arms

again, opened his palms toward the monsters, ready.

"Petey," Astrid said more urgently.

Now monstrous bodies shifted. They moved almost as one, some clumsy, some like lightning, but all moving as if they were Disney animatronics operating off the same signal. They turned to face Sam and Astrid.

One after another their mouths opened. Sounds came from those mouths. Grunts and hisses, hoots and growls; sounds like steel dragged on porcelain, sounds like the chirping of crickets, sounds like mad dogs barking. Not words, but sounds that wanted to be words, were struggling to be words.

It was a chorus of fury and frustration. And it stopped as suddenly as if someone had yanked the plug from a stereo.

The monsters glared at Sam and Astrid, as though they were to blame for the silencing.

Sam cursed softly.

"Walk backward. Down the hall," Sam ordered. "They'll have to come at us one by one and Pete won't be in the line of fire."

"Sam . . ."

"Not really a good time for a debate, Astrid," Sam said through gritted teeth. "Back slowly away."

She did. He followed, one foot directly behind the other, arms up, his mutant's weapons at the ready.

But no way he'd get them all if they came. No way. He could get a few, maybe, if they could even be burned. How did you burn a creature made of magma?

Step by step till they were halfway down the hall. Ten feet. Fifteen. The monsters would have to come at him down that hallway. That gave him all the advantage he was going to get. Pete was out of the direct line of fire.

"Call him again. Louder this time."

"He doesn't always respond."

"Try."

"Pete," Astrid shouted, fear giving volume to her voice. "Petey, wake up! Wake up, wake up!"

Through the doorway Sam saw the floating creatures, all those that didn't have wings anyway, suddenly land with convincing weight on the floor. The floorboards jumped from the impact.

The six-winged creature was first. Fast as a dragonfly it zoomed straight for Astrid.

A scorching green-white light shot from Sam's hands. The winged thing burst into flame. But it already had too much momentum.

Sam dropped, reached back to yank Astrid down, found that she had already ducked. The flaming corpse, wings shriveled like burning leaves, blew over their heads.

Mary Terrafino blundered into the hallway. "What is happening!"

"Mary! Back! Backbackback!" Sam yelled.

Mary jumped back into her room as the mustard-colored, eyeless dog with antennae attacked, feet clicking and scrabbling on the hardwood.

It had two tubes on its head. Sam was sure it hadn't had

them just moments earlier.

Something pale blue shot from the tubes. Slime covered one of Sam's hands, thick as oatmeal, sticky as rubber cement.

With the other hand, Sam fired again. The thing burned, slowed, but did not stop.

And now all the nightmares were pushing and shoving to get through the door, jostling for the chance to attack, and then—

Then they were gone.

Simply gone.

All but the still-sizzling remains of the six-winged bug and the goo-spraying canine. Astrid rushed into Little Pete's room. Sam was only a step behind. Little Pete was sitting up in bed, eyes open, unfocused.

Astrid threw herself onto the bed and put her arms around him.

"Oh, Petey, Petey," she cried.

Sam crossed quickly to the window. The curtain that had been singed was now burning. He yanked at it, pulled it down to stomp on it, and in the process knocked a shelf full of nesting dolls to the floor. Sam stamped the fire out. One foot crushed one of the gaily painted red nesting dolls. The outer doll splintered. The doll nestled within rolled free into the flame.

Sam stamped it all out.

"You have a fire extinguisher?" he asked. He was trying to wipe the mucousy substance from his hand and not having much luck. "Just to be safe, we should—"

But then, through the window he saw something almost as frightening as the monsters. There was a girl standing across the street. She was gazing up at him.

She had huge dark eyes, and an abundance of brown hair pulled back into a ponytail.

The girl from his dream.

Sam ran from the room, tumbled down the steps, and burst out onto the street.

The girl was nowhere to be seen.

Sam ran back inside to face a terrified Mary and Astrid, who, to his amazement, was taking notes on a pad of paper even as she hugged her brother.

"What in the—" Sam began.

"They were adapting, Sam," Astrid interrupted urgently. "Did you see? They were changing as we watched them. Altering their physical shapes. Evolving."

She scribbled, wiped tears from her face, and scribbled some more.

"What is going on?" Mary Terrafino asked in an abashed, diffident whisper, like she was intruding.

Sam turned to her. "Mary. You don't talk about this."

"It's him, isn't it?" Mary asked, looking at Little Pete, who was yawning now and beginning to drift back to sleep. "There's something about him."

"There are a lot of things about him, Mary," Sam confessed wearily. "But it stays between us. I need to be able to trust you on this."

Mary nodded. She seemed torn between staying and

arguing and returning to the relative sanity of her room. Sanity won out.

"This isn't right," Astrid whispered as she laid her brother back on his pillow.

"You think?" Sam asked shrilly.

Astrid stroked Little Pete's forehead. "Petey, you can't do that again. You might hurt someone. You might hurt me. And then who would take care of you?"

"Yeah, no more monsters, Petey," Sam said.

"No more monsters," Astrid echoed.

Little Pete closed his eyes. "No more monsters," he said through a huge yawn.

"I made him be quiet," Little Pete added.

"Made who be quiet?" Sam asked.

"Petey. Who?" Astrid pleaded. "Who? Who was it? What did he want to say?"

"Hungry," Little Pete said. "Hungry in the dark."

"What does that mean?" Astrid pleaded.

But Little Pete had fallen asleep.

FOURTEEN

"SHE'S BEEN LIKE this ever since." Bug—the visible Bug—waved his hand at Orsay, who sat knock-kneed and slump-shouldered on the front steps of Coates Academy.

Caine stared down at her with more than casual interest. He touched the top of Orsay's head and noted the way she flinched. "Been there. I think," he said.

Diana yawned. She was still dressed in her silk pajamas with a robe pulled around her as if it was cold. It was never really cold in the FAYZ.

Bug swayed back and forth, barely able to stay awake.

"What was happening when she started zoning out?" Caine asked Bug.

"What?" Bug snapped his head forward, jerking himself awake. "She was in one of Sam's dreams. Something about cans of food. Then all of a sudden there's this, like, creepy light show going on in one of the other rooms in the house and then it was like Orsay was on drugs or something."

"What do you know about drugs?" Diana asked.

Bug shrugged. "Joe junior, my big brother, he got high a lot."

Caine knelt down in front of Orsay. Gently he lifted her face. "Snap out of it," he said.

There was no response. So he slapped her once, hard but with no malice. His palm left a pink stain on her cheek.

Orsay's eyes flickered. She looked like a person waking up many hours too early.

"Sorry," Caine said. He was very close to her. Close enough to inhale her breath. Close enough to hear her heart pounding like a cornered rabbit's. "I need to know what you saw."

The corner of her mouth turned down, like a crudely drawn cartoon of fear and sadness and something else.

"Come on," Caine cajoled. "Whatever dreams you had, I've had worse. Terrible stuff you don't even want to know about."

"They weren't terrible," Orsay said in a small voice. "They were . . . overpowering. They made me want more."

Caine shifted his weight away from her. "Then why are you all freaked out?"

"In his dreams . . . in his dreams the world . . . Everything is so . . ." She formed her hands as if trying to make a shape out of something that defied definition.

"Sam's dreams?" Caine demanded, half skeptical, half angry.

Orsay looked sharply at him. "No. No, not Sam. Sam's dreams are easy. There's no magic in them."

"Then tell me about them. That's what I sent you to find out."

Orsay shrugged. "He's . . . I don't know. Like, worried. He's distracted," she said dismissively. "He thinks he's screwing up and, anyway, he just wants to get away from it all. And of course, he thinks about food a lot."

"Poor baby," Diana said. "All that power. All that responsibility. Boo-hoo."

Caine laughed. "I guess being the boss isn't what Sam thought it would be."

"I think it's exactly what he thought it would be," Diana argued. "I don't think he ever wanted any of this. I think he just wanted to be left alone." That last sentence she spoke pointedly.

"I don't leave people alone when they screw with me," Caine said. "Useful information, Diana."

He stood up. "So. Sam is running scared. But not scared of me. Good. He's worried about his silly job as mayor of loserville. Good." He tapped the top of Orsay's head. "Hey. Anything about the power plant in Sam's dreams?"

Orsay shook her head. She was off again, off in some zombie trance reliving some strange hallucination of her own or maybe someone else's.

Caine clapped his hands together. "Good. Sam isn't obsessing over the power plant. The enemy," he said with a grand flourish, "is looking inward, not outward. In fact, we could strike at any time. Except."

He stared hard at Diana.

"I'll get him," she said.

"I can't do it without Jack, Diana."

"I'll get him," she said.

"You want Jack? I'll get him," Drake said.

Caine said, "You're thinking of the old Jack, Drake. You have to remember that Jack has powers now."

"I don't care about his powers," Drake snarled.

"Diana will give me Jack," Caine said. "And then we will turn off the lights and feed the—" He stopped very abruptly. He blinked in confusion.

"Feed?" Drake echoed, puzzled.

Caine almost didn't hear him. His brain seemed to trip, to skip a step, like a scratch in a DVD when the picture pixilates for a moment before starting up again. The familiar grounds of Coates Academy swam before his eyes.

Feed?

What had he meant?

Who had he meant?

"You can all go," he said, distracted.

No one moved, so he made it clear: "Go away. Go away and leave me alone!"

Then he added, "Leave her."

With Diana and Drake gone, Caine knelt before Orsay again. "You saw him, didn't you? You felt him there. He touched your mind. I can tell."

Orsay didn't deny. She met his gaze, unflinching. "He was in the little boy's dreams."

"The little boy?" Caine frowned. "Little Pete? Is that who you mean?"

"He needed the little boy. The dark thing, the gaiaphage, he was . . ." She searched for a word, and when she found it, it surprised her. "He was learning."

"Learning?" Caine gripped her arm tightly, squeezing meaning from her. She flinched. "Learning what?"

"Creation," Orsay said.

Caine stared at her. He should ask. He should ask what she meant. What would the Darkness create? What would he learn from the mind of a five-year-old autistic?

"Go inside," Caine whispered. He let go of her arm. "Go!"

Alone, he searched his mind, his memory. He stared into the trees at the edge of the campus as though the explanation might be hiding there in the early morning shadows.

"And then we will turn off the lights and feed the—"

He had not just misspoken. It wasn't just . . . nothing. There had been a definite idea there, something tangible. Something that needed doing.

Hungry in the dark.

It felt like someone had a rope wrapped around his brain. Someone he couldn't see, someone standing far off in the dark, invisible. The rope disappeared into gloom and mystery, but at this end it was attached to him.

And out there, the Darkness held the other end. Yanked it whenever it liked.

Like Caine was a fish on a hook.

He crawled up onto the step. The granite was cold. He felt exposed and ridiculous sitting there, almost doubled over, beads of sweat forming on his brow.

It still had its hook in him. It was playing him, letting the line go slack, letting him think he was free, then yanking back hard, making sure the hook was still set, wearing him out.

Playing him.

Caine flashed on a memory almost forgotten. He saw his "father," seated in a deck chair with salt spray darkening his tan jacket, holding the long, supple pole, sawing it back and forth.

Caine had gone fishing that one time, with his "father." It hadn't been a Tom Sawyer, Huck Finn kind of experience. Caine's father—the man he'd grown up calling his father— was not a man for small, intimate moments, for worms in a bucket and bamboo poles.

They were on a trip down to Mexico. Caine's "mother" had been left to shop in Cancún, and Caine had been granted the high privilege of accompanying his father on what amounted to a business trip disguised as a father-son fishing trip.

Caine and his father; a kid named Paolo and his father; a girl named . . . well, he couldn't recall her name. The three fathers were doing business and fishing for swordfish aboard a seventy-foot power boat.

The girl, what was her name?

Oh, my God, her name had been Diana. Not the same Diana, of course, a very different girl, not very attractive, red hair, bulging eyes, not at all the same.

Diana had led them, Caine and Paolo, down into the tight forward space where the anchor and ropes and so on were stored. There she had produced a joint, a small, tightly rolled marijuana cigarette.

Paolo, an Italian kid a couple of years older than Caine, had shrugged and said, "No problem," using his American slang. Caine had felt trapped. Trapped on the boat. Trapped in the company of the two kids. Trapped into getting high.

Trapped.

It wasn't Caine's favorite feeling.

He'd sat there in that dark, damp, cramped space taking hits of the joint and wishing he was anywhere else.

Paolo had tried to hook up with the girl, the pre-Diana Diana. She'd discouraged him and eventually Paolo had gone off in search of food. The girl had sidled up beside Caine and made it clear that she'd like to make the most of their privacy and the drug's effects.

Caine had rebuffed her, but she'd said, "Oh, you think you're too cool, right? You think you're out of my league, don't you?"

"You said it, not me."

"Yeah? Guess what? Your dad needs my dad. What if I go up on deck and tell my dad you forced me to smoke pot? I do that and guess what? Your dad loses this deal and he blames you."

Her eyes shone with triumph. She had him. She had her hook in him, no different from the loudly laughing men up on deck and their stupid fish.

She was sure of it, that Diana.

But Caine had laughed. "Go ahead."

"I will," she said.

"Fine. Go."

He had come to realize a basic truth that day: You can't be trapped by other people, you can only be trapped by your own fear. Defy and win.

On that day, that day on the boat, Caine had been less afraid than the girl. And he'd known intuitively that he held the winning hand.

Defy and win.

The problem now was that Caine was truly, deeply afraid of the creature in that mine. Afraid all the way down to his bones. Afraid down to the smallest, farthest, most secret recesses of his mind.

He couldn't bluff the Darkness. The Darkness knew he was afraid.

There was a rope wrapped tightly around his mind and soul. The other end of that rope was held by the dark thing at the bottom of that mine shaft. Caine imagined himself cutting that rope, picking up an ax, raising it high above his head, bringing it down with all his might. . . .

Ruthless and unafraid. Like he had been with Diana.

With both Dianas.

"Have to," he whispered to himself.

"Have to cut it," he said.

"Maybe I will," he muttered.

But he doubted very much that he could.

"He's hungry," Little Pete said.

"You mean you're hungry," Astrid corrected automatically. Like Little Pete's major problem was bad grammar.

She was in Sam's office at town hall. People were coming and going. Kids with requests or complaints. Some Astrid dealt with herself. Some she wrote down for Sam.

One thing Sam was right about: This couldn't go on. Kids coming in to ask for someone to arbitrate sibling rivalries, or asking whether it was okay for them to watch a PG-13 DVD, or asking Sam to decide whether they could stop wearing their retainer. It was ridiculous.

"He's hungry," Little Pete said. He was hunched over his Game Boy, intent on the game.

"Do you want something to eat?" Astrid asked absent-mindedly. "I could maybe find something."

"He can't talk."

"Sure you can talk, Petey, when you try."

"I won't let him. His words are bad."

Astrid looked over at him. There was a slight smile on Little Pete's face.

"And he's hungry," Little Pete said, whispering now. "Hungry in the dark."

"Because Sam said so, that's why," Edilio said for maybe the millionth time. "Because if we don't pick the food, we're all going to get very, very hungry, that's why."

"Can I do it another time?" the kid asked.

"Little dude, that's when everyone wants to do it: some other time. But we got melons need picking. So just get on the bus. Bring a hat, if you have one. Let's go."

Edilio stood holding the front door of the house, waiting for the kid to find his *Fairly OddParents* cap. His mood, already gloomy, was not improving as the morning wore on. He had twenty-eight kids on the bus, all complaining, all wanting to go to the bathroom, all hungry or thirsty, squabbling, whining, crying.

It was almost eleven already. By the time he got them to the fields it would be noon and they'd be asking for lunch. He was determined to tell them to pick their lunch. Pick your lunch, it's right there in front of you. Yes, I mean melons. I don't care if you don't like melons, that's your lunch.

Thirty kids, counting himself. If they worked hard for four hours they could harvest maybe seventy, eighty melons each. Which sounded like a lot until you divided it by three hundred-plus hungry mouths and you started to realize that it took a whole lot of cantaloupe before you felt full.

What worried Edilio was the way so many of the melons were already rotting in the field. The way the birds were getting at them. And the fact that no one was thinking far enough ahead to wonder what they should be planting for the next season.

Food rotting. No planting. No irrigating.

Even if they harvested the available crops, it was just a matter of time before everyone was starving. Then, good luck keeping it all together.

It turned out he'd been optimistic. It was almost one in the afternoon before they made it to the field after a hellishly unpleasant bus trip during which a full-on fistfight broke out between two sixth graders.

Sure enough, the first words out of the kids' mouths were, "I'm hungry."

"Well, there's your lunch," Edilio said, sweeping his hand toward the field and feeling great personal satisfaction at being able to rub their noses in it.

"Those round things?"

"They're called cantaloupes," Edilio said. "And they're very tasty, actually."

"What about zekes?" one of the girls asked.

Edilio sighed. "That's the cabbage field, not here. That's, like, a mile from here."

But no one moved. They all lined up obediently but kept close to the bus and far from the edge of the field.

Edilio sighed. "Okay. Let the wetback show you how."

He sauntered out into the field, bent over, gave a twist to one of the melons, and held it up high so they could see.

It was luck that saved him. The fact that he dropped the melon.

He looked down at the cantaloupe and saw the dirt move.

Edilio leaped, a wild reaction that almost tripped him, but he caught his footing and ran.

He ran faster than he had ever run before, boots slamming down on the seething worms and faster, faster, faster until he sprawled, facedown, in the dust.

The dust beyond the field.

He yanked his feet toward him and frantically examined his boots. There were chew marks on the sides, on the heels. But no holes.

The worms had not penetrated.

Edilio looked at the shocked faces of the kids around him. He had been seconds away from impatiently ordering them into the field. Most wearing sneakers. None with experience seeing what the zekes looked like.

He'd been one hesitation away from ordering forty-nine kids to their deaths.

"Get back on the bus," Edilio said shakily. "Get back on the bus."

"What about lunch?" someone asked.

FIFTEEN

SAM TOOK THE list from Astrid. He scanned the first couple of matters and nearly crumpled it up.

"The usual?" he asked her.

Astrid nodded. "The usual. I think you'll especially enjoy the—"

Computer Jack burst in like he was in a hurry.

People weren't supposed to just come busting in, but Jack wasn't just people.

"What is it, Jack?" Sam asked him as he slid into the oversized leather chair behind what had once been the real mayor's desk and briefly was Caine's.

Jack was agitated. "You should let me turn on the phones."

Sam blinked. "What? I thought you had an emergency the way you came in here."

"Everybody keeps asking me when I'm going to fix the phones," Jack said in apparent agony. "Everybody asks me, and I keep having to come up with stupid lies. They think I failed."

"Jack, we've been over this. I'm really grateful for the work you have done, man, no one else could ever have pulled it off. But, dude, we have other issues, okay?"

Jack flushed. "You asked me to do it. I told everyone I was going to do it. Then you won't let me do it. It's not fair." His glasses almost seemed to steam up from the heat of his indignation.

"Listen, Jack. You really want Caine and Drake to be able to dial up anyone they want down here? You want Caine to be able to reach out to kids? Threaten them? Sweet-talk them? Maybe offer to give them food in exchange for guns or whatever? Look how well he fooled everyone the first time around."

"You just want to be in control of everything," Jack accused.

The accusation stung. Sam started to yell but choked it off. For a few seconds he just struggled with his temper, unable to speak.

Of course I want to control things, he wanted to say. Of course he didn't want Caine filling kid's heads with lies. Kids were desperate enough to listen to anyone who offered an easier life, even Caine. Did Jack not understand how close they all were to disaster? Did Jack not get how tenuous Sam's control of the situation had become?

Maybe not.

"Jack, kids are scared. They're desperate," Sam said.

"Maybe you don't see that because you're busy with other things. But we are about this far"—he held up thumb and forefinger about an inch apart—"from total disaster. You want Caine to know that? You want kids talking to him or Drake at three in the morning, spilling their guts, telling him all of our business? You really want Caine knowing how bad things are?"

Astrid stepped in to cut off Sam's increasingly angry rant. "Jack, what happened to get you all worked up?"

"Nothing," Jack said. Then, "Zil. He's busting on me in front of everyone, talking about how now that I'm a mutant and all, my brain must not work as well."

"Say what?" Sam asked.

"He says people who get powers, their IQ drops, they get stupid. He said, 'Exhibit A: poor old Jack, formerly Computer Jack, who can pick up a house but can't get the phones to work.'"

"You know, Jack, I'm sorry if he hurt your feelings, but I kind of have stuff to deal with here," Sam said, beginning to get really exasperated. "You're the tech genius. You know it, I know it, Astrid knows it, so who cares what Zil thinks?"

"Look, why don't you just work on the internet thing you're trying to do?" Astrid suggested.

Jack shot her a poisonous look. "Why, so you can not use that, either? Make me look like an even bigger fool?"

Sam was ready to snap at Jack, tell him to shut up, go away, stop bothering him, but that would be a bad idea, so he took a deep breath, summoned all his patience, and said, "Jack, I cannot make promises. I'm dealing with a lot of stuff. First priority, before we worry about techie stuff, is—"

"Techie stuff?" Jack interrupted. His voice was shocked and indignant.

"That's not a diss. I'm just saying—" But whatever he was about to say was forgotten when Edilio appeared in the doorway. He didn't rush in as Jack had done. He just stood there looking pale and solemn.

"What?" Sam asked.

"The zekes. They're in the melon field now."

"They're spreading," Astrid said.

"I could have got all those kids killed," Edilio said. He looked like he'd seen a ghost. He was trembling.

"Okay. Enough," Sam said, standing up, pushing his chair back sharply.

Finally.

Finally something he could actually do.

He should have been worried. And he was. But the emotion that filled his mind as he strode purposefully from the room was relief. "The list is going to have to wait, Astrid. I'm going to kill some worms."

Two hours later Sam stood at the edge of the melon field. Dekka was beside him. Edilio had driven them there in the open Jeep, but he was not stepping foot on the ground.

"How you see this playing out?" Dekka asked.

"You lift them, I burn them," Sam answered.

"I can only reach a little area at a time. A circle, maybe

twenty feet across," Dekka said.

The word had spread that Sam was going to throw down with the zekes. So other kids had piled into cars and vans and now a couple of dozen watched from a safe distance. Some, looking like tourists or sports fans, had brought cameras.

Howard and Orc arrived as well. Sam was relieved. He'd sent word to Howard that he might need Orc's help.

"T'sup, Sammie?" Howard asked.

"More worms. We're going to see if we can do some pest control."

Howard nodded. "All right. And what do you want with my boy?" He jerked his thumb toward Orc, who stood leaning back against a car hood, his weight almost flattening the tires and denting the sheet metal.

"We can't kill all the zekes," Sam said. "But Astrid thinks they may be smarter than your average murderous mutated worm. So we're sending a message: don't mess with us."

"Still not seeing what Orc is here for."

"He's our canary," Sam said.

"Our what?"

"Coal miners in the old days would carry a canary down with them," Sam said. "If there was poison gas, the canary would die first. If the canary was okay, the miners knew it was safe."

Howard took a moment to digest that idea. He laughed sardonically. "I used to think you were soft, Sam. Now here you are all cold and hard, wanting to send Orc in there to get chewed up."

"It took them a while to get to his face last time," Sam said. "If we see any worm activity, he comes right out."

"Cold and hard," Howard said with a smirk. "I'll talk to my boy. But he doesn't work for free. You know that. Four cases of beer."

"Two."

"Three."

"Two, and if you argue anymore, I'll show you just how cold and hard I can be."

With the deal done, Sam looked over at Dekka. "You ready?"

"I am," she said.

"Let's do it."

Dekka raised her hands high over her head. She aimed her palms at the nearest edge of the melon field.

Suddenly, in a rush, melons, vines, and a cloud of dirt rose into the air, a dark pillar. Worms could be clearly seen, writhing within the ascending cloud.

Sam raised his own hands to shoulder height. He spread his fingers.

"This is going to feel good," he muttered.

Blazing fire shot in two green-white bolts from his palms.

Melons exploded like soggy popcorn. Vines crisped. Clods of dirt smoked and melted in midair.

The worms died. They died popping open from the super-heated steam of their own blood. Or they died shriveling up like ash curlicues, like Fourth of July snakes. Some did a little of each.

Sam raked his flamethrower up and down the pillar, aiming anywhere he saw movement. In places where he lingered, the dirt grew so hot, it glowed red and formed flying droplets of magma.

"Okay, Dekka, let go!" Sam yelled.

Dekka released her hold. Gravity worked again. And the whole molten, smoking pillar fell back to earth. It sent up a shower of sparks as it crashed. Some of the kids who were standing too close yelped as they were hit by droplets of what was almost lava.

Sam and Dekka both backed away hastily, but too late to save Sam a burn that went through his jeans and sizzled a teardrop-shaped spot onto his thigh.

"Water bottle," he yelled. He grabbed the proffered bottle and doused the spot. "Okay, that hurt. Man. Ow."

"I saw some very crispy zekes," Howard commented.

"Let's go again, Dekka. If you're up for it."

"I like melon," Dekka said. "I'm not giving it up for these worms."

They moved a distance to the left and repeated the whole sequence. Then to a third location and did it again.

"Okay, message sent," Sam said when they were done. "Let's see if they got it. Howard?"

Howard waved Orc over. The boy-monster lumbered wearily toward the field.

"First go into an area we blasted," Sam instructed him.

Orc did. If his stone feet were bothered by the scorching heat of the singed soil, he showed no sign of it.

"Okay," Sam said. "Now farther. Past the burned part. Try to pick a melon."

"Someone ought to beer me," Orc grumbled.

"I don't have any with me," Sam said.

"Figures," Orc said. He plodded into fresh, unburned dirt. He leaned down to grab a melon and came back up with two worms writhing around his hand.

Orc flung the worms away and moved with some speed back onto safer ground.

Sam felt deflated. He had failed. Even at this.

In the process he'd used the promise of beer to turn an alcoholic kid into human bait.

"Not maybe my proudest day," he said to himself.

The crowd, disappointed, shot sidelong looks of worry at Sam. He ignored them all and climbed into the Jeep beside Edilio.

"You want my job, Edilio? he asked.

"Not a chance, man. Not a chance."

Nothing stuck to the FAYZ wall. Lana had discovered that fact. She had put on gloves and tried to tape a target to the barrier. The tape didn't stick. Neither did rubber cement.

No one was going to be mounting posters of their favorite bands on the barrier.

She tried spray paint. It was fun to try. Fun to imagine that the barrier could be covered in graffiti. But spray paint sizzled a bit as if it had been sprayed onto a hot frying pan. Then it evaporated and disappeared, leaving no trace.

It was frustrating. Lana needed a target. And the notion of shooting at the wall appealed to her.

In the end she had dragged a chaise lounge from the pool area over to the tennis courts, where the barrier was most easily accessible. She leaned the chair up against the barrier—you could at least lean things against it—and taped a target to the chair.

It was not a bull's-eye. It was a copy of a photo she'd found. A picture of a coyote.

Then she took the pistol out of her backpack. It was heavy. She had no idea what caliber it was. She'd found it in one of the houses she'd previously occupied. Along with two boxes of ammunition.

She had figured out how to load it. She'd gotten pretty fast at that. The clip held twelve bullets. There was one extra clip. It was easy to slide the old clip out and pop the new one in. She'd managed to pinch her finger pretty badly the first time she tried, but she was the Healer, and that had certain advantages.

But she needed to be able to do more than hold it and load it.

She raised the gun in one hand. But it was too heavy to hold very steady with just her hand. So she gripped it with both hands. Better.

She took aim at the coyote picture.

She squeezed the trigger.

The gun kicked in her hand.

The explosion was so much louder than it was on TV or in movies. It sounded like the whole world had blown up.

She walked forward, feeling a little shaky, to check the target. Nothing. She had missed. The FAYZ wall behind the target was unscathed, of course.

Lana took aim more carefully. She'd watched Edilio training his people. She knew the basics. She centered the front target in the middle of the rear target, made sure the top edge of front and back targets were level. Then she lowered the gun until the sights rested just beneath the coyote's head.

She fired.

When she walked forward this time she found a hole in the target. Not precisely where she had aimed. But not too far off, either.

The hole in that paper filled her with pleasure.

"Looks like you have a boo-boo, Pack Leader."

Lana fired two clips' worth of ammunition at the target. She hit only half the time, but that was better than hitting not at all.

When she was done she could barely hear for the ringing in her ears. Her hands were sore and bruised. She could easily heal the bruising. But she kind of liked the feeling and what it represented.

Lana carefully reloaded both clips, slid one back into the gun, and put the gun in her backpack.

Come to me. I have need of you.

She slung the pack over her shoulder. The sun was going down, casting pale orange shadows against the gray of the FAYZ wall.

Tomorrow. She would be there soon.

SIXTEEN

SHE DIDN'T WANT to cut off her hair. She liked her hair long. But Diana took Caine's threat seriously. She had to deliver Jack.

So she stood before the mirror and lifted the electric clippers she'd found in the bedroom closet of the former headmaster. There was no point in subtlety, no need to fool with scissors and mirror for hours.

The clippers made a strangely pleasing buzz. They changed pitch each time she pushed the blade into a tuft of hair.

In less than fifteen minutes her dark hair was in the sink and spilling out onto the floor. Her head was covered in a half-inch-long black burr that made her look like Natalie Portman in *V for Vendetta*.

She scooped the hair into a trash can and rinsed the sink.

Next she began removing the last traces of makeup from her eyes. There was nothing much she could do about the sculpted eyebrows. However, there was plenty she could do about clothing. Laid out on her bed was a black World of

Warcraft T-shirt two sizes too big, a gray hoodie, a pair of baggy boy's jeans, and a pair of boy's sneakers. She kept her own underthings. There was such a thing as getting too deep into the part, after all.

She dressed quickly and stood back to check the results in the full-length mirror that hung behind the closet door.

She was still obviously a girl. From a distance she might pass, but up close, no way.

She analyzed the problem. It wasn't her body; that was covered effectively. The problem was that she simply had a girl's face. The nose, the eyes, the lips, even the teeth.

"Not much I can do about my mouth," she whispered to her reflection. "Except not smile."

Then, as if arguing with her own reflection, she said, "You never smile, anyway."

She rummaged in the bathroom until she found some medical supplies. Moments later she had a white bandage on the bridge of her nose. That helped. She could pass. Maybe.

She stepped out into the hall. No one there, which wasn't surprising. Dinner, such as it was, had come and gone. Kids were hungry and weak, and no one had energy for much except lying in their rooms.

Diana knew better than to take a car. A guard was being kept at the entrance to Coates again. They'd be sure to stop her and summon Drake.

Drake might let her go. She was, after all, following Caine's orders.

But then again, he might not. What better time to arrange an "accident" for Diana?

So she took a side door out of the dormitory, the door nearest the woods. She was acutely conscious of the crunch of her oversized boy sneakers on gravel and then grateful for the softer sound of pine needles and moldering leaves.

It was a long walk to skirt the gate. The woods were dark. Straight overheard, when she looked at the sky, she could see the rich blue of evening. But night fell early under the trees.

It took her an hour to work her way through brambles and over gullies. She was afraid she wouldn't be able to find her way back to the road—woods were woods, to Diana, one tree like the next. But at last, as night crept up on twilight, she climbed a slippery embankment and stepped onto blacktop.

She had no brilliant plan for getting to Jack. She couldn't exactly knock him on the head and carry him to Caine. She would have to rely on other means. Jack had always had a crush on her, not that he would ever act on it.

A pity she looked like a boy now.

It was all downhill until she hit the highway. There at last were widely separated pools of light cast by the ever fewer functioning streetlights, and a faint glow from the empty storefronts that hadn't yet burned out their last lightbulbs.

She was footsore and weary when she reached Perdido Beach and she badly needed a rest. It was going to be a long night, of that she was sure.

Diana walked down Sherman Avenue and onto Golding Street, looking for an empty house. They weren't hard to find. Few homes showed any glimmer of light, and this one house was so shabby, so run-down, that she was convinced no one would be staying here.

The lights were off inside and repeated efforts yielded only one functioning light bulb, a Tiffany-style lamp in the cramped and overstuffed living room. There was a roll-armed easy chair decorated with lace doilies and she sagged into it gratefully.

"Some old lady lived here," she said to the echoing emptiness.

She put her feet up on the coffee table—something the previous resident would no doubt have frowned on—and considered how long she should wait before risking the streets again. Jack's place was only a few blocks away, but it would mean passing through the more densely populated center of town.

"I would sell my soul for some TV," she muttered. What was that show she used to watch? Something with doctors and all kinds of soap opera plots. How could she have forgotten the name? She'd watched it every . . . every what? What night was it on?

Three months and she'd forgotten TV.

"I suppose my MySpace and Facebook pages are still up, somewhere, back in the world," she mused aloud. Messages and invitations piling up unanswered. Where are you, Diana? Can I be your friend? Did you read my bulletin?

What ever happened to Diana?

Diana is _____. Fill in the blanks.

Diana is . . .

She wondered what everyone in the FAYZ wondered: Where were all the adults? What had happened to the world? Was everyone "out there" dead and the only life here in this bubble? Did people in the outside world know what had happened? Was the FAYZ like some giant, impenetrable egg plopped on the Southern California coastline? Was it a tourist attraction? Were busloads of the curious lining up to have their pictures taken in front of the mysterious sphere?

Diana is . . . lost.

She got up to search the kitchen. As far as she could see in the deep gloom the shelves were empty. They had been cleaned out, of course, Sam would have seen to that, marshalling his resources.

The refrigerator was empty, too.

Diana is . . . hungry.

But she found a working flashlight in the kitchen junk drawer. With this she explored the only other room, the old lady's bedroom. Old lady clothing. Old lady slippers. Old lady knitting needles stuck through a ball of yarn.

Would Diana still be here, trapped in the FAYZ when she was old? "You're already old," she told herself. "We're all old now." But that wasn't quite true. They'd been forced to act older, to behave in ways that were very adult. But they were all still kids. Even Diana.

There was a book beside the old lady's bed. Diana was sure it was a Bible, but when she shone the light on it, she saw a reflection from glossy raised lettering. It was a romance novel. Some half-undressed woman and a kind of creepy guy in what looked like a pirate outfit.

The old woman had been reading romances. The day she poofed out of the FAYZ she was probably thinking, I wonder if spunky Caitlin will find true love with handsome Pirate guy?

That's how I should reach out to Jack, Diana thought. Play the beautiful damsel in need. Save me, Jack.

Would Computer Jack respond to her now? Would he buy the act? Would he be her pirate?

"Just call me Caitlin," Diana said, and smirked.

She tossed the book aside. But that felt wrong, somehow. So she picked it up and placed it carefully back where the old woman had left it.

She went out into the night looking for a kid who was very strong—and, she hoped, very weak.

Astrid plugged the cable into her computer and the other end into the camera Edilio had brought at her request. He'd told her a number of kids had taken pictures. The best of the photographers was an eleven-year-old named Matteo. This was his camera.

iPhoto opened and she clicked import. The pictures began to open, flashing through the viewer as they loaded.

The first half dozen or so were of kids standing around. Shots of the field. A greedy close-up on some melons. Sam with the look of cold anger he sometimes wore. Orc slouched against a car hood. Dekka self-contained, unreadable. Howard, Edilio, various people.

Then the moment when the ground rose up.

The moment when Sam fired.

Once the photos had loaded, Astrid began to go back over

them, starting with Dekka's suspension of gravity. The boy had used a good camera and he'd gotten some very good shots. Astrid zoomed in and could clearly see individual worms suspended in midair. Or mid-dirt.

Then came a spectacular shot that captured the first blast of Sam's power.

Several more, taken in just a few seconds, snapped quickly, some shaky, but some perfectly focused. Matteo knew how to use a camera.

Astrid clicked ahead, but then she froze. She backed up. She zoomed in tight.

A worm was turned toward the camera, twisted around so that its toothy mouth was aimed at the camera. Nothing unusual except that the next worm she panned over to was doing the same thing. The same direction, the same expression.

And the next worm.

She found nineteen separate images of worms. All were turned toward the camera. Pointing in the direction of the attack.

Aiming their devil grins at Sam.

With shaking hand she moved the mouse to an earlier album. She opened the photos she had taken of the dead zeke Sam had brought her. She zoomed in on the ugly thing, scanning carefully over the head.

Sam came into the room. He stood behind her and put his hands on her shoulders.

"How are you, babe?" He had started calling her that. She was still deciding whether or not she liked it.

"Rough evening," she said. "I just got past a two-hour Petey meltdown. He noticed Nestor."

"Nestor?"

"His nesting doll, remember? The little red things in his room, one doll fits exactly inside the other? The other night you stomped on it."

"Oh. Yeah. Sorry."

"Not your fault, Sam." She wasn't sure she liked him calling her "babe," but she did like the feel of his lips on her bare neck. But after a few seconds she pushed him away. "I'm working."

"What is it you're seeing?" Sam asked.

"The worms. They were looking right at you."

"I was the guy cooking them," Sam said. "For all the good it did."

Astrid twisted around to look up at him.

"Oh, I know that look," Sam said. "Go ahead, genius, tell me what it is I missed."

"With *what* are they looking at you?" Astrid asked.

Sam took a beat. Then, "They don't have eyes."

"No. I just checked again. They don't have eyes. But somehow, in the middle of being levitated in midair and getting hit with blasts of light energy, they all twist around in midair to stare—at least it looks like they're staring—in the same direction. At you."

"Great. So somehow they can see. I think what matters is that I killed a bunch of them and they didn't get the message."

Astrid shook her head. "I don't think you did anything

to them. I'm not sure it's 'them.' What if they're like ants? I mean, what if there really aren't individual worms? What if they're all part of one superorganism? Like a hive."

"So there's a queen worm somewhere?"

"Maybe. Or maybe it's not so hierarchical, less differentiated."

He kissed the nape of her neck, sending pleasant shivers down her spine. "This is all great, Astrid. How do I kill them?"

"I have two ideas on that. One is a practical suggestion. You'll like it. The other is crazier. You won't like the crazy idea."

It was time to get Little Pete ready for bed. She stood up and called to him, using the trigger phrase he understood. "Beddy boody, beddy boody."

Little Pete gave her a hazy look, as if he had heard her but had not understood. Then he got up from his chair and headed obediently up the stairs. Obedient not to Astrid's authority, really, but to what was, in effect, programming.

"I have to go do a walk-through in town, and you have to get Petey to bed," Sam said. "So give me the short version."

"Okay," Astrid said. "SUVs running just on their rims, no tires. The zekes can't eat through steel. That's the practical suggestion."

"That could work, Astrid," he said excitedly. "Four-by-fours, on their steel rims, use hooks on poles to snag melons or cabbages or whatever. It would take practice, but unless the zekes can fly, the pickers would be pretty safe riding in the truck." He grinned at her. "This is why I keep you around, despite your annoying superior attitude."

"It's not a superior *attitude*," Astrid teased back. "It's actual superiority."

"So, what's the crazy suggestion?"

"Negotiate."

"What?"

"They're too smart to be worms. They're predatory and they shouldn't be. They're territorial and they couldn't possibly be. They move and act as one, at least some of the time, and there's no way. They were looking at you, but they don't have eyes. I have no proof, obviously, but I have a feeling."

"A feeling?"

"I don't think they're zekes. I think they're Zeke."

"Talk to the superworm?" Sam said. He shook his head and looked down at the ground. "No offense, but the SUV tractor thing is why you're the smartest person in the FAYZ. The other part? That's why even though you're smart, you're not the one in charge."

Astrid resisted the urge to say something cutting in response to his condescension. "You need to keep your mind open, Sam."

"Negotiate with a killer worm brain? I don't think so, babe. I think maybe your brain is overheating. I have to go."

He tried to kiss her, but she dodged it. "Good night. Let's hope Petey doesn't have any interesting nightmares tonight, huh? Oh wait, nothing to worry about there, it's probably just my overheated brain."

Computer Jack clicked through a dizzying number of windows at an amazing speed. The mouse cursor flew across the virtual page, opening, closing, pushing aside.

It wouldn't work.

It could work. Maybe. But not without more gear. A serious server. A serious router.

He'd found one server with nowhere near the capacity he wanted. It was old, not exactly state-of-the art, but it was functional. And there were certainly enough PCs and Macs in town that could be strung together, and enough for everyone to have his own 'puter, with plenty of spares that could be cannibalized for parts.

But he did not have a serious router. A router was the difference between a true internet and just being able to share a computer between several people.

A large-capacity router. That was the Holy Grail.

Jack could see a day when all of Perdido Beach had WiFi. Then kids would start blogs, and they'd start databases, and post pictures, and maybe he would set up some version of MySpace or Facebook, a social networking site. And maybe a YouTube, and maybe even a Wiki. WikiFAYZ.

It could be done. But not without more and better gear.

He pushed back from his desk. Which turned out to be a mistake. The chair, and him in it, went flying, slid, caught on a dropped sweater, tipped over, and luckily twisted sideways just before his head would have slammed into a closed door.

He was still getting used to his strength. So far it had been of no practical use to him. In fact, it was more dangerous than helpful.

Jack picked himself up and righted the chair.

There was a knock at the door. At least, maybe it was a knock. It sounded more like a woodpecker.

"Who is it?"

"The Breeze."

"What?"

"Brianna."

Jack opened the door and there she was. She was wearing a dress. It was blue and short and had thin straps. He blurted the first thing that popped into his head. "How can you run in that?"

"What?"

"Um—"

"I can run—"

"I didn't—"

"No biggie—"

"I need a router," he said.

That put an end to the confusing cross-talk.

"A what? A router?"

"Yes," Jack said. "I can't, uh, you know, make it all work without a serious router."

Brianna considered that for a moment, then, "Do I look stupid in this dress?"

"No. You don't look stupid."

"Thanks," she said with heavy sarcasm. "I'm so glad to know I don't look stupid."

"Okay," he said, and felt stupid himself.

"Well, I was just going to the club. I have some batteries. That's all."

"Oh. Good."

"And?"

Jack shrugged, mystified. "And . . . so . . . have fun?"

Brianna stared at him for a very long five seconds without looking away. And then she was a blur. Gone.

He closed the door and went back to the computer he was using to run an analysis of the antique server.

About five minutes later he began to wonder if he had missed something in his brief conversation with Brianna.

Why had she come by?

Even six months ago Jack never thought about girls. Now they tended to show up more and more often in his thoughts. Not to mention some very embarrassing dreams.

In the good old days he might have Googled up an explanation. Not now. His parents had never really talked to him about puberty, about the fact that as his body changed, so did his thoughts. He knew enough to know things were changing for him, but he didn't know whether or not it was something he could stop.

He needed a router.

Or he needed to find Brianna and . . . and talk to her. Maybe about the router.

An idea hit him with such force, he felt as if it had stopped his heart for a second: Had Brianna been asking him to go with her to the club? Where people danced?

No. That was crazy. She wouldn't have come to ask him

to go to a dance. Would she?

No.

Maybe.

The computer screen called to him. It had always been better than candy to Jack. Better than anything. He longed desperately to be able to get back online, back to Google. Back to Gizmodo. Back to . . . to more sites than he could list.

Jack did have a free pass to Albert's club. He had spent part of a day helping Albert set up the sound system—easy work—and had earned a sort of VIP pass. So if Brianna was there, and she actually did want him to be there, too, well, he could go.

He made the decision very suddenly and acted on it very suddenly, in a hurry lest he change his mind. He leaped for the door and crushed the door handle in overeager fingers. Now it wouldn't turn, but it was easy enough to rip the door open. There was some damage, but nothing major.

The club was loud—the sound system seemed to be working just fine—and crowded with too many kids. Albert was holding a line of them at the door.

"Sorry, folks, but the maximum occupancy is seventy-five," Albert said. Then he spotted Jack. "Jack, how's it going?"

"What? Oh, fine." Jack was confused as to how to proceed. He didn't want to wait in line if Brianna wasn't even inside.

"You look like a man with a question," Albert prompted.

"Well, I'm kind of looking for Brianna. We had this . . . it's a . . . tech thing. You wouldn't understand."

"Breeze is already inside."

One of the kids in the line said, "Of course she is, she's a freak. They always get in."

A second kid nodded. "Yeah, the freaks don't wait in lines. Bet she didn't have to pay, either."

Albert said, "Hey, she got here a little before you guys did and she waited. And she paid." Then to Jack. "Go ahead in."

"See?" the first kid crowed. "He's one, too."

"Dude, he set up my sound system," Albert said. "What have you done for me other than stand here and bust on me?"

Jack, embarrassed, slid past Albert and into the room. About half the kids were dancing. The rest were camped out in chairs and sitting on tables talking. It took Jack a while to adjust to the lighting and the noise.

He searched for Brianna while trying to look casual. He spotted Quinn, dancing all alone, and Dekka, sitting silent, brooding in a corner.

Standing near Dekka but not with her was a kid Jack thought at first seemed familiar. A boy, maybe twelve, no older, with a shaved head, and a bandage on his nose. Jack noticed the boy because the boy was staring at him. The instant Jack made eye contact the boy looked away.

Jack heard a rising chorus of happy, encouraging shouts and clapping hands. He followed the sound and there was Brianna. She was dancing alone—no one could possibly have danced with her—keeping her own accelerated beat ten times faster than the music.

Her dress sort of floated around her, not quite attached, a blue cloud. Jack found the effect utterly fascinating. Brianna wasn't what people would call beautiful, she was more in the "cute" category. But there was something about her that made her hard to ignore. And not just the fact that she was the Breeze.

"Go, Breeze," someone yelled.

But another voice yelled, "Quit showing off, stupid mutant."

Brianna stopped dead. Her dress settled back into place. "Who said that?"

Zil. The same jerk who had picked on Jack over the phones.

"Me," Zil said, stepping forward. "And don't bother trying to look tough. I'm not scared of you, freak."

"You should be," Brianna hissed.

Suddenly there was Dekka, up off her chair, hand extended between Brianna and Zil. "No," she said in her deep voice. "None of that."

Quinn joined her. "Dekka's right, we can't be having fights and stuff here. Sam will shut this place down."

"Maybe we should have two different clubs," a seventh grader named Antoine said. "You know, one for freaks and one for normals."

"Man, what is the matter with you?" Quinn demanded.

"I don't like her acting like she's so cool, is all," Zil said, stepping beside Antoine.

"You should be on our side, Quinn. Everyone knows you're a normal," another kid, Lance, said. "Well . . . kind of normal. You're still Quinn."

"Knock it off," Dekka growled.

"I can take care of myself," Brianna snapped at Dekka. "I can handle both these little twerps, slap them both down so fast, they wouldn't even see it happening."

"Be cool," Dekka said to her. "Why don't you just have a good time and not put on a show?"

For a second Brianna looked as if she might challenge Dekka. But Dekka never flinched, just waited.

Brianna sighed theatrically. "Okay. The Breeze is not into making trouble. The Breeze is all about a good time." She made a sort of curtsy to Dekka, which Dekka accepted with a nod.

The music rose again and kids went back to dancing or hanging around.

"Hey, Jack," Brianna said. "You came."

"Yeah."

"So. You think you could beat Dekka?" she asked.

The question startled him. His mouth dropped open.

"Kidding. Just kidding," Brianna said. "Dekka's actually very cool. Not as cool as me, of course."

"No one is as cool as you," Jack blurted.

Brianna accepted this as though it were only her natural due. "You want to dance?"

"I don't know how," Jack said.

"Really?"

"Really."

"I could teach you."

"I'd be too embarrassed."

Brianna shrugged. "It's not like anyone is going to laugh at you."

"Yes, they would."

Brianna shook her head. At normal speed. "No way. Everyone is hoping you'll fix the phones and the internet and all. Everyone likes you. Well, not exactly likes, but everyone hopes you'll do it."

"I told you I fixed the phones already," Jack said.

Brianna's eyes narrowed. "Jack-O, watch what you say about that. It's supposed to be a secret, right?" Then she shifted focus to someone just behind Jack's shoulder. "What did you hear?"

Jack twisted to see the shaved-head kid shrugging. "What? I didn't hear anything."

That voice. Jack knew that voice.

"That's right you didn't hear anything," Brianna said pointedly. "And you better not repeat what you didn't hear."

He knew that voice.

He stared at the kid with the voice.

And suddenly, he *saw*.

"So come dance with me," Brianna said, tugging at Jack's arm.

He pulled away. "I uh . . . I have to go," he said, unable to tear his gaze away from the shaved-head "boy."

"No one will laugh at you," Brianna pleaded.

But Jack just shook off her hand and fled toward the door.

"Okay, fine, forget you," Brianna yelled. "Jerk. Computer Jerk." Then, loud enough for everyone to hear, she said, "I guess he's scared of girls."

SEVENTEEN

22 HOURS

DIANA FOLLOWED JACK from the McClub. It was a relief to get away from Brianna and Dekka. Both girls knew Diana well. Neither had any reason to like her.

Fortunately, Dekka had eyes only for Brianna, and Brianna was focused on Jack. There had been a terrifying moment when Brianna had spoken directly to Diana, but she'd quickly looked down at the ground and Brianna had not recognized her.

Jack was moving, ignoring Albert's polite "Good night," walking quickly away from the club. Not quite running but looking as if he wanted to.

She caught up with him. "Jack."

He stopped. He looked around, fearful that someone might overhear. "Diana?" he whispered.

"Mmmm. Yep. Like the new hairdo?" She rubbed her hand over her brush cut.

For a boy with the strength of ten grown men, he looked awfully nervous.

"What are you doing here?"

"I need you, Jack."

"You? You need me?"

She tilted her head to the side and sized him up. "So, you like Brianna, huh? And here I thought I was the girl of your dreams."

Flesh tones were all blue in the harsh streetlight, but Diana was sure he was blushing.

"Come on," she said. "Let's walk on the beach. We'll have some privacy there."

He followed her obediently, as she knew he would. He might have a crush on cute little Brianna, but Diana had missed none of the covert looks Jack had sent her way over the months she'd known him. She still had some power over him. They climbed the low sea wall and labored across the sand under the night sky. Diana wished she could live down here, close to the beach. As shabby and damaged as Perdido Beach was, it was still so much more alive than the Fear Factory, as some kids called Coates Academy.

"What is it you want?" Jack asked. His voice sounded desperate.

"So. You got the cell phones working. I was wondering what was taking you so long," Diana said. "You always used to tell me it would be fairly easy."

"I can't talk about it," he said miserably.

"Sam won't let you do it, will he? Why?" When he didn't answer, she provided her own explanation. "Because we'd be able to use it, too. Interesting. Poor Caine: always underestimating his brother."

Jack plodded along beside her. The strength in his limbs drove his feet too deep into the sand.

"Caine knows about you now, of course, about you being a mutant. With a serious power, no less."

"He knows?" Jack's voice rose an octave.

Diana smiled to herself. Still scared. Good. "Yep. He knows everything. He knows it's not your fault you ended up over here. He knows that was me."

"Did he make you cut off your hair?"

The question caught Diana off-guard. She laughed. "Oh, Jack. No. Caine forgave me. You know how he is. He gets mad, but really he's very forgiving."

"That's not how he seemed to me," Jack said.

Diana chose not to argue that point. "How's the internet project going?"

"I need a decent server. I need a serious router."

"Are those pieces of equipment?"

The question allowed Jack a moment of superiority. She heard the familiar pedantic tone in his voice. "Yes, those are pieces of equipment."

"Have you looked everywhere?"

"Yeah."

"Did you look at Coates when you were still with us?"

"Of course. I know every piece of technology at Coates, and probably every one here in Perdido Beach."

So, Diana thought, that was the bait she had to lay out for Jack. Of course. What else? He might lust for Diana, and long for Brianna, but Jack's true love was made of silicon.

"Even if you got a router, what makes you think Sam would let you set up your own internet?"

The long, long hesitation was all the confirmation Diana needed.

At last he said, "I don't know."

"I know Sam is a nice guy," Diana conceded. "Nicer than Caine. But Caine has always had respect for what you can do, Jack. Even back before the FAYZ. You know he always let you do your thing."

"Maybe," Jack muttered.

"I mean, put it this way: do you imagine, even for a second, that Caine would give you a job as hard as setting up the cell phone system and then just blow you off?"

His silence was eloquent.

"We need you, Jack," Diana said. "We need you back."

"I have stuff to do here."

She put her hand on his arm and he stopped walking. She came around to stand face-to-face with him. She stood too close. Close enough that she could be sure that the hard drive he had in place of a heart was whirring away.

She stroked his face with her fingers. Not too overt, not really a promise, just enough to disorient him, poor boy.

"Come back, Jack," Diana breathed. "Caine has a job for you. The biggest job you can imagine. The ultimate technological challenge." She spoke the last three words slowly, pausing dramatically.

Jack's eyes widened. "What is it?"

"Something only you can do," she said. "Only you."

"Can't you tell me?" he pleaded.

"It's huge, Jack. Beyond anything you've tried so far. Bigger computers. Far more complex programs. Maybe too much— even for you."

He shook his head, but barely. "It's a trick. You're just trying to get me to go back so Caine and Drake can teach me a lesson."

"Don't flatter yourself, kid," Diana said. Time to close the deal. Time to make him believe. "You're only good for one thing. You're not Courageous Jack or Fighting Jack or even Lover Jack, although I know you have your sad little fantasies. You're Computer Jack. Sam won't let you do what you can do. Caine will. And Jack?"

"Yes."

"So very much technology. Such a huge challenge. And only you can do it."

"I . . . I have to think about . . ."

"No, Jack. It's right now. Right now, or never."

She turned and began to walk away. Jack stood there, hesitating. But she knew. She had seen it in his eyes.

"Hey. Someone's been in my room," Zil Sperry said, coming down the stairs at a run.

Hunter Lefkowitz was splayed out on the couch, one leg up on the back, one leg touching the floor, both arms behind his head. He was watching a DVD of *Superbad*. He'd watched it at least ten times before. He knew every joke.

"How can you tell, man? The mess your room is in?"

Hunter said, barely paying attention.

Zil came around and hit the power button on the side of the TV. "Not finding that real funny, freak. Someone was in my room. Someone took something that belonged to me."

Hunter shared the house with three other boys, Zil, Charlie, and Harry. They'd been friends back before the FAYZ. They were all seventh graders, and the thing that had united them was their love of the San Francisco Giants. Perdido Beach was definitely Dodgers territory, with maybe a scattering of Angels fans. But Zil and Charlie had moved here at various times from the Bay Area, Harry had come from Lake Tahoe, and Hunter just plain liked the Giants.

So they had banded together to irritate other kids at school by ostentatiously dressing up in the orange and black. They'd gotten together on summer afternoons to watch games.

But there were no pro sports in the FAYZ. No TV, either. The four of them no longer had the one shared interest that had bound them together.

And lately distance had grown between Hunter and the other three for a reason unique to the FAYZ: Hunter was a freak. The other three were normals. At first they'd all talked about it together, like, no big deal, they'd probably all get powers eventually, it was just that Hunter was first.

But as the weeks had worn on, none of the other three had changed at all, whereas Hunter was rapidly becoming a potentially powerful mutant. That had bothered Zil.

It had bothered him more with each passing day.

"Hey man, turn the set back on," Hunter demanded,

pointing angrily at the set.

"Give it back, Hunter," Zil demanded.

"Give what back, jerkwad?"

Zil hesitated. Then, "You know what."

Hunter sighed heavily and sat up. "Okay, so you're accusing me of stealing something and you won't even tell me what it is? Man, you must be awfully bored to be starting some beef with me over nothing."

"Beef!" Zil cried accusingly.

Harry came wandering in from the dining room, where he was building a complicated LEGO design, attracted by the sound of raised voices.

"What's going on?" Harry asked.

"Moof boy here stole something from my room," Zil said.

"You're lying," Hunter shot back. "And don't be calling me names."

"Moof? You're a mutant freak. Why shouldn't I call you that?"

"What's going on?" Harry asked again, bewildered.

"Give it back," Zil said. "Give it back."

"You stupid moron, I don't even know what you're talking about!" Hunter was on his feet now, red in the face.

"The jerky," Zil said. "You called me jerkwad. Then you said 'beef.' So stop trying to be clever. You know exactly what it was, because you stole it. I had a piece of beef jerky."

"That's what this is about?" Hunter was incredulous. "First off, why were you holding out on us, man? I thought we shared—"

"Shut up, you mutant freak of nature," Zil shouted. "I don't share anything with you. I might share stuff with humans, but not with chuds."

They'd had disagreements before. Even arguments. And this was not the first time Zil had harped on Hunter's powers. But this was more intense, and now it was starting to seem like a fight they'd managed to sidestep in the past was now unavoidable. The question in Hunter's mind was, could he win? Zil was bigger and stronger. But if there had to be a fight, then, okay, Hunter would have that fight. He couldn't back down.

"Step back, Zil," Hunter warned.

"Shut your fat mutant face, you subhuman chud freak," Zil shot back. He balled his fists, tense, ready.

"Last chance," Hunter warned.

Zil hesitated, but only for a second. He spun and grabbed a long, bronze poker from in front of the fireplace.

Hunter recoiled in shock. Zil could kill him with the poker. This wasn't just a fistfight.

He raised his hands, palms out.

Harry moved with surprising speed, trying to get between the two of them, trying to calm them down, maybe, or maybe just get out of the way

Then Harry screamed.

He clawed at his neck.

He turned, slowly, and stared in horror at Hunter. Harry's glasses slid off the end of his nose. His eyes rolled up in his head, and he crumpled to the floor.

Hunter and Zil both froze. They looked down at Harry.

"What happened?" Zil asked. "What did you do to him?"

Hunter shook his head. "Nothing. Nothing, man, I didn't do anything."

Zil dropped to his knees and touched Harry's neck. "It's hot. His skin is hot."

Hunter backed away. "I didn't do anything, man."

"You freak! You murdering freak! You killed him."

"He's not dead, he's breathing," Hunter protested. "I didn't mean to . . . He jumped between us—"

"It was me you were trying to kill," Zil yelled.

"You were going to hit me with that poker!"

"What did you do, man? Did you turn on your magic microwave hands and fry his brains?"

Hunter was looking at his own palms, appalled, not wanting it to be true, needing for it not to be true. He hadn't meant . . . Harry had been his friend . . .

"Oh, my God, you murdering mutant freak!"

"I'll get Lana. She'll save him," Hunter said. "He'll be okay. He'll be fine."

But as he watched, a massive blister was forming on the back of Harry's neck, right at the base of his skull. The blister was six inches across, as big as an orange, a hairy sac full of liquid.

Hunter ran from the room. His former friend's shouted accusations followed him: "Murdering freak! Murdering freak!"

Sam was asleep in the extra bedroom at Astrid's house. He heard the sound of someone vomiting in the adjoining bathroom.

He was beyond weary, but nevertheless he dragged himself up out of bed, grabbed a T-shirt, and tapped at the bathroom door. "Hey," he said.

"What?" Mary's voice, shaky.

"You okay?"

"Oh, I'm sorry. Did I wake you up?"

"Sounded like you were ralphing. Are you sick?"

"No. No, I'm fine."

He could have sworn he heard a sob in her voice, a catch. "You sure?"

Her voice steadied. "Yeah, I'm fine, Sam. Go back to sleep. Sorry I woke you."

Sam thought that was a good suggestion. He climbed back into bed and arranged the pillows the way he liked them. He stared at the clock. Midnight. He closed his eyes. But he knew that sleep wasn't coming back anytime soon. Instead there came a rushing freight train loaded with worries and fragments of worries. And his old friend, hunger. It was hard to fall asleep when your stomach was twisting into knots.

He heard the toilet flush and the bathroom light went off.

What if Mary was sick? Who could he get to take over running the day care? Astrid had to deal with Little Pete, so it couldn't be her. He started running down the list of people he could trust to behave in a mature fashion and cope.

The only kids he could think of to take over for Mary would probably just do the job so they could get into the day care's oatmeal supplies.

He'd been dreaming, he realized. Junior Mints. He'd been dreaming about . . .

. . . Junior Mints.

That was it, the thing nagging at the edge of his consciousness. Junior Mints.

"I'm going nuts from hunger, that's what it is, I'm slowly but surely going nuts."

He forced his eyes closed, but the nagging in the back of his head was yammering louder now, not letting go, demanding attention.

Alton and Dalton fighting over whom they belonged to. Who had taken them.

Did it ever occur to you it might be one of the other kids standing guard?

No. Heather B and Mike J were at the guardhouse. And Josh was asleep the whole time.

What do you mean Josh was asleep?

Junior Mints. The map with the power plant at its center. The memory of the day of the battle.

Bug, the chameleon.

Bug.

The power plant.

Sam jumped out of bed like he'd been shot from a cannon.

He pulled on jeans and searched frantically for his shoes under the bed. He slipped them on and ran to Astrid's room. He didn't knock, just threw open the door.

She was asleep, a tangle of blond hair on a pillow.

"Astrid. Wake up."

She didn't move, so he took her bare shoulder, feeling an illicit thrill despite his frenzy. "Wake up."

Blue eyes snapped open. "What? Is it Petey again?"

He was suddenly extremely aware of the fact that he had never been in her bedroom before. But this was not the time.

"Bug. He took the Junior Mints."

She stared at him. "You woke me up for that?"

"At the power plant. Alton and Dalton. They were both telling the truth. Neither of them took the candy, or Josh, either. Someone else was there. Someone they didn't see."

"Why would Bug be at the power plant?" Astrid wondered. Then her eyes widened as she understood.

"Because I'm an idiot, that's why," Sam said angrily. "I have to get Edilio. You're in charge till I get back."

"You may be wrong," Astrid said.

He was already on his way out. He pounded down the stairs and out into the frosty night air. He found Edilio at the firehouse, where he stayed most nights.

"Who's on guard at the plant?" Sam asked Edilio after he'd shaken him out of a sound sleep.

"Josh, Brittney D, um, Mickey, and Mike Farmer."

"Mike's solid," Sam said. "The other three?"

Edilio shrugged. "Man, I work with what I got. Mickey's the one who was playing around with a gun and shot a hole in the floor of his house, killed the washing machine in the basement. Brittney may be cool. She's motivated. Josh? I don't know, man."

They piled into the Jeep. It took them an hour of crisscrossing the town before they had rounded up Dekka, Brianna, Taylor, Orc, and a handful of Edilio's soldiers. They added a sedan and a giant Escalade to the convoy. Orc snoozed in the back of the Escalade.

They had ten kids in the three vehicles. They paused in front of the town hall. Sam stood on the sidewalk, where he could be heard by everyone.

"I'm sorry to drag you all out of your warm beds, but I think Caine is going to make a move on the power plant," he said.

"Let me run out there and warn them," Brianna begged.

"If you run ten miles at high speed you'll be dead on your feet. Hungry as you are?"

"Man, the Breeze can do ten miles in, like, a minute." She snapped her fingers.

Sam hesitated. It was true. Brianna could get there long before any of them. It was also true she'd be exhausted by it. He'd seen her when she had done those kind of distances. She wasn't just worn out by it, she'd looked close to death.

"Go. But stay out of trouble." The last four words were said to a whoosh of air.

He was probably overreacting, Sam told himself. Missing Junior Mints was not a very good reason to panic. He was going to look like an idiot.

But his instincts told him he was right. He was right because if he were Caine, that's what he would have done.

He should have seen it. He should have seen it and been prepared. Just like he should have been prepared for the raid on Ralph's.

They drove away from the plaza. Past the graveyard Edilio had built, the one with far too many gravestones. Past the burned apartment building, the damaged preschool, the half-destroyed church.

Sam told himself he'd been running as fast as he could, just keeping up with trivia, and trying to deal with the threat of starvation. It didn't help. If Caine was after the power plant. . . .

They drove two blocks more, and suddenly, right in the middle of the dark street, caught in the headlights, was Zil, running and waving his arms like a crazy person.

"What do I do?" Edilio asked.

Sam cursed under his breath. "Pull over. Let's see what it is."

Edilio hit the brakes. Zil rushed over, breathless, panting, flushed. He leaned on the window as Sam rolled it down. "It's Hunter, man. The freak killed Harry."

Dekka made a sort of growling noise in her throat that made Zil take a step back. But he wasn't apologizing. "That's right, he's a freak. One of you people. And he used his freak powers to kill Harry. For nothing."

"Have you found Lana?" Edilio asked.

"I don't know where she is."

"Funny how you don't call the Healer a freak," Dekka pointed out.

"Lana's at Clifftop," Sam said. "Great. Now I really could use Brianna. Okay, we're going to have to hope I'm just being paranoid about the power plant. Edilio, drop me at Hunter and Zil's place. Tell your crew to head back to the plaza, hang around there, wait for us. Then you'll have to head up to Clifftop and see if you can find Lana. All right?"

"Yep."

"Dekka, why don't you stay with me to see what this is about."

"I'm going to go get some other normals," Zil said. "Normals gotta know what's happening."

Sam pointed his finger out of the window at him. "You're going to run around waking people up out of a sound sleep? No. You come with us."

"No way, man. You and Dekka? You're both freaks. Freaks always back each other up."

"You're being an idiot, Zil," Sam said. "I'm not going to have you running around and stirring up trouble."

"What are you going to do? Fry me?" Zil spread his hands in a gesture that was simultaneously defiant and innocent.

"This is bull," Sam said. "Get in, Zil. We're wasting time arguing."

"No way, man. No way." Zil turned and began to walk quickly away.

"You want me to stop him?" Dekka asked.

"No," Sam said.

"He's going to make trouble."

"Sounds like Hunter already made trouble. Let's get going, Edilio. Hopefully Breeze gets to the plant and at least wakes them up. The more I think about it, the more I think I overreacted. I don't think Caine will start a war tonight."

"We may have our own war, right here in town," Edilio said.

EIGHTEEN

PATRICK FIGURED IT was all a party. His master was up in the middle of the night, and that was fun. Plus, now she was climbing into a pickup truck.

Quinn was behind the wheel. Albert sat beside him. The backseat would normally have been a little cramped for Lana and Cookie, who was a very big kid, but Quinn had his seat pulled all the way forward so he could reach the pedals. Patrick climbed in and lay across Cookie's lap.

"You want to put the dog in the back?" Albert suggested.

"And have him bark at everything we pass? Wake everyone up?"

"Okay," Albert said. He gave the dog a dirty look. Lana didn't like that about Albert, that he didn't like dogs, but this wasn't the time to have that argument.

At least Albert wasn't joking about eating Patrick. She'd heard that from more than one person.

The four of them—five, if you counted Patrick—had met

up at a muffler shop on the highway. There was a heavy-duty four-by-four, extended-cab pickup parked there that Albert figured would be just right for the cross-country travel and the gold.

"Guess I better see if I know how to drive this thing," Quinn said.

"You said you know how to drive," Albert accused.

"I do. I've driven Edilio's Jeep, anyway. But this is bigger."

"Great," Albert muttered.

Quinn turned the key and the engine roared. It seemed way too loud, like it would wake up the whole town.

"Yikes," Quinn said. He put it into drive, and the beast lurched forward, bumped across a curb, and fishtailed out onto the highway.

"Hey, let's not get killed, huh?" Albert yelled.

Quinn steadied the truck and it went off at a sedate thirty miles an hour straight down the center of what had once been a busy highway.

"You seem a little cranky, Albert," Quinn said playfully. "Are you going to tell me what this trip is all about? I mean, it's, what, three A.M.? We're not going to kill a guy, right?"

"You're getting paid, aren't you?" Albert snapped.

"You haven't told him?" Lana said from the backseat. "Albert, he has to know what's going on."

When Albert didn't answer, Lana said, "We're going after gold, Quinn."

She saw Quinn's eyes framed in the rearview mirror.

"Um. What?"

"Hermit Jim's shack. The gold," Lana explained.

Lana saw Quinn's eyes again, more worried. "Excuse me, but last time we were out there, we were getting chewed on by coyotes."

"You know how to handle a gun now. And you have a gun with you," Albert said calmly. "And Cookie has a gun. You're both trained."

"That's right," Cookie agreed. "But I don't want to shoot no one. Unless they mess with the Healer."

"And we need gold *why*?" Quinn asked a bit shrilly.

"We need money," Albert said. "You can only get so far with barter. We need a system, and the system works better if you have a basis for the currency."

"Uh-huh."

"Okay, look, take the fish business, right?" Albert began.

"It hasn't been much of a business," Quinn grumbled. "I barely caught enough yesterday to make bait."

"You'll have good days and bad days," Albert said impatiently. "Some days you'll have a lot of fish. So let's say you want to trade some fish for oranges."

"Sounds good, actually. You know someone with oranges?"

"You have enough fish that you want to trade some for oranges, and some for bread, and some for a kid to clean your room for you. That's three different places you have to go with your fish in your hand to pay someone."

"Is anyone else really starving right now?" Quinn joked. "I mean, dude: oranges? Bread? Stop."

Albert ignored him. "What you do if you have money, instead of just trading things, is you can have a market where everyone brings what they have to sell, right? All in one place. And everyone is walking around with pieces of gold, not their fish, or a wheelbarrow full of corn or whatever, trying to make deals."

Quinn said, "Either way, I'm standing around with my fish. Either I'm walking around selling them at this market of yours, or I'm standing still and people are coming to me to trade, but either way—"

"No, man," Albert interrupted impatiently. "Because you're selling your fish to someone who sells it to other people. You need to be out fishing, because that's what you're good at. Not selling fish. Catching fish."

Quinn frowned. "You mean, I'm selling them to you."

"Could be," Albert agreed. "Then I sell them to Lana. That way, Quinn, you're doing what you do and I'm doing what I do, and to make all that work out easy peasy we need money of some kind."

"Yeah, well, since I'm doing this all night there may not be any fish tomorrow, either," Quinn grumbled. Then he asked the question Lana expected. "Why are you coming along, Healer?"

The use of her "title" bothered Lana; she wasn't quite sure why. And the question on top of the title bothered her. She didn't like the question. She shifted in her seat and stared out of the window.

"She's coming because I need a guide," Albert said. "And

I'm going to pay her. When I get the gold. Which brings us to a little something called credit."

Poor Albert, Lana thought as Albert launched into a lecture on the usefulness of credit. Smart kid. He'd probably end up owning the FAYZ some day. But he knew nothing of her reasons for going on this trip.

All the gold in the world wouldn't be enough to pay her for what she was planning to do. Gold couldn't touch the cold dread that filled her heart. And gold wouldn't be any use to her if she failed.

"There's more than money in the world," Lana said, thinking she was speaking only to herself.

"Like what?" Albert asked.

"Like freedom," Lana said.

At which point Albert went on, talking about how money could buy freedom. Lana supposed he was right, in most cases. But not in this one.

Not in this case.

She couldn't bribe the Darkness. But maybe, maybe . . . maybe she could kill it.

Caine sat silent, biting his thumb, chewing at the ragged nail.

Panda was driving. Computer Jack was squeezed in the backseat between Diana and Bug. They were the lead car. The second car, an SUV, was behind them, Drake and four of his soldiers. All were armed.

They drove cautiously. Caine insisted on it. Panda had gotten better at driving, more confident, but he was still just thirteen. He still drove scared.

The SUV behind, urged on no doubt by Drake, practically hung on their bumper, impatient.

Down Highway 1, past abandoned businesses, weaving around crashed cars and overturned trucks. All the debris of the FAYZ, the litter left behind by all the disappeared.

They turned onto the power plant road.

"Don't drive us off the road," Caine cautioned. "It's a long drop."

"Don't worry," Panda said.

"Uh-huh," Caine said. There was a cliff to the left, a hundred-foot drop to the ocean rocks below. Caine wondered if he could use his powers to stop the car falling in the event that it did topple over. That kind of thing might be worth practicing, to see if he could use his telekinetic power to suspend a falling object with him inside. It would take just the right balance.

"What was that?" Panda cried.

"What was what?"

"I saw it, too," Diana said.

"Saw what?" Caine demanded.

"Like a blur. Like something shooting past us."

There was silence. Then, Caine cursed. "Brianna. Faster, Panda!"

"I don't want to run off—"

"Faster," Caine hissed.

The walkie-talkie crackled. Drake's voice. "You guys see that?"

Caine keyed his own set. "Yeah. Brianna. Either that or a tornado."

"She'll get there before us," Diana said.

"She's already there," Caine agreed.

"Don't you think maybe we should do this some other time?" Diana asked.

Caine laughed. "Just because Brianna is zipping around? I'm not worried about that girl." It was phony bravado. Brianna "zipping around" could mean that an ambush was waiting. Or it could mean that Sam had been alerted and was already on his way.

He keyed the walkie-talkie. "Drake. They may be ready when we get there."

"Good. I'm in the mood for a fight," Drake answered.

Caine twisted halfway in his seat to see Diana. Her nearly bald head was distracting. It had the strange effect of focusing his attention on her eyes and lips. He winked at her. "Drake's not worried."

Diana said nothing.

"You worried, Panda?" Caine asked. Panda was too terrified to answer. His fingers were white from gripping the wheel.

"Nobody's worried but you, Diana," Caine said.

Caine hadn't asked Jack. He was going to be careful with Jack for a while. At least until the computer genius had given him what he needed.

"Coming up on the gate," Bug said.

There was a brick guardhouse beside a tall chain-link

fence. Lights were blazing everywhere. Spotlights atop the guardhouse, trained down along the fence line in both directions. And beyond the gate the vast bulk of the power plant itself, humming, vibrating, a sinister presence in the night. It was bigger than Caine had imagined, and was comprised of several buildings, the largest of which looked like a prison. It could almost be a small city of its own. The parking lot was half full of cars, glittering in the glow.

"There's Brianna!" Caine cried, and pointed at the girl, doubled over, clutching the fence, tugging ineffectually at it. She glanced back fearfully at them, face blue-white in the headlights. She shouted something that Caine did not hear.

In obvious frustration she rattled the chain link, unable to open it, unable, it seemed, to get the attention of anyone in the guardhouse. If anyone even *was* in the guardhouse.

Panda slammed on the brakes and the car skidded.

Caine leaped out and raised his hands toward Brianna. But in a blur she was gone only to reappear halfway up the hill to the right.

"Hello, Brianna, long time no see," Caine called to her.

"Hello, Caine. How's that leg where Sam burned your skin off?"

Caine smiled at her. "Everyone out of the car," he said in a whisper. "Now!"

Panda, Jack, and Diana piled out. Bug may have piled out or not, Caine didn't see him, but with Bug, that didn't mean much.

"Whatcha up to?" Brianna asked. She was chewing gum,

trying to act nonchalant. But Caine could see that she had not yet recovered from the exertion. She would be tired. Hungry, too, no doubt. He wished he had some food to offer her. Like a bone for a dog. Test her loyalty.

But they had not brought any food.

"Oh, not much, Brianna," Caine answered. He dropped his hands to his waist, arms crossed over his chest, and turned his palms toward the car behind him. Then, in a swift motion he rotated his arms up over his head and brought them down.

The car jumped up off the ground. It was yanked into the sky like it was a giant's yo-yo that had run out its string.

The car inscribed a tight arc, twenty, thirty feet in the air, and hurtled down toward Brianna.

The car smashed the dirt with shocking violence. The windshield and all the other windows shattered into a million glittering pieces. Like someone had set off a hand grenade inside. Two of the tires blew out. The hood popped clear off, twirled in the air, and crashed.

Brianna was standing twenty feet away from the impact.

"Wow. That was cool, Caine," Brianna mocked. "I'll bet that seemed really fast to you, huh? Car flying through the air all lightning quick? Why don't you try again?"

"She's baiting you, Caine," Diana said, stepping up beside him. "She's stalling. Not to mention that whoever is on guard inside may have heard that."

Drake's car had come to a stop just behind theirs. He leaped from the car and went racing toward Brianna, unspooling his whip hand as he went.

Brianna laughed and gave Drake the finger. "Come on, Drake, you can catch me." Drake lunged at her, but suddenly she was behind him.

"Knock it off, Drake," Caine yelled. "You can't catch her. And all we're doing is making noise and wasting time."

"The gate's locked," Brianna taunted, suddenly just out of arm's reach in front of Caine. When she came to a stop she quivered like an arrow hitting a target.

"Gate?" Caine said. He aimed his hands at the shattered car. It came up off the ground and flew, tumbling, through the air, spraying bits of glass like a comet's tail.

The car smashed into the gate, ripped the gate from its mooring, wrapping chain link around itself, and carried the twisted mess for forty feet before hitting the parking lot and skidding into a parked minivan.

It made enough noise to wake a deaf person.

"And now," Caine said, "it's open. Good-bye, Brianna."

The girl glared at him and was gone.

"Drake, leave two guys in the guardhouse," Caine ordered. "Let's go get this over with."

Edilio pulled the Jeep into Zil, Hunter, Lance, and Harry's driveway. Sam and Dekka jumped out. The front door of the house was ajar.

"Edilio? Go. Find Lana. Maybe pick up Taylor on the way, huh, if she's in the plaza still? She could help you search."

"You sure you don't want me to—"

"Get Lana." He slapped his hand on the hood, a signal to hurry. Edilio gunned it into reverse and then took off down the street.

"How do we play this?" Dekka asked.

"We see what's what. If Hunter's gone nuts, lift him off the ground, keep him from running away. Bounce him off the ceiling, if you need to. I'm not looking to hurt him, just talk to him," Sam said. He knocked on the open door, which swung away from him. "Hunter. You in there?"

No answer.

"Okay, it's Sam, and I'm coming in." He purposely did not mention Dekka. Dekka was a weapon he'd as soon keep in reserve. "I'm hoping there won't be any kind of problem."

Sam took a deep breath and stepped inside.

A painting of an attractive but serious-looking woman with luxuriant red hair hung in the entryway. Someone, presumably one of the current residents, had defaced the painting with a mustache carefully drawn on with a black Sharpie.

The hallway was a mess—a Frisbee on the side table, a dirty gym sock hanging from a chandelier, a mirror badly out of alignment and cracked. Not much different from most of the residences in a FAYZ without parents.

The first room, on the left, was a formal dining room, dark. The kitchen was ahead, down the hall, past the stairs. The family room was ahead and to the right. Dekka poked her head into the dining room, peered under the table, and whispered, "Clear."

Sam advanced to the family room.

The family room was an even bigger mess than the hall-way: DVDs strewn here and there, long-emptied soda cans, some sort of bright yellow Nerf projectiles, family photos— the red-haired woman again, and what was probably her husband—knocked over on the mantel, dust thick on book-shelves.

At first Sam didn't see Harry. He had fallen between the couch and a heavy coffee table. But one step closer, and he came into view.

Harry was lying facedown. There was a deflating blister on the back of his neck. It reminded Sam of a balloon three days after a party.

Sam pushed the table aside, but it was wedged. "Dekka?"

Dekka raised one hand, and the table lifted off the floor. Sam gave it a shove. It floated aside till it was out of Dekka's field, then it crashed to the floor.

Sam knelt beside Harry. Carefully avoiding the blister, he pressed two fingers against Harry's neck. "I'm not feeling anything," Sam said. "You try."

Dekka glanced around, searching for what she needed, and came up with a small, mirrored box. She twisted Harry's head to the side and held the mirrored surface close to the boy's nostrils.

"What are you doing?" Sam asked.

"If he's breathing, you'd see it. Condensation."

"I think he's dead," Sam said.

They both stood up then and took a couple of steps back. Dekka set the box aside, careful, like Harry was asleep and she didn't want to wake him.

"What do we do about this?" Dekka wondered.

"That's a very good question," Sam said. "I wish I had a very good answer."

"If Hunter killed him . . ."

"Yeah."

"The freak-versus-normal thing . . ."

"We can't let it get like that," Sam said forcefully. "If Hunter did this . . . I mean, I guess we have to hear what he says about it."

"Maybe talk to Astrid, huh?" Dekka suggested.

Sam laughed mirthlessly. "She'll say we should have a trial."

"We could, you know, just make this go away," Dekka said.

Sam didn't answer.

"You know what I'm saying," Dekka said.

Sam nodded. "Yes. I do. We're trying to keep from starving. Trying to stay ready in case Caine starts something. The last thing we need is some big argument between freaks and normals."

"Of course Zil won't shut up about it, no matter what we do," Dekka pointed out. "We could say we got here, Harry wasn't here, we found nothing. But Zil would never believe it, and a lot of kids would go along with him."

"Yep," Sam said. "We are stuck with this."

They stood side-by-side, staring down at Harry. The blister still slowly, slowly deflating.

Then Sam led the way back out to the driveway. Edilio roared up ten minutes later with Dahra Baidoo in the passenger seat.

"Hey, Dahra," Sam said. "Thanks for coming."

"I couldn't find Lana," Edilio said. "She's not in her room at Clifftop. Her dog was gone, too. I got Taylor bouncing around, looking for her everywhere. The rest are still hanging out in the plaza in case we need them."

Sam nodded. He was used to Lana's strange and sudden relocations. The Healer was a restless girl. "Dahra, take a look, huh? Inside. On the floor."

Edilio looked quizzically at Sam. Sam shook his head and avoided making eye contact.

Dahra was back in less than a minute. "I'm not Lana, but even she couldn't do anything here. She's not Jesus," she snapped. "She doesn't raise the dead."

"We were hoping he wasn't dead," Dekka said.

"He's dead, all right," Dahra said. "Did either of you notice that the skin on his neck wasn't burned? The hair around it wasn't singed? The blister must have welled up from inside. Which means something cooked him from the inside out. That leaves you out as a suspect, Sam: I've seen your handiwork. You leave people looking like marshmallows that got dropped in the coals."

"Hey," Edilio blurted angrily. "You got no reason to be harshing on Sam."

"It's okay, Edilio," Sam said mildly.

"No. He's right," Dahra said. She touched Sam's shoulder.

"Sorry, Sam. I'm tired and I don't like seeing dead bodies, okay?"

"Yeah," Sam acknowledged. "Head on home. Sorry to drag you out."

She peered quizzically at Sam. "What are you guys going to do about this?"

Sam shook his head. "I don't know, but whatever I do, it'll probably make everyone mad. Edilio can drive you home."

"No reason, it's a five-minute walk." Dahra patted his shoulder again and took off.

When she was gone, Sam said, "I guess we're going to talk to Hunter."

"You guess? Man, this ain't something can be let slide," Edilio said. "This is killing."

"Orc killed Betty," Sam pointed out. "And Orc's still free."

"You weren't in charge then," Edilio said. "We didn't have a system."

"We still don't have a system, Edilio. We have me being pestered by everyone with a problem," Sam said. "That's not a system. You see a Supreme Court around here, somewhere? I see me and you and about a dozen others even giving a damn."

"You saying we're going to have it where kids can kill someone and that's okay?"

Sam slumped. "No. No. Of course not. I'm just . . . Nothing."

"I'll get my guys, go look for Hunter," Edilio said. "But I gotta know: What if he won't come? Or what if he tries to hurt one of my guys?"

"Come get me if that happens," Sam said.

Edilio did not look happy about that instruction. But he nodded and left.

Dekka watched him go. "Edilio's a good guy," she said.

"But?"

"But, he's a normal."

"There aren't going to be lines like that, between freak and normal," Sam said firmly.

Dekka almost, but didn't quite, laugh. "Sam, that's a great concept. And maybe you believe it. But I'm black and I'm a lesbian, so let me tell you: From what I know? Personal experience? There are always lines."

NINETEEN

THEY DROVE THE SUV through the hole in the fence, veered around the twisted mess of chain link, and raced to a skidding halt in the parking lot of the power plant.

The sheer size of the power plant was intimidating. The containment towers were as tall as skyscrapers. The big turbine building was blank and hostile, like a giant windowless prison.

A door, almost insignificantly small, stood open. No light shone from inside, but Caine could make out a shape crouching within.

"Hey! What are you doing here?" a young voice challenged.

Caine didn't recognize the kid, couldn't really see him. The plant was very loud, so Caine pretended he couldn't hear. He cupped a hand to his ear and yelled, "What?"

"Stop! Don't come any closer."

"Come closer? Okay." Caine kept walking. Diana and Jack

hung back, but Drake was striding quickly to catch up. Drake had an automatic pistol in his real hand. His whip slithered and squirmed at his side, a snake anxious for a chance to strike.

"Stop! I said stop!"

The doorway was just a hundred feet away now. Caine never faltered.

"Stop, or I'll shoot," the voice cried, scared, almost begging.

Caine stopped. Drake stood beside him.

"Shoot?" Caine demanded, sounding puzzled. "Why on earth would you shoot me?"

"That's we're opposed to do."

Caine laughed. "You can't even say it right. Who are you, anyway? If you're going to shoot me, I should know your name."

"Josh," the answer came. "It's me, Josh."

"It's 'me Josh,'" Caine mimicked.

Drake snarled, "You better step off, me Josh, or me Whip Hand is going to hurt you."

The sudden explosion of bullets was deafening. Josh's firing was wild, bullets shattering the glass of parked cars far off to their right.

Caine dropped to the pavement.

Drake never flinched. He raised his pistol, took careful aim, and fired.

Bang. Bang. Bang.

With each shot he advanced a step.

Josh whinnied in terror.

Bang. Bang. Bang.

Each time the noise was stunning. Each time fire flashed from the barrel of the pistol, lighting Drake's blank, cold eyes.

Then Drake broke into a run. Straight for the door, pistol held level, firing carefully, precisely even as he ran.

Josh fired back, but again the bullets went wild into the night, missing even the parked cars, doing nothing to stop Drake.

Bang. Bang.

Click.

Caine stayed on the ground, staring, rapt, at Drake as he calmly ejected his ammunition clip. The clip clattered on the concrete.

Drake held the pistol with the delicate end of his tentacle and fished a second clip out of the hunting vest he was wearing. Using his hand he slammed the clip into place.

Josh fired again. More careful, this time.

Bullets sparked the pavement near Drake's feet.

Drake raised the gun carefully, fired and moved, fired and moved, fired and now Josh was gone, running back inside the building, screaming for help, screaming that someone better help him.

Caine stood up, feeling shamed by Drake's cold-blooded performance. He hurried now to catch up to Drake, who was through the doorway and inside the building.

Another loud bang, the sound different this time, muffled.

The doorway was a bright rectangle from the muzzle flash.

A cry of pain.

"I give up! I give up!"

Caine reached the doorway and entered the turbine room. There, on the floor between massive, howling machines, pitilessly lit by eerie fluorescent light, lay Josh. He sat, stunned, in a black pool of his own blood. One leg was twisted at an impossible angle.

Caine felt a flash of anger. Josh was a kid, no more than ten. What was Sam thinking, putting kids in this position?

"Don't shoot me, don't shoot me!" Josh begged.

Drake raised high his whip hand and brought it down with sound-barrier-shattering speed on Josh's upraised hands.

Josh screamed and writhed in agony. The screaming didn't stop.

"Leave him," Caine snapped. "Get to the control room."

Drake turned a feral snarl on Caine, teeth bared, eyes wild. Contempt and fury were in those eyes. Caine raised his hands, ready, waiting for his lieutenant to turn his whip against him.

Instead Drake kicked the prostrate boy in his damaged leg and plowed ahead. Josh crawled sobbing toward the door to the outside.

It all seemed unnatural, nightmarish. Drake stalking ahead, his gun smoking, his whip twitching. Caine heard Drake's soldiers coming up behind, and Diana and Jack bringing up the rear.

"Door's locked," Drake called back.

Caine caught up to him and tried the doorknob himself. It was heavy steel set into a heavy steel frame, obviously a door meant to withstand explosion or attack. If he hit it with a direct shock-wave of telekinetic power, it might bust open. But in the confined area of the hallway it might also reverb and knock him on his butt. "It won't be locked for long."

Caine glanced around, searching for something heavy enough for his purposes. Back in the turbine room he found a rolling steel tool chest, four feet tall, strongly built.

Caine raised the chest off the floor and hurled it through the air, down the hall. It slammed into the locked door.

He was immensely gratified by the spectacle of Drake flattened to the wall to avoid getting hit by the wrenches and sockets and screwdrivers that flew like shrapnel from the chest.

The tool chest was crumpled, the door barely scratched.

Caine drew the chest back and hurled it forward again. This time more tools spilled out and the chest was crushed to half its size. But the door was undamaged.

Caine felt Diana's hand on his arm. "Hey. Why don't you see what Jack can do."

Caine was torn between the fear of failing if he continued to batter away ineffectually, and the fear of being shown up by the computer geek. This had become as much a contest between him and Drake as it was an attack on the power plant.

"Show us what you got, Jack," Caine said.

Computer Jack advanced uncertainly, urged on by Diana.

He placed his hands against the door and tried to get a good grip on the floor with his sneakers. He pushed against the door, and his feet slid away beneath him. He fell to one knee.

"It's too slippery," Jack said.

"We have to be through that door before Sam shows up," Caine said. "We need hostages, and we need that control room."

His gaze rested on a heavy wrench. "Look out."

Caine levitated the wrench, lifted it to the ceiling, turned it vertical, and with a sudden sweep of his hands plunged the wrench into the floor. It crunched through tile and concrete and stood like a climbing piton that had been hammered into a cliff face.

Caine repeated the move three more times, driving heavy-gauge stainless steel into the floor.

"Okay, use those."

Jack braced his feet against the tools, placed his hands against the door, and heaved with all his might.

Edilio did not find Hunter. Instead he found Zil and a crowd of a dozen kids. They in turn had found Hunter. They had Hunter cornered on the porch of the house Astrid and Mother Mary shared.

Why Hunter had gone there, Edilio could guess: Astrid would be calm and reasonable. She would shelter him, for a while at least.

The scene, however, was anything but calm or reasonable.

Astrid was wearing a nightgown. Her blond hair was untethered and wild. She stood at the top of the porch stairs and stabbed an angry finger at Zil.

Hunter was behind Astrid. Not exactly cowering, but not getting out in front of her, either.

Zil and his friends, who—Edilio noted with a sinking heart—were all normals, were angry. Or most were angry, some were just goofing around, glad of an excuse to get out and run around town in the middle of the night.

Most had some kind of weapon or other, baseball bats, tire irons. One, Edilio noted grimly, carried a shotgun. The kid with the shotgun, Hank, had been a quiet kid back in the old days. He didn't look quiet now.

Edilio pulled his Jeep up to the curb. He hadn't had time to round up any of his own people, he was alone. All eyes registered Edilio's arrival, but no one stopped yelling.

"He's a murdering chud," Zil was yelling.

"What do you want to do? Lynch him?" Astrid demanded.

That stopped the flow for a second as kids tried to figure out what "lynch" meant. But Zil quickly recovered.

"I saw him do it. He used his powers to kill Harry."

"I was trying to stop you from smashing my head in!" Hunter shouted.

"You're a lying mutant freak!"

"They think they can do anything they want," another voice shouted.

Astrid said, as calmly as she could while still pitching her voice to be heard, "We are not going down that path, people, dividing up between freaks and normals."

"They already did it!" Zil cried. "It's the freaks acting all special and like their farts don't stink."

That earned a laugh.

"And now they're starting to kill us," Zil cried.

Angry cheers.

Edilio squared his shoulders and stepped into the crowd. He went first to Hank, the kid with the shotgun. He tapped him on the shoulder and said, "Give me that thing."

"No way," Hank said. But he didn't seem too certain.

"You want to have that thing fire by accident and blow someone's face off?" Edilio held his hand out. "Give it to me, man."

Zil rounded on Edilio. "You going to make Hunter give up his weapon? Huh? He's got powers, man, and that's okay, but the normals can't have any weapon? How are we supposed to defend ourselves from the freaks?"

"Man, give it a rest, huh?" Edilio said. He was doing his best to sound more weary than angry or scared. Things were already bad enough. "Zil, you want to be responsible if that gauge goes off and kills Astrid? You want to maybe give that some thought?"

Zil blinked. But he said, "Dude, I'm not scared of Sam."

"Sam won't be your problem, I will be," Edilio snapped, losing patience. "Anything happens to her, I'll take you down before Sam ever gets the chance."

Zil snorted derisively. "Ah, good little boy, Edilio, kissing up to the chuds. I got news for you, dilly dilly, you're a lowly normal, just like me and the rest of us."

"I'm going to let that go," Edilio said evenly, striving to regain his cool, trying to sound calm and in control, even though he could hardly take his eyes off the twin barrels of the shotgun. "But now I'm taking that shotgun."

"No way!" Hank cried, and the next thing was an explosion so loud, Edilio thought a bomb had gone off. The muzzle flash blinded him, like camera flash going off in his face.

Someone yelled in pain.

Edilio staggered back, squeezed his eyes shut, trying to adjust. When he opened them again the shotgun was on the ground and the boy who'd accidentally fired it was holding his bruised hand, obviously shocked.

Zil bent to grab the gun. Edilio took two steps forward and kicked Zil in the face. As Zil fell back Edilio made a grab for the shotgun. He never saw the blow that turned his knees to water and filled his head with stars.

He fell like a sack of bricks, but even as he fell he lurched forward to cover the shotgun.

Astrid screamed and launched herself down the stairs to protect Edilio.

Antoine, the one who had hit Edilio, was raising his bat to hit Edilio again, but on the back swing he caught Astrid in the face.

Antoine cursed, suddenly fearful. Zil yelled, "No, no, no!"

There was a sudden rush of running feet. Down the walkway, into the street, echoing down the block.

Edilio struggled to stand. It wasn't easy. His legs did not

want to stay where he put them.

Astrid had a hand over one eye but was steadying Edilio with the other.

"You okay?" Astrid asked. "Did he shoot you?"

"I don't think so." Edilio patted himself down, searching for but not finding any wounds except for a growing knot on the crown of his head.

His vision cleared enough to notice the red welt where the bat had caught Astrid in the eye. "You're going to have a shiner."

"I'm okay," Astrid said, shaky but strong.

Zil's mob was gone. Disappeared. It was just the three of them left, Edilio, Astrid, and Hunter.

Edilio picked up the shotgun and cradled it carefully. "I guess that could have been worse. No one got shot."

Astrid said, "Hunter, go inside and get some ice for Edilio's head."

"Yeah. No problem," Hunter said. He hurried away.

With Hunter out of hearing Astrid said, "What are you going to do?"

"Sam said bring Hunter in."

"Arrest him?" Astrid asked.

"Yeah, because all of a sudden I'm like the sheriff, too," Edilio said bitterly, touching the lump on his head. "I must have forgot the day where I signed up for that."

"Did Hunter really kill Harry?"

Edilio nodded, a movement which sent bright shards of pain stabbing into his brain.

"Yeah. Killed him. Maybe it was an accident like Hunter says, but either way I better take him and keep him in Town Hall."

Astrid nodded. "Yeah. I'll talk to him. Make him see it's the only way."

The two of them went inside. Hunter was not in the kitchen making ice packs. The sliding glass door to the backyard was open.

Brittney Donegal recoiled from the door when the banging started. Mickey Finch and Mike Farmer were already across the room, back by the plant manager's office. They were waiting for Brittney to give them some guidance because neither of them had a clue.

Brittney was twelve years old, overweight, with a pimply face adorned by overbearing black horn-rim glasses. She wore sweat pants pulled up too high, and a pink frilly blouse that was at least one size too small. Her indifferent brown hair was yanked to either side in pigtails.

She had braces on her teeth—braces that had not been adjusted in three months. Braces that were accomplishing nothing now, but that she could not figure out how to remove.

Brittney had kind of had a crush on Mike Farmer, but he wasn't exactly impressing her.

"We gotta get out of here, Britt," Mike whined.

"Edilio said anything ever happens, we're supposed to lock this door and sit tight," Brittney said.

"They got guns," Mike cried.

Another crashing impact. They all jumped. The door did not budge.

"So do we," Brittney said.

"Josh is probably already heading back to town, safe, I bet," Mickey said. "Mike's right, we have to get away."

Brittney wanted nothing more than to run away. But she figured she was a soldier. That's what Edilio had said. Their job was to protect the power plant.

"I know we're all just kids," Edilio used to say. "But we may need kids to step up, someday, be more than just kids."

Brittney had been in the square the day of the big battle. It was Edilio who had killed the coyote that was all over her, snapping at her throat, then seizing her leg in a jaw like a bear trap.

She had no scars from the coyote bite on her leg. The Healer had cured all that. And she had no scar from the bullet that had burned a crease across her upper arm. The Healer had taken all the wounds away. But Brittney's little brother, Tanner, was one of the kids buried in the plaza.

Edilio had dug his grave with the backhoe.

Brittney had no romantic feelings for Edilio, but what she had went a lot deeper. She would rather burn for eternity in the hottest fires of Hell than let Edilio down.

Brittney had no scars, but she did still have nightmares, and sometimes not when she was asleep. Mike had been there that day, too, hurt worse than her. But it had left Mike scared and timid, while it had left Brittney mad and determined.

"Anyone comes through that door, I'm shooting them," Brittney said in a loud voice, loud enough that she hoped to be heard by whoever was on the other side.

"Not me, I'm getting out of here," Mickey said. He turned and ran.

"You want to run, too?" Brittney challenged Mike.

"Lana's not exactly here right now," Mike said. "What if they shoot me? I'm just a kid, you know."

Brittney tightened her grip on her machine gun. It hung from a strap over her shoulder. She'd long since gotten used to the weight of it. She had test-fired it four times, following Edilio's training program. The first time she'd dropped it and burst into tears and Edilio had asked her if she wanted to quit.

But then Tanner had made his presence known, a soft voice that spoke to her when she was scared and told her not to worry, that he was in Heaven with Jesus and the angels. And he was so happy, not hurt or afraid or lonely anymore.

The next time she'd held on as the gun kicked in her hands. After that she'd more or less hit what she aimed at.

"If that's Caine out there, I'm going to get him," Brittney said.

"I hate him," she said. "I mean, I hate what he did. Hate the sin, not the sinner. And I'm going to shoot him so he won't hurt anyone else."

The banging had stopped. Now something different was happening. The door seemed to be bulging inward. It creaked and groaned. There was a loud snap.

It was going to give way.

"Run away, Mike," Brittney said. He was weak. Well, kids were, sometimes. She had to forgive that. "But leave your pistol."

"Where do you want me to put it?"

Brittney stared at the door. It was bulging, straining. Something or someone very, very strong was pushing against it.

"On the floor. Underneath the last console. Back where no one can see it."

"You should come," Mike pleaded.

Brittney's finger curled around the trigger. "No. I don't think I'm going to do that."

She heard his footsteps retreating down the hallway. She expected the door to give way in a few seconds. And then she figured she would be in Heaven with her little brother.

"Lord? Please help me to be brave," Brittney said. "In Jesus' name. Amen."

"It's okay if I die, Tanner," she said, in a different sort of prayer, one she knew her dead brother could hear. "As long as Caine dies first."

TWENTY

BRIANNA **HAD** **NOT** found Sam on the road to the power plant as she raced back to town. He was not on any of the roads. The only vehicle she had seen had Quinn, Albert, Cookie, and Lana out for a ride in a giant pickup truck. She'd thought about stopping them, telling them to go to the power plant, but none of the four was much of a fighter. Quinn and Cookie were both supposed to be soldiers, but the person she needed to find was Sam, not his useless old surfing buddy.

Sam wasn't at the gas station. He wasn't at town hall or in the plaza. He wasn't anywhere she looked.

And Brianna was burning out fast. The speed was exhausting. Not as tiring as it should have been, probably, given that she had just run something like fifteen miles or so, dodging back and forth, up and down streets and alleyways. But exhausting. And the hunger was like a lion inside her, tearing at her insides.

Her sneakers were in tatters. Again. They didn't build

Nikes for going as fast as a race car.

Then she heard a loud bang. It was hard to guess where it had come from. But then suddenly there were kids running. Slow. Very slow. But as fast as they could run, poor things.

"What's going on?" she demanded, screeching to a stop.

No one answered. If anything, they seemed scared of her.

It was clear, though, that they were running away from, and not toward something. So she zipped back up the street and in less time than it would have taken a normal heart to beat twice she was standing in Astrid's open doorway.

"Hey. Anybody home?"

Astrid came out, followed by Edilio. It was obvious that neither was having a good night. Astrid had a red welt on the side of her face next to her eye. Edilio was rubbing his head gingerly and holding a massive shotgun.

"Where is Sam?" Brianna demanded. "What happened to you guys?"

"You missed the fun," Edilio said sourly.

"No. No, I didn't. You did!" Brianna yelled. "Caine is attacking the power plant."

"What?"

"He's there. He and Drake and some other guys."

"What about our kids up there?" Edilio demanded.

"I didn't see any of them. Look, Caine threw a car through the front gate. He's real serious about this."

"You know where Hunter lives?" Edilio asked.

Brianna nodded. But too fast to be seen. So she said, "Yeah."

"Go there. Sam was there last I saw him. Tell him I'm getting my guys. It'll take me half an hour to get everyone assembled again. Tell Sam I'll meet him at the highway."

"Your shoes," Astrid said, pointing down at Brianna's feet. "What size do you wear?"

"Six."

"I'll get you a pair from my closet." But before Astrid could move, Brianna was up the stairs and back, sitting on the porch and tying on a pair of New Balance.

"Thanks," she said to s startled Astrid.

"Don't forget to—," Astrid said, but between "don't" and "forget" Brianna had arrived at Hunter's house.

Dekka was just coming down the steps looking like a thundercloud. The girl barely flinched when Brianna appeared suddenly before her.

"Hi, Breeze," Dekka said. She almost smiled.

"Sam in there?"

"Yep."

Brianna appeared suddenly before Sam, who took it less calmly than Dekka had.

"Sam. Caine. He's at the plant. I already found Edilio, he's getting his guys together. Give me a gun, I'll go keep Caine busy."

Sam cursed loudly. It took a while before he was ready to stop. Then, "I knew it! I knew it, and I let myself get distracted."

"Sam. Give me a gun."

"What? No, Breeze, I need you. And not dead."

"I can get back there in, like, two minutes," Brianna pleaded.

Sam put a hand on her shoulder. "Breeze? You have a job. You're the messenger. Right? We have other people for fighting. Go help Edilio get the troops together. Then go see if you can find Lana. I don't know where she is and we're going to need her."

"She's driving around in a truck with Quinn and Albert," Brianna reported.

"What?"

"They're in a truck, heading out on the highway."

Sam threw up his hands. "Maybe they heard about Caine, somehow. Maybe they're on the way there."

"Yeah, I don't think so. Albert wouldn't be with them. Also, someone smacked Astrid."

Sam's face froze. "What?"

"She's fine, but there was some kind of problem over at her house."

"Zil," Sam said through gritted teeth. He kicked savagely at a chair. Then, "Go, Breeze. Do what I told you to do."

"But—"

"I don't have time to argue, Breeze."

"Guys? Guys?" Quinn reached across to shake Albert's shoulder. He had fallen asleep.

"What? I'm awake. What?"

"Dude, we are lost."

"We're not lost," Lana said from the backseat.

Quinn glanced in the rearview mirror. "I thought you were asleep, too."

"We're not lost," Lana said.

"Well, all due respect, we're not exactly *not* lost, either. This isn't even a dirt road anymore, it's just, like, you know, flat. And not even all that flat." They had left the highway and turned onto a side road. From there onto a dirt road. And that had gone on and on forever, without so much as a twinkle of light anywhere. Then the dirt road had become more and more dirt and less and less road.

"If the Healer says we're not lost, we're not lost," Cookie grumbled.

"It's not far," Lana said.

"How do you know? I couldn't find my way back here in the middle of the day. Let alone at night."

She didn't answer.

Quinn glanced down at the road, then back into the rearview mirror. The only light came from the dashboard, so he could see only the faintest outline of her face. She was looking out of the window, not the direction they were traveling but northeast.

He couldn't read her expression. But he got a feeling off her. It was in the occasional sigh. In the absent way she stroked Patrick's ruff. The distant tone of her voice when she spoke.

"You okay?" Quinn asked.

She didn't answer. Not for a while. Too long. Then, "Why wouldn't I be?"

"I don't know," he said.

Lana said nothing.

Albert, by contrast, was easy to read. Albert—when he managed to stay awake—was all about the goal. He focused his gaze straight ahead. Sometimes Quinn noticed him nodding to himself, as if he was commenting on some internal dialogue.

Quinn was envious of Albert. He seemed to be so sure of himself. He seemed to know just where he wanted to go, who he wanted to be.

For his part, Cookie had his own goal: to serve Lana. The big ex-bully would do anything Lana told him to do.

There were two kinds of kids in the FAYZ, Quinn reflected, and the types were not "freak" and "normal." They were kids who had been changed for the worse, and the kids who had been changed for the better. The FAYZ had changed them all. But some kids had become more than they were. Albert was one of those. Cookie, in a very different way, was another.

Quinn knew himself to be the first type. He was one of the kids who had never recovered from the FAYZ. The loss of his parents was like a wound that had never healed. Never stopped hurting. How could it?

It went beyond the loss of his mom and dad, too, a loss that encompassed everything he had known, everything he had been. He'd been cool, once. The memory brought a sad smile to his lips. Quinn was cool. One of a kind. Everyone knew him. They didn't all like him, they didn't all get his act, but Quinn had carried an aura of specialness with him.

And now . . . now he was an afterthought in the FAYZ.

Kids knew he had betrayed Sam to Caine. They knew that Sam had taken him back. They knew that he had gone a little crazy on the day of the big battle. Maybe more than a little crazy.

The memories of his mom and dad, his old life, they were far away. Like photos in an old album. Not quite real. Someone else's memories, his pain; someone else's life, his loss.

The memories of the battle—those couldn't even be called memories because weren't memories something from the past? That day might have happened three months ago, but it wasn't the past to Quinn, it was right here, right now, always. Like a parallel life happening simultaneously with this life. He was driving through the night and feeling the gun buck buck buck in his hands and seeing the coyotes and the kids, all mixed up together, all crisscrossing, weaving through the arcs of the bullets.

Finger off the trigger. Too close to shoot. He'd hit the kid. He couldn't do it, couldn't take that chance, and so the coyote had leaped, jaws open, and—

And that wasn't long ago and far away to Quinn. It was right now. Right here.

"Okay," Lana said, bringing him back to reality. "Slow down, we're almost there."

The headlights lit scruffy bushes and dirt and scatterings of rock. Then a wooden beam, badly charred. Quinn swerved to avoid it.

He stamped on the brakes. Then, much more slowly crept forward again.

The headlights illuminated a section of wall, just a few feet. Charred wood was everywhere. Two blackened cans of fruit or beans or whatever lay on their sides in the dirt.

Despite himself Quinn wondered if there was anything edible left. He remembered that terrifying night spent cowering in the cabin, waiting for the coyotes to drag them out and kill them.

That was when Sam had finally revealed the extent of his powers. For the first time he had been able to control the devastating light that shot from his hands.

Quinn stopped the vehicle. He put it into park.

"It was here," Quinn said softly.

"What happened here?" Albert asked.

Quinn killed the lights, and the four of them climbed from the SUV. It was silent. So much quieter than the last time Quinn had been there.

Quinn slung his machine pistol over his shoulder and fished a flashlight from under the seat. Albert had a flashlight of his own. The two beams stabbed here and there, highlighting this jagged beam, that singed bit of rug, a kitchen utensil, a twisted metal chair.

"This is where we met Lana for the first time," Quinn said. "We'd escaped from Caine. Run away into the woods up north. Decided to go back to town and make a fight of it. Anyway, Sam decided."

He bent down to pick up a hefty number-ten can. The label was charred. It might be pudding, though. Roasted pudding, maybe, but the can looked intact. He walked it back to the

SUV and tossed it into the back.

"How was it destroyed?" Albert pressed.

"Partly it was Sam. First time he ever used his power deliberately. Not out of panic, or whatever, just cold-blooded, knowing what he was doing. You should have seen that, man." Quinn recalled the moment perfectly. It was the moment when his old friend was clearly revealed as something far, far beyond Quinn. "Partly the coyotes had set the place on fire."

"Where's the gold?" Albert asked, not really caring about the story.

Quinn waited for Lana to show the way, but she seemed rooted to where she stood. Looking down at the brown, dead remains of Hermit Jim's quirky attempt to keep a lawn in the midst of this dry, empty land. Cookie stood just behind her, big pistol stuck in his belt, ready, scowling at the threatening night, ready to lay down his life for the girl who had saved him from agony beyond enduring.

Patrick was busily running around to anything remotely vertical, smelling carefully. He didn't mark anything himself, just smelled. He seemed subdued, tail down almost between his legs. The scent of Pack Leader must still be strong.

"This way," Quinn said when it was clear that Lana wasn't going to respond.

He threaded his way through the wreckage. There wasn't much, really; most of it had burned down to ash. But the surviving bits of shattered lumber were stuck with nails, so Quinn moved cautiously.

He bent down when he reached what seemed like the right

place and began pushing two-by-fours and shingles aside. He was surprised to find the plank floor mostly intact. It had been singed but not consumed by the fire. He found the hatch.

"Let me see if I can get it open." He tried, but the fire had warped the hinges. It took both of them, him and Albert, to raise the hatch. One hinge broke, and the hatch flopped awkwardly to one side.

Albert aimed his flashlight down into the hole.

"Gold," Albert said.

Quinn was a little surprised by Albert's matter-of-fact tone. He'd half expected a Gollum-like "My precioussss," or something.

"Yeah. Gold," Quinn agreed.

"It didn't melt," Albert said. "Heat rises and all that. Like they taught us in school."

"Let's start loading, huh? This place gives me the creeps," Quinn said. "Bad memories."

Albert reached down and lifted out a brick. He set it down with a thud. "Heavy, huh?"

"Yeah," Quinn said. "What are you going to do with it all?"

"Well," Albert said. "I'm going to see if I can melt it down and make coins or something out of it. Except I don't have any kind of coin mold. I had thought about using muffin tins. I have a cast-iron muffin tin that makes the small-sized muffins."

Quinn grinned and then laughed. "We're going to use gold muffins for money?"

"Maybe. But, actually, I found something better. One of the kids searching houses found where the guy had made his own ammunition. He found some bullet molds."

They kept busy lifting the gold out and onto the ground. They stacked it crisscross, like kids playing with blocks.

"Gold bullets?" Quinn stopped laughing. "We're going to make gold bullets?"

"It doesn't matter what shape they are, so long as they're consistent. All the same, you know?"

"Dude. Bullets? You don't think that's maybe, you know . . . weird?"

Albert sighed, exasperated. "Gold slugs, not the gunpowder part, just the slug part."

"Jeez, man, I don't know." Quinn shook his head.

"Thirty-two caliber," Albert said. "That was the smallest size the guy had."

"Why isn't Cookie helping us?" Quinn wondered.

In answer, Lana, from somewhere outside, said, "Guys, I'm going to look around for food. Cookie will help me."

"Cool," Quinn said.

In a few minutes they had all the gold up out of the hole.

They began walking the gold to the truck, a few bars at a time. The gold bars were not big, but they were heavy. By the time Albert and Quinn had finished hauling the gold they were sweating despite the chill of the night.

Albert climbed in and pulled a canvas tarp over the gold.

"Listen, man," Albert said as he worked to tie down the corners, "this isn't something we want anyone talking about.

Right? This is just between the four of us here tonight."

"Hold up, dude. You're not telling Sam?"

Albert climbed down to stand face-to-face with Quinn. "Look, I'm not trying to get over on Sam. I have the most total respect for Sam. But this plan works better if it all comes out at once."

"Albert, I'm not going to lie to Sam," Quinn said flatly.

"I'm not asking you to lie to Sam. If he asks you, tell him. If he doesn't ask . . ."

When Quinn still hesitated, Albert said, "Look, man, Sam is a great leader. Maybe he's our George Washington. But even Washington was wrong about some things. And Sam doesn't get what I'm talking about. How people all have to work."

"He knows people have to work," Quinn argued. "He just doesn't want you getting over on everyone, making yourself the rich guy."

Albert wiped sweat from his forehead. "Quinn, why do you think people work hard? Just to get by? You think your folks worked just to get by? Did they buy just enough food? Or did they get just barely enough house? Or a car that barely runs?" Albert's voice was urgent. "No, man, people like a good life. They want more. What's wrong with that?"

Quinn laughed. "Dude, okay, you've thought about all this and you're probably right. I mean, what do I know? Anyway, look, am I going to go running straight to Sam and tell him what we did? No. As far as I know, I don't have to do that."

"That's all I'm asking, Quinn," Albert said. "I wouldn't ever ask you to lie."

"Uh-huh," Quinn said cynically. "What about the Healer? She . . ." He looked around, suddenly aware that he hadn't heard her or Cookie in quite a while.

"Lana!" he yelled.

Then, "Healer!"

The night was silent.

Quinn aimed the flashlight into the truck cab. Maybe she was in there. Asleep, maybe. But the cab was empty.

He swiveled the light around the area, picking out the poles that had once held Hermit Jim's water tower.

"Lana? Lana? We're ready to go," Quinn yelled.

"Where is she?" Albert wondered. "I don't see her or Cookie. Or her dog."

"Lana! Healer!" Quinn shouted. No answer came.

He and Albert exchanged looks of horror.

Quinn leaned into the truck, intending to sound the horn. She'd have to hear that. He froze when he saw the Post-it note. He tore it from the steering wheel and read it aloud by flashlight.

"'Don't try to follow us,'" Quinn read. "'I know what I'm doing. Lana.'"

"Okay," Albert said, "Okay, now we have to tell Sam."

TWENTY-ONE

JACK STRAINED AGAINST the door.

It was built strong. Very strong. Steel in steel.

But it creaked and groaned, and Jack could see the seam between door and jamb growing.

His strength was shocking to him. He'd done very little to learn to control it. He hadn't really tested it much. In fact, he kept forgetting he had it because it was not, it never would be, part of who he really was.

Jack had grown up being a brain. He liked being a brain. He wore the geek label proudly. He had no interest in being some superstrong mutant. In fact, even as he pushed against the door, he was wondering if there wasn't an electronic control of some sort on the door. Wondering where the control panel might be. Wondering whether he could cut a wire, or solder another wire, and open the door. Wondering whether it might be computer-controlled, in which case it would be a question of hacking.

Those thoughts engaged Jack's mind. And that gave Jack pleasure.

Pushing on a steel door like some kind of ox? That was stupid. It was what stupid people did. And Jack was not stupid.

"Keep at it, Jack," Caine encouraged him. "It's starting to give."

Jack heard Diana saying to Drake, "I told you he was strong. And you thought you'd just go and pick him up and bring him to Coates? Hah."

The door would give way in another few seconds, Jack could feel it.

"When it goes, Jack, you need to drop to the floor," Caine said.

Jack would have asked why, but the exertion was popping the veins in his neck, squeezing his lungs, bulging his eyes, and generally making it hard to imagine engaging in conversation.

"Soon as it goes, Jack, drop to the floor," Caine reiterated. "Someone in there might start shooting."

What? Shooting?

Jack lessened his effort.

"Don't slack off," Drake warned. "We'll take care of whoever is on the other side."

Jack heard the sound of a gun being cocked. And a low, mean laugh from Drake.

He wedged his feet tight. One more big push. And drop.

Suddenly he was scared. Getting shot at was not part of the deal.

He shoved hard. All his might.

The door collapsed suddenly, but not the way Jack had expected. It snapped at the top hinge and the deadbolt broke. The door was still in the doorway, bent at an angle but held in place by one hinge. Another push and it would swing in.

The sound of the gun was shocking.

Jack dropped to the floor. He covered his head, covered his ears.

He yelled, "Don't kill me, don't kill me!" but no one could possibly have heard because now the firing was coming from both sides. Whoever was in the control room was firing short bursts through the gaps. BlamBlamBlam!

Drake was firing back in rapid-fire single rounds.

Bullets pinged off the steel and ricocheted in the hallway.

Drake yelled, Caine yelled, Jack yelled, and from beyond the doorway a girl's voice was screaming in rage and fear.

Then Caine struck. He hit the weakened door with a blast of his own.

The steel door exploded inward.

It skidded across the floor beyond and knocked the legs out from under a girl who kept firing as she fell, spraying automatic weapons fire wildly in the air.

Jack hugged the ground, sobbing, "Don't kill me!" Drake leaped over him, gun in one hand, whip hand unfurled.

Lying on his side, Jack saw a crazy tableau, the girl, unable to move, her legs twisted at impossible angles but bringing the still-firing gun around toward Drake.

Drake's whip hand snapping.

The girl pointed her gun straight at Drake's chest.

Click.

Empty.

Drake's whip connected.

A scream of pain.

Another.

"Stop it!" Diana cried.

Caine, accidentally kicking Jack's head as he rushed into the room.

Again, the lash of Drake's whip, and now he was yelling in wild glee, crowing and cursing.

Jack crawled forward, blinded by tears. He knew the girl. He knew her. Brittney. She'd been in history with him. Three rows back.

Again Drake struck.

The empty gun fell from Brittney's hand.

She was cut, bleeding, legs shattered from the impact of the door, her face a mess of tears and blood and Diana screaming abuse at Drake and Caine saying nothing to stop the psychopath and Jack wanting to cry, "I'm sorry, I'm sorry," but unable to find the words.

Diana reached Drake and grabbed his whip hand at the shoulder. "Enough, you sick piece of—"

Drake spun around, face-to-face with Diana. He bared his teeth and roared at her, roared like an animal, spit flying.

"She's right: enough," Caine said at last.

"Keep your girlfriend out of my face!" Drake bellowed at Caine.

Caine looked coldly at Drake. "I let you have your fun. We're not here for your entertainment."

Jack was stunned. He was unable to tear his eyes away from Brittney. She moaned, tried to move, then slumped to the floor. Unconscious or dead. Jack didn't know which.

She'd been in his class.

He *knew* her.

"Get to work, Jack," Caine said.

Diana turned bloodshot eyes on Jack, eyes full of hatred and sorrow. She brushed tears away. "Jack's hurt."

"What?" Caine demanded. "Jack?"

Jack wasn't hurt. He started to get up, ashamed of cowering on the floor. But his left foot gave way. He looked down, mystified, and saw that his pants, from the knee down, were soaking red.

"He's losing a lot of blood," Diana said.

It was the last thing Jack heard before the floor rushed up and smashed him in the face.

Lana heard Quinn's shouts. She heard the truck's horn. She was no more than two or three hundred feet away, just beyond the reach of the stabbing flashlight beams.

Cookie walked stolidly beside her, quiet, though he must have had his doubts.

Lana hoped Quinn and Albert wouldn't come after her. She didn't want to have to explain what she was up to.

Patrick, too, heard the honking horn, so she whispered, "Quiet boy. Shhh."

Lana had made sure to wear sturdy boots—a big improvement over the last time she had walked this route. She had her heavy pistol in her shoulder bag, which was another major improvement. And she had Cookie.

If Pack Leader found them out here, Lana intended one of them—she hoped it was she, not Cookie—to shoot him in the face.

Also in her bag was a bottle of water, a can of button mushrooms, and an entire cabbage. Not much food, especially for a guy Cookie's size, but then she expected to find at least a few cans of something in the shed at the mine. Hermit Jim would have stashed at least some food there.

She hoped.

The last time she had walked this path she'd gone in search of Jim's truck, hoping to use it to get to Perdido Beach. By that point she had found the gold and figured out that the eccentric hermit was a prospector. She had followed tire tracks to the tumble-down, abandoned mining town hidden in a crease of the hills. She'd found Jim's truck but not the keys. Then she had found Jim himself, dead in the mine shaft.

She knew now where the keys were.

Back then, back before so much had happened, she would have been terrified of digging through the pockets of a corpse. But that was the old Lana. The new Lana had seen things that were so much worse.

She knew where to find the keys. And where to find the truck. And she remembered the big LPG—liquid petroleum gas—tank Jim used to fire the smelter.

Her plan was simple: Retrieve the keys. With Cookie's help, load the gas tank into Jim's truck. Drive the truck and the tank to the mine entrance. Open the valve on the gas and let it seep into the mine shaft.

Then light a fuse and run.

She didn't know if the explosion would kill the thing in the mine. But she hoped to bury it under many tons of rock.

The Darkness had called to her in her dreams and in her waking dreams as well. It had its hook in her and she knew it was drawing her in.

Come to me. I have need of you.

It wanted her.

"Hello darkness, my old friend," Lana half sang, half whispered. "I'm coming to talk with you again."

TWENTY-TWO

JACK WOKE TO pain.

He'd been moved. Someone had turned him over. He sat up too suddenly. His head swam, and for a moment he thought he would pass out again.

One leg of his trousers had been crudely ripped to expose the wound. There was a blue, blood-soaked bandage tied around his lower thigh. It hurt. It burned like someone was sticking a red-hot poker into his flesh.

Diana was beside him. It took him a moment to make sense of her shaved head. "I found these in one of the offices. Take them." She transferred four Advil from her hand to his. "It's twice the regular dose, but I doubt it will kill you."

"What happened?" he rasped.

"Bullet. But it just grazed you and kept going. It cut a kind of neat little furrow. It'll hurt, but the bleeding's already stopped."

"Okay, Jack, snap out of it," Caine said. He sounded harried and worried. Things weren't going quite as he had planned. "You know what you're here for."

Two of Drake's soldiers returned, loudly abusing Mickey Finch and Mike Farmer, who had their hands tied behind them. They'd been found hiding in offices. Cowering under desks. "Oh good," Caine said breezily, "the hostages are here."

"We told them to throw down any guns they had, and this retard just did," one of the goons crowed. "All we had was a shotgun and a pistol and this kid had a machine gun and he still gave up. Little wussy. The other one didn't have a gun."

Mickey and Mike looked miserable and very afraid. Their expressions grew bleaker still when they saw Brittney on the floor in a puddle of blood.

Drake strode toward them, pushed Mike aside, and grabbed the machine gun. He ran his tentacle over the stock, over the cocking mechanism, holding it almost reverently. There was an expression not far from love in his cold, blue eyes. "I like this. The girl's gun was a piece of crap, but this is cool. Very cool."

"Maybe you two should get a room," Diana said.

"None of the freaks has power enough to mess with me if I'm carrying one of these," Drake said.

"Yeah, not even Caine," Diana agreed brightly. "Now you can be the boss, right?"

Jack stood rooted in place watching all this, still unable to focus on his so-called job.

How had he let himself be dragged into this? There was a

girl not ten feet away from him who might die, if she wasn't dead already. He could take three steps and be standing in her blood, as he was sitting in his own.

"Jack," Caine said. "Snap out of it. Get to work. Now!"

Jack moved like he was in a dream, shaking his head, his ears still ringing from the gunfire. His leg burned. And the material of his trousers, wet, clung to him. He stepped gingerly to the nearest computer console and sat down heavily in a swivel chair. The monitor was old. The look of the software was old. The computer didn't even have a mouse, it was all keyboard-controlled.

His heart sank further still. Old software meant all kinds of keystrokes, nothing he was used to. He slid open a drawer hoping to find a manual, or at least a cheat sheet.

"How's it look?" Caine asked. He laid his hand on Jack's shoulder, a friendly gesture meant to reassure Jack. For the first time in his life it occurred to Jack that he wanted to spin around and punch Caine. Punch him hard.

"It's totally unfamiliar software," Jack said.

"Nothing you can't handle, though. Right?"

"I can't do it very fast," Jack said. "I have to work through it."

The hand on his shoulder tightened its grip. "How long, Jack?"

"Hey, I'm hurt, all right? I got shot!" When Caine just stared at him, he lowered his voice. "I don't know. It depends."

He could sense Caine's tension, the bottled-up rage that fed on fear. "Then don't waste time."

Caine released him and turned back to Drake. "Put the hostages in the corner."

"Uh-huh," Drake said absently. He was still fondling the submachine gun.

Caine strode quickly up to him and smacked the barrel of the gun. "Hey. Take care of business. Brianna could be back here at any second. If it's not her, it'll be Taylor. You'd better not be screwing around."

Brittney lay on the floor, not moving, not making a sound. Was she alive? Jack wondered. Given how badly she was hurt, and knowing now how much pain even a grazing wound could cause, he wondered if she might not be better off dead.

Jack found an ancient loose-leaf binder, smallish, with torn page ends sticking out here and there, festooned with age-curled Post-it notes marking pages.

He started to work his way through it. He was looking for a guide to the function keys. Without that he had nothing. The lack of a mouse was crippling: he'd never seen, let alone used, a computer without a mouse. It was amazing that such things still existed.

"Diana," Caine ordered. "Read our two hostages. I don't want to find out they're hiding some power. Drake? How's it going?"

"I'm going to string the wire," Drake said.

"Good," Caine said.

Jack stole a glance and saw that Drake was holding a spool of bare wire, quite thin but strong looking. He was surveying the doorway, looking for something.

Drake shrugged, dissatisfied with what he was seeing. He began to wrap one end of the wire around the broken middle hinge where it was still attached to the wall. It was a tall door with three hinges, one that was just above head level, one at ankle height, one splitting the difference.

Drake stretched the wire from the hinge to a heavy metal filing cabinet against the wall. He passed the spool through a drawer handle and pulled it tight. He cut the wire with a pair of needle-nose pliers and wrapped the wire back on itself, tightening it further.

Diana stepped back from the two hostages and said, "They're both clear. The one may be a one bar, but at that level he doesn't even know what powers he has. If he even has anything at all useful."

"Good," Caine said.

Diana sauntered over and flopped into the swivel chair closest to Jack. She stared moodily at the monitor in front of her.

"What's Drake doing?" Jack whispered.

Diana turned her languid eyes on him. "Hey. Jack wants to know what you're doing, Drake. Why don't you tell him?"

"Jack is supposed to be working," Caine interrupted. "He's busy."

Jack turned hastily back to the notebook. There it was: a list of function keys. He frowned and began to work his way through the keys, pressing, seeing the results, moving on methodically to the next key.

Drake had finished with the wire. He ducked beneath it and disappeared down the hallway from the direction they had come, uncoiling wire as he went.

"I'm in the main directory," Jack announced. "This is so old. This is, like, DOS or something."

Despite himself he was becoming fascinated by the challenge at hand. It was computer archaeology. He was deciphering a language that was pre-Windows, pre-Linux, pre-everything. It took his mind off the pain. Mostly.

"I hope you weren't too madly in love with Brianna, Jack," Diana said.

"What? No. No way." Jack could feel himself blushing. "No. That's stupid."

"Uh-huh."

He felt his way, step by step, through the directory, looking for controls that might not even be there, commands that might not even exist.

Drake reappeared. He was whistling happily to himself. "Slice and dice," he said. "Slice and dice."

"Good," Caine said. "That's one. Now set up for Taylor. Remember, we don't want anyone shooting Jack or hitting any of the equipment."

"I know what I'm doing," Drake said. He pointed his tentacle at one of his two thugs. "You. Bring the shotgun." When the boy had complied, Drake spent a few minutes moving him around the room, checking sightlines. "Okay. You have a simple job. You see Taylor popping in here, you shoot."

The kid looked pale. "I have to shoot her?"

"No, you have a choice," Drake said. "You can shoot her or not. It's up to you."

The kid breathed a sigh.

"Of course, if you don't shoot her?" Drake snapped his whip arm. The tentacle wrapped around the boy's throat. "If you don't shoot her? If you forget, or get distracted, or miss? I'll whip you till I see bone."

Drake laughed happily and unwrapped his arm. "I believe we are ready," he announced. "Taylor has a load of buckshot waiting for her. And if little Brianna decides to breeze on in at a hundred miles an hour, she'll hit the wires."

"And set off an alarm?" Jack asked.

Drake laughed like that was the funniest thing he'd ever heard.

"Slice and dice," Drake said. "Slice and dice."

Jack didn't look at Drake. He looked at Diana. Her eyes were windows on darkness.

"Get back to work, Jack," Caine said.

The McClub was closed down. There was a sign on the door that said, "Sorry, We Are Closed. Will Reopen Tomorrow."

Duck didn't know why he had been drawn there. Of course it was closed—it was after midnight. He had just craved company. Hoped someone was hanging around. Pretty much anyone.

In the three days—well, technically four, since it was tomorrow already—since Duck had fallen through the bottom of the swimming pool, his life had actually managed to get worse. First off, he had lost his private oasis of calm. The pool was obviously unfixable. He had spent some effort looking for another pool, but no other spot had been nearly as great as the one he had lost.

In the second place, no one believed him. He had become a joke. Kids didn't bother to go and check out the pool to see if the hole was really there. And of course Zil and his punk friends didn't exactly step up to validate Duck's story.

When he'd tell people about this weird, un-asked-for power, they'd demand he demonstrate. But Duck didn't want to demonstrate. It meant getting mad, for one thing, and he wasn't naturally an angry person.

More importantly, it meant falling into the ground. And Duck had not enjoyed that the first time around. It had been sheer luck that he had passed out before he fell right on past the cave. He could have kept falling until he reached the molten core of the earth. That was the image in his head, anyway. Falling through the ground, down through the crust and the mantle and the whatever other layers there were that he had probably learned about in school but couldn't recall now, all the way down to the big melted metal and rock core.

In his mind's eye that would look like the scene at the end of *The Lord of the Rings*. He would be like Gollum, swimming for a few seconds in all that lava, then incinerated.

But that image was almost a relief compared to the other possibility: that he would simply be buried alive. That he would fall a hundred feet into the ground and have no way of extricating himself. He would slowly suffocate as the dirt walls of the hole filled in, clods falling onto his upturned face, dirt filling his eyes, his mouth, his nose . . .

He grabbed the handle of the McClub door to steady himself. The images were waking nightmares. They were in his thoughts more and more often.

It didn't help that no one else took the problem seriously. Kids laughed at his story. They thought the whole thing was funny. The part about falling through the bottom of the pool. The part about the cave. The radioactive side cave. The blue bats. The emergence from the waves, half naked and shivering. The way he'd had to climb the cliff up from the beach, forcing himself to grin happily lest anger cause him to fall and keep on falling. Climbing had been the easiest part. He'd felt light with relief.

He had told the story and kids roared with laughter. The first day or so he'd played along. He enjoyed making people laugh. But he'd gone very quickly from being a funny storyteller to being an object of ridicule.

"Your power is the power to gain so much weight, you actually sink into the ground?" That had been Hunter, who thought himself a real comedian. "So, you're basically *Fatman*?"

After that it was open season: Fatman led to Fall-through Boy, the Spelunker, the Sinker, the Miner, and the one he heard most often, the Human Drill.

Kids didn't get it: It wasn't funny. Not really. Not if you thought about it. Not if you spent the night tossing and turning, barely able to sleep because you worried that you might get angry in some dream and fall to a slow, agonizing death.

Hunter had also ridiculed his tale of the blue bats. "Dude—or should I call you the Human Drill? Dude, bats sleep during the day and fly at night. Your blue bats? According to you, they woke up when it got light. How do you figure? Plus, no one but you has ever seen them."

"They're blue, like the sky, so you wouldn't see them flying overhead or through the water," Duck had pointed out to no avail.

He let go of the club door. Probably better that it was closed. He was lonely, but maybe loneliness wasn't as bad as the ridicule.

Duck looked around, feeling lost. It was late. No one was out. In the old days his parents would have grounded him for a year if they'd found out he was wandering the streets at night.

No one was in the plaza. It was a creepy place at night. The graves were there. The shattered outline of the church dark against the stars. The burned remains of the apartment building. There were a couple of lights on in town hall—no one bothered going around and turning out lights. The streetlights were still on, although some had burned out and others, especially the ones in the plaza, had been broken either by the battle or by vandals.

The plaza was a place of ghosts now. Ghosts and long shadows.

Duck headed wearily toward home. So-called home. It meant passing by the church. It at least was dark. It was lit nowadays only on meeting nights because the original lighting system had not survived. Lights were strung from the town hall on an extension cord. Someone usually remembered to yank the cord out of the socket when they were done.

Rubble, some of it massive chunks of masonry, blocked the sidewalk on the church side. No one had ever cleaned it up. Probably no one ever would. Duck walked down the middle of the street, mistrusting the shadows on either side.

He heard a scuffling sound in the church. A dog, probably. Or rats.

But then, an urgent whisper, "Hey! Hey, Duck!"

Duck stopped. The voice was coming from the direction of the church.

"Dude!" the whisper, louder now.

"What? Who is that?" Duck asked.

"It's me, man. Hunter. Keep it down. They'll kill me if they find me."

"What? Who?"

"Duck, man, come here, I can't be yelling back and forth."

Reluctantly—very reluctantly because he expected some trick—Duck crossed the street.

Hunter was crouched behind a piece of rubble that still held a portion of stained-glass window. He stood up when Duck approached, which brought his face into the light. He didn't look as if he was planning a prank. He looked scared.

"What's up?" Duck asked.

"Come back here, man, so no one can see us."

Duck climbed over the rubble, skinning his shin in the process.

"Okay," Duck said, once he was in Hunter's rubble hide-away. "What?"

"Can you hook me up, dude? I didn't catch any dinner."

"Uh . . . what?"

"I'm hungry," Hunter said.

"Everybody's hungry," Duck pointed out. "I drank a jar of gravy for dinner."

Hunter sighed. "I'm starving here. I didn't get dinner. I barely got any lunch. I was trying to save up."

"Why are you here?"

"Zil. He and the normals are after me."

Duck had the definite feeling he was either being elaborately punked, or had wandered into someone else's crazy dream. "Man, if you're here to bust on me, just get it over with."

"No, man. No way. I'm sorry about all that, you know, teasing you and all. I was just trying to get along with them, you know?"

"No. I don't know what you're talking about, Hunter."

Hunter hesitated, looking like he might try to bluster. But then he collapsed. He sat down hard on the ground. Duck knelt awkwardly beside him. The awkwardness was compounded when he heard the telltale sniffle. Hunter was crying.

"What happened, man?" Duck asked.

"Zil. You know Zil, right? We were having an argument. He goes totally nuts. He tries to kill me with a fireplace poker. So what am I supposed to do?"

"What did you do?"

"I was totally in the right," Hunter said. "I was totally in the right. Only I didn't get Zil because Harry came rushing in. He got in between us."

"Okay."

Hunter sniffled again. "No, man. Not okay. Harry goes down. He hits the floor. I wasn't even aiming at him, he didn't do anything. You have to help me, Duck," Hunter pleaded.

"Me? Why me? All you ever do is pick on me."

"Okay, okay, that's true," Hunter admitted. He had stopped crying. But his voice was, if anything, even more urgent. "But, look, we're on the same side, here."

"Um . . . what?"

"We're freaks, man. You aren't getting this, are you?" Irritation helped Hunter's self-control. The sniffling stopped. "Dude, Zil is running around getting normals to come out against us. All of us."

Duck shook his head in confusion. "What are you talking about, man?"

Hunter grabbed his arm and held it tight. "It's us against them. Don't you get that? It's freaks against normals."

"No way," Duck scoffed. "First of all, I didn't hurt anyone. Second of all, Sam is a freak and Astrid's a normal, and so is Edilio. So how is it that all of them are trying to get us?"

"You think they won't come after you next?" Hunter said, not exactly answering. "You think you're safe? Fine. Go on. Run away home. Play pretend. It's us against them. You'll see, when it's you hiding out from them."

Duck disengaged himself from Hunter's grip. "I'll see if

I can bring you something to eat, dude. But I'm not getting involved in your troubles."

Duck climbed back out of the rubble and headed down the street.

Hunter's hissed words followed him. "It's freaks against normals, Duck. And you're a freak."

Jack was sweating like he was in a sauna. His leg hurt. Hurt bad.

But more, the wires.

The wires.

Brianna would never see them. She would come rushing on, as fast as a speeding bullet. She would hit the wires at that speed and she would be sliced into pieces. Like a wire cheese cutter going through a brick of Swiss.

The image was painfully clear in Jack's mind.

He could see Brianna hitting the wire. And being cut in half. Legs still running for another few steps before they realized they were no longer carrying a body.

"Take down the wires," Jack said. The words were out of his mouth before he knew it. He hadn't planned it. He'd just blurted it.

No one heard him except Diana.

He glanced at her and saw a flicker of a smile.

But Drake was busy and Caine was ranting and neither heard him.

Jack pulled his hands away from the keyboard.

"You have to cut down the wires," Jack said, choking on the words.

And now Caine froze. And now Drake whirled.

"What?" Drake demanded.

"Take the wires down," Jack said. "Or else I—"

The whip landed on his neck and back. Like the bullet wound, but so much worse for being on such tender skin.

Jack cried out in shock at the pain.

Drake was coiled to strike again, but Caine yelled, "No!"

Drake seemed ready to ignore the order, but contented himself with wrapping his tentacle around Jack's throat. He squeezed, and Jack felt blood pounding in his head.

Caine walked over and in a reasonable voice said, "What's the problem, Jack?"

"The wires," Jack said, barely able to form sounds. "I don't like what you're doing."

Caine blinked. He was honestly puzzled. He looked at Diana for an explanation.

Diana sighed. "Puppy love," she said. "It looks like Jack's gotten over me. There's another girl playing the leading role in Jack's shameful dreams."

Caine laughed, disbelieving. "You've got a thing for Brianna?"

"I don't . . . it's not like . . ." Jack squeezed the words out.

"Oh, come on, Jack. Don't be an idiot," Caine cajoled him. "Let him go, Drake. Jack's just losing focus. He's forgetting what's important."

Drake withdrew his tentacle, and Jack breathed in deep. His neck and back burned so badly, he forgot the lesser wound on his thigh.

"Jack, Jack, Jack," Caine said, sounding like a disappointed teacher. "Bad things happen sometimes, Jack, you have to accept that."

"Not Brianna," Jack said.

Jack saw color rising in Caine's face, a warning sign. But he knew Caine needed him. Caine wouldn't kill him, he was sure of that, no matter how mad he got. Drake might let his rage take over, but Caine wouldn't.

"You think she'd defend you?" Caine asked. "She'll come zooming in here, maybe carrying a gun, shoot anyone she sees, Jack. Now, get back to work and let me take care of making the big decisions."

Jack turned back to the keyboard. He started to rest his hands on the keys. But he couldn't do it. He froze there with his fingertips half an inch above the keys.

Not Brianna. Not her. Not like that.

"I could talk to her," Jack said. "I could maybe get her to come over to your side."

"Let me just deal with this," Drake pleaded. "I guarantee you, he'll get back to work."

"That's right, Drake," Diana said. "Torture him into it. You'll never know if he gets pissed off enough to maybe flood this room with radiation. Until your hair starts falling out."

That had not occurred to Jack. But it did now. Diana was right, they wouldn't really know what he was doing.

Caine was biting his thumb again, his habit when frustrated.

"Drake, cut the wires. Jack, figure out how to turn the lights off in Perdido Beach or I'll tell Drake to not only put the wires back up, but whip you till he gets too tired to lift his arm."

Jack carefully concealed his feeling of triumph.

Drake started to object, but Caine snapped, "Just do it, Drake. Just do it."

Jack felt a wave of some warm feeling flow through him. Something unlike anything he'd ever felt before. There was still the searing pain on his neck and back, and the all-but-forgotten pain on his leg. But the pain was secondary to this feeling of . . . something. He didn't know quite what to call it.

He had stepped up to protect someone else. Brianna might never know it, but he had just taken a big risk for her. In fact, he had risked his life for her.

Diana drawled, "Our little geek is growing up."

Jack began tapping away at the keyboard.

"But still so naïve," Diana added.

The word bothered Jack, vaguely. He kind of knew what it meant, the word "naïve." But now he was into the directory he needed, and there were commands to be learned, sequences to be deciphered.

TWENTY-THREE

"THEY'LL HAVE SOMEONE on the gate," Sam said. "It's just around this bend. Stop here."

Edilio braked, and the other two vehicles came to a stop behind them. Dekka driving Orc and Howard in a hefty SUV. A handful of Edilio's soldiers in the third car. All the people Sam could round up. He'd tried others, but these were the ones who came when they learned they were to do battle with Caine and Drake.

Fear of Caine, and especially Drake, ran deep in Perdido Beach.

Sam turned in his seat so he could see Brianna and Taylor in the back. "Okay, girls, here's our problem: I need to know where Caine's goons are. I have to figure he left at least a couple of guys on the front gate. Armed, of course. They'll have instructions to shoot anyone who comes down this road."

"I can pop in and out before they can shoot me," Taylor said. She wasn't quite eager.

"Sam, I can plow past that gate and take a little tour inside the facility and be back in thirty seconds," Brianna argued. "They most likely won't even see me."

"If you're going so fast, they don't see you, how you going to see them?" Edilio asked.

She pointed at her face. "Fast eyes, Dillio, very fast eyes."

Sam and Edilio both grinned. But it didn't last long.

"Okay, listen to me, Breeze," Sam said. "Do not go anywhere but to the gate. That's not a suggestion, that's me telling you."

"I can do it all in no time," Brianna argued.

"Breeze, I need you to hear me on this: do not go into that plant."

Brianna pouted. "You're the boss, boss."

"Okay," Sam said. "Take off—" He stopped, realizing he was talking to air.

"Long gone," Edilio commented. "Girl doesn't hang around."

"I can help, too," Taylor said, a little resentful.

"You'll get your chance," Sam said.

Dekka was climbing out of the SUV. "Did you send Breeze?"

"Yeah. She should be back any second now," Edilio said.

"I'm ready to do this," Dekka said. "Driving with Orc in the back? Boy is farting something terrible."

"Cabbage," Taylor said.

"Any second now. You know Brianna," Edilio said.

The four of them waited. Sam kept his eyes on the road. Not that he would see her when she got back.

"Taking a while," Taylor said. "I mean, for her."

No one spoke after that. Not as two minutes passed. Then three minutes. Five interminable minutes.

"Oh, my God," Dekka whispered. "Brianna." She closed her eyes and seemed to be praying.

"She'd be back by now," Sam said heavily. "If she was coming."

He felt sick to his stomach. Sick down to his bones.

Lana felt the dread growing on her. She was prepared. She knew it was coming.

"What is this place?" Cookie asked, feeling something, too, no doubt, but only the ghosts, not the living, seething evil that was now so close.

"It used to be a mining town," Lana said. "Gold miners, back in, like, the 1800s or whatever."

"Like cowboys?"

"I guess so."

They walked through the ghost town, the shabby, tumbledown wreck of a place that had no doubt once been someone's dream of a future metropolis. The mines had mostly played out back in the late 1800s.

It was still possible to make out where the main street had been. And Lana supposed if you really thought about it, you'd be able to figure out which of the piles of sticks was the hotel, the saloon, the hardware store, or whatever. Here and there a tenuous wall or rickety chimney still stood outlined in silver. But roofs had mostly collapsed long ago, storefronts had pancaked. Maybe it was an earthquake or something that had tumbled the weakened structures. Maybe it was just time.

Only one building seemed more or less intact, the rough-hewn warehouse where Hermit Jim had hidden his gas-fired gold smelter and his pickup truck.

"That's where we're going," Lana said, nodding in the direction of the structure.

Lana's gaze was drawn beyond the building to the trail that led up the side of the hill. She knew she would have to walk up that trail, up that hill to the mine shaft, and dig the keys from the mummified miner's pocket.

Not her favorite idea. Being even this close to the thing in the mine shaft laid shadows on her soul. She could feel it up there, the Darkness, and she had the terrible feeling that it could sense her closeness as well.

Did the Darkness know she was coming?

Did it know why?

Did *she* know? For sure?

"I know why I'm here," Lana said. "I know."

"Of course," Cookie said. He seemed to think she was rebuking him.

Patrick was quiet, cowed. He remembered, too.

They were in the warehouse. Lana checked the propane gas tank. There was a gauge that showed it half full. That should be enough.

She knelt and checked the support for the tank. It rested on a sort of steel frame, rusted, but not, thankfully, bolted down to the ground or anything. The cradle rested on dirt. Good.

"What we have to do, Cookie, is get this tank into that

truck. In a little while I'm going to get the keys. We'll back
the truck up to the tank. But first, let's see how it all works,
huh?"

"You got it, Healer."

She pressed her leg against the bottom edge of the tank,
finding it came to the top of her thigh. She walked to the
pickup truck and compared the height of the tailgate.

Good. Good. They were very close to being the same
height. The tank was maybe two inches lower, which meant
it would have to be lifted. Lifted and shoved. But there would
be a system, had to be, because Hermit Jim would have had to
carry the tank in his truck to get refills.

"Cookie. Look around for a toolbox."

First things first. She made sure the nozzle was off.

Then she rummaged in the toolbox Cookie had retrieved
until she found a wrench that fit the pipe fitting. The coupling that attached the hose to the tank was frozen up.

"Let me give it a try," Cookie suggested.

Cookie was at least twice Lana's weight. The coupling
gave way.

Lana pointed to the rafters. A heavy chain hung down
from a series of pulleys. There was a hook on the end of the
chain, and an eyebolt on the gas tank's frame.

"Jim would have had to refill the tank from time to time.
That's how he got the tank into his truck."

Cookie hauled the hook down. The chain clanked and
came easily, rolling through the well-oiled pulley.

Cookie hoisted himself heavily up onto the framework
and attached the hook to the eyebolt.

"Okay. Good," Lana said. "Now I'm going up to get the key."

Something in her tone must have worried Cookie. "Well, um, Healer, we should go with you. Me and Patrick. It's not safe out there."

"I know," Lana said. "But if something goes wrong, I want to know I have someone I trust who can take care of Patrick."

That was the wrong thing to say if her goal was to soothe Cookie. His eyes were wide, his chin trembling.

"What's going to go wrong?"

"Probably nothing."

"Okay, I have to go with you," Cookie said.

Lana laid her hand on his big forearm. "Cookie, you have to trust me on this."

"At least tell me what the problem is," he pleaded.

Lana hesitated. A big part of her wanted Cookie and Patrick, too, along for the walk to the mine entrance. But she was worried about Patrick. And even more, she was worried about what might happen to Cookie.

In the old days Cookie had been a big, dumb bully, a sort of second-tier Orc. He was still not exactly a genius. But his heart had been transformed by days of suffering, and whatever meanness had once been in him was gone. There was now in Cookie a sort of purity, he seemed so innocent to Lana. An encounter with the Darkness might end all that. The creature in the mine had left its stain on her soul, and she didn't want that same thing to happen to her trusting and loyal protector.

Lana retrieved her bag. From it she drew a letter, neatly

sealed in a white business envelope. She handed it to Cookie. "Look, if something does happen, you take this to Sam or Astrid. Okay?"

"Healer . . ." He was reluctant to take it.

"Cookie. Take." She placed it in his hand and closed his fingers around it. "Good. Now, listen, I need you to do something else while I'm gone."

"What?"

She forced a smile. "I'm so hungry, I could eat Patrick. Look around this dump and see if you can find something to eat. I'll be back in fifteen minutes."

She turned toward the door and plunged out into the night before he could argue any further.

Lana slipped her hand into her bag, wrapped her fingers around the cold plastic grip of the pistol. She pulled it out and let it hang by her side.

She was going to get the key from the dead miner. If Pack Leader showed up to stop her, she would shoot him.

And if . . . and if she could not bring herself to come back out of that cave, if she found herself instead walking deeper into it, deeper, toward the Darkness, unable to resist, well . . .

Taylor was not Brianna. Breeze had an image of herself as a superhero. Taylor knew she was just a girl. Like any other girl except that she had the strange ability to think of a place and appear there instantaneously.

And now Brianna was very late getting back. The Breeze was never late. Brianna didn't know how to be late.

Something had happened to her.

So it was Taylor's turn. She felt it, knew it. But Sam didn't ask her. He stood there staring down the road, like he was willing Brianna to appear.

Dekka was more upset than Taylor had ever seen her. Dekka was normally a rock, but the rock had some cracks in it now.

Edilio kept a poker face. Eyes straight ahead, waiting for orders. Patient.

No one wanted to pressure Sam. But everyone knew that with each passing minute, it was becoming harder to act.

It was up to Taylor. Sam didn't want to send her. So it was up to her.

She would do anything for Sam. Anything. She supposed she was kind of in love with him, even though he was older than her and was totally into Astrid.

Sam had saved Taylor's life. He had saved her sanity.

Caine had decreed that uncooperative freaks at Coates be kept under control. He had figured out that most powers seemed to focus through a kid's hands, and with Drake's help he had moved quickly and decisively.

It was called plastering. It involved encasing a kid's hands in a block of cement. The blocks weighed forty pounds. The sheer weight rendered kids helpless. At first Caine's flunkies had fed them in dishes on the ground, like dogs. Taylor and the others, including Brianna and Dekka, had lapped up bowls of cereal and milk like animals.

Then trouble had broken out between the kids left in

charge at Coates while Caine went down to grab control in Perdido Beach.

The feedings had grown less frequent. And then they had stopped altogether. Taylor had eaten weeds poking up through gravel.

Sam was the reason she wasn't dead.

She owed him. Everything.

Even, she realized with a sinking in the pit of her stomach, the life he had given back to her.

"I'll be right back," she said.

Before Sam or anyone else could speak, she was gone. Just down to the end of the road so she could see the gate, not far, not as far as she was capable of teleporting.

One second she was with Sam and Edilio and Dekka. A millisecond later she was alone in the dark, her friends just out of sight behind her.

It was like changing a TV channel. Only she was inside the TV.

Taylor took a shaky breath. The gate was just fifty yards away. The power plant beyond was bright and intimidating.

They would expect her to either bounce into the guardhouse or directly into the plant. She wouldn't do either.

A split second later she was on the hillside above the guardhouse, tripping because she had materialized on a steep slope.

She caught herself, glanced around quickly, saw no one, and bounced to a dark shadowed place behind a parked delivery truck just off to one side of the gate.

"Ah!"

A shout of surprise and Taylor knew she had made a bad choice.

Two kids, two of Drake's thugs, both armed with rifles were right there, right next to her, hiding behind the truck. Waiting in ambush.

Surprise slowed their reactions. She could see it in their eyes.

"Too slow," Taylor said.

They shouted, swiveled their guns, and she was gone.

She appeared three feet from Sam, who was still staring down the road.

"Taylor. What are you doing?" he asked.

He hadn't realized she was gone. She laughed in relief. "Two guys with guns behind a big truck, just past the gate, to the left. I don't think anyone's actually in the guardhouse. It's an ambush. If you guys went toward the guardhouse, these guys would be able to shoot you in the back. They saw me."

Now it was Sam's turn to be a little stunned.

"You . . ."

"Yeah."

"You shouldn't . . ."

"Had to. And look, I didn't see Brianna anywhere."

"Load up," Sam ordered. He leaped into the Jeep. "Dekka?"

"On it," Dekka said, breaking into a run for her own vehicle.

Edilio shouted to his guys to load up as well.

"Thanks," Sam said over his shoulder.

Taylor felt amazingly happy over that one word

acknowledgment. "I could . . . ," she began, not really wanting Sam to say yes.

"No," he said firmly. "And keep your head down." To Edilio he said, "Straight to the gate, but pull over before you reach it. We have to move fast before they can figure out what to do. But, remember, there'll be one more guy out there. The one that Taylor *didn't* see."

"Yep," Edilio said. "We're ready for that."

Taylor wondered what they were talking about, but it wasn't time for twenty questions.

The Jeep careened around the curve and hurtled down the hill to the gate. Edilio slammed on the brakes. Dekka's SUV barely had time to avoid piling into them. The third vehicle followed more slowly.

Sam jumped out. Dekka leaped while her own car was still moving.

Both pelted down the hill.

Taylor heard Sam yelling instructions to Dekka. Seconds later the truck, tons of steel, floated up off the ground.

Taylor saw the two thugs gaping up at it.

Sam raised his hands. "Guys?" he said to the two startled thugs. "Way I see it, you have a choice. Drop your guns, run away, and live. Or point those guns my way and burn."

The two guns clattered on the pavement. The two boys stuck their arms in the air.

"You have anything we can eat?" one asked.

Dekka dropped the truck back into place.

It made a huge noise, smashing, bouncing but remaining upright.

"Have you seen Brianna?" Dekka asked them.

"No," the boy said.

"But if she tried to go after them inside, she's not coming back," the other said, trying to sound tough, even though his hands were in the air.

"Taylor," Sam said. "Double-check the guardhouse."

Taylor bounced into the guardhouse. She was on a hair trigger, ready to bounce back out again. But she saw no one inside.

Outside, through the window, she saw Edilio's soldiers piling out of the last car, machine guns ready. Howard stepped out of the SUV, scared, cringing. And slowly, like he was an old man with arthritis, came Orc. Howard was a tiny shadow beside him.

Taylor bounced to them.

"No one's in the guardhouse," Taylor reported. "And no Brianna."

Dekka looked at Sam. "If anyone's hurt that girl, they don't get the chance to walk away."

"Dekka, we need to play this smart," Sam said.

"No, Sam," Dekka said with sudden, savage ferocity. "Anyone who hurts that girl dies."

Taylor expected Sam to put Dekka in her place. Instead, he said, "We all love her, Dekka. We'll do what's right."

Taylor bounced next to Dekka. She put her hand on Dekka's strong shoulder. The girl was trembling.

TWENTY-FOUR

18 HOURS, 1 MINUTE

SAM WISHED CAINE would come out after him. That would be best. That would be the thing. A straight-up fight, out in the open. Last time they'd had that fight, Sam had won.

But Caine wasn't going to step outside.

The fight had barely begun and already he had lost Brianna.

Poor Breeze.

"What do we do?" Edilio asked. He was at Sam's side. Edilio was always at his side, and Sam was profoundly grateful for that. But right this moment, standing here in the shadow of the hulking power plant, with images of Brianna filling the next hole in the town plaza, he wished Edilio would shut up and leave him in peace.

But Sam was the guy who made decisions. Win or lose. Right or wrong. Life or death.

"I should have brought Astrid along," Sam said. "She knows the plant better than either of us do."

"They gotta be in the control room," Edilio said. "Whatever Caine is up to, he'd want to have the control room."

"Yeah."

"Only two ways in, as far as I remember. Either in through the turbine building or back through all the offices. They'll have both covered."

"Yeah."

"Kind of narrow hallways from either direction. Come through the turbine room, maybe they won't want to get crazy and do anything that messes up the plant, right?"

Sam looked at him sharply. "You're right. That makes sense. I should have thought of it. Caine doesn't want the plant destroyed."

Edilio shrugged. "Hey, man, I'm not just your good-looking Mexican sidekick."

Sam smiled. "You're not Mexican. You're Honduran."

"Oh, yeah," Edilio said dryly. "Sometimes I forget." Then, serious again, he said, "Caine didn't come here to wreck the place. He came here to take it over, use it somehow. Boy doesn't want to sit in the dark any more than we do."

"But he'll do what he has to," Sam said.

"Yeah. If the other choice is him coming out peacefully and letting us lock him up, or . . ."

Howard sidled up. "We standing around here all night or what? Orc's, like, let's do this or let me go home and go to sleep."

"I kind of thought we'd take a couple of minutes to think it over," Sam snarled. "We've probably lost Breeze. But if you'd rather just have Orc go barreling in there alone, fine."

"No, man," Howard said, backing down quickly.

Sam laid his hand on Edilio's shoulder and gave it a little squeeze. "He may have hostages."

"Yeah," Edilio agreed. "My guys. Mike and Mickey and Brittney and Josh."

"Okay, as long as we understand," Sam said. He made eye contact with Edilio. Edilio gave just the slightest nod in return.

"Here's my plan. Taylor bounces in, carries a shotgun, starts to blast. One, two, three rounds, then bounces out. At that point we hit them all together, straight through the turbine room."

"Yep," Edilio said. "Straight through the turbine room."

Looking perfectly casual, Edilio slung his knapsack off his shoulder and began rummaging inside. He called over to a kid named Steve, one of his soldiers. "Hey, Steve, man, where's my Snickers bar? I had it right here in my backpack."

Steve frowned and headed over. The pockets of his cargo pants were bulging.

Edilio drew a gun—too big, too brightly colored, and too plastic to be real from his backpack. He pumped it once, leveled it at waist level, and fired.

A thin stream of watered-down yellow paint sprayed thirty feet.

At the same time Steve drew twin cans of spray paint from his pants, aimed, and fired.

Edilio and Steve both sprayed in a circle, twirling, hitting kids and cars and foliage.

"There!" Sam yelled.

Bug was almost completely invisible at night. But a lot less invisible with a spray of yellow paint across his chest.

Bug bolted, looking like nothing more than a dancing, racing streak of fluorescence. He pelted away, yelling, "Open the door! Open the door!"

Dekka took a stance. "Make it look good, but not too good," Sam whispered.

Suddenly Bug tripped. Gravity had ceased to exist, but he stumbled out of Dekka's range, regained his feet, and hit the door.

"Nice," Sam said.

The door opened, and Bug fell into the darkness beyond.

"You think he heard?" Edilio asked.

"Yeah. He'll be blurting it to Caine right about now. So we go in hard and fast."

"How?" Edilio asked.

"Right through the wall," Sam said grimly. "Howard! Orc!" he yelled. He pointed at the turbine room door, which had slammed shut behind Bug. "Take out that door. Edilio, grab your best guy and go with them. Make lots of noise. Make it look good. Everyone else with me."

"Lots of noise," Edilio echoed in a worried voice.

Sam tightened his grip on Edilio's shoulder. "If I were ever going to have a Mexican sidekick, you'd be the guy."

"Yeah, right."

"Ready?"

"Nope."

"So let's go," Sam said. Then, louder, "Let's go!"

They raced for the door that Bug had taken. Across the parking lot at a crazy run. Edilio, Steve, and one other soldier, half pushing Orc ahead of them as Howard drifted strategically slower and fell behind in relative safety.

Sam, Dekka, and the remaining soldiers kept pace, then peeled off, dodging left and racing along the building.

Taylor stayed behind with two guys guarding the rear.

Orc ran straight for the door. He plowed into it like a bull, full-speed, heedless. The sound of the impact echoed around the parking lot.

The metal door crumpled but did not give. Orc reared back and kicked it with his stone foot. He fell on his back, but the door flew open.

Gunfire erupted from inside.

Orc stayed flat. The others dodged aside.

Edilio began firing through the doorway, an earsplitting din. The muzzle flash was like a strobe light.

Sam and Dekka raced away, hugging the wall.

"About here, I think," Sam said, panting.

The two of them stepped away from the wall, and Sam raised his hands.

Blistering green fire exploded from Sam's upraised palms. The brick wall glowed red. Almost immediately the masonry began to crack, and then Dekka made her own move. Gravity beneath the wall ceased to exist.

The wall began to crack. Flakes of mortar and stone flew

straight up in the air. Some of the smaller chunks caught fire and burned as they rose. The wall was coming apart, but too slowly.

"Orc!" Sam yelled.

The boy-monster rolled to his feet and came at a rush.

"Dekka, off!" Sam yelled.

The green fire died, gravity returned with a rain of dirt and gravel, and through it ran Orc. He hit the weakened wall with one massive shoulder. The cinder block collapsed in like a fallen pie crust.

Orc backed up, then hit it again and he was through. Sam dashed after him, but unlike Orc he was not immune to the heat he had himself created. It was like rushing into an oven. He brushed against a bit of red-hot brick and yelped in pain.

Sam froze.

Inside, beyond the cinderblock wall, was not the control room. Instead of breaking through to the control room and catching Caine off guard, he was in an outer room filled with old-style metal filing cabinets.

The whole plan had just fallen apart. The diversion was now pointless.

Dekka was right behind Sam. "So much for the element of surprise," she said.

No time for regrets, Sam told himself, but it was a bitter moment. Surprise might have saved lives. Surprise might have allowed them to rescue the hostages.

"The next wall should be easier," Sam said. "Take cover!"

Dekka jumped behind a row of filing cabinets as Sam

attacked the inner wall. The temperature in the filing room went from stifling to dangerous in seconds.

Sam's light burned away paint and wallboard in a few seconds, but beyond it, inside the wall, was a barrier of dull, gray metal.

"It's a radiation shield," Sam yelled to Dekka. "Lead."

The lead melted quickly at the touch of Sam's probing fire. Liquid lead dribbled down the wall and pooled, instantly igniting anything it touched.

But now the file room was too hot for anyone. The air was gone, and Sam was woozy, unfocused, forgetting what he was doing.

"Orc! Grab him!" Dekka yelled as she dove back outside, gasping for breath.

Sam felt himself lifted off his feet. It was curiously pleasant. Outside, the shock of cold air on his face snapped him back to reality.

He glanced to his right. Gunfire still kept the turbine room doorway clear. Edilio was flattened against the wall, unable to do anything but reload and keep firing blindly. His soldiers had been ordered back to safety behind parked cars.

The attack was failing.

Sam stood up, fighting nausea and dizziness. He faced the wall again. He could shoot through the outer wall, through the room beyond, and hit the lead shield. But his deadly light was diffused at that distance. And he had no room to ply the blowtorch back and forth and widen the hole.

He raised his hands and unleashed the power. The lead

sheath melted quickly. But too late, Sam knew. Too late for surprise. Too late.

And in the end, too little.

A red-rimmed hole about the size of a manhole cover dripped melted lead like tears.

Then a familiar voice cried, "Sam!"

Sam ignored it.

"Sam, in three seconds I'm pushing one of my hostages into this hole you've made," Caine yelled. "One!"

Sam widened the gap as much as he could, working the edges, melting lead.

"Two!"

He couldn't stop, Sam told himself.

But if he didn't stop, he had no doubt, none, that Caine would make good on his threat. Caine could literally hurl one of the hostages into the fiery hole Sam was burning.

Sam dropped his hands. The light died.

"That's better," Caine yelled.

"Come out now, Caine, and maybe I let you walk away in one piece," Sam blustered.

"Here's the thing, brother," Caine called back. "I have two of your people. Give a shout-out, kids."

"It's me, Sam. It's Mike Farmer! Mickey's here, too. And Britt, she's . . . she's hurt."

Sam shot a look at Dekka. She stared back at him, stone faced. Caine had said two hostages. So he was counting Brittney as dead.

And no mention of Brianna. The Breeze was not a hostage.

At the same time, Sam told himself, Mike hadn't listed her, either. So at least she wasn't lying defeated in that room.

The gunfire at the doorway had ceased. Edilio still stood ready, but not knowing what to do next.

"Let them go, Caine," Sam said wearily.

"I don't think I'm going to do that," Caine answered.

Sam ran his hand through his hair, beside himself with frustration.

"What is it you want?" Sam asked. "What do you think you're doing?"

"I have the power plant, that's obvious," Caine said. "Stupid of you to lose it, Sam."

Sam had no answer to that.

"What I'm going to do, Sam, is turn off the power to Perdido Beach."

"You do that, you'll be sitting in the dark, too," Sam shouted back.

"You'd think so, wouldn't you?" Caine said with a laugh. "But it turns out that's not true. It seems we can turn off some parts of the grid from here and not affect other parts."

"I think you're bluffing, Caine. I've seen the control room. It would take you a week to make any sense out of it."

Caine laughed easily. "Oh, man, you are right about that, brother. Hey, it would probably take me a month. And Diana's no better at the techie stuff. And Drake, well, you know Drake. But . . ."

Sam knew what was coming next. He closed his eyes and hung his head.

"Fortunately, our mutual friend Computer Jack, here, he's

pretty much got it whipped. In fact . . . How's it going, Jack? Got it yet?"

There was a murmur, barely audible. Then, Caine again, taunting. "Guess what, Sam?"

Sam refused to answer.

"Jack here says the lights just went off in Perdido Beach."

Caine laughed, a wild, triumphant sound.

Sam caught Taylor's eye. She teleported over to him. "Check it out," he said. The girl nodded once and disappeared.

"You sending Brianna to check it out?" Caine shouted. "Or Taylor?"

Sam said nothing. He waited.

Taylor popped back into view, right beside him.

"I bounced to a bend in the road where you can see town," she reported.

"And?"

TWENTY-FIVE

DUCK HAD ARGUED with himself all the way home. Hunter's problem was not his problem, he told himself. Okay, maybe he was a freak now, too, like Hunter, but so what? He had some stupid, useless power—why did that mean he had to buy a piece of Hunter's grief?

Hunter was a jerk. And all the people Duck liked were normals. Mostly. He liked Sam, of course, in a sort of distant way. But, man, how was he suddenly supposed to be choosing sides in a fight he didn't even know was happening?

However, he didn't like the idea of just leaving Hunter hiding out hungry in the rubble outside the church. That seemed kind of harsh.

By the time he had reached the relative safety of his home, Duck had talked himself out of doing anything one way or the other. And then he talked himself into the opposite position. And back again.

He found himself looking in the kitchen cupboards. Just to

see. Just to see if it was even possible to help Hunter out.

There wasn't much to see in the kitchen. Two cans of veg-gies. A jar of hot dog relish, but not even the sweet kind. A half-empty bag of flour and some oil. He'd learned how to cook a sort of nasty-tasting tortilla with the flour and a little water and oil. It was the current popular favorite in the FAYZ, something even the most kitchen-impaired could kind of fig-ure out.

He didn't want to even think about what they'd all be eat-ing in a week. From what Duck had heard, there was food in the fields, but no one wanted to pick it if there were zekes. He shuddered at the thought.

But he supposed he could spare the hot dog relish. Not exactly something good for you, but Hunter had sounded pretty desperate. And nowadays everyone was eating things that would have made them gag before.

Duck had a sudden vision of actual hot dogs. The real thing, steaming hot, nestled in a tender white bun.

Duck's aunt was from Chicago. She had taught him about genuine Chicago hot dogs with, what was it? Seven toppings? He wondered if he could remember them all.

Mustard. Relish. Onions. Tomatoes.

His mouth was watering at the thought. But then his mouth would have watered at the idea of a real hot dog topped with Brussels sprouts.

He made up his mind. It wasn't about freaks versus nor-mals. It was about whether he could just leave Hunter out there cowering all through the night.

No. He'd bring him the relish and then, if Hunter needed a place to hide, he'd let him stay in the basement here at the house.

Duck slipped the relish into the pocket of his jacket and headed with great reluctance back into the night.

It took only a few minutes to reach the church.

"Hunter. Yo, Hunter," he called in a hoarse whisper.

Nothing.

Great. Perfect. He was being punked after all.

He turned and started to walk away. But around the corner came a group of seven, maybe eight kids. It took him only a second to spot the baseball bats.

Zil was in the lead.

"There's one!" Zil shouted, and before Duck could even react the seven boys were rushing him.

"What's up?" Duck asked.

The boys surrounded him. There was no denying their menacing attitude, but Duck was determined not to give them an excuse to start swinging.

"What's up?" Zil mocked. "The Human Drill wants to know what's up." He gave Duck a shove. "One of your kind killed my best friend, that's what's up."

"We're sick of it," another boy chimed in.

Various voices muttered agreement.

"Guys, I didn't hurt anyone," Duck said. "I'm just . . ."

He didn't know what he was just. The hostile eyes around him narrowed.

"Just what, freak?" Zil demanded.

"Walking, man. Anything wrong with that?"

"We're looking for Hunter," Hank said.

"We're going to kick his butt."

"Yeah. Maybe rearrange his nose," Antoine said. "Like maybe it would look better sticking out the side of his face."

They laughed.

"Hunter?" Duck said, working to sound innocent.

"Yeah. Mr. Microwave. Killer chud."

Duck shrugged. "I haven't seen him, man."

"What's that in your pocket there?" Zil demanded. "He's got something in his pocket."

"What? Oh, it's nothing. It's—"

The baseball bat swung with unerring accuracy. Duck felt the blow on his hip where the relish hung in his jacket pocket. The soggy sound of wet glass shattering.

"Hey!" Duck yelled.

He started to push his way through them, but his feet wouldn't move. He looked down, uncomprehending, and saw that he had sunk up to his ankles in the sidewalk.

"Okay, stop making me mad," he cried desperately.

"Stop making me mad," Zil repeated in a taunting, sing-song voice.

"Hey, man, he's sinking!" one of them yelled.

Duck was up to mid-calf. Trapped. He met Zil's contemptuous gaze and pleaded, "Come on, man, why are you picking on me?"

"Because you're a subhuman moof," Zil said, adding, "duh."

"You want Hunter, right?" Duck asked. "He's in there, man, behind all this stuff."

"Is that so?" Zil said. He nodded to his gang, and all together they climbed into the rubble in search of their true prey. Someone, Duck didn't see who, smashed the stained glass fragment with his bat.

Duck took a deep breath. "Happy thoughts, happy thoughts," he whispered. He had stopped sinking, but he was still trapped. He squirmed his foot this way and that. Finally he pulled one foot free—minus the shoe. The other foot came out easier, and he managed to keep the shoe.

Duck took off at a run.

"Hey, get back here!"

"He lied, man, Hunter's not here!"

"Get him!"

Duck ran all-out, yelling, "Happy thoughts, happy thoughts, ah hah hah hah!" desperate to keep anger at bay, forcing his mouth into a grin.

He made it across the street. He was well out in front of the mob, but not far enough ahead that he would be able to get inside his house and lock the door before they caught him.

"Help! Someone help me!" he cried.

His next step landed hard.

The step after that broke the curb.

The third step plowed down through the sidewalk and he fell hard.

His chin hit concrete and crunched through it like a rock through glass.

He was falling into the earth again. Only this time he was facedown.

Zil and the others immediately surrounded him. A blow landed on his back. Another on his behind. Neither blow hurt. It was like they were hitting him with straws rather than bats. Then they could no longer reach him because he had fallen all the way through the cement and was sinking through the dirt.

"Scratch one chud," Duck heard Zil crow.

Then, "What happened, man?"

"All the lights went out," someone said, sounding scared.

There was a frightened curse, and the sound of running footsteps.

Duck Zhang, facedown in dirt, kept sinking.

Mary was lying in bed, in the dark, running her hands over her belly, feeling the fat there. Thinking, just a few more weeks of dieting, maybe. And then she'd be there. Wherever "there" was.

The water bottle beside her bed was empty. Mary climbed wearily from her bed. She opened the bathroom door and flipped on the light. For a moment she saw someone she did not recognize, someone with sunken cheeks and hollow eyes.

Then sudden, total darkness.

In the basement of town hall, in the gloomy space kids called the hospital, Dahra Baidoo held Josh's hand.

He wouldn't stop crying.

They'd brought him from the battle at the power plant. One of Edilio's soldiers had dropped him off.

"I want my mom, I want my mom." Josh was rocking back and forth, deaf to any words Dahra had, lost and ashamed.

"I want my mom," he cried.

"I just want my mom."

"I'll put on a DVD," Dahra said. She had no other solution. She'd seen kids like this before, too many to keep track of. Sometimes it was all just too much for some kids. They broke, like a stick bent too far. Snapped.

Dahra wondered how long it would be before she was one of them.

How long until she was holding herself and rocking and weeping for her mother?

Suddenly, the lights went out.

"I want my mom," Josh wept in the dark.

At the day care John Terrafino lay zoned out, one eye half open, watching a muted TV while he fed a bottle to a cranky ten-month-old. The bottle wasn't filled with milk or formula. It was filled with water mixed with oatmeal juice and a small amount of puréed fish.

None of the baby care books had recommended this. The baby was sick. Getting weaker every day. John doubted the baby, whose name was also John, would live very long.

"It's okay," he whispered.

The TV blinked off.

Astrid had gotten Little Pete to bed, finally. She was exhausted and worried. Her eye hurt where the baseball bat had caught her. She had a gruesome bruise in yellow and black. Ice had helped, but not much.

She needed to sleep; it was one in the morning, but it wasn't going to happen. Not yet. Not until she knew Sam was okay. She wished she could have gone to the power plant with him. Not that she would have been much help, but she would at least have known.

Strange how, in just three short months, Sam had come to feel like a necessary part of her life. More than that, even. A necessary part of *her*. An arm, a leg. A heart.

She heard a noise from the street. Running. She tensed, expecting to hear the pounding of feet on her porch. But no one approached.

Was it Hunter coming back? Or was Zil still running around looking for trouble? There wasn't anything she could do about it. She had no powers, or none that mattered, anyway. All she could do was threaten and cajole.

By the time she reached the window, the street was empty and quiet.

She hoped Hunter was hiding somewhere. They'd have to figure out what to do about that situation and it would be very tricky. Explosive, maybe. But it wasn't going to be solved tonight.

What was happening with Sam? Had he managed to stop Caine?

Was he hurt?

Was he dead?

God forbid, she prayed.

No. He wasn't dead. She would feel it if he was.

She wiped away a tear, and sighed. No way she could sleep. Not happening. So she sat herself down in front of the computer. Her hands were shaking as she touched the keyboard. She needed to do something useful. Something. Anything to keep from thinking about Sam.

At the bottom of the screen were the usual icons for Safari and Firefox. Web browsers that, when opened, would just remind her that she was not connected to the internet.

Astrid opened the mutation file. There were all the bizarre pictures. The cat that had melded with a book. The snakes with tiny wings. The seagulls with raptor talons. The zeke.

She opened a Word document and began to type.

> The one constant seems to be that mutations are making
> creatures—humans and nonhumans—more dangerous.
> The mutations are almost all in the form of weapons.

She paused and thought about that for a moment. That wasn't quite right. Some kids had developed powers that seemed to be essentially useless. The truth was, Sam wished more mutants had developed what he called "serious" powers. And there was Lana, whose gift was definitely not a weapon.

> Weapons or defense mechanisms. Of course it may be that I simply
> have not observed enough mutations to know. But it would not
> exactly be surprising if mutations tended to be survival mechanisms.
> That's the whole point of evolution: survival.

But was this evolution? Evolution was a series of hits and misses over the course of millions of years, not a sudden explosion of radical changes. Evolution built on existing DNA. What was happening in the FAYZ was a radical departure from the billion years' worth of code in animal DNA. There might be genes for speed, but there was no gene for teleportation, or for suspension of gravity, or for telekinesis.

There was no DNA for firing light from the palms of your hands.

The fact is, I don't

The screen went blank. The room was dark.

Astrid stood up and went to the window. She pulled back the curtains and looked out at total darkness. Not a light on in the street.

She let herself out onto the porch.

Darkness. Everywhere. Not a single light from the surrounding houses.

Someone a few doors down yelled in outrage, "Hey!"

Caine had reached the power plant. Sam had failed.

Astrid stifled a sob. If Sam was hurt . . . If . . .

Astrid felt fear like icy fingers reaching through her nightgown. She stumbled into the kitchen. She opened the junk drawer and found, after some searching, a flashlight. The light from it was faint and failed in seconds.

But in the few seconds of light she found a candle.

She tried to light it from the stove. But the gas ran unlit because it required electricity to fire.

Matches. A lighter. Surely there were some matches somewhere.

But there was no way to find them without light. She had a candle and no way to light it.

Astrid felt her way to the stairs and climbed to Little Pete's room. The Game Boy was beside his bed, where he always left it. If he woke up and found it missing, he would go nuts. He would . . . there was no telling what he would do.

She carried the Game Boy down the stairs and used the light from the LED to search the junk drawer. No matches, but there was a yellow Bic lighter.

She struck a flame and lit the candle.

She had avoided thinking about Sam for the last few moments, intent on her search. But there was no escaping the fact that Sam had rushed off to stop Caine. And he had not succeeded. The only question now was: Had he survived?

A line from an old poem bubbled up from Astrid's near-photographic memory. "The center cannot hold," she whispered to the eerily lit kitchen. The verse played in her head.

> *Things fall apart; the center cannot hold;*
> *Mere anarchy is loosed upon the world,*
> *The blood-dimmed tide is loosed, and everywhere*
> *The ceremony of innocence is drowned;*
> *The best lack all conviction, while the worst*
> *Are full of passionate intensity.*

"Things fall apart; the center cannot hold," Astrid repeated.

The center, maybe. But surely, even here in the FAYZ, God listened and watched over His children.

"Please let Sam be okay," she whispered to the candle.

She made the sign of the cross on her chest and knelt before the kitchen counter as if it were an altar.

"Saint Michael the Archangel, defend us in battle. Be our defense against the wickedness and snares of the devil."

In the old days when she had said this prayer, the devil was a creature with horns and a tail. Now in her mind the devil had the same face as Caine. And when the prayer went on to speak of "the evil spirits who prowl about the world seeking the ruin of souls," the picture in her mind's eye was of a dead-eyed boy with a snake for an arm.

TWENTY-SIX

"**WHAT IS IT** you want, Caine?" Sam's voice, calling from outside. He sounded angry, frustrated. Defeated.

Caine bowed his head. He savored the moment. Victory. Just four days had passed since he had regained some measure of control over himself. And now he had beaten Sam.

"Four days," he said, just loudly enough for those in the room to hear. "That's how long it took me to defeat Sam Temple." Caine locked eyes with Drake. "Four days," Caine sneered. "What did you accomplish in the three months I was sick?"

Drake met his gaze, then wavered, and looked down at the floor. There was red in his cheeks, a dangerous glitter in his eyes, but he could not meet Caine's triumphant scowl.

"Remember this when you finally decide it's time to take me on, Drake," Caine whispered.

Caine turned to the others and beamed happiness at his crew. Jack, still at the computer, a sloppy, bloody mess, but so engaged in his work that he was barely aware of what was going on. Bug, drifting in and out of view. Diana pretending to be unimpressed. He winked at her, knowing she wouldn't respond. Drake's two soldiers, lounging.

"What do I want?" Caine yelled back through the charred hole in the wall. Then, carefully enunciating each word for emphasis. "What. Do. I. Want?"

And then, Caine drew a blank. For a moment, just a moment before he recovered, he couldn't think of what he wanted. No one else heard the hesitation. But Caine felt it.

What *did* he want?

He searched for an answer and found one that would do. "You, Sam," Caine purred. "I want you to walk in here all by yourself. That's what I want."

The hostages, Mickey and Mike, looked at each other in disbelief. Caine could guess what they were thinking: their big hero, Sam, had failed.

Sam's voice was muffled but audible. "I would, Caine. To tell you the truth, it would probably be a relief." He sounded weary. He sounded beaten. Luscious, wonderful sounds to Caine's ears. "But we all know how you act when there's no one there to stop you. So, no."

Caine let out a loud, theatrical sigh. He smiled ear to ear. "Yeah, I thought you'd take that attitude, Sam. So I have an alternative. I have a trade in mind."

"Trade? What for what?"

"Food for light," Caine said. He put his hand to his ear as if listening. To Diana, he whispered, "Hear that? That's the sound of my brother realizing he's beaten. Realizing he just became my . . . what's a good word? Servant? Slave?"

Sam yelled, "Looks to me like you're the one in trouble, Caine."

Caine blinked. A warning light was flashing in the back of his mind. He had just made a mistake. He didn't know what, but he had made a mistake.

"Me?" Caine yelled. "I don't think so. I own the light switch, brother."

"Yeah, I guess you do," Sam shouted. "And I've got you surrounded. And if you're short on food up at Coates, my guess is you don't have a lot with you here. So I'm guessing you'll get hungry pretty soon."

Caine's smile froze.

"Well, there's an unexpected development," Diana said dryly.

Caine bit his thumbnail and yelled, "Hey, brother of mine, do I have to remind you that I have two of your people hostage in here?"

There was a long silence and Caine braced himself, thinking that Sam might launch another attack. Finally, Sam spoke. He sounded both more grim and more confident. "Go ahead, Caine, do whatever you want with the hostages. Then you won't have hostages anymore. And you'll still be hungry."

"You think I won't turn the hostages over to Drake?" Caine threatened. "You'll be able to listen to them scream." He could feel the color rising in his cheeks. He knew Sam's answer. It wasn't long in coming.

"Two seconds after I hear anyone yelling, in we come," Sam said. "It will be bloody, and I'd like to not have that. But you know I have enough people with enough power to do it."

Caine chewed his thumbnail. He glanced at Diana, willing her to have some solution, some helpful idea. He carefully avoided making eye contact with Drake.

"So, I have a better idea," Sam yelled. "How about I give you ten minutes to get out of there? And I give you my word you can go back to Coates."

Caine squeezed out a laugh that was half snarl. "Not happening, Sam. I'm holding this place. And you can go back to a very dark town."

There was no answer.

The silence was eloquent. Sam didn't need to say anything else. And Caine had nothing left to say. It felt as if there was a band tightening around his chest. Like he had to fight for each breath.

Something was not right. Something was very much not right. The fears that lived in his nightmares were rising now, like an incoming tide inside his head. He was in a trap.

"Stay tight," Drake muttered as his soldiers exchanged skeptical, worried looks.

Diana swiveled in her chair. "So what now, Fearless Leader? He's right: we don't have any food."

Caine winced. He ran a hand through his hair. His head felt hot.

He turned quickly, feeling as if someone was sneaking up behind him. No one there but the girl, Brittney, on the floor.

How had he not seen this coming? How had he not realized he would be trapped here? Even if he could somehow reach his people at Coates, they were far fewer in number than the number of kids Sam could command.

And none would come. Not here. Not with Sam surrounding the place.

Sam could have fifty people sitting outside the power plant within a few hours. And what could Caine do?

What could he *do*?

They had taken the power plant. They had turned off the lights in Perdido Beach. But now they were trapped. It was impossible.

Caine frowned, trying to concentrate. Why had he done it? In the space of a minute he had gone from crowing triumph to dismal humiliation.

What he had done? It made no sense. It gained him nothing. All he had thought was: Take the plant. Take it, and hold it. Then . . .

Then . . .

Caine felt himself sinking, mind swirling down and down as if a pit had opened beneath him.

The realization was sudden and sickening. He hadn't taken the power plant in order to get food for his people, or even to show his power over Sam. He hadn't been following his own desires at all.

Caine, the color all drained from his face now, stared at Drake.

"It's for him," Caine said. "It's all for him."

Drake narrowed his eyes, uncomprehending.

"He's hungry," Caine whispered. It hurt him to see the dawning realization in Diana's eyes as he said the words, "He's hungry in the dark."

"How do you know?" Drake demanded.

Caine spread his hands, helpless to explain. Words would not come.

"It's why he let me go," Caine said, more to himself than to Diana or Drake. "It's why he released me. For this."

"Are you telling me we're living out some fever dream of yours?" Diana was poised between laughing and crying, incredulous. "Are you telling me we did all this because that monster out in the desert is in your head?"

"What does he need us to do?" Drake asked, eager, not angry. A dog anxious to please his true master.

"We have to bring it to him. We have to feed him," Caine said.

"Feed him what?"

Caine sighed and looked at Jack. "The food that brings the light to his darkness. The same thing that brings light to Perdido Beach. The uranium."

Jack shook his head slowly, understanding but not wanting to understand. "Caine, how do we do that? How do we take uranium from the core? How do we move it for miles across the desert? It's heavy. It's dangerous. It's radioactive."

"Caine, this is crazy," Diana pleaded. "Drag radioactive uranium across the desert? How does this help you? How does this help any of us? What is the point?"

Caine hesitated. He frowned. She was right. Why should he serve the Darkness? Let the creature feed itself. Caine had problems of his own, his own needs, his own—

A roar so loud, it seemed to vibrate the walls, filled the room. It knocked Caine to his knees. He clapped his hands over his ears, trying to block it out, but it went on and on, as he cringed and covered himself and fought the sudden desire to void his bowels.

It stopped. The silence rang.

Slowly Caine opened his eyes. Diana looked at him like he had gone crazy. Drake stared incredulous, on the edge of laughing. Jack merely looked worried.

They hadn't heard it. That inhuman, irresistible roar had been for Caine alone.

Punishment. The gaiaphage would be obeyed.

"What is going on with you?" Diana asked.

Drake narrowed his eyes and smirked openly. "It's the Darkness. Caine is no longer running things. There's a new boss."

Diana gave voice to Caine's own thoughts.

"Poor Caine," she said. "You poor, screwed-up boy."

For Lana each step seemed too loud, like she was walking on a giant bass drum. Her legs were stiff, knees welded solid. Her feet felt each pebble as though she were barefoot.

Her heart pounded so hard, it seemed the whole world must be able to hear it.

No, no, it was just her imagination. There was no sound

but the soft cornflake crunch of sneakers on gravel. Her heart beat for her ears only. She was no louder than a mouse.

But she was convinced it could hear her. Like an owl listening and watching for prey in the night, it watched and it waited, and all her stealth was like a brass band to it, him, the thing, the Darkness.

The moon was out. Or what passed for the moon. The stars shone. Or something very like stars. Silvery light illuminated tips of brush, the seams of a boulder, and cast deep shadows everywhere else.

Lana picked her way along, holding herself tight. The gun was in her right hand, hanging by her side, brushing against her thigh. A flashlight—off for now—stuck up from her pocket.

You think you own me. You think you control me. No one owns me. No one controls me.

Two points of light winked in the shadows ahead.

Lana froze.

The twin lights stared at her. They did not move.

Lana raised the gun and took aim. She aimed at the space directly between the two points of light.

The explosion lit up the night for a split second.

In that flash she saw the coyote.

Then it was gone and her ears were ringing.

From back down the trail she heard a wooden door creaking, slamming. Cookie's voice. "Lana! Lana!"

"I'm okay, Cookie. Get back inside. Lock the door! Do it!" she yelled.

She heard the door slam.

"I know you're out there, Pack Leader," Lana said. "I'm not so helpless this time."

Lana started moving again. The explosion, the bullet—which almost certainly had missed its target—had settled her down. She knew now that the mutant coyote leader was there, watching. She was sure the Darkness also knew.

Good. Fine. Better. No more sneaking. She could march to the mine and take the key from the corpse. And then march back to the building where Cookie waited with Patrick.

The gun felt good in her hand.

"Come on, Pack Leader," she purred. "Not scared of a bullet, are you?"

But her bravado faded as she drew near the mine entrance. The moonlight painted the crossbeam above the entrance with faintest silver. Below it a black mouth waiting greedily to swallow her up.

Come to me.

Imagination. There was no voice.

I have need of you.

Lana clicked the flashlight on and aimed the beam at the mouth of the cave. She might as well have pointed it at the night sky. The beam illuminated nothing.

Flashlight in her left hand. Pistol heavy in her right. The smell of cordite from the shot she'd fired. The crunch of gravel. Limbs heavy. Mind in something like a dream-state now, all focus narrowed down to a simple task.

She reached the mine shaft entrance. There above it,

perched on the narrow ledge, stood Pack Leader snarling down at her.

She aimed her flashlight and swung the pistol to follow the beam, but the coyote darted away.

He's not trying to stop me, Lana realized. He's just observing. The eyes and ears of the Darkness.

Into the mine entrance. The beam searched and stopped when it found the object.

The face was like a shrunken head, yellow skin taut against bones that waited patiently to emerge. The rough, patched denim seemed almost new by comparison with the ancient-looking mummy flesh and sere-grass hair.

Lana knelt beside him. "Hey, Jim," she said.

She now had to choose between the gun and the light. She laid the gun on Jim's collapsed chest.

She found his right front pocket. Wrangler jeans. The pocket loose. Easy enough to reach in. But the pocket was empty. She could reach the hip pocket easily enough as well, but it was also empty.

"Sorry about this." She seized the waist of his jeans and rolled him toward her, exposing the other hip pocket. The body moved oddly, too light, too easily shifted, so much weight evaporated.

Empty.

"Human dead."

She knew the voice instantly. It wasn't a voice you ever forgot. It was Pack Leader's slurred, high-pitched snarl.

"Yes, I noticed," Lana said. She was proud of the calmness

of her tone. Inside, the panic was threatening to engulf her, just one pocket left, and if the keys weren't there?

"Go to the Darkness," Pack Leader said.

He was a dozen feet away, poised, ready. Could she reach the gun before Pack Leader could reach her?

"The Darkness told me to pick this guy's pockets," Lana said. "The Darkness says he wants gum. Thinks maybe Jim has a pack."

During her time as Pack Leader's captive, Lana had come to respect the coyote leader's ruthless determination, his cunning, his power. But not his intelligence. He was, despite the mutation that allowed speech, a coyote. His frame of reference was hunting rodents and dominating his pack.

Lana shoved the corpse away from her, rolling it back to reveal the remaining pocket. The gun clattered onto the rock, Hermit Jim between Lana and the weapon.

No chance now that she could reach it before Pack Leader could reach her.

Lana fumbled for and found the pocket.

Inside, something cold and hard-edged.

She drew the keys out, squeezed them tight in her fist, then thrust them into her own pocket.

Lana leaned out over poor, dead Jim and swept the flashlight until she found the gun.

Pack Leader growled deep in his throat.

"The Darkness asked for it," she said.

Her fingers closed on it. Slowly, knees creaking, she stood up.

"I forgot. I have to get something," she said. She walked directly toward the coyote.

But this was too much for Pack Leader.

"Go to Darkness, human."

"Go to hell, coyote," Lana answered. She did not move the light, did not telegraph her move, just snapped the gun up and fired.

Once. Twice. Three times. BangBangBang!

Each shot was a bolt of lightning. Like a strobe light.

There was an entirely satisfying coyote yelp of pain.

In the strobe she saw Pack Leader leap. Saw him land hard, far short of his objective.

She was past him and running now, running blind and heedless down the path and as she ran she screamed. But not in terror.

Lana screamed in defiance.

She screamed in triumph.

She had the key.

TWENTY-SEVEN

BRIANNA WOKE.

It took a while for her to make sense of where she was.

Then the pain reminded her. Pain all down her left arm, left hip, left calf, left ankle.

She had been wearing a denim jacket over a T-shirt, shorts, and sneakers. The hoodie was burned away on her left shoulder and arm, a skid burn. A three-inch oval was gone from her shorts on the same side.

The skin beneath was bloody. She had hit the roof at high speed. The concrete had been like sandpaper.

It hurt amazingly.

She was on her back. Staring up at the bogus stars. Her head hurt. Her palms were scraped raw but nowhere near the scraped-to-the-meat injuries on her side.

Brianna picked herself up, gasping from the pain. It was like she was on fire. She looked, expecting almost to see actual flames.

It was scary bright on the roof of the power plant. So she could see the wounds all too clearly. The blood looked blue in the fluorescent light. Her injuries weren't life-threatening, she reassured herself, she wasn't going to die. But oh, man, it hurt and it was going to keep on hurting.

"Happens when you slam concrete at a couple hundred miles an hour," she told herself. "I should wear a helmet and leathers. Like motorcycle guys."

That thought offered a welcome distraction. She spent a few seconds contemplating a sort of superhero outfit for herself. Helmet, black leather, some lightning-bolt decals. Definitely.

It could have been worse, she told herself. It would have been worse if she were anyone else on earth, because when she had hit the deck her body wanted to go tumbling out of control. That would have broken her arms and legs and head.

But she was the Breeze, not anyone else. She'd had the speed to slam palms and feet against concrete fast enough— barely—to turn a deadly tumble into an extremely painful skid.

She limped at regular speed over toward the edge of the roof. But the way the building was constructed the edges sloped away, round-shouldered, rather than forming a nice, neat ninety-degree angle. So she couldn't see straight down, though she could see the gate and the parking lot, all blazing bright. Beyond, the dark mountains, the darker sea.

"Well, this was a stupid idea," Brianna admitted.

She had attempted to fly. That was the fact of it. She had

tried to translate her great speed into a sort of bounding, leaping version of flight.

It had made perfect sense at the time. Sam had ordered her not to enter the power plant's control room. But by the same token she had to try to get the lay of the land, to see where all of Caine's people might be positioned. She'd thought: What would be better than the view from on top of the turbine building?

She'd been toying for a long time with the idea of flying. She'd worked out the basic concept, which amounted to running real fast, leaping onto something a little high, then jumping to something higher still. It wasn't rocket science. It was no different from leaping from rock to rock while crossing a stream. Or perhaps like taking a set of stairs two at a time.

Only in this case the "stairs" had been a parked minivan, and a low administrative building, with the final "step" being the turbine structure itself.

The first two steps had worked fine. She had accelerated to perhaps three hundred miles an hour, leaped, slammed off the roof of the minivan, landed on the admin building, kept almost all of her speed, taken six blistering steps to regain whatever speed she'd lost, and made the jump to the roof of the massive concrete hulk.

And that's when things had gone wrong.

She was just short of landing on the flat part of the roof and instead hit the shoulder. It was more like belly-flopping than it was the sort of airplane-landing-on-runway situation she was looking for.

She'd seen the concrete rushing up at her. She'd motored her feet like crazy. She'd managed to avoid sliding off and falling all the way to the ground, but her desperate lunge had ended with an out-of-control impact that had come very close to killing her.

And now, now, having reached this perch, she couldn't actually see much of anything.

"Sam is going to kill me," Brianna muttered.

Then, as she bent a knee, "Ow."

The roof was a few hundred feet long, one third as wide. She trotted—slowly—from one end to the other. She found the access door easily, a steel door set in a brick superstructure. This would lead down to the turbine room and from there to the control room.

"Well, of course there would be a door," Brianna muttered. "I guess I should pretend that was my plan right from the start."

She tried the doorknob. It was locked. It was very locked.

"Okay, that sucks," Brianna said.

She was desperately thirsty. Even more desperately hungry. Thirst and hunger were often extreme after she had turned on the speed. She doubted she'd find any food up on this roof the size of a parking lot. Maybe water, though. There were massive air conditioners, each the size of a suburban home. Didn't air conditioning always create condensation?

She zipped at a moderate speed over to the closest AC unit, ow, ow, owing as she ran. Brianna let herself in. Found a light switch. Her heart leaped when she spotted the Dunkin'

Donuts box. In a flash she was there. But there was nothing inside but some tissue paper smeared with the crusty remains of pink icing and a half dozen brightly colored sprinkles.

Brianna licked the paper. It had been so long since she'd tasted anything sweet. But the result was just a sharpening of the pain in her stomach.

She found what she hoped was a water pipe, white plastic. She looked around for a tool and found a small steel box containing a few wrenches and a screwdriver. In seconds she had popped the pipe and was filling her stomach with ice cold water. Then she let the water pour over the burns on her skin and cried out at the agony of it.

She next carried the screwdriver—it was large and heavy—to the steel door. She inserted it into the gap between the handle and the frame and pushed. There was no give. Not even a little.

In frustration she stabbed at the door. The screwdriver made a spark and a scratch. Nothing more.

"Great. I'm trapped on the roof," she said.

Brianna knew she needed medical attention. A visit with Lana would be great. Failing that, she needed bandages and antibiotics.

But all of that was nothing compared to the hunger. Now that the adrenaline rush was wearing off, the hunger was attacking her with the ferocity of a lion. She had started the night hungry. But then she had run perhaps twenty-five miles. On a very empty stomach.

It was a ridiculous situation to be in. No one knew she was

up here. She probably couldn't yell loud enough to make herself heard over the noise of the plant. Even if she could, she probably wouldn't want to because if Sam had failed, somehow, then the guy who heard her would be Caine.

Then she spotted the pigeon.

"Oh, my God," Brianna whispered. "No."

Then, "Why not?"

"Because, ewww."

"Look, it's no different from a chicken."

She retrieved the donut box. She tore the paper into little strips. She found an ancient newspaper and tore it up as well. She found a wooden pallet and with a saw from the toolkit, and superhuman speed, she soon had a small pile of wood.

It was unfortunate that none of the workmen had left matches behind. But steel struck with super speed against cement made sparks fly. It was tedious work, but she soon had a fire going. A cheerful little fire in the middle of the vast roof.

And now there were two pigeons, dozing and cooing in their sleep. One was gray, the other kind of pink.

"Pink," she decided.

The chances of a regular kid catching them was close to zero. But she was not a normal person. She was the Breeze.

The pigeon never had time to flinch. She grabbed it, hand around its golf ball head. She swung it hard, snapping its neck.

Two minutes in the fire burned off most of the feathers. Five minutes more and the bird burst open.

That was the end of her patience. She used the screwdriver to pry slivers of meat from the pigeon's plump breast and pop them into her mouth.

It had been weeks since she had tasted anything half as good.

"The Breeze," she said, squatting by her fire. "Scourge of pigeons."

She lay back, savoring her meal.

In a minute she would get up and figure out how to escape this rooftop trap.

But with food in her stomach the weariness of a day spent running at insane speeds over insane distances caught up with her.

"I'm just going to rest my . . ."

Duck sank, facedown, mouth full of dirt and rock.

He was choking, gagging. No way to breathe.

His head was pounding. Blood pounding in his ears. His chest heaved, sucking desperately on nothing.

It was over.

He was going to die.

Wild with panic, he thrashed. His arms plowed through packed dirt with no more effort than if he had been swimming in water.

He was no longer acting consciously, legs and arms kicking in a sort of death spasm as his brain winked out and his lungs screamed.

"Duck! Duck! You down there?"

A voice from a million miles away.

Duck tried to sit up, very quickly. He had managed to turn himself over. But his head slammed into dirt, and he took a shower of gravel in the face for his efforts. He tried to open his eyes, but dirt filled them. He spit dirt out of his mouth and found that he could breathe. His thrashing had made a space for him.

"Duck! Dude! Are you alive?"

Duck wasn't sure he knew the answer. He cautiously moved his arms and legs and found that he could, within limits.

Sudden, overwhelming panic. He was buried alive!

He tried to scream, but the sound was choked off and now he was falling again, falling through the earth.

No. No. No.

He had to stop. Had to stop the anger.

It was the anger that had sent him plummeting toward the center of the earth.

Think of something not angry, not fearful, he ordered himself.

Something happy.

Buried alive!

Happy . . . happy . . . the swimming pool . . . the water . . . floating . . .

Duck stopped sinking.

That was good. Good! Happy. Floating. Happy, happy thoughts.

Cookies. He liked cookies. Cookies were great.

And . . . and . . . and Sarah Willetson that time she smiled at him. That was nice. That had given him a nice, warm feeling, like maybe someday girls would like him.

Also, how about watching TV, watching basketball on TV? That was a happy thought.

He was definitely no longer sinking.

No problem. Just be happy. Be happy to be buried alive.

"Duck?" It was Hunter's voice calling down to him. It sounded like Hunter was at the bottom of a well. Of course it was the other way around: Duck was at the bottom of the well.

"Happy, happy," Duck whispered.

He was not buried alive, he was sitting down in the movie theater. He was in the seats with the railing right in front where he could rest his feet. And he had popcorn. Buttered, of course, extra salt. And a box of Cookie Dough Bites.

Previews. He loved the previews. Previews and popcorn and oh, look, there was a Slushee in the seat's cup holder. Blue, whatever flavor that was supposed to be. Blue Slushee.

What was the movie? *Iron Man*.

He loved *Iron Man*.

And Slushees. Popcorn. Swimming pools. Girls.

Something was scraping against his face, against his arms and legs and chest.

Don't think about that, it might make you unhappy and mad, and boy, those are not helpful emotions. They drag you down.

Way down.

Duck laughed at that.

"Duck. Dude." Hunter's voice. It sounded closer now, clearer. Was he watching *Iron Man*, too?

No, Sarah Willetson was. Sarah was sitting beside him, sharing his popcorn and oh, excellent, she had a bag of peanut M&M's. She was pouring some into his hand. Happy little football shapes in bright colors.

The scraping had stopped.

"Dude?"

The voice was close now.

Duck felt a breeze.

He opened his eyes. There was still dirt in his eyes. He brushed it away. The first thing he saw was Hunter. Hunter's head.

The *top* of Hunter's head.

Slowly Hunter's face turned up toward him with an expression of pure awe.

"Dude, you're flying," Hunter said.

Duck glanced around. He was no longer buried alive. He was out of the hole. He was across the street from the church, out of the hole, and floating about five feet in the air.

"Whoa," Duck said. "It works both ways."

"We should just get out. Take Sam's deal. Walk away," Diana was saying.

"I'm in the root directory," Jack was saying.

Brittney knew she should be in pain. Her body was a wreck. She knew that. Her legs were broken. The control room door, blown from its hinges, had done that. She knew she should be in agony. She wasn't.

She should be dead. At least one bullet had hit her.

But she wasn't dead. Not quite.

So much blood, all around her. More than enough to kill her. Had to be.

And yet . . .

"No one's leaving," Caine said.

It was like being in a dream. Things that she should feel, she didn't. It was like the way sometimes, in a dream—cause and effect went backward, or sideways, things not making sense.

"We have no food," Diana said.

"Maybe I could go for some," Bug said.

"Yeah, right. Like you'd come back here if you found any," Drake sneered. "We're not here to feed ourselves. We're here to feed him."

"Do you capitalize it when you say 'him,' Drake?" Diana's sarcasm was savage. "Is he your god now?"

"He gave me this!" Drake said. Brittney heard a loud crack, the bullwhip sound of Drake's arm.

With infinite caution, Brittney tested her body. No, she could not move her legs. She could only rotate one hip, and that only a little.

Her right arm was useless. Her left arm, though, worked.

I should be dead, Brittney thought. I should be with Tanner in Heaven.

I should be dead.

Maybe you are.

No. Not before Caine, Brittney thought.

She wondered if she had become a healer, like Lana. Everyone knew the story of how Lana had discovered her power. But Lana had been in terrible pain. And Brittney was not.

Still, she focused her thoughts, imagined her useless right arm healing. She concentrated all her mind on that.

"Trapped," Diana said bitterly.

"Not for long. We bust out of here and bring him what he needs," Drake said.

"Gaiaphage. That's what Caine calls it when he's ranting," Diana said. "Shouldn't you know your god's name?"

Brittney did not feel any change in her arm.

A terrible suspicion came to her. There was an awful silence from within her own body. She listened. Strained to hear, to feel, the ever-present thump . . . thump . . .

Her heart. It was not beating.

"Gaiaphage?" Jack said, sounding interested. "A 'phage' is another word for a computer virus. A worm, actually."

Her heart wasn't beating.

She wasn't alive.

No, that was wrong, she told herself. Dead things don't hear. Dead things cannot move their one good hand, squeezing the fingers ever so slightly so no one would notice.

There could be only one explanation. Caine and Drake had killed her. But Jesus had not taken her up into Heaven to be reunited with her brother. Instead, He had granted her this power. To live, still, a while, though she was dead.

To live long enough to accomplish His will.

"A phage is code. Software that sort of eats other software," Jack said in his pedantic way.

Brittney had no doubt what God had chosen her to do. Why He had kept her alive.

She could still see, barely, though one eye was obscured. She could see across the floor to where Mike had left the pistol, just the way she had told him to.

She would have to move with infinite patience. Millimeter by millimeter. Imperceptible movements of her hip and arm. The gun was underneath the table, far in a corner, seven, eight feet away.

Satan walked the earth in this evil trinity of Caine, Drake, and Diana. And Brittney had been chosen to stop them.

Watch me, Tanner, she prayed silently. I'm going to make you proud.

Quinn and Albert were silent as they drove back to Perdido Beach.

The truck was heavier by many pounds of gold.

Lighter by two kids and a dog.

Finally Quinn spoke. "We have to tell Sam."

"About the gold?" Albert asked.

"Look, man, we lost the Healer."

Albert hung his head. "Yeah."

"Sam has to know that. Lana's important."

"I know that," Albert snapped. "I said that."

"She's more important than some stupid gold."

For a long time Albert didn't respond. Then, finally, "Look,

Quinn, I know what you think. Same as everyone else. You
think I'm just all about me. You think I'm just into being
greedy or whatever."

"Aren't you?"

"No. Well, maybe," Albert admitted. "Okay, maybe I want
to be important. Maybe I want to have a lot of stuff and be in
charge and all that."

Quinn snorted. "Yeah. Maybe."

"But that doesn't make me wrong, Quinn."

Quinn didn't have anything to say to that. He was sick at
heart. He would be blamed for losing Lana Arwen Lazar. The
Healer. The irreplaceable Healer. Sam would be disgusted
with him. Astrid would give him one of her cold, disappointed looks.

He should have stuck to fishing. He liked that. Fishing. It
was peaceful. He could be alone and not be bothered. Now,
even that was ruined with him having Albert's guys working
under him. Having to train them, supervise them.

Sam was going to blow up. Or else just borrow Astrid's
cold, disappointed look.

They bounced out onto the highway.

"The streetlights are out," Albert said.

"It's almost morning," Quinn said. "Maybe they're on a
timer."

"No, man. They aren't on a timer."

They reached the edge of Perdido Beach. It began to dawn
on Quinn that something very big was very wrong. Maybe
even something bigger and wronger than losing the Healer.

"Everything's dark," Quinn said.

"Something's happened," Albert agreed.

They drove down pitch-black streets to the plaza. It was eerie. Like the whole town had died. Quinn wondered if that's what had happened. He wondered if the FAYZ was in some new phase. Just he and Albert left, now.

Quinn pulled the truck up in front of the McDonald's.

But just as Quinn was pulling up to park, he spotted something. He turned the truck around to aim the headlights at town hall.

There, spread across one wall, in letters two feet tall, was spray-painted graffiti. Bloodred paint on the pale stone.

"'Death to freaks,'" Quinn read aloud.

TWENTY-EIGHT

THE PICKUP TRUCK'S battery was dead. It had been sitting for more than three months.

But Hermit Jim was a prepared guy. There was a gasoline-powered generator and a charger for the battery. It took an hour for Lana and Cookie to figure out how to start the generator and hook up the battery. But finally Lana turned the key and after several attempts the engine sputtered to life.

Cookie backed the truck up to the gas tank.

It took some hard, sweaty work to shift the tank into the truck's bed.

By the time they were done, so was the night. Lana cautiously opened the warehouse's door and looked outside. In the shadow of the hills it wasn't possible to speak of true dawn, but the sky was tinged with pink, and the shadows, still deep, were gray and no longer black.

A dozen coyotes lounged in an irregular circle, a hundred feet away. They turned to stare at her.

"Cookie," Lana said.

"Yeah, Healer?"

"Here's what I want you to do. I'm taking the truck, right? You should hear an explosion. Wait ten minutes after that. I'll be back. Maybe. If not, well, you need to wait until the sun is all the way up—coyotes are more dangerous at night. Then walk back to the cabin, and from there head home."

"I'm staying with you," Cookie said firmly.

"No." She said it with all the finality she could manage. "This is my thing. You do what I say."

"I ain't leaving you to those dogs."

Lana said, "The coyotes won't be the problem. And you have to leave. I'm telling you to. Either the explosion happens or it doesn't. Either way, if I don't come back, I need you to get to Sam. Give him the letter."

"I want to take care of you, Healer. Like you took care of me."

"I know, Cookie," Lana said. "But this is how you do it. Okay? Sam needs to know what happened. Tell him everything we did. He's a smart guy, he'll understand. And tell him not to blame Quinn, okay? Not Quinn's fault. I would have figured out some other way to do it if Quinn and Albert hadn't helped."

"Healer . . ."

Lana put her hand on Cookie's beefy arm. "Do what I ask, Cookie."

Cookie hung his head. He was weeping openly, unashamed. "Okay, Healer."

"Lana," she corrected him gently. "My name is Lana. That's what my friends call me."

She knelt down and ruffled Patrick's fur the way he liked. "Love you, boy," she whispered. She hugged him close and he whimpered. "You'll be okay. Don't worry. I'll be right back."

Quickly, before she could lose her resolve, she climbed into the truck. She fired up the engine and nodded to Cookie.

Cookie swung open the creaking door of the warehouse.

The waiting coyotes got to their feet. Pack Leader ambled forward, uncertain. He was limping. The fur of one shoulder was soggy with blood.

"So, I didn't kill you," Lana whispered. "Well, the day is young."

She put the truck into the lowest gear and took her foot off the brake. The truck began to creep forward.

Slow and steady, that would be the way, Lana knew. The pathway to the mine entrance was a mess of potholes, narrow, crooked, and steep.

She turned the wheel. It wasn't easy. The truck was old and stiff with disuse. And Lana's driving experience was extremely limited.

The truck advanced so slowly that the coyotes could keep up at a walk. They fell into place around her, almost like an escort.

The truck lurched crazily as she pulled onto the path. "Slow, slow," she told herself. But now she was in a hurry. She wanted it to be over.

She had an image in her mind. Red and orange erupting

from the mouth of the mine. Debris flying. A thunderclap. And then the sound of collapsing rock. Tons and tons and tons of it. Then billowing dust and smoke and it would be over.

Come to me.

"Oh, I'm coming," Lana said.

I have need of you.

She was going to silence that voice. She was going to bury it beneath a mountain.

There was a sudden jolt. Lana glanced into her mirror and saw the deformed, scarred face of Pack Leader. He had jumped into the back of the truck.

"Human not bring machine," Pack Leader said in his unique snarl.

"Human do whatever she likes," Lana yelled back. "Human shoot you in your ugly face, you stinking, stupid *dog*."

Pack Leader digested that for a while.

The truck lurched and wallowed and crept up the hillside. More than halfway now.

Come to me.

"You're going to be sorry you invited me," Lana muttered. But now, with the mine shaft entrance in view, she found she could scarcely breathe for the pounding in her chest.

"Human get out. Human walk," Pack Leader demanded.

Lana couldn't shoot him. That would break the window behind her and that would allow the coyotes to come at her.

She had reached the entrance.

She put the truck into reverse. She would have to turn the

truck around. Her hands were white, tendons straining, as she gripped the steering wheel.

Pack Leader's evil face was in her way as she turned to check her backward course. He was inches away, separated by nothing but a pane of glass.

He lunged.

"Ahh!"

His snout hit the glass. The glass held.

Lana was sure the glass would hold. The coyotes had not yet grown hands or learned to use tools. All they could do was bang their snouts into the glass.

You are mine.

"No," Lana said. "I belong to me."

The bed of the truck crossed the threshold into the mine. Now the coyotes were getting frantic. A second coyote leaped and landed on the hood. He got the windshield wiper in his teeth and ripped savagely at it.

"Human, stop!" Pack Leader demanded.

Lana drove the truck backward. The back wheels rolled up and over the mummified corpse of the truck's owner.

The truck was all the way inside now, as far as it would go. The mine shaft ceiling was mere inches above the cab. The walls were close. The truck was like a loose cork in the shaft. The coyotes, feeling the walls closing in, had to decide whether to be trapped by the truck. They opted to slither out of the way, back to the front of the truck where they took turns leaping on and off the hood, snarling, snapping, scrabbling impotently at the windshield with their rough paws.

The truck stopped moving, held tight. The doors would no longer open.

That was fine. That was the plan.

Lana twisted around in her seat, aimed carefully to avoid hitting the big tank in the back, and fired a single shot.

The rear window shattered into a million pieces.

Shaking with fear and excitement Lana crawled gingerly out of the cab into the bed of the truck. This excited the coyotes even more. They tried to shove themselves through the gap between the sides of the truck and the mine shaft walls, trying to get at her. One furious head jammed sideways between roof and a crossbeam.

They yapped and snarled and Pack Leader cried, "Human, stop!"

Lana reached the valve of the LPG tank. She twisted it open. Immediately she smelled the rotten-egg odor of the gas.

It would take a while for the gas to drain out. It was heavier than air, so it would roll down the sloping floor of the mine shaft, like an invisible flood. It would sink toward the deepest part of the mine. It would pool around the Darkness.

Would he smell it? Would he know that she had sealed his fate? Did he even have a nose?

Lana paid out the fuse she'd made. It was a hundred feet of thin rope she'd soaked in gasoline. She'd kept it in a Ziploc bag.

She took a coil and tossed it into the dark of the mine. It didn't have to reach far.

She carried the rest with her, back into the cabin of the

truck. She stepped on the brake, turning on the brake lights and illuminating the shaft in hellish red. It was impossible to see the gas, of course.

Lana waited, hands gripping the steering wheel. Her thoughts were a jumble of disconnected images, wild jump-cuts of her captivity with the coyotes and her encounters with the Darkness.

The first time she had—

I am the Gaiaphage.

Lana froze.

You cannot destroy me.

Lana could barely breathe. She thought she might pass out. The Darkness had never before spoken its name.

I brought you here.

Lana reached into her pocket and fingered the lighter. It was simple physics. The lighter would light. The gasoline-soaked rope would burn. The flame would race down the rope until it reached the gas vapor.

The gas would ignite.

The explosion would shatter the ceiling and walls of the shaft.

It might even incinerate the creature.

It might kill her, too. But if she survived, she would be able to heal any burns or injuries. That was her bet: if she could simply stay alive for a few minutes, she would be able to heal herself.

And then she would be truly healed. The voice in her head would be gone.

You do my will.

"I am Lana Arwen Lazar," she cried with all the shrill force she could manage.

"My dad was into comic books, so he named me Lana for Superman's girlfriend Lana Lang."

You will serve me.

"And my mom added Arwen for the elf princess in *The Lord of the Rings*."

I will use your power as my own.

"And I never, ever do what I'm told."

Your power will give me shape. I will feed. Grow strong again. And with the body I will form using your power, I will escape this place.

Your power will give me freedom.

Lana was shaking. The gasoline smelled, and the fumes were making her woozy.

Now or never. Now.

Never.

"Pack Leader!" Lana shouted. "Pack Leader! I'm going to blow this mine to hell, Pack Leader. Do you hear me?"

"Pack Leader hears," the coyote sneered.

"You get yourself and your filthy animals out of here or you'll die with the Darkness."

Pack Leader leaped heavily onto the hood. His fur was up, the ripped mouth slavering. "Pack Leader fears no human."

Lana snapped the pistol up and fired. Point-blank range.

The sound was stunning.

In the glass there was a hole surrounded by a star pattern, but the glass did not blow out like the rear window had.

Blood sprayed across the glass.

Pack Leader yelped and jumped clumsily from the hood, hit. Hurt.

Lana's heart jumped. She'd hit him. A solid, direct hit this time.

But the glass was still there. It was supposed to shatter. It was her only escape route.

Your power will give me freedom.

"I'll give you death!" Lana raged.

Lana took the pistol and used it like a hammer, beating on the glass, breaking it out, but only a little at a time. She kicked at it, frantic. It gave, but too slowly.

The coyotes could take her if they made a concerted attack.

But the coyotes held off. The injury of their leader had left them confused and rudderless.

Lana kicked, crazy now, panicked.

You will die.

"As long as you die with me!" Lana screamed.

A big section of the safety glass gave way, folding out like a stiff-frozen blanket.

Lana began pushing through. Head. Shoulders.

A coyote lunged.

She fired.

She pushed the rest of the way out, scratched, skin ripped, oblivious to the pain. On hands and knees on the hood. She had to fumble for the rope. Rope in one hand, greasy. Gun in the other, stinking of cordite.

She fired wildly. Once, twice, three times, bullets chipping rock. The coyotes broke and ran.

She laid the pistol on the hood.

She fumbled the lighter from her pocket.

No.

She struck the lighter.

The flame was tiny and orange.

You will not.

Lana brought the flame toward the rope's end.

Stop.

Lana hesitated.

"Yes," Lana breathed.

You can not.

"I can," Lana sobbed.

You are mine.

The flame burned her thumb. But the pain was nothing, nothing next to the sudden, catastrophic pain like an explosion in her head.

Lana cried out.

She clasped her hands over her ears. The lighter singed her hair.

She dropped the rope.

She dropped the lighter.

Lana had never imagined such pain. As if her brain had been scooped out and her skull filled with burning, white-hot coals.

Lana screamed in agony and rolled off the hood.

She screamed and screamed and knew that she would never stop.

TWENTY-NINE

"**WE CAN WAIT** him out," Edilio said to Sam. "Just sit tight here. You could even catch a few Zs."

"Do I look that bad?" Sam asked. Edilio didn't answer.

"Edilio's right, boss," Dekka said. "Let's just sit tight and wait. Maybe Brianna will . . ." She couldn't finish, and turned away quickly.

Edilio put his arm around Sam's shoulders and drew him away from Dekka, who was now sobbing.

Sam gazed up at the massive pile of cement and steel that was the power plant. He scanned the parking lot, looking past the parked cars to the sea beyond. The black water twinkled here and there, faint pinpoints of starlight, a rough-textured reflection of the night sky.

"When's your birthday, Edilio?"

"Cut it out, man. You know I'm not stepping out," Edilio said.

"You don't even consider it?"

Edilio's silence was answer enough.

"Where's this all end, Edilio? Or does it never end? How many more of these fights? How many more graves in the plaza? You ever think about it?"

"Sam, I dig those graves," Edilio said quietly.

"Yeah," Sam said. "Sorry." He sighed. "We're not winning. You know that, right? I don't mean this fight. I mean the big fight. Survival. We're not winning that fight. We're starving. Kids eating their pets. We're breaking up into little groups that hate each other. It's all going out of control."

Edilio glanced at Howard, who was a discreet distance away but listening in. Two of Edilio's guys were within earshot as well.

"You need to cut this out, Sam," Edilio said in an urgent whisper. "These people are all looking to you, man. You can't be talking about how we're screwed."

Sam barely heard him. "I need to get back to town."

"What? Are you messing with me? We're kind of in the middle of something here."

"Dekka can keep an eye on Caine. Besides, if he busts out, that's good, right?" Sam nodded as if he had convinced himself. "I need to see Astrid."

"You know, maybe that's not a bad idea," Edilio said. He left Sam and went to Dekka, drew her aside, and spoke urgently to her. Dekka shot a tear-stained glance at Sam, worried.

"Come on, I'll drive you back to town," Edilio said.

Sam followed him to the Jeep. "What did you tell Dekka?"

"I told her with the lights out, you needed to check on what's happening in town."

"She buy that?" Sam asked.

Edilio didn't answer directly. And he didn't look Sam in the eye. "She's tough. Dekka will handle things here."

They drove in silence to Perdido Beach.

The plaza was full of kids milling around. That many kids hadn't been together in one place since the Thanksgiving feast.

Sam felt a hundred pairs of eyes on him as he pulled up with Edilio.

"This doesn't look like a fiesta," Edilio said.

Astrid came out of the crowd, ran to the car, and threw her arms around Sam. She kissed him on the cheek, and then on the lips.

He buried his face in her hair and whispered, "Are you okay?"

"Better now that I know you're alive," Astrid said. "We have some very scared, angry kids here, Sam."

As if she had given a cue, the crowd rushed forward to surround the three of them.

"The lights are out!"

"Where have you been?"

"We're out of food!"

"I can't even turn on the TV!"

"I'm scared of the dark!"

"There's a mutant freak murderer running loose!"

"The water isn't working!"

Those that weren't shouting accusations were asking plaintive questions.

"What are we supposed to do?"

"Why didn't you stop Caine?"

"Where's the Healer?"

"Are we all going to die?"

Sam pushed Astrid gently, reluctantly away and stood alone to face them. Each question hit home. Each was an arrow aimed at his heart. They were the same accusations he had thrown at himself. The same questions he had asked himself. He knew he should put an end to it. He knew he should call for quiet. He knew that the longer he went without answering, the more scared the kids would get.

But he had no answers.

The assault of anger and fear was deafening. A seething wall of angry faces pressed all around. It left him numb. He knew what he should do, but he couldn't. Somehow he had convinced himself that kids would understand. That they would cut him some slack. Give him some time.

But they were terrified. They were on the edge of panic.

Astrid was turned to face the crowd, back against the hood, pressed from all sides. She was yelling for quiet, ignored.

Edilio had reached into the backseat of the Jeep to slide his gun forward onto his lap. Like he thought he might have to use it to save Sam or Astrid or both.

Zil appeared, pushing his way through the crowd, five other kids acting like a star's bodyguard, shoving people out of the way. He was cheered by some, booed by others. But when he raised his hand the crowd quieted, at least a little, and leaned forward in anticipation.

Zil stuck one fist on his hip and pointed at Sam with his

other hand. "You're supposed to be the big boss."

Sam said nothing. The crowd hushed, ready to watch this one-on-one confrontation.

"You're the big boss of the freaks," Zil yelled. "But you can't do anything. You can shoot laser beams out of your hands, but you can't get enough food, and you can't keep the power on, and you won't do anything about that murderer Hunter, who killed my best friend." He paused to fill his lungs for a final, furious cry. "You shouldn't be in charge."

Suddenly, there was silence. Zil had laid the challenge out there.

Sam nodded, as if to himself. Like he was agreeing. But then, moving as slowly as an old man, he climbed up onto the passenger seat of the Jeep, and stood where everyone could see him.

Sam felt anger building inside him. Resentment. Rage.

It wouldn't be good to let it out. He knew that. He kept his voice calm, kept his expression blank. He now towered over Zil. "You want to be in charge, Zil? Last night you were running around trying to get a lynch mob together. And let's not even pretend that wasn't you responsible for graffiti I saw driving into town just now."

"So what?" Zil demanded. "So what? So I said what everyone who isn't a freak is thinking."

He spit the word "freak," making it an insult, making it an accusation.

"You really think what we need right now is to divide up between freaks and normals?" Sam asked. "You figure that will get the lights turned back on? That will put food on people's tables?"

"What about Hunter?" Zil said. "Hunter murders Harry with his mutant freak powers and you don't do anything."

"I had kind of a busy night," Sam said, his voice now poisonous with sarcasm.

"So let me and my boys go find him," Zil said. "You're so busy not getting any food, and not stopping Caine and all, not keeping the lights on, so me and my crew will get Hunter."

"And do what with him?" It was Astrid. The crowd had backed up just enough to give her some breathing room. "What's your big plan, Zil?"

Zil spread his hands in a gesture of innocence. "Hey, all we want to do is get him before he hurts someone else. You want to, like, give him a trial or whatever? Fine. But let us go and get him."

"No one is stopping you from finding him," Sam said. "You can walk around town all you like. You can admire your graffiti and count the number of windows you broke."

"We need guns," Zil said. "I'm not going up against a killer freak without guns. And your wetback friend there says we regular people can't carry guns."

Sam glanced down at Edilio to see how he had registered the insult. Edilio looked grim but calm. Calmer than Sam felt.

"Hunter is a problem," Sam acknowledged. "We have a big list of problems. But you trying to make trouble between people with powers and people without powers is not helping anything. Neither is calling people names. We have to stick together."

When Zil didn't immediately answer, Sam went on, looking past Zil to speak to the whole group. "Here's the thing, people: We have some serious problems. The lights are off. And it seems like that's affecting the water flow in part of town. So, no baths or showers, okay? But the situation is that we think Caine is short of food, which means he's not going to be able to hold out very long at the power plant."

"How long?" someone yelled.

Sam shook his head. "I don't know."

"Why can't you get him to leave?"

"Because I can't, that's why," Sam snapped, letting some of his anger show. "Because I'm not Superman, all right? Look, he's inside the plant. The walls are thick. He has guns, he has Jack, he has Drake, and he has his own powers. I can't get him out of there without getting some of our people killed. Anybody want to volunteer for that?"

Silence.

"Yeah, I thought so. I can't get you people to show up and pick melons, let alone throw down with Drake."

"That's your job," Zil said.

"Oh, I see," Sam said. The resentment he'd held in now came boiling to the surface. "It's my job to pick the fruit, and collect the trash, and ration the food, and catch Hunter, and stop Caine, and settle every stupid little fight, and make sure kids get a visit from the Tooth Fairy. What's your job, Zil? Oh, right: you spray hateful graffiti. Thanks for taking care of that, I don't know how we'd ever manage without you."

"Sam . . . ," Astrid said, just loud enough for him to hear. A warning.

Too late. He was going to say what needed saying.

"And the rest of you. How many of you have done a single, lousy thing in the last two weeks aside from sitting around playing Xbox or watching movies?

"Let me explain something to you people. I'm not your parents. I'm a fifteen-year-old kid. I'm a kid, just like all of you. I don't happen to have any magic ability to make food suddenly appear. I can't just snap my fingers and make all your problems go away. I'm just a kid."

As soon as the words were out of his mouth, Sam knew he had crossed the line. He had said the fateful words so many had used as an excuse before him. How many hundreds of times had he heard, "I'm just a kid."

But now he seemed unable to stop the words from tumbling out. "Look, I have an eighth-grade education. Just because I have powers doesn't mean I'm Dumbledore or George Washington or Martin Luther King. Until all this happened I was just a B student. All I wanted to do was surf. I wanted to grow up to be Dru Adler or Kelly Slater, just, you know, a really good surfer."

The crowd was dead quiet now. Of course they were quiet, some still-functioning part of his mind thought bitterly, it's entertaining watching someone melt down in public.

"I'm doing the best I can," Sam said.

"I lost people today . . . I . . . I screwed up. I should have figured out Caine might go after the power plant."

Silence.

"I'm doing the best I can."

No one said a word.

Sam refused to meet Astrid's eyes. If he saw pity there, he would fall apart completely.

"I'm sorry," he said.

"I'm sorry."

He jumped down. The crowd parted. He walked away through shocked silence.

Not that many kids came up to congratulate Zil on exposing Sam Temple as a helpless, useless fraud. Not as many as he had a right to expect.

But Antoine was with him, and Lance, Hank, and Turk. The four of them had become his crew. His boys. These four had been with him last night as he woke up the town of Perdido Beach.

It had been a dizzy, crazy, wild night. Zil had gone from being just a guy to becoming a leader. The way the others looked at him had changed. Lightning quick. One minute they were his equals, now he was clearly in charge.

That was cool. Very cool. Zil was the "Sam" of the normals, now. And the normals were still by far the majority.

So why didn't more kids crowd around him now? There were a few nods, some pats on the back, but there were also some very suspicious looks. And that wasn't right. Not when he, Zil Sperry, had stood up face-to-face with Sam Temple.

As if reading his thoughts, Lance said, "Don't worry, they'll come around. They're just shaken up right now."

"They're still scared of Sam," Hank said. "They should be scared of us."

Hank was a short, skinny, angry kid, with a face like a

rat. Hank talked constantly about kicking butt, to the point where Zil could barely stop himself from pointing out that Hank was practically a midget and wasn't going to kick anyone's butt.

Lance was a different story. Lance was tall, athletic, good looking, and smart. Zil could hardly believe Lance was being so respectful to him, letting Zil take the lead and make the decisions. Back in the old days Lance had been one of the most popular kids in school—not at all like Hank, who was generally despised.

"Hi."

Zil looked around and found himself face-to-face with a girl he knew vaguely. Lisa. That was her name. Lisa something.

"I just wanted to tell you that I totally agree with you," Lisa something gushed.

"Really?" Zil had very little experience talking to girls. He hoped he wouldn't start blushing. Not that this girl was beautiful or anything, but she was cute. And she was wearing a short skirt and makeup; almost none of the girls in the FAYZ seemed to bother trying to look nice and "girly" anymore.

"The freaks are totally out of control," Lisa said, nodding her head constantly like a bobble-head doll.

"Yes, they are," Zil agreed, almost wary, not knowing why this girl was talking to him.

"I'm really glad you're standing up to them. You're, like, totally brave."

"Thanks." Zil found his own head bobbing up and down

now in response to her. Then, not knowing what else to say, he forced an awkward smile and started out of the church.

"Can I—" Lisa began.

"What?"

"I mean, are you guys going to do anything? Because maybe I could help," Lisa said.

Zil felt a moment of panic. Do something? Like what? They'd already tagged town hall and busted some windows. Unless Hunter showed up, what was there to do?

Then it dawned on Zil. If he did nothing now, he would lose everything. Lance and Hank and Turk and even Antoine would drift off, or just settle into being another bunch of dudes doing nothing much and slowly starving.

It wasn't over. It couldn't be over.

"Actually, I could use your help," Zil said to Lisa. "I have plans."

"What are you going to do?" Lisa asked eagerly.

"I'm going to put real humans back in charge. Get rid of the chuds. Run things for us, not for them."

"Yeah!" Turk said.

"The six of us, here? We're just the start," Zil said.

"Absolutely," Hank agreed.

"Zil's crew," Turk said.

Zil waved that off modestly. "I think maybe we should call ourselves the Human Crew."

THIRTY

CAINE HAD FALLEN asleep, exhausted, on the plant manager's couch. He woke slowly. Disoriented. Not sure where he was. He opened his eyes and everything around him, the dusty furnishings of the office, seemed to vibrate.

He rubbed his eyes and sat up.

Someone was sitting in the plant manager's chair. A green man. Green from some inner light, like chemicals were burning inside him putting off a sickly glow.

The man had no face. His shape was rough, like a clay model only half completed. When Caine looked closer he could see millions of tiny crystals, some no larger than a period, some almost as big as a sugar cube. The mass of crystals was constantly in motion, like frenzied ants crawling over each other.

Caine closed his eyes. When he opened them again the apparition was gone.

A hallucination. Caine had gotten used to hallucinations.

He got to his feet, but he was shaky. He felt sick, like he had the flu or something. His face was beaded with sweat. His shirt was sticky on his skin.

He needed to throw up, but there was nothing in his stomach.

Through the glass he could see the control room. Diana, asleep or dozing in her chair, her feet up on the table. She looked strange without her hair. Caine loved Diana's hair.

Jack had his head down on the same table, his face puffy, lips babylike as he snored.

The two hostages leaned into each other, asleep.

The dead girl, Brittney, lay on the floor in a heap. Someone had moved her. It looked like someone had tried to push her under the counter, out of the way. The pool of her blood was now a smear.

The only one awake was Drake. He leaned against a wall, unblinking, whip arm coiled around his waist, a machine gun in his other hand.

Caine staggered. He righted himself, squared his shoulders, wiped the drool from his mouth. He had to look strong. Drake looked strong, like he was the one in charge.

Caine wondered how long it would take for Drake to finally decide to come after him. He hadn't done so during Caine's long months incapacitated. But now that Caine was giving the orders again, he knew Drake was chafing.

Caine steadied himself and started toward the control room. He got as far as the office door when the memory storm swept over him, almost knocked him to his knees. He grabbed the door and held on to it, shaking.

It came to him as hunger. Hunger deeper than anything he had ever felt himself. As if he had nothing inside his skin but a roaring, starving tiger.

Hungry in the dark.

Caine whimpered. He caught himself before he did it again, but the desperate sound was out of his mouth. Had Drake heard?

Leave me alone, Caine pleaded silently with the voice in his head. I'm doing what you want, but leave me alone.

Caine, looking down at the floor, saw Drake's feet. Drake had arrived soundlessly. Or maybe Caine had been beyond hearing anything.

"You okay?" Drake asked.

"I'm fine," Caine snapped.

Drake said, "Good. I'm real glad about that."

Caine pushed past him, making sure to dig a hard shoulder into Drake.

"What are you all doing asleep?" Caine demanded in a loud voice. "Sam could be outside right now, waiting for a chance to come back after us."

"We won't have to worry about Sam for long," Drake said. "Not once *he's* fed."

Caine kicked Jack's chair. He kicked the nearest of the hostages. "Wake up. All of you. It's almost daylight outside. Sam may be planning something."

"What is your problem?" Diana demanded. "Did your monster overlord wake you up? Did he crack his crazy-brain whip and make you jump?"

"Shut up!" Caine said savagely. "I don't need this from you. Has anyone searched for food?"

"You don't think in the last three months Sam's people have searched this place for food?" Diana said, but with less overt hostility than usual.

"That's not what I asked," Caine yelled. "I asked whether any of you stupid, lazy idiots bothered to look for something to eat. It's a yes-or-no answer."

"No," Diana answered for all of them.

"Then get off your butts and go look," Caine said.

Diana sighed and got to her feet. "I wouldn't mind a little walk."

Jack got up as well. So did Drake's two gunmen. The four of them disappeared down various hallways.

"Just don't go outside the building," Caine yelled after them.

Caine pulled Drake aside. "Has Jack got it worked out yet?"

"I think so. He was looking smug right before he fell asleep."

Caine nodded. "We should move out as soon as we can."

"Shouldn't we try to take Sam out first?" Drake asked.

Caine snorted a laugh. "You say that like it's easy. If we could start by taking Sam down, we'd have an easy time of it." He shook his head. "No. That's not how we do this. If they catch us, we use the uranium to make them back off."

Despite himself, Drake grinned. "Threaten to drop it on them?"

"Threaten to smash it open," Caine said. "Threaten to launch it into the air and smash it open."

"And everyone will glow in the dark," Drake said, as if that was a happy thought.

"I'll only have one hand free," Caine said. "So you may finally get a chance to use that gun you love so much."

"Should we send Bug to Coates?" Drake asked. "Bring more of our people?"

"They wouldn't come," Caine said flatly.

There was a commotion and Caine glanced aside to see Computer Jack storming down the hallway trailed by Diana, who tried unsuccessfully to hold him back. Like a two-year-old trying to hold a bull.

"You!" Jack bellowed.

He waved his fist in the air and Caine could see naked wires, like hair-thin snakes in his fingers.

"You said you took these down!" Jack cried accusingly.

"Oh, gee, I must have missed some," Drake said. "Hey, did you find your girlfriend while you were looking around?"

Jack froze. "What?"

Drake had his arm uncoiled, ready to use. "She must have been doing pretty good speed when she hit the wire. Breezed right through them. Oh wait, I said that wrong. The wire breezed right through the Breeze."

"She . . . what . . ." Jack gasped.

"Cut her right in half," Drake said, laughing with sheer glee. "It was kind of neat to see. You'd have found it interesting, all her insides, sliced right in half. Like a meat cleaver went through her."

"I'm going to kill you," Jack whispered.

"You don't have the—"

But Jack had tossed Diana aside and was running straight at Drake.

Drake managed to lash him once with his whip hand, but only once. Jack hit him like a linebacker. Drake went flying across the room, flying like he'd stepped out in front of a bus.

Drake landed hard, but rolled to his feet. He lashed again. There was a loud crack, and a tear appeared in Jack's shirt.

Jack never slowed down but went straight for Drake. But then, suddenly, he couldn't move. He motored his legs, but could not advance.

Caine with one raised hand held him with an irresistible force.

"Let me go, Caine," Jack yelled.

"He's yanking your chain, you idiot," Caine yelled. The temptation to let Jack kill Drake was strong. It would solve a major problem—sooner or later Drake was going to challenge Caine. But for now, Drake was still necessary in a battle.

Drake slashed at Jack with his whip, but the whip stopped in midair, hitting an invisible barrier.

"Both of you knock it off," Caine yelled.

"You touch me, I'll kill you!" Drake shrieked at Jack.

"I said shut up, both of you!" Caine bellowed. He pushed both palms out, one aimed at Jack, the other at Drake. Both boys went flying backward. Jack landed hard on his back. Drake, lighter and without Jack's superhuman strength, hit the wall and crumpled at its base.

Caine caught a movement out of the corner of his eye and saw the backs of the two hostages as they bolted from the room.

Caine twisted to aim for them, but they were out of his line of sight. He heard footsteps pelting away. "Get them!" he yelled.

But Drake was slow getting up and Jack would be no help. Drake's two thugs stood stock still, paralyzed. Caine realized that they were loyal to Drake, awaiting *his* orders and not Caine's.

He spun, raised his hands, lifted both the punks off the floor, and hurled them bodily down the hallway after the hostages.

"Bring them back!" Caine bellowed.

"Look out!" Diana cried.

Gunfire erupted. Insanely loud. Caine heard bullets fly past his ear like buzzing dragonflies.

Brittney!

Not dead. Just playing dead and slowly, slowly working her way toward a gun she must have known was stashed under the counter.

She was still in a heap on the floor, unable to stand, unable even to sit up, lying on her side firing.

Caine leaped aside as bullets flew.

He slammed heavily into the table, rebounded, and fell to his knees. He brought his palms up, but the barrel of the gun moved faster.

But faster still, was Drake's whip hand. It snapped and wrapped around Brittney's wrist. The gun fired, but the bullets hit wall and ceiling.

Caine, enraged, aimed his full power at the girl. She skidded across the floor and hit the wall, so quickly that Drake was still attached and was drawn along with her.

Caine jumped to his feet, holding his focus on Brittney, raised her from the ground, suspended in midair.

"You piece of—" Brittney said, and then she was a bullet herself, rocketing through the air.

She flew through the hole Sam had burned earlier.

That had not been Caine's intention. The girl was lucky.

Or someone was looking out for her.

Outside, standing faithful guard, Dekka heard the eruption of gunfire from the control room.

She leaped toward the wall just as something flew through the burned-out hole. It landed with the unmistakable sound of a human body hitting the ground.

Dekka stared, too stunned to react.

Then, off to her right, gunfire from inside the turbine building. Bright yellow flashes outlined the doorway.

She broke her trance and ran toward the door. Edilio's soldiers jumped up off the ground and fell in behind her.

"Orc! Orc!" Dekka shouted.

She heard rather than saw the monster stir. He'd been asleep in the back of the SUV. The springs squeaked as he clambered out.

Two of Caine's gunmen appeared as shadows in the doorway. Their guns aimed at the fleeing forms.

Gunfire and one of the shapes fell without even crying out. Collapsed onto his face and did not move. The other ran, ran, ran.

"I got him! I got him!" someone cried, more terror than pride in his voice.

"Taylor!" Dekka yelled. "Distract them!"

"Bouncing!" Taylor yelled back and disappeared.

"Oh, my God, I think I killed him," the voice moaned.

Dekka raised her hands and both gunmen floated up off the ground. One smacked the top of the doorway. The other slid back inside, out of Dekka's reach. The firing stopped. The running hostage collapsed, gasping, behind a vehicle.

One second Taylor was running beside Dekka.

A split second later she was staggering, still half running, across the control room of the power plant.

"You stupid psycho!" Caine screamed at Drake.

Drake had gone bone white, all but his cold gray eyes. "I just saved your life!"

"You were being an idiot! You pushed Jack just to watch him squirm," Caine yelled. "And look what happened. I'm busy keeping you two apart and look what happened, you stupid thug!"

"Hey!" Diana yelled.

It took Taylor a moment to recognize her. Her head was practically shaved.

"Hey!" Diana yelled again, pointing at Taylor. "We have company!"

Caine whirled and swung his deadly hands up, but Taylor bounced across the room to appear in a far corner, behind him.

"Jack, you traitor!" Taylor yelled, and bounced out of the room.

Taylor popped back, right in Dekka's face. "They're freaking out in there. We should hit them now!"

Dekka came to a stop. She added quickly in her mind. She had Orc and Taylor and herself. She had three of Edilio's guys. The hostages were no longer an issue.

But Caine and Drake were still alive. Still very, very dangerous. Plus at least two gunmen, maybe more.

"No," she said, feeling deflated. "Not without Sam."

"We should go now, right now!" Taylor yelled. She pointed at the bloody mess on the ground. "Look what they did. Look what they did! Look at what those animals did!"

Dekka put a calming hand on the girl's shoulder. "We go in now, we'll lose," she said. And even if Sam were there . . . She'd never seen Sam acting the way he had earlier. Like the fire had gone out in him.

"You're just scared," Taylor said.

"Don't be up in my face, Taylor," Dekka warned. "We don't have the power. Simple as that. We attack now, we'll lose. Sam will have more bodies for Edilio to bury. I don't know if Sam can . . ." She stopped herself. Too late.

"What about Sam?" Taylor demanded.

Dekka shrugged. "Nothing. Boy's just tired, is all. I think maybe he doesn't need another fight tonight."

Taylor looked like she might argue some more. Then her shoulders sagged. "Yeah. Whatever."

"You head back to town. Tell Sam what went down. Tell him what you saw inside there."

"It'll take me a few minutes. I can't do it all in one bounce," Taylor said.

"Then get going."

Taylor disappeared and Dekka kicked furiously at the dirt. It had all happened too fast for her to do much more than watch.

Mike Farmer was creeping from behind the truck where he'd hidden. Mickey was facedown and terribly still. The remains of Brittney were a nightmare.

Dekka felt a flash of anger at Sam. He had run off and left her in charge. Well, she didn't want to be in charge. Sam wasn't the only one who was hanging on by his fingernails.

Brianna . . . The thought was like a knife to the stomach, twisting, twisting.

She had never even told Brianna how she felt. And now it was too late.

Something landed on the pavement next to Dekka. She stared at what looked a great deal like chicken bones. Cooked chicken bones.

Dekka looked up. She moved back and back to get a clear view.

Ten stories up, eerie in the blazing light atop the turbine building, someone was waving her arms. Very fast.

Time seemed to stand still. Dekka couldn't breathe. She stared hard, not wanting to be wrong, not willing to believe until she was sure.

"Breeze?" Dekka whispered, amazed.

Dekka lowered her head for just a moment and thanked God. Brianna. Alive.

Alive and as impatient as ever, by the look of it.

No way Brianna could hear her over the noise of the plant. How Brianna had managed to get herself up there was a mystery, but judging from her frantic semaphore of waving arms, she wanted to get down.

Dekka waved. She even displayed a rare smile. Brianna, alive.

Brianna stuck her hands on her hips as if to say, "What's keeping you?"

Dekka considered for a moment. Then she pointed to a spot just at the base of the wall, well away from the door where Caine's boys crouched hidden with guns.

Brianna nodded.

Dekka raised her hands.

Brianna leaped into midair. And stayed in midair. No gravity dragged her down.

Dekka took a deep breath. She switched off her power for a second and Brianna fell. On again and Brianna stopped falling. Off. On. Until Brianna floated just a few feet off the pavement.

Dekka released her and Brianna landed lightly, taking the shock in her knees. Dekka steadied her.

"What is going on down here?" Brianna demanded. "I heard guns. Woke me up."

"Good to see you, too, Brianna," Dekka said dryly. "Everyone thought you were dead."

"Well, I'm not. Duh."

Dekka shook her head in tolerant amazement.

They joined Mike behind the truck, leaving Edilio's soldiers in place watching the door, guns leveled.

Mike was surprised. "Hey, Drake told Jack you were dead! Jack totally lost it believing him."

Brianna grinned. "Oh he did, did he?"

"Totally. He went all Aragorn on Drake. Tried to kill him. That's how we . . . I mean, how I, got away." He burst into tears then, weeping uncontrollably and covering his face with his hands.

"You have a thing with Computer Jack?" Dekka asked. She carefully modulated her voice, giving nothing away of her inner turmoil. This was no time to burden Brianna with feelings she wouldn't reciprocate. Feelings that might even make her mad at Dekka. The two of them hadn't exactly been friends while they were at Coates. Dekka wasn't sure Brianna even knew Dekka was gay.

"I didn't think I did," Brianna answered, looking pleased with herself. "I guess I do."

"Okay," Dekka said, swallowing hard. The important thing was Brianna was alive. And Mickey and Brittney were not.

Dekka was in charge here, she had to make some decisions. "You going to tell me how you came to be up on the roof?"

"Um . . . no. But here's the thing: There's a door up there that leads down inside. If I had a crowbar or something, I could get it open, get in and out of there before they know it. Smack the—"

"No, no," Mike said through heaving sobs. "The wires are still up."

"What wires?" Brianna demanded.

"Drake. He stretched wires all over the place so if you came in, they'd cut you up."

Dekka noted the look of shock on Brianna's usually cocky face.

"That's why Jack was trying to kill Drake," Mike said. "Jack told him he had to take them all down, and Drake pretended like he did, but he didn't."

Dekka said, "Guess it's a good thing Jack likes your act, Breeze. Mike here got away."

Brianna had no answer.

"Don't let it shake you up, girl," Dekka said. "You had a bad day. We've all had a very bad day." She sat down beside Mike and put her arm around his shoulders. "I'm so sorry about Mickey. I know you guys were buds."

Mike shook her off. "You don't care about Mickey. You care about her because she's a freak, like you."

Dekka decided to let that go. Couldn't blame Mike for being a little crazed. Couldn't really blame him if he fell apart completely.

To Brianna, Dekka said, "You had a close call. But right now the important thing is you start listening to other people and not do crazy stuff that leaves you trapped on a roof when we need you. Or worse yet, sliced up."

"Yeah," Brianna said, abashed. Then, recovering a little of her usual sass, she added, "Thanks, *Mom*."

Dekka loved that. Brianna's wild recklessness. She loved that. So much the opposite of Dekka herself. She didn't let Brianna know she loved it because right now Dekka was in charge, responsible. But Brianna wouldn't be Brianna without the crazy part.

Alive. She was alive.

And had a thing for Jack.

But alive.

COME TO ME. I have need of you.

"I can't breathe," Lana said, although if she spoke with her mouth, she heard no sound from it, nor did she feel her tongue and lips moving.

The gas compound deprives you of oxygen.

Yes. That was it. The gas. One spark and . . . somewhere she had a lighter. One spark and she would be free. Dead. Dead-free.

She laughed and the laughter became crimson daggers stabbing into her brain. She clutched her head and cried out in pain. She heard no sound. She did not feel her hands pressed against her temples.

Crawl to me.

Body not working. Was it? Was she on her hands and knees? Was her body still real?

Was she blind, or was it too dark to see?

Had she been unconscious? How long?

Moving, she was sure she was moving. Only maybe it was a breeze blowing past her.

I expel the carbon-hydrogen compound.

The . . . what? Carbon . . . what? Her mind was reeling, swirling, round and round and as it swirled out came the knives of pain to stab at her, to torture her. Head exploding. Heart hammering in her chest, trying to escape, ripping her ribs apart to get out of her.

No, all hallucination. Madness and lies.

But the pain was real. She could feel that, the pain. And the fear.

The oxygen-nitrogen mix flows.

Air. Replacing the gas. It did nothing to lessen the pain in her head. But her heart slowed.

She could see again, just a little, the headlights of the truck throwing the faintest light down the mine shaft to where she lay face down on rock. Lana brought her hand up in front of her face. Fingers. She could not quite make them out, but she knew they were there.

She touched her face. She could feel her hand. She could feel her cheek. Wet with tears.

Come to me.

No.

But she was on hands and knees now, moving. The rock tore the flesh of her palms and knees.

No. I won't come to you.

But she came. Moved. Hands and knees. Crawled.

Had it ever been possible to resist it?

No.

I am the gaiaphage.

You are mine.

I am Lana Arwen Lazar. My mother named me for . . . For something. Someone . . . My . . .

I hunger.

You will help me feed.

Leave me alone, Lana protested feebly as her arms and legs kept moving, her head hung down like a dog. Like . . . like someone . . .

I am the gaiaphage.

What does that mean? Lana asked.

She had more sense of herself now. She could reach into her memory and remember who she was and why she was here. She could recall the foolish hope she had nurtured of destroying the Darkness. The gaiaphage.

But now she saw its hand in everything she had done. From the start it had been calling to her. Twisting her thoughts and actions to its will.

She'd never had a chance.

And now she crawled.

Superman's other girlfriend, Lana. Aragorn's true love, Arwen. Lazar, shortened from Lazarevic. Lazarus, who rose from the dead. Lana Arwen Lazar. That's who she was.

She was unable to stop crawling. Down and down the mine shaft.

Come to me.

I have need of you.

What need? Why me?

You are the Healer.

You have the power.

Are you hurt? A flicker of hope at the thought that the creature might be wounded.

Lana's limbs were so heavy now, she could barely move. Barely slide her knees two inches across rough stone. Barely push her palms forward. But her eyes now registered the faint green glow she had remembered always from her first trip down this awful mine shaft.

A glow like luminescent watch dials. A glow like the glow-in-the-dark stars Lana's dad had pasted to her ceiling when she was little.

The thought of her father tore at Lana's soul. Her mother. Her father. So far away. Or dead. Or, who knew? Who would ever know?

She imagined them seeing her. As if she were bacteria on a slide and her mother and father were looking down through a gigantic microscope. Seeing their daughter like this. Crawling in the dark. Terrified. Hungry. So afraid.

Crawling toward the Darkness. Slave to the gaiaphage.

She stopped moving, commanded by the voice in her head. She panted, waiting, sweat pouring off her.

Place your hand on me.

"What?" she whispered. "Where? Where are you?"

She swung her weary head around, peering into the radioactive dark, seeing nothing but faintly glowing rock.

No. Looking closer, forcing herself to look, she saw that

it was not rock. Her unwilling eyes seemed to bore into the faint green glow and there began to see not a single mass of rock but a seething, pulsating swarm. Thousands, maybe millions of tiny crystalline shapes, hexagons, pentagons, triangles. The largest were perhaps half the size of her smallest fingernail. The smallest were no bigger than a period on a page. Each sprouted countless tiny legs, so that what Lana saw appeared as a vast ant colony, an insect hive, all green and glittering, pulsing like an exposed heart.

Place your hand on me.

She resisted. But she knew, even as she fought the gaiaphage's will, that she was doomed to lose. Her hand moved. Trembling, it moved. She saw her fingers dark against the green glow.

She touched it, felt it, and it was like touching rough sand on the beach. Only this sand moved, vibrated.

For a moment there was only that simple sensation.

Then, the gaiaphage showed her what he wanted.

She saw creatures. A creature of living fire. A clockwork snake. Monsters.

And she saw a Russian nesting doll.

One doll . . . inside another . . . inside another . . . and another . . .

Now she knew him, knew in a moment of blinding clarity what he was. Now she could feel his hunger. And now she sensed his fear.

He needed her, this foul creature made of human and alien DNA, of stone and flesh, nurtured on hard radiation in the depths of space and now in the depths of the earth. The glowing food had all been consumed in the thirteen years the gaiaphage had grown and mutated down here in the darkness.

It was hungry. Food was coming. When the food came, he would be strong enough to use Lana's power to create a body. He had used her power to give Drake his whip hand, to make a monster of him. He would use her now, once he had fed, to create a monstrous body of his own. Bodies inside of bodies, bodies that could be used and then cast aside as another emerged.

To move.

To escape the mine. That was his goal.

To walk the FAYZ and destroy all who resisted him.

Sam's day was a series of wild mood swings.

Taylor bounced in to tell him that Mickey Finch had been killed escaping from Caine. But that Mike Farmer had survived. And now Caine was without hostages.

Then a fire broke out in a house where two five-year-olds shared a place with two nine-year-olds. One of the nine-year-olds had been smoking pot.

Fire Chief Ellen got the fire truck to the scene in time to keep the fire from spreading to the house next door. Water pressure still held strong at that end of town.

The kids had all made it out alive.

Then, as he was standing on the street with the sun rising and smoke pouring from the burned house, trying to decide how, or if, he should punish a kid for smoking weed and starting a fire, he felt a slight gust of wind.

"Hey, Sammy," Brianna said.

Sam stared at her. She grinned at him.

Sam breathed a big sigh of relief. "I should kill you, disappearing like that."

"Come on," Brianna said, stretching her arms wide, "Hug it out."

She embraced Sam—quickly—then stepped back. "That's all, big boy, I don't want Astrid mad at me."

"Uh-huh."

"So, when do we go take out Caine and get the lights back on?"

Sam shook his head. "Can't do it, Breeze."

"What? What?" What do you mean you can't do it? He's sitting there with no hostages. We can take him."

"There are other issues," Sam said. "We've got trouble here between freaks and normals."

Brianna made a dismissive sound. "I'll run around and slap some of them a few times, they'll get over themselves, and we'll get busy at the power plant." She leaned close. "I found a way in through the roof."

That was interesting news. Interesting enough to make Sam reconsider. "A way into what? The turbine room?"

"Dude, there's a door on the roof. I don't know where it goes, but it has to go into the turbine room. Probably."

Sam tried to shake himself out of his funk, but he couldn't quite do it, couldn't quite focus. He felt deflated. Weary beyond belief. "You're hurt," he observed.

"Yeah, and it stings, too. Where's Lana? I need some cur-
ing. Then we can do some butt-kicking."

"We lost Lana. She took off."

That piece of news rocked even Brianna's eager confidence.
"What?"

"Things are not going well," Sam said.

He felt Brianna's worried gaze. He wasn't setting a good
example. He wasn't exactly taking charge. He knew all that.
But he couldn't shake off the indifference that sapped his
every attempt to formulate a plan.

"You need some rest," Brianna said at last.

"Yeah," Sam said. "No doubt."

The voices were familiar. Dekka. Taylor. Howard.

"Sun's coming up," Taylor said. "The sky's turning gray."

"We have to do something about Brittney and Mickey,"
Dekka said.

"I don't deal with dead bodies." Howard.

"I guess we could, you know, send them back to town for
Edilio to bury," Dekka said.

Taylor sighed. "Things are bad back there. I've never seen
Sam like that. I mean, he's just . . ."

Dekka said, "He'll get over it." She didn't sound too sure of
that. "But yeah, maybe this isn't the time to ask him to speak
at a burial."

"Maybe we could just cover them up. You know, haul
Mickey over here, maybe just put a blanket over them or
something for now."

"Yeah. One of these cars around here must have a blanket in the trunk. A tarp. Something. Get Orc to pop some trunks open, huh?"

Which was how Brittney ended up nestled next to Mickey, under the shelter of a painter's drop cloth.

She felt no pain.

She saw no light.

She heard, but barely.

Her heart was still and silent.

Yet she did not die.

Albert had no time to waste. He and Quinn had finally told Sam about their gold mission. About Lana going off with Cookie.

They'd found Sam listless, not as mad as either of them had expected. He'd listened with his eyes closed and a couple of times Albert thought he might have nodded off.

It had been a relief not to have Sam rage at them. But also disturbing. After all, they were delivering very bad news. Sam's nonreaction was unreal. Sam wasn't acting like Sam.

All the more reason for Albert to get his act together. He'd sent a disbelieving Quinn off to fish.

"I don't care how tired you are, Quinn: we have a business to run."

And then he'd gotten down to work.

The problem for Albert was melting the gold. The melting point for gold was three times higher than the melting point for lead, and nothing Albert could find achieved that temperature. Certainly none of the equipment at his McDonald's, none of which was working now anyway, with the power out.

Albert despaired until, rummaging through the hardware store looking for a solution, he noticed the acetylene torch.

He hauled two torches and all the spare acetylene tanks he could find to the McDonald's. He locked the door.

He placed a large cast-iron pot on the stove and heated it to maximum. It wouldn't melt the gold, but it would slow down the cooling process.

He placed one of the gold bars into the pot, fired the torch, and aimed the blue pencil point flame at the gold. Instantly the metal began to sweat. Then to run off in a tiny river of molten gold.

An hour later he popped his first six gold bullets from the bullet mold.

It was exhausting work. Hot work. But he got so he could produce twenty-four bullets an hour. He worked without pause for ten hours straight and then, exhausted, starving and dehydrated, he counted out 224 of the .32-caliber bullets.

Kids knocked on the door, demanding to be let in for the McClub. But Albert just posted a sign saying, "Sorry: We Are Closed This Evening, Please Come Back Tomorrow."

He drank some water, ate a meager meal, and did some calculations. He had enough gold to produce perhaps four thousand bullets, which, equally distributed, would mean just over ten bullets for each person in Perdido Beach. The job would take weeks.

But he didn't have nearly enough acetylene to manage it. Which would mean that in order to melt all the gold he would need the help of the one person least likely to want to help: Sam.

Albert had seen Sam burn through brick. Surely he could melt gold.

In the meantime Albert intended to distribute a single bullet to each person. Sort of as a calling card. A sign of what was coming.

And then, a paper currency backed up by the gold, and finally, credit.

Despite his weariness, Albert hummed contentedly as he sat with a yellow legal pad and a pen, writing out possible names for the new currency.

"Bullets" was obviously not the appropriate term. He wanted people thinking "money," not "death."

Dollars? No. The word was familiar, but he wanted something new.

Euros? Francs? Doubloons? Marks? Chits? Crowns?

Alberts?

No. Over the top.

Units?

It was functional. It meant what it said.

"The problem is, whatever we call them, we don't have enough," Albert muttered. If there were going to be just four thousand of the new . . . whatevers . . . they'd obviously have to be worth a lot, each one. Like, to start with, ten slugs should . . .

Slugs?

They were slugs, after all.

To start with, if a kid had the original ten slugs he was given, then each slug would have to be worth more than, say, a single one-can meal. So he needed, in addition to the slugs, smaller units. A currency that would be worth, say, one tenth of a slug.

But any attempt to make up paper currency would just send everyone running to find a copier. He needed something that could not be duplicated.

An idea hit him. A memory. He ran for the storeroom that had long since been cleaned out of food. There were two boxes on the wire shelves. Each was filled with McDonald's Monopoly game pieces—tickets—from some long-forgotten promotion.

Twelve thousand pieces per box. Hard to counterfeit.

He would have enough to make change for four thousand slugs at a rate of six Monopoly pieces per slug.

"A slug equals six tickets," Albert said. "Six tickets equals a slug."

It was a beautiful thing, Albert thought. Tears came to his eyes. It was a truly beautiful thing. He was reinventing money.

THIRTY-TWO

BUG WAS LEERY now. Sam's people knew about him. They had since the big battle of Perdido Beach. But now they had begun to take countermeasures. The sudden attack with spray paint had shaken Bug's self-confidence.

So when Caine drew him aside, careful not to let Drake overhear, and gave him a new assignment, Bug was dubious.

"They're out there waiting for anyone who comes out," Bug argued. "Dekka's out there for sure. Bunch of kids with guns. And probably Sam, hiding somewhere maybe."

"Keep your voice down," Caine said. "Listen, Bug, you're doing this: the easy way or the hard way. Your choice."

So Bug was doing it. Not liking it, but doing it.

He began by drifting into invisibility. Even when he was visible, kids tended to overlook him. They would forget he was there. Once he'd faded, they seldom seemed to remember him.

He stood in the corner of the control room for a while, out

of sight. Making sure no one—by which he meant Drake—was going to miss him.

Things had calmed down a little since it became clear that Sam's people were not going to rush in, guns and laser hands blazing.

But the room was still tense. Drake and Caine paranoid, waiting for attack from outside, or from each other. Diana sullen, sleepy. Computer Jack obviously in pain from his injuries, popping Advil like crazy, but still pecking away at the keyboard. Drake's bully boys had found some guy's handheld game and were taking turns playing it till the batteries failed. Then they'd go off in search of more batteries.

No one missed Bug.

So he slipped out of the room, inches away from Drake, fearing the sudden lash of his whip as he held his breath.

Outside, things were better than he'd expected. Dekka was sitting in the front seat of a car, half dozing, half arguing with Taylor and Howard. Orc was at the far edge of the parking lot idly smashing car windshields with a tire iron. And two, no three, kids with guns, concealed behind cars, around corners, all waiting for trouble. All bored, too.

And in very bad moods. Bug heard fragments of grousing as he passed.

"... Sam just takes off and leaves us here and ..."

"... if you're not some powerful freak, no one gives a ..."

" ... I swear I am going to cut off my own leg and eat it, I'm so hungry ..."

" ... rat doesn't taste as bad as you'd think. The trouble is, finding a rat ..."

Bug slipped past them and reached the road. Easy-peasy, as they used to say back in kindergarten.

From there it was a long, long walk. With nothing to eat.

Bug felt like his stomach was trying to kill him. Like it had become this enemy inside him. Like cancer or whatever. It just hurt all the time. He'd found his mouth watering when he heard the kid talking about eating a rat.

Bug would eat a rat. In a heartbeat. Maybe he wouldn't have even the day before, but now, he hadn't eaten in a very long time. Maybe the time had come to start eating bugs again. Not as a dare, but simply for a meal.

He wondered how long you could go without food before you died. Well, one way or another, he was going to get some food. He'd managed to slip into Ralph's before, and it was kind of on the way to Coates.

Had to eat, man. Caine had to understand that.

He'd get to Coates and find the freaky dream girl in plenty of time.

Bug reached into his pocket and pulled out the map Caine had drawn onto a piece of printer paper. It was pretty good, pretty clear. It led from Coates, down around the hills, out into the desert. An "X" marked something Caine had labeled "Ghost Town." A second "X," almost on top of the town, was labeled "Mine."

On the map was a written message to anyone who challenged Bug. It read:

Bug is following my orders. Do what he says. Anyone who tries to stop him deals with me. Caine.

Bug was to gather up the dreamer, Orsay, and, using what-ever guys he could round up at Coates, get her to the "X" labeled "Mine."

"I don't know if it dreams or not," Caine had said. "But I think maybe all its thoughts are dreams, kind of. I think maybe Orsay can get inside its head."

Bug had nodded like he understood, though he didn't.

"I want to know what it plans for me," Caine instructed Bug. "You tell her that. If I bring it food, what will it do to me? You tell Orsay that if she can tell me the dreams of the Dark-ness, the gaiaphage, I will cut her loose. She'll be free."

Then Caine had added, "Free from me, anyway."

It was an important mission. Caine had promised Bug first choice of any food they got in the future. And Bug knew he'd better succeed. People who failed Caine came to bad, bad ends.

It was a very long walk to Ralph's. The place was still guarded. Bug could see two armed kids on the roof, two by the front door, two by the loading dock in back. And the place was hopping, kids crowding at the door, pushing and yelling.

Many were there to get their daily ration of a couple of cans of horrible food, doled out by bored fourth graders who had already grown cynical.

"Dude, don't try and play me," one was saying as he turned a girl away. "You were here two hours ago getting food. You can't just change clothes and trick me."

Others were not there to get food but electricity. Ralph's

was on the highway, outside of the town proper. Obviously it still had electricity, because extension cords had been strung through the front door and power strips attached. Kids were lined up charging iPods, rechargeable flashlights, and laptops.

Bug would tell Caine about the electricity at the store. That would earn him some brownie points. Caine would get Jack to find a way to cut it off.

The fact that the power was still on meant that the automatic door also still worked. Bug had to be careful to follow someone else in.

The store was an eerie place. The produce section, which was the first thing he saw, was empty. Most of the rotting produce had been shoveled out, but they had not done a thorough job. A big squash was so rotted, it had been reduced to a liquid smear. There were corn-on-the-cob leaves scattered, onion skins, and on the floors a sticky gray goo that was the residue of the cleanup effort.

The meat section stank, but it was empty nonetheless.

Shelves were acres of emptiness. All the remaining food was gathered into a single aisle in the middle of the store.

Careful to avoid brushing against any of the half dozen or so workers, Bug walked along the aisle.

Jars of gravy. Packets of powdered chili mix. Jars of pimentos and pickled onions. Artificial sweetener. Clam juice. Canned sauerkraut. Wax beans.

In a separate section with its own guard was a slightly more inviting shelf. A sign read, "Day Care Only." Here, there were cylinders of oatmeal, cans of condensed milk, boiled pota-toes, and cans of V8 juice, though not many.

Things were bad in Perdido Beach, Bug reflected. The days of candy and chips were definitely gone. Not even a cracker to be seen, let alone a cookie. He'd been really lucky to score that handful of Junior Mints on his spy mission to the power plant.

That was luck. And now, Bug had some more luck. It was purely by chance that he discovered the secret of Ralph's. He had dodged aside to avoid a couple of kids and ended up cow-ering in front of the swinging doors that led to the storeroom area. A swing of the door had revealed two kids manhan-dling a plastic tub filled with ice.

Bug couldn't enter the storeroom without pushing the door and risking discovery. But he figured it might be worth it: anything someone else wanted to hide was something Bug wanted to find out about.

He took a deep breath, ready to run for it if necessary. He pushed the swinging door open and slid through. The kids with the bin were gone. But he heard movement around the corner, behind a wall of cartons marked "plastic cups."

There was the work area that had once belonged to the butchers. Now four kids, in rubber aprons that dragged to the floor, were wielding knives.

They were cutting up fish.

Bug stood and stared, not believing what he was seeing. Some of the fish were big—maybe three feet long—silver and gray, with white and pink insides. Other fish were smaller, brown, flat. One of the fish looked so ugly, Bug figured it must be deformed. And two of the fish didn't look like fish at all, but rather like soggy, featherless blue birds, or maybe like bats.

The aproned kids were chatting happily—like people who were eating well, Bug thought bitterly—as they sliced open the fish and, with many cries of, "Ewww, this is so gross," sluiced the fish guts into big, white plastic tubs.

Others then took the cleaned fish, cut off their heads and tails, and scraped the scales from them under running water.

Bug hated fish. Really, really hated it. But he would have given anything, done anything, to have a plate full of fried fish. Ketchup would have helped, but even without it, even knowing that ketchup might never be seen again, the idea of a big plate of hot anything seemed wonderful.

It made Bug want to swoon. Fish! Fried, steamed, micro-waved, he didn't care.

Bug considered his options. He could grab a fish and run. But although people couldn't see him easily, they'd sure be able to see a fish flying through the store and out the door. And those kids at the door and on the roof probably weren't good shots, but they didn't have to be when they were firing machine guns.

He could try to conceal a fish down his pants or under his shirt. But that assumed the kids with the gutting knives were slow to react.

A kid Bug recognized came in: Quinn. One of Sam's

friends, although at one point, he'd been with Caine.

"Hey, guys," Quinn said. "How's it going?"

"We're almost done," one answered.

"We had a good day, huh?" Quinn said. There was obvious pride in his tone. "Did you guys all get some to eat?"

"It was, like, the most delicious thing I've ever eaten in my entire life," a girl said fervently. She almost choked up with emotion. "I never even used to like fish."

Quinn patted her on the shoulder. "Amazing what tastes good when you get hungry enough."

"Can I take some home for my little brother?"

Quinn looked pained. "Albert says no. I know this looks like a lot of fish, but it wouldn't even be a mouthful per person in the FAYZ. We want to wait till we have some more frozen. And . . ."

"And what?"

Quinn shrugged. "Nothing. Albert just has a little project he's working on. When he's ready, we'll tell everyone that we have a little fish available."

"You'll catch more, though, right?"

"I'm not counting on anything. Listen, though, guys, you know you have to keep this to yourselves, right? Albert says anyone tells about this, they lose their job."

All four nodded vigorously. The price of disobedience was losing access to a fried-fish meal. That would be enough to scare most kids into behaving.

One of the guys looked around, like he was suspicious. He looked right at Bug, though his eyes slid right over him. Like he sensed something but couldn't put his finger on it.

The hunger was terrible. It had been bad when all Bug hoped to get was a can of beets. But the mere existence of fresh fish . . . he was imagining the smell. He was imagining the flavor. He was slavering, drooling, his stomach . . .

"If you give me some fish, I'll tell you a secret," Bug said suddenly.

Quinn jumped about a foot.

Bug turned off his camouflage.

Quinn reached for one of the knives and yelled, "Guards! Guards, in here!"

Bug held out his hands, showing he had no weapon. "I'm just hungry. I'm just so hungry."

"How did you get in here?"

"I want some fish. Give me some fish," Bug pleaded. "I'll tell you everything. I'll tell what Caine's doing. I am so hungry."

Quinn looked profoundly uncomfortable. Even nervous. Two armed kids rushed into the room. They looked to Quinn for direction, and pointed their guns without any real conviction.

Quinn said, "Oh, man. Oh, man."

"I just want to eat," Bug said. He broke down crying. Sobbing like a baby. "I want some fish."

"I have to take you to Sam," Quinn said. He didn't seem to be happy about the idea.

Bug fell to his knees. "Fish," he begged.

"Give him one bite," Quinn said, making his decision.

"One single bite. One of you go and bring Sam and Astrid. They can decide whether to give this little creep any more."

One of the guards took off.

Quinn looked down at the weeping Bug. "Man, you have picked a bad time to switch sides."

His surfboard was still leaning against the washing machine in the tiny room off the kitchen. A Channel Island MBM.

Sam wanted to touch it, but couldn't bring himself to. It was everything he had lost in the FAYZ.

His wetsuit hung from a peg. The can of wax was on the rickety shelf next to the laundry detergent and the fabric softener.

The ball of light was still there in his bedroom. Still floating in the air, just outside of Sam's bedroom closet.

He hadn't been back to his old home in a long time. He'd forgotten the light would be there.

Strange.

He passed his hand through it. Not much of a sensation.

He remembered when it first happened. He'd been scared of the dark. Back then. Back when he was Sam Temple, some kid, some random kid who just wanted to surf.

No. That wasn't true, either. He'd already stopped being just some random kid. He'd already been School Bus Sam, the quick-thinking seventh grader who had taken the wheel when the bus driver had had a heart attack.

He'd been that.

And he'd been the kid who had freaked out, not

understanding that the argument between his mother and stepfather was no big thing. He'd thought his stepfather was going to hit his mother.

So, by the time Sam, in a panic, had created the light that would not die, he had already been School Bus Sam, and the person who'd burned a grown man's hand off.

Not some random teenager.

He hated this house and hated this room. Why had he come here?

Because everyone knew he hated it, so they wouldn't come looking for him here. They'd search for him everywhere and not find him.

The stuff he had in his room—the clothes, the books, the old school notebooks, the pictures he had taken once with a waterproof camera while he was surfing—none of it meant anything to him. Some other kid's stuff, not his. Not anymore.

He sat on the end of his bed, feeling like an intruder. A strange feeling since this was the only place he'd stayed in the last three months that he had any real claim to.

He gazed at the ball of light. "Turn off," he said.

The ball did not respond.

Sam raised his palms, aimed them toward the light, and thought the single word, Dark.

The light disappeared.

The room was plunged into darkness. So dark, he couldn't see his hand in front of his face. All over town, kids were sitting in the dark, just like this. He supposed he could go around and create little light balls in every house in town. Sam, the electrician.

He was no longer afraid of the dark. That realization surprised him. The dark almost felt cozy, now. Safe. No one could see him in the dark.

There was a list in his head, a list that kept scrolling and scrolling. Words and phrases. One after another. Each representing a thing he should be doing.

Zekes. Caine and the power plant. Little Pete and his monsters. Food. Zil and Hunter. Lana and . . . whatever. Water. Jack. Albert.

Those were the headlines. Buzzing around those great big things were thousands of smaller things, like a nest of hornets. Kids fighting. Dogs and cats. Broken windows. Grass. Gasoline that needed to be rationed. Trash piling up. Toilets plugged. Teeth needing to be brushed. Kids drinking. Bedtimes. Mary throwing up. Cigarettes and pot.

Things to do. Decisions to make.

No one listening.

And what about Astrid?

And what about Quinn?

And what about kids talking more openly about stepping off when the Big One-Five rolled around?

And around and around and around it whirled through his head.

He sat in the dark on the end of his bed. He wanted to cry. That's what he wanted to do. But there wouldn't be anyone to come and pat him on the shoulder and tell him everything would be okay.

There was no one. And things wouldn't be okay.

It was all coming apart.

He imagined himself facing a tribunal. Stone faces glaring at him. Accusations. You let them starve, Sam. You let normals turn against freaks.

Tell us about the death of E.Z., Mr. Temple.

Tell us what you did to save the kids at the power plant.

Tell us how you failed to find a way out of the FAYZ.

Tell us why, when the FAYZ wall came down, we found kids dead in the dark.

They were down to eating rats, Mr. Temple.

We have evidence of cannibalism.

Explain that to us, Mr. Temple.

Sam heard soft footsteps in the family room. Of course. There was one person who would know where he was hiding.

The bedroom door opened with a squeak. A flashlight found his face. He closed his eyes to block the light.

The flashlight snapped off. Without a word she came and sat beside him.

For the longest time neither of them spoke. They sat side by side. Her leg was against his.

"I'm feeling sorry for myself," he said at last.

"Why?"

It took him a few beats to realize she was kidding. She knew the list in his head as well as he did.

"Whatever vitally important thing you came here to tell me?" he said. "Just don't, okay? I'm sure it's absolutely life or death. But just don't."

He could sense her hesitation. With sinking heart he realized he had guessed correctly. There was some new crisis. Some new thing that absolutely demanded Sam Temple's attention, his decisiveness, his leadership.

He didn't care.

Astrid remained silent. Silent for too long. But she seemed to be rocking back and forth, just slightly. And he almost thought he heard her whispering.

"What are you doing?" he asked.

"I'm praying."

"What for?"

"A miracle. A clue. Food."

Sam sighed. "What food?"

"A Quiznos. Turkey, bacon, and guacamole."

"Yeah? If God gives you a Quiznos, can I have a bite?"

"No way. You have to pray for your own food."

"Three hundred kids are praying for food. And yet, we have no food. Three hundred kids praying for their parents. Praying for this all to be over."

"Yeah," she admitted. "Sometimes it's hard having faith."

"If there's a God, I wonder if he's sitting in the dark on the end of his bed wondering how he managed to screw everything up."

"Maybe," Astrid said with just a little bit of a laugh.

Sam was not in a laughing mood. "Yeah? Well to hell with your God."

He heard a sharp intake of breath. It gratified him. Good.

Let her be shocked. Let her be so shocked, she went away and left him to sit here alone in the dark.

Neither of them spoke for a long while. Then Astrid stood up, breaking the slight physical contact between them.

"You don't want to hear this," Astrid said, "but they couldn't find you, so they found me. And now I've found you."

"I really don't care," Sam warned.

But Astrid would not stop. "Bug has come over to our side. He was on a mission for Caine. They have a freak who can see dreams and Caine wanted Bug to get her, take her to some mine in the hills. Some monster."

"Yeah?" Sam said. Not like he cared. Like he was just being polite.

"And Cookie showed up. He had to walk all the way back to town. He walked through the night. He had a note from Lana."

Nothing. Sam had nothing to say to that.

Astrid sat quiet for a second then added, "Bug says they call it the gaiaphage. Lana calls it the Darkness."

Sam covered his face with his hands. "I don't care, Astrid. Handle it yourself. Pray to Jesus and maybe He'll handle it."

"You know, Sam, I've never thought you were perfect. I know you have a temper. But I've never known you to be mean."

"I'm mean?" He laughed bitterly.

"Mean. Yes, that was mean."

Their voices were rising swiftly. "I'm mean? That's the worst you can throw at me?"

"Mean and self-pitying. Does that make it better?"

"And what are you, Astrid?" he shouted. "A smug know-it-all! You point your finger at me and say, 'Hey, Sam, you make the decisions, and you take all the heat.'"

"Oh, it's my fault? No way. I didn't anoint you."

"Yeah, you did, Astrid. You guilted me into it. You think I don't know what you're all about? You used me to protect Little Pete. You use me to get your way. You manipulate me anytime you feel like it."

"You really are a jerk, you know that?"

"No, I'm not a jerk, Astrid. You know what I am? I'm the guy getting people killed," Sam said quietly.

Then, "My head is exploding from it. I can't get my brain around it. I can't do this. I can't be that guy, Astrid, I'm a kid, I should be studying algebra or whatever. I should be hanging out. I should be watching TV."

His voice rose, higher and louder till he was screaming. "What do you want from me? I'm not Little Pete's father. I'm not everybody's father. Do you ever stop to think what people are asking me to do? You know what they want me to do? Do you? They want me to kill my brother so the lights will come back on. They want me to kill kids! Kill Drake. Kill Diana. Get our own kids killed.

"That's what they ask. Why not, Sam? Why aren't you doing what you have to do, Sam? Tell kids to get eaten alive by zekes, Sam. Tell Edilio to dig some more holes in the square, Sam."

He had gone from yelling to sobbing. "I'm fifteen years old. I'm fifteen."

He sat down hard on the edge of the bed. "Oh, my God, Astrid. It's in my head, all these things. I can't get rid of them. It's like some filthy animal inside my head and I will never, ever, ever get rid of it. It makes me feel so bad. It's disgusting. I want to throw up. I want to die. I want someone to shoot me in the head so I don't have to think about everything."

Astrid was beside him, and her arms were around him. He was ashamed, but he couldn't stop the tears. He was sobbing like he had when he was a little kid, like when he had a nightmare. Out of control. Sobbing.

Gradually the spasms slowed. Then stopped. His breathing went from ragged to regular.

"I'm really glad the lights weren't on," Sam said. "Bad enough you had to hear it."

"I'm falling apart," he said.

Astrid gave no answer, just held him close. And after what felt like a very long time, Sam moved away from her, gently putting distance between them again.

"Listen. You won't ever tell anyone . . ."

"No. But, Sam . . ."

"Please don't tell me it's okay," Sam said. "Don't be nice to me anymore. Don't even tell me you love me. I'm about a millimeter from falling apart again."

"Okay."

Sam heaved a huge sigh. Then another. Then, "Okay. Okay. Tell me what's in Lana's letter."

THIRTY-THREE

HUNTER WAS HUNGRIER than he would have thought possible. He'd been hungry for a long time, living on the slimy, tasteless, awful stuff they handed out at Ralph's. Three cans of goo a day. That's what kids called it. Only sometimes the word wasn't "goo" but something harsher.

But now he was far beyond that. Now the days of three cans of goo seemed like the good old days.

After leaving Duck he'd been spotted and chased by Zil's friends. He'd barely escaped. And in order to get away, he'd had to go the one direction they didn't expect: out of town.

He had crossed the highway. Running, scared, feeling he was being chased even when he wasn't. Feeling like at any minute Zil and his thug friends might catch him. And then . . . and he didn't want to think too hard about what came then.

It seemed so crazy. So impossible. Zil had never been like his best friend or anything, but they had shared a house. They had been buddies. Not close, but buddies. Guys who would chill and watch a game or check out girls or whatever. Zil and him and Harry and . . .

And of course that was the problem: Harry.

He hadn't meant to hurt Harry. It wasn't really his fault. Was it?

Was it?

Hunter had slunk across the highway and it was like it was a border or something. Like he was crossing from one country into another. Perdido Beach on one side, something else on the other.

He thought at first about going to Coates. But Coates wasn't the answer to any question that Hunter could think of. Coates meant Drake and Caine and that deceptive witch, Diana. Mostly, Drake. Hunter had seen Drake at the Thanksgiving Battle. Back at the time Hunter had not even known he was developing powers. He was a bystander, mostly getting in the way of the guys who were doing the real fighting. Standing there watching in sheer, wild-eyed terror as Sam fired massive jolts of energy from his hands and Caine picked up things and people and threw them around.

And the coyotes. They were part of it, too.

But it was Drake who had haunted Hunter's nightmares. Whip Hand, he called himself, and that was accurate enough. But it wasn't the whip hand that terrified Hunter. It was the sheer, insane violence in the boy. The madness.

No. Not Coates. He couldn't go there.

He couldn't go anywhere.

Hunter had spent the remainder of the night hiding in one

of the abandoned homes that nestled up against the hills.

But he had not slept well. The fear and the hunger made sleep impossible.

Well, Hunter told himself, if he was still this desperate in two days, he had a solution. Not a good solution, maybe, but a solution. In two days Hunter would turn fifteen. Fifteen was the poof, the big step-off. Later to the FAYZ.

He had heard all about how to survive. How to stay in the FAYZ, fight the temptation. But he'd also heard that lately more and more kids were saying, forget it: I hit fifteen, I am out of here.

They said at the moment of the poof you were tempted with the one thing you wanted most. By the one person you missed most. If you could reject that temptation, you stayed in the FAYZ. If you gave in . . . well, that was the thing. No one knew what happened if you went for it.

Hunter knew what would tempt him to accept. A cheese-burger. Or a slice of pizza. Not candy, it wasn't about candy. Not anymore. It was all about meaty goodness now.

If some demon came to him with a rack of Applebee's ribs, Hunter had no serious doubt that he would reach for it, what-ever the consequence.

He would trade his life for an In-N-Out Double-Double. The only hesitation in his mind was whether the demon would actually let him eat it or would just zap him into non-existence, still hungry.

Hunter hid in the house all night and well into the morning, afraid to step outside. But no matter how hard he searched, he found nothing to eat. Nothing. The house had been cleaned out completely. The cupboards were all open, the refrigerator door wide open, all the telltale signs that Albert's gatherers had been through.

Nothing. To. Eat.

Hunter stood vacant, hopeless, in the living room. He stared at the backyard and thought about the grass and weeds. Weeds were plants, after all. Animals ate them. They would at least fill his stomach.

Grass and weeds. Boiled. He could do that.

Then he saw the deer.

It was a doe. Hyper alert, with a face that managed to be both cute and stupid. The doe blinked her big black eyes.

A deer. As big as a calf.

Hunter was moving toward the back door before he'd thought through what he was doing or why.

He moved swiftly. He opened the back porch door. The deer, startled, took off in a bounding run. Hunter raised his hands and thought, Burn.

The deer did not fall over dead. Instead, it made a squealing sound Hunter had not known deer could make. The deer kept running, but one leg dragged.

Hunter aimed again and thought, Burn.

The deer stumbled. Its front legs kept motoring, but its hind legs were immobilized. It fell on its face.

Hunter ran to it. He found the deer still alive. Struggling. She looked at him with her big, soft eyes and for a moment he hesitated.

"I'm sorry," he said.

He aimed his hands at her head. In seconds she had stopped thrashing. The dark eyes turned opaque.

She smelled like a steak on the grill.

Hunter burst into tears. He sobbed wildly, out of control. It was like what he'd done to Harry. Poor Harry. And now this poor animal, who was just hungry herself.

He didn't want to eat the deer. It was crazy. She'd been alive, munching weeds just a minute earlier. Alive. Now dead. And not just dead, but partly cooked.

He told himself he would not eat the deer. But even as he was telling himself he wouldn't, couldn't, shouldn't . . . he was finding the biggest knife in the kitchen.

Orsay Pettijohn was no longer hungry for dreams. She was hungry for food.

Since coming to Coates she had eaten barely enough to stay alive. The situation was desperate. Kids were going into the surrounding woods looking for mushrooms, chasing squirrels and birds. One boy had made a trap and managed to catch a raccoon. The raccoon had bitten the boy repeatedly before being beaten to death with a piece of rebar.

A girl named Allison had collected a bowl full of mushrooms. She had reasoned that cooking them would make them safe. She microwaved them till they were rubbery but fragrant.

Orsay had smelled them cooking and had been driven nearly crazy by the smell. One of the boys had attacked

Allison, beaten, her and stolen the mushrooms as Allison wept and cursed.

Within a few minutes the boy was vomiting. Then he began raving, crying, shouting at things that weren't there. He'd fallen silent after a while. No one had entered his room since to see if he was dead or alive.

Some kids had gathered grass and weeds and boiled them. They had not gotten very sick, just a little. But they hadn't really gotten full, either.

Kids were thin. Their cheeks were hollow. They didn't look like starvation victims yet, because the serious hunger was only a few days old. But soon, Orsay knew, bellies would bloat and hair would turn red and crisp, and deadly resigned lethargy would set in. She had done a report once on famine, never imagining it would be something she would experience.

More and more kids made dark jokes about cannibalism.

Orsay was less and less sure she wouldn't go along.

Unless, of course, she herself was the meal.

She was lying in her bungalow, in the woods, out behind the school, watching an old download of a show that seemed to be from another planet. The download came with a commercial for Doritos. The characters ate food all the time. It was impossible to believe that world had ever been real.

Suddenly, Orsay was aware of another person in the room. She didn't see him or hear him. She smelled him.

He smelled like . . . like fish. Her stomach rumbled and her mouth watered.

"Who's there?" she demanded, frightened.

Bug appeared slowly. He emerged from the background of Mose's shabby room.

"What do you want?" Orsay demanded, not really afraid of Bug now that she knew it was him. The smell, the fat, luscious aroma of fish, had her slavering like a hungry dog.

"I need you to do something," Bug said.

"Did Caine send you?"

Bug hesitated. He glanced aside and for a few seconds faded into the background again. Then he reappeared. His face was twisted into a very un-Bug-like expression of determination. He glanced warily over his shoulder as if fearing that some second version of himself was lurking, listening. "They have fish."

"I can smell it," Orsay whimpered.

"I brought some for you," Bug said.

Orsay felt like she might faint. "Can I have it?"

"First you have to promise you'll do what I say."

Orsay knew Bug was a little creep. Who knew what he would want her to do? But she also knew she wasn't going to resist. There was just about nothing she wouldn't do for food. Fish would be much, much better than the other type of meat kids were considering.

"What do I have to do?" Orsay asked.

"We have to take a walk. Then you have to do your thing. There's some, like, creature or whatever. They want you to watch its dreams. See what it wants."

"The fish," Orsay whispered urgently. "Do you have it with you?"

Bug drew a Ziploc bag out of the pocket of his hoodie. Inside was white, crumbly, smashed-up fish. Orsay lunged for it, tore the packet open with trembling fingers, and ate it like an animal, sticking her mouth into the bag.

She didn't stop until she had turned the bag inside out and licked the plastic clean. "Do you have any more?" she begged.

"First, you do your thing. Then we go back to town and talk."

"We're doing this for the Perdido Beach kids?" Orsay asked.

Bug snorted. "We're doing this for whoever gives us the best offer. Right now, Sam's guys have some fish. So we're with them. But if Drake gets hold of us, somehow, we've been on his side all along. Right?"

"I'm too weak to walk a long way," Orsay said.

"We only have to get as far as the highway. A guy will be there with a car."

THIRTY-FOUR

EDILIO DROVE THE creepy little mutant, Bug, and the girl he'd brought along with him. He wasn't happy about having to do this. Mostly he wanted to stay in town. Nightfall could bring trouble. And Sam . . . well, Sam wasn't acting like Sam.

Sam had looked like a zombie listening to Quinn and Albert's confession last night.

And then, this morning, Bug told his story. It was every kind of bad news rolled into one shamefaced confession after another, and Sam had just stared. Fortunately Astrid had stepped up.

Sam, Edilio, Brianna, Taylor, Quinn, Albert, Astrid—the seven of them in Astrid's living room, listening as Bug alternately groveled and whined.

Then, Astrid read Lana's letter.

Sam:

I'm going to try to kill the Darkness. I'd explain what that means, but I don't even know. I only know that it's

the scariest thing you can imagine. I guess that's not too
helpful.

I had no choice. It had its hooks in me, Sam. It was
in my head. It's been calling to me for days. It needs me
for something, I don't know what. But whatever it is, I
can't let it happen.

Hopefully I'll be fine. If not, take care of Patrick.
Cookie, too.

—Lana

"I knew she was having some problems," Quinn said, sounding guilty. "I didn't know about this, though. I mean . . . it's like Lana used me and Albert so she could get back out to the desert."

"That would be putting a convenient spin on your own sneakiness, Quinn," Astrid had snapped.

"She brought up the gold to me," Albert said thoughtfully, not at all intimidated by Astrid's anger. "It was a good suggestion. So I jumped at it. But it came from her, originally. Maybe what we need to think about is whether Lana is working with this creature."

"No," Quinn said.

Everyone waited for him to explain. He shrugged and repeated, "No." And then he added, "I don't think so."

"We need Lana," Sam said, finally breaking his gloomy silence. "It almost doesn't matter if she's helping this thing. Friend or enemy, we need Lana."

"Agreed," Albert said, as though the conversation were one between him and Sam, like it was just the two of them debating what to do. For a guy who had been caught breaking various rules, Albert didn't seem too worried.

But then he wouldn't, would he? Edilio reflected. He had food. Food was power now. Even Astrid wasn't really going after Albert, although she obviously didn't like him much.

"We need to know what this creature is," Albert said.

Sam looked at Bug, who had been ordered to remain visible. "What's this Orsay girl's thing?"

Bug shrugged. "She sees people's dreams, I think."

"And Caine wants her to spy on the creature." Almost despite himself Sam was becoming more engaged. Edilio had seen the wheels begin to turn again in his friend's head. It was a huge relief. "If Caine wants it, maybe we want it, too," Sam had said, and one by one the others nodded agreement. "Albert's right: we need to know what we're dealing with."

Which was how Edilio had ended up playing chauffeur to Bug and this strange girl.

"What'd you say your name was?" Edilio asked, making eye contact with her in the rearview mirror.

"Orsay."

She probably wasn't bad looking, under normal circumstances. But right now she looked terrified. And gaunt. Her hair was all over the place. And although Edilio wasn't one to complain, one or both of them back there smelled, and not just like Quinn and Albert's fish.

"Where you from, Orsay?"

"I lived at the ranger camp. In the Stefano Rey."

"Huh. That's kind of cool."

She didn't look as if she agreed. Then she said, "You have a gun."

Edilio glanced at the machine pistol on the seat beside him. Two full clips rattled with each bump. "Yeah."

"If we see Drake, you have to shoot him."

Edilio pretty much agreed. But he had to ask, anyway. "Why?"

"I've seen his dreams," Orsay said. "I've seen inside him."

They were off-road, heading vaguely toward the hills. They had found Hermit Jim's shack—Edilio had a good sense of direction—but none of them had ever been to this mine shaft. All they had were the directions Caine had given Bug. The sun was setting behind the hills, turning them an ominous dark purple. Night would come too soon. No way Orsay could do whatever it was she was supposed to do in time for them to get back to town before full night fell.

"What exactly are you supposed to be doing?" Edilio asked.

"What do you mean?"

"I mean, you're a freak, right? Bug wasn't too clear."

Bug looked up at the sound of his nickname. Then, as if in response, he faded from view.

"I can see dreams. I told you," Orsay said, and looked out of the window.

"Yeah? You wouldn't want to see my dreams. They're kind of boring."

"I know," the girl said.

That got Edilio's full attention. "Say what?"

"Long time back. You and Sam and Quinn and a girl named Astrid. And the other one. I saw you hiking through the woods."

"You were there, huh?" Edilio said. He pursed his lips, not at all happy with the idea that some girl could see his dreams. He'd said his dreams were boring. Mostly they were. But sometimes, well, sometimes they weren't something he wanted a stranger sitting in on. Especially a girl.

He squirmed in his seat.

"Don't worry," Orsay said with a trace of a smile. "I'm used to . . . you know. Whatever."

"Uh-huh," Edilio muttered.

The Jeep bounced and rattled as they went though a rocky patch. They had the top up and buttoned tight. It was dusty and Edilio didn't trust Bug not to drop off and simply disappear.

Then, too, there were the coyotes. Edilio kept an eye out for them.

They were closing in on the hills. There was the fold formed by a spur, just like Caine had shown on the map he'd drawn for Bug.

There was a bad look about the place. The shadows seemed deeper than they should be for the middle of the day.

"I'm not crazy about this," he said to no one.

"Do you have family?" Orsay asked.

The question surprised Edilio. People tended to avoid talking about family. No one knew what had happened to the families. "Sure."

"When I'm scared I try to think about my dad," Orsay said.

"Not me," Bug said.

"Not your mom?" Edilio asked.

"No."

"Because me, I think about my mom. In my mind, you know, she's like beautiful. I mean, I don't know if she was . . . is . . . in reality? Right? But in here," Edilio tapped his head. "In here she's beautiful." He tapped his chest. "In here, too."

They rounded the end of the rocky spur and there, in pitiless sunlight, a ghost town lay revealed.

Edilio put on the brakes.

"That look like what Caine told you?" he asked Bug.

Bug nodded.

"Okay."

"Caine said go through the town. Past a building that's still standing. Up a path. Mine shaft."

"Uh-huh," Edilio said. He knew what he was supposed to do. But he didn't like it. Not at all. Less, now that he was here. He was not a superstitious person, at least he didn't think so, but there was something very wrong about this ghost town.

He put the Jeep into gear and crept ahead, no more than ten miles an hour. The last thing he wanted to do was have to figure out how to change a tire.

"I don't like this place," Orsay said.

"Yeah. Let's not go here for spring break," Edilio said.

Through the town.

Past the ramshackle building.

The path was narrow, but the Jeep managed it at a crawl.

"Stop!" Orsay cried.

Edilio slammed on the brakes. They came to rest beside a high outcropping of rock. If this had been an old Western, Edilio thought, this is where the ambush would take place.

He lifted the gun. It was a reassuring weight in his hand. He checked to make sure it was cocked. Thumb on the safety. Finger resting on the trigger guard, just like he taught his recruits.

He listened but didn't hear anything.

"Why did we stop?" Edilio asked Orsay.

"Close enough," she whispered. "I . . ."

Edilio twisted in his seat. "What is it?"

What he saw shocked him. Orsay's eyes were wide, glittering whites showing all around.

"What's with her?" Bug asked in a quivering voice.

"Orsay. Are you okay?" Edilio asked.

Her only answer was a moaning sound so unearthly that at first Edilio didn't realize it was coming from her. It seemed to generate from her chest, a sound too deep for this frail girl. It was something closer to an animal growl.

"Girl's crazy," Bug moaned.

Orsay began to tremble. The trembling escalated until she was shaking, in spasm, like a person being electrocuted. Her tongue protruded from her mouth, gagging her.

She was biting her tongue. Like she was trying to bite it off.

"Hey!" Edilio slammed the glove compartment open and yanked everything out with frantic fingers, screwdriver, flashlight, a thick digital tire gauge. He grabbed the tire gauge and pushed his way into the backseat. He yelled, "Grab her, hold her!" to Bug, who instead shrank away.

Edilio grabbed her by the hair, there was nothing else he could hold with one hand, twisted his fist into her hair until he had a firm purchase, yanked her head forward, and shoved the tire gauge between her teeth.

Her jaws clamped hard, so hard, they cracked the plastic of the tire gauge. Blood flowed from her mouth, but her teeth no longer closed on her tongue.

"Hold that in her mouth!" Edilio yelled at Bug.

Bug just stared, paralyzed.

Edilio yelled a curse and said, "Do it or I swear I will shoot you!"

Bug snapped out of his trance and grabbed Orsay's head with his hands.

Edilio threw the Jeep into reverse and began backing up as fast as he could go, down the path. The first he noticed of the coyotes was when he felt a bump and heard a canine yelp of pain.

One hand on the wheel, yelling in fear, Edilio smashed the Jeep into an embankment. He threw it into drive, advanced a few feet to get clear, threw it, gears grinding into reverse again as a huge, snarling face appeared beside him. Coyote teeth slavered and tore at the plastic.

Edilio snap-aimed and fired. The burst was short, maybe five rounds, but more than enough to dissolve the coyote's head into red mist.

Down they bumped, down the path, smashing and jolting. Edilio could barely hold the wheel.

Then, suddenly, they were on flat terrain. He spun the wheel as two coyotes hurled themselves at the plastic sheath. The impact of their bodies was so great, it pushed the plastic in and slammed Edilio's arm, knocking his hand off the wheel, stunning him.

But his foot was on the gas pedal and he floored it. The Jeep plowed straight toward a building. Edilio grabbed the wheel, slammed on the brakes, twisted hard, fish-tailed into a two-wheel turn, and roared away from the ghost town.

The coyote pack followed for a while, then fell away as it became clear that they would never catch the speeding car.

Bug still had Orsay in a headlock. But she was making more reasonable sounds, now, seeming to ask to be freed.

"Let her go," Edilio ordered.

Bug released Orsay.

She wiped blood with the back of her hand. Edilio found a rag in the debris of the glove compartment and handed it back to her.

"It told me to chew my tongue off," she gasped at last.

"What?" Edilio snapped. "What? Who?"

"Him. It. He told me to chew my tongue off and I couldn't resist," she cried. "He didn't want me to be able to tell you."

"Tell us what? What?" Edilio demanded, desperate and confused.

Orsay spit blood onto the floor of the Jeep. She wiped her mouth again with the rag.

"He's hungry," she said. "He needs to feed."

"On us?" Bug cried.

Orsay stared at Bug. Then she actually laughed. "No. Not on us. Ow. My tongue."

"On what? On what?"

Orsay ignored Bug and spoke to Edilio. "We don't have much time," she said. "Food is coming. People are bringing it to him. And when he feeds he grows strong, and that's when he will use her."

"Use who?" Edilio demanded, knowing the answer before he asked the question.

"I don't know her name. The girl. The one with the healing touch. He can use her to give him legs and arms. To give him a body.

"He's weak now," she added. "But if he gets what he wants . . . becomes what he wants to become . . . then you will never stop him."

"Hungry in the dark," Little Pete said.

He was tucked into his bed, but his eyes were bright.

"I know, Petey. We're all hungry. But it's not really dark," Astrid said wearily. "Go beddy boody. Nap time."

It had been a very long night and morning. She wanted Pete to take a nap so she could catch some sleep as well. She could barely hold her head up. It was hot in the house with the power off and the air-conditioning dead. Hot and stuffy.

She had been badly shaken by Sam's meltdown. She wanted to be sympathetic. She was sympathetic. But more, she was frightened. Sam was all that really stood between the relative decency of Perdido Beach and the violent psychopathy of

Caine and Drake and Diana.

Sam was all that protected Little Pete, and Astrid herself.

But he was breaking down. PTSD, she supposed, post-traumatic stress disorder. What soldiers get after they spend too much time in combat.

Everyone in the FAYZ probably had it to one extent or another. But no one else had been in the middle of every violent confrontation, every new horror, and also been saddled with all the endless, endless details. There had been no downtime for Sam. No break.

She remembered Quinn laughing about how Sam never danced. She loved him, but it was true that Sam was lousy at relaxing. Well, if she ever got the chance, she would have to help him find a way.

"He's afraid," Little Pete said.

"Who?"

"Nestor."

Nestor was the nesting doll Sam had accidentally crushed. "I'm sorry Nestor got broken. Go to sleep, Petey."

She bent over to kiss him on his forehead. Of course he gave no response. He didn't hug her or ask her to read him a story, or say, "Hey, thanks for taking care of me, sis."

When he spoke, it was only about the things in his head. The world outside meant little or nothing to him. That included Astrid.

"Love you, Petey," she said.

"He has her," Little Pete said.

She was already out of the door when that last statement registered. "What?"

Pete's eyes closed.

"Petey. Petey." Astrid sat down beside him and put her hand on his cheek. "Petey . . . is Nestor talking to you?"

"He likes my monsters."

"Petey. Is . . ." She barely knew how to ask the question. Her brain was fried. She was beyond exhausted. She lay down beside her brother and cuddled close to his indifferent body. "Tell me, Petey. Tell me about Nestor."

But Little Pete was already asleep. And in seconds, so was Astrid.

It was in sleep that she began to fit together the pieces of the puzzle.

THIRTY-FIVE

TWENTY-ONE HOURS WITH no food. Not a bite.

No likelihood of food suddenly appearing.

Jack's stomach no longer growled or rumbled. It cramped. The pains would come in waves. Each pain would last a minute or so, and stretch out over the course of an hour. Then there would be a reprieve of an hour, sometimes an hour and a half. But when the pain came back, it was worse than before. And lasted longer.

It had started in earnest after about twelve hours. He'd been hungry before that, hungry for a long, long time, but this was different. This wasn't his body saying, "Hey, let's eat." This was his body saying, "Do something: we're starving."

A new round of pains was just beginning. Jack dreaded it. He wasn't good with pain. And this pain was worse, somehow, than the pain in his leg. That pain was outside. This pain was inside.

"Have you figured it out yet?" Caine demanded. "Have you got it, Jack?"

Jack hesitated. If he said yes, then the next round of this nightmare would begin.

If he said no, they would sit here and sit here and sit here until they all starved.

He didn't want to say yes. He knew now what Caine planned. He didn't want to say yes.

"I can do it," Jack said.

"You can do it now?"

"I can withdraw a single-fuel rod from the pile," Jack said.

Caine stared at him. Almost as if this wasn't the answer he wanted.

"Okay," Caine said softly.

"But I have to start by lowering the control rods all the way. This will stop the reaction, which means it turns off all electricity."

Caine nodded.

Diana said, "You mean, there won't be any power for anyone. Not just Perdido Beach."

"Unless someone restarts the reactor," Jack said.

"Yeah," Caine said, but distracted, like his head was somewhere else.

"I can lift out a power rod. It's twelve feet long. Actually it contains pellets of uranium 235. It's like a very long, thin can filled with pebbles. It's extremely radioactive."

"So your plan is to kill us all?" Diana said.

"No. There are lead-lined sheaths they use to carry the rods. They aren't totally effective, but they should shield us for the time we need. Unless . . ."

"Unless?" Caine demanded.

"Unless the sheath is damaged. Like if you drop it."

"Then what happens?" Diana demanded.

"Then we're hit with massive doses of radiation. It's invisible, but it's like someone is shooting tiny bullets at you. They blow millions of tiny holes through your body. You get sick. Your hair falls out. You vomit. You swell up. You die."

No one said anything.

"So we don't drop it," Drake said finally.

"Yeah. We carry it for miles and we don't drop it," Diana said. "While Sam and Dekka and Brianna are coming at us. I can't see how that would be a problem."

Jack said, "The closer you are, the deadlier it is. So if you're a couple feet away, you're dead real quickly. If you're farther away, you die slowly. If you're far enough away, maybe you don't die until you develop cancer. And if you're even farther away, you're safe."

"I choose farther away," Diana said dryly.

"How long to get ready?" Caine asked.

"Thirty minutes."

"It's late enough now we should wait for dark," Caine said. "How do we get out?"

Jack shrugged. "There's a loading dock behind the reactor."

Caine sagged into a chair. He bit savagely at a thumbnail. Drake watched, making no attempt to disguise his contempt.

"Okay," Caine said at last. "Jack, get everything ready. Drake, we'll need a diversion. You attract Sam's attention out front. Then you catch up with us."

"Let's just grab a truck," Drake suggested.

"We can't go up the coast road. They'll see us right away," Caine said. "We have to go overland. There are trails going up over the hills. We find a way to the highway. Cross it. Then get a vehicle and head into the desert."

"Why should we sneak?" Drake asked. "We'll have the uranium, right? Who is going to mess with us? Who is going to take a chance on you dropping it?"

"Let me ask you something, Drake," Caine said. "If you were Sam, and you saw me and you and Diana and Jack all together marching up the coast road, and you saw that I was carrying this big, dangerous radioactive thing around, what would you do?"

Drake frowned.

"Oh, look: Drake's trying to think," Diana said.

"This is why I run things and you don't, Drake. Let me explain it in terms you might grasp. If I'm Sam, and I see the four of us, and I figure I can't go after us . . ." Caine held up four fingers. One by one he subtracted them. He left the middle finger up.

"He takes the rest of us out," Drake said. He gritted his teeth, and his eyes blazed with suppressed rage.

"So if the three of you want to just walk out of here all bold and brave, let me know," Caine said, meeting Drake's glare with one of his own. Then he leaned close to Drake, almost embracing him. He brought his mouth to Drake's ear and whispered, "Don't start thinking you can take me down, Drake. You're useful to me. The minute I start thinking you're no longer useful . . ."

He smiled, patted Drake's gaunt cheek, and with a hint of his old swagger said, "We're going to reshuffle the deck. Sam thinks he holds all the cards. But we're going to change everything."

"We're going to feed the monster who has his hooks in your head," Diana said coldly. "Don't try to dress it up. We're feeding a monster and hoping it will show its gratitude by letting go of your leash."

"Let it go, Diana," Caine said. The bluster was gone.

Diana glanced to see that Drake was out of earshot. "Bug's not coming back. You know that."

Caine chewed at his thumb. Jack had the unsettling thought that he might be hungry enough to eat his own finger.

"You don't know that," Caine said. "He might have had trouble finding Orsay. He wouldn't turn against me."

"No one's loyal to you, Caine," Diana said. "Drake is itching to take you down. No one at Coates is rushing to bail you out. You only have one person who actually cares about you."

"You?"

Diana didn't answer. "I know it has a hold on you, Caine. I've seen it. But that monster of yours isn't loyal to *you*, either. It will use you and throw you away. It will be everything and you will be nothing."

"Most of what I have to say is speculative," Astrid began.

Sam, Astrid, Edilio—almost from the start, they had been a team. They'd fought Orc when he was calling himself Captain Orc and trying to dominate the FAYZ. They'd fought

Caine and Pack Leader. They had learned to survive the Big One-Five.

Now, the picture of something much more terrible was becoming clear.

"From what Edilio has said, what Lana's letter said, what we've learned of Drake's story from Lana in the past, and all the little things we've pieced together."

She glanced at Little Pete, who sat in a chair by the window, looking out at the slowly sinking sun and nodding mechanically. "And from what I've been able to guess from my brother. Something . . . maybe some type of freak, a mutated human. Maybe a mutated animal . . . maybe something else entirely that we don't understand at all . . . is in that mine shaft."

"This thing, this gaiaphage, has the ability to reach out, mind-to-mind, and influence people. Maybe especially people it has had some contact with. Like Lana," said Sam.

"Or like Orsay," Edilio interrupted. "Someone with that kind of mind, you know? Like, sensitive, or whatever."

Astrid nodded. "Yes. Some may be more vulnerable than others. I am sure, now, that it is in contact with Little Pete."

"They talk?" Edilio asked skeptically.

Astrid rolled her head, stretching her neck forward, trying to shake off the tension that tightened her jaw. Sam was struck by how beautiful she still was. Despite everything. But he saw as well how delicate she seemed, how thin and fragile. She had lost weight, like everyone. Cheekbones more prominent than before, eyes bruised by exhaustion and worry. There was a welt just in front of her temple.

"I don't think they talk, not like you mean," Astrid said. "But they can feel each other. Petey's been trying to warn me . . . I didn't understand."

"Short version," Sam said in a low voice. "What do you think?"

Astrid nodded. "You're right. I'm sorry, I'm not . . ." Her voice trailed off. But she shook her head vigorously and refocused. "Okay, it's some mutant creature. Origin unknown. It has great power to influence minds. That power is greater over people who've already encountered the creature. Like Lana. Drake."

"And possibly Caine," Astrid added.

Sam said, "You think Caine has had a run-in with this gaiaphage?"

"You asked for the short version. So I'm leaving out the epistemology."

Sam recognized Astrid's favorite ploy: dazzling people with polysyllables. He managed a faint smile. "Go ahead. Leave out the . . . whatever it was."

"Suddenly," Astrid went on, "after months of relative quiet, Caine reemerges. We know from Bug that he was in some kind of a coma, or delirium, before that. But suddenly, he's better. And the first thing he does is charge off to take over the power plant."

"At the same time, Lana begins to feel the gaiaphage calling to her. And Petey is starting to talk about something being hungry in the dark."

"Orsay says the thing is expecting to be fed soon," Edilio said.

"Yes. And then, there's Duck."

Sam's eyebrows shot up. "Duck?" He had not expected this.

"No one listened much to his story. Me included," Astrid admitted. "But he kept saying there was a cave down there that glowed. Like from radioactivity. He said like something from *The Simpsons*."

"Yeah?" Edilio prompted.

"The power plant is at the center of the FAYZ," Astrid said. "We know it was going into meltdown when Little Pete reacted by creating this . . . this bubble. But why were things changing even before that? How did Little Pete acquire that kind of power?"

"The accident thirteen years ago," Sam said, realizing it even as he said it.

"The accident. We've always said it was a meteorite that hit the plant. But maybe it wasn't just a meteorite. Maybe there was more to it."

"Like what?"

"Some people theorize that life on Earth grew from a simple organism that reached this planet by comet or meteorite. So, let's say something as simple as a virus was alive on the object that hit the power plant. Virus plus radiation equals mutation."

"So that's what this gaiaphage is?" Sam asked.

"Please don't act like I just told you the answer, okay?" Astrid said. "Because I'm totally off in guesswork. And it doesn't really explain much, even if it's true. Big 'if.' Really big 'if.'"

"But?" Sam prompted.

"But maybe this thing that's been living under the ground for thirteen years has been living on radiation. Feeding on it. Think about a virus that could survive thousands of years in the environment of space. The only possible food source would be hard radiation."

The next part was hard for Astrid. Sam could see the way her lip quivered. "The power company lied: they never cleaned up all the radiation from the accident. It's been under our feet all this time, seeping into the water, being absorbed into the food we eat."

Astrid's father had been an engineer at the power plant. She must be wondering whether he had known of the deception.

"They may not even have known they didn't get it all," Sam said. "The people who worked there—they probably didn't know."

Astrid nodded. The quiver stopped. The tight anger in her expression remained. "As the gaiaphage mutated, so did some of us. Maybe some kind of synthesis. I don't know. But one safe guess is that the gaiaphage began to run out of food. It needs more. It can't get to it, it can only attempt to make others do its will. I think—I believe—that the meltdown Little Pete stopped was caused by someone at the plant. Obeying the gaiaphage. Attempting to blow up the plant, which would spread radiation everywhere, kill everything nearby... except for the creature that lives on radiation."

"Little Pete stopped the meltdown. Created the FAYZ. But

he did not destroy the gaiaphage. And the gaiaphage is still hungry."

"Hungry in the dark," Little Pete said.

"Caine's going to feed it," Sam said.

"Yes."

"And then?"

"And then, the gaiaphage will survive and adapt. It can't go on living in a hole in the ground, relying on others. It needs to be able to escape. To move freely. And to survive attacks from us."

"Maybe it's good if it comes out to fight," Edilio said. "Maybe we can kill it."

"It knows what powers we have," Astrid said. "And it has had some help imagining ways to build a body that would be invulnerable."

"Help? Help from who?"

Sam put his hand on Edilio's arm, calming him. "From someone who doesn't know what he's doing," he said.

"Nestor," Little Pete said.

"Try some, dude. What are you, three years old?" Antoine tried to pass the joint to Zil. Zil waved it off.

"I've tried it before," Zil said. "I didn't like it."

"Yeah, right." Antoine took a long pull off the joint and began coughing like he was hacking up a lung. He coughed so violently, his knee hit the coffee table and knocked over Zil's water.

"Hey," Zil yelled.

"Oh, sorry, man," Antoine said when he could speak again.

Lance took a hit, made a face, and handed it off to Lisa. She giggled, smoked, coughed, then giggled some more.

Zil had never had a girlfriend before. Girls didn't like him. Not like, *like*. He had never been one of the popular kids.

In the old days Zil was mostly known for the strange lunches his mother packed for him. They were always vegan, organic, and always very "green," with nothing disposable, nothing prepackaged. Unfortunately much of what his mother packed for his lunch smelled. Vinegar dressing for salads, tapenade or hummus reeking of garlic, stuffed grape leaves.

Zil loved his mom and dad, but the coming of the FAYZ had been liberating in one way: he'd finally been able to eat all the cookies and chips he'd wanted. He'd even done what his parents would have considered unforgivable: he had eaten meat. And he'd liked it.

Of course now he would give anything to have a gooey wad of hummus and some whole wheat pita bread.

He had no food. What he had were stomach pains. And his crew. His posse. The Human Crew. All of whom, he realized, were losers. Except for Lance. Lance being there kind of made them look cooler than they were. He even managed to look cool by the flickering candlelight.

"The freaks have food," Turk said for the thousandth time. "They always have food. Regular kids are going hungry, but the freaks always have enough."

Zil doubted that, but there was no point arguing about it. It wasn't some crazy story about the freaks having food that made him hate them. It was their superior attitude. But whatever.

"I heard Brianna caught some pigeons and ate them," Lisa said, then giggled. Zil wasn't sure if she always giggled, or was mostly giggling because she was high.

She was drawing on a pad, perching a small flashlight on her lap and using a Sharpie to do variations on the letters "H" and "C" for Human Crew. She had a version that Zil kind of liked where the "H" and the "C" were sort of joined, slanted to one side, all hard edges.

Antoine had found the weed in his parents' bedroom. While conducting yet another desperate search for food.

"That's what I'm saying," Turk said, pointing at Lisa like she was evidence. "They have their ways of getting food. The freaks all work together." Turk was not smoking. He was staring at Zil. Like Zil might have some solution. Like Zil was going to have some kind of plan.

Zil didn't have a plan. Zil just knew that freaks were running things in the FAYZ. And not just in Perdido Beach, but up the hill at Coates, too. And now at the power plant. Freaks running everything. Well, freaks and their helpers, like Edilio and Albert and Astrid.

And the other thing Zil knew was that things were a mess. People were starving. And if the freaks were in charge, who else's fault could it be?

"They have food, I guarantee you," Turk said.

"Yeah, well, we have tree," Antoine said, and laughed at his own wit.

The front door opened and Zil reached for his baseball bat, just in case. It was Hank. Hank came in, stepped right up to Antoine, who was easily twice his size, and said, "Put that away."

"What are you, the po-po?"

"This is not about getting stoned," Hank said. "That's not what Zil is about. That's not what the Human Crew is."

Antoine looked blearily at Zil. Zil was surprised at hearing himself referred to as if he had some larger meaning. It was flattering. Also confusing.

"Yeah, put away the weed, man," Zil said.

Antoine made a dismissive noise.

To everyone's amazement, Hank knocked the joint from Antoine's hand.

Antoine rose from the couch, looking like he might flatten little Hank. But Zil said, "No. No fighting between ourselves."

Lance said, "Yeah. That's right," but he didn't sound too sure.

It was left to Turk to settle the matter. "Hank's right. Zil's not about us acting like everyone else, like kids. Zil's about us dealing with the freaks. If we sit around getting high, Zil's not going to be able to deal with the problem. He needs us to be cool."

"Yeah," Lance agreed. "But be cool about what?"

"I found Hunter." Hank delivered the news with quiet pride. Like he was presenting a straight-A report card to his parents.

Zil jumped to his feet. "You found him?"

"Yeah. He's across the highway, hiding out in a house over there. And you'll never guess what he's got there."

"What?"

"Food. The mutant freak killed a deer. Then he cooked it with his freak powers and last I saw he was cutting it up with a knife."

"Keeping it all for himself," Turk said. "Just him and the other freaks. They'll eat venison, the rest of us can go boil some grass or whatever."

Zil's mouth watered. Meat. Actual meat. And not rat or pigeon, but something that was almost like beef.

"I've eaten venison," Lance said. "It's good."

"Has to be better than dog," Antoine said. "Although I'd eat some more dog right now, if I had any."

"What do we do?" Lance asked Zil.

Every eye, even Lisa's, turned to Zil. "What do you think we do?" Zil asked rhetorically, stalling for time.

"We go get him!" Antoine said.

Zil slapped Antoine on the shoulder and laughed. "Yeah." Then he high-fived Hank. "Good work, man. Venison is on the menu."

"Right after we hang Hunter," Hank said.

That stopped the conversation cold.

"Say what?" Lance asked.

Hank looked coldly at Lance. "You think the freak is just going to give us the food? He'll kill us, if he gets the chance. Freaks don't care about us, don't care if we starve. Anyway, he's a murderer, right? What are you supposed to do with a murdering freak?"

Zil swallowed hard. Hank was pushing this thing too far. It was one thing busting on Sam, trying to get some respect for normals.

To Zil's relief, Lance spoke up. "Dude, I don't think we want to, like, kill the guy ourselves."

"It was Zil's idea," Hank said. "That first night. Why did we have a rope with us if we weren't going to execute justice on Hunter?"

The rope had not been Zil's idea. But should he admit that? He'd just figured on giving Hunter a beating. He wanted Hunter to cry and confess that he'd stolen that last shred of beef jerky. He hadn't been thinking about actually killing Hunter. That was just talk.

"You think Sam and Edilio and all of them are going to let us just execute Hunter?" Lance argued.

Hank smiled. It was a strange, little-boy smile. Innocent. "They're all gone. Dekka's at the power plant, right? And Sam and Edilio just blew out of town in that Jeep. The whole bunch of them, off trying to deal with Caine, I guess."

Zil's heart was pounding. His mouth was dry. They weren't really going to do this, were they?

But Hunter had meat. And how else were they going to get the food from Hunter?

Turk said, "We can't just take out Hunter."

"Right," Zil blurted.

"We have to give him a trial first," Turk said.

And Zil found himself nodding. And he found himself grinning, like that had been his idea all along. And maybe it had been. Maybe it was what he had known in his heart had to happen.

Yes, Zil told himself. You're soft-hearted, but you know it's what's got to be, Zil. You know it's what has got to be.

Every face was turned toward him expectantly. Lisa, not so bad looking, really. Not when she smiled at him like he was some kind of rock star.

"We'll have a trial. Because the Human Crew is not just about doing random violence," Zil said, sounding as though he believed it. Setting aside the fact that random violence, smashing windows and such, was all they'd done so far. "This has got to be about justice. Otherwise the other normals, our people, will be weird about it. So, we have to have a trial. Then we deal with Hunter. Give him justice. And we share some of the deer meat around, right?"

"Yeah," Lance agreed.

"Bring kids over to our side," Zil said. "It'll be like, hey, Zil gave us justice and food."

"It will be the truth," Turk said.

THIRTY-SIX

DRAKE CREPT TO the hole in the exterior wall. The rim of the hole was still a little warm to the touch. He kept his face in the shadows, looked left, looked right.

Caine wanted a diversion? Fine, he'd get a diversion.

Drake saw Dekka in a lawn chair, head down, maybe dozing. He saw a tarp covering what could only be bodies. He saw two kids playing thumb war. Their guns were leaned against a car. He did not see Sam or his shadow, Edilio. He didn't see Brianna.

The sun was dropping out over the water. Night would fall soon. Caine had warned him to do nothing before Jack turned off the reactor.

"You'll see the lights in the parking lot go out," Jack had said in his usual know-it-all voice. "And you'll hear the turbines suddenly slow down."

Sam had to be out there somewhere, just beyond the narrow slice of parking lot that Drake could see. Had to be. Sam wouldn't have left Dekka all alone with nothing but a couple of idiot sixth graders.

Drake wanted to be the one to take Sam down. If he took Sam down, then no one would ever be able to argue with his claim to be the boss. When the big dogs fight it out, it's the winner who rules. Caine had missed his shot at Sam. Drake wouldn't miss his.

But no matter how long he looked, he saw no evidence of Sam or anyone else worth worrying about.

Just as he was turning away Orc stomped heavily into view. He headed toward the edge of the parking lot, toward some high grass.

Drake laughed silently. The monstrosity had to take a pee.

Okay, so it was Orc and Dekka and a couple kids with rifles. It would be foolish to take any of them lightly. Drake had fought Orc once before and not entirely won the battle. Of course he hadn't been cradling a machine gun then.

Drake rested his left hand on the rim of the hole. Hot but not too hot. He formed his hand into a bridge, then laid the barrel of the gun on his hand. He squatted to get into position. He laid his cheek against the cool plastic stock, closed his left eye, and lined up the rear and forward sights. He wrapped the tip of his tentacle around the trigger.

He shifted the sights left an inch. Another inch. And now they were lined up on Dekka.

Not yet. Wait until Jack had turned off the reactor. Then wait ten minutes more.

But it had better be soon. The sun was casting long purple

shadows and if the parking lights went out, Drake wouldn't have much ability to aim.

Dekka dozing. Looked like she was drooling.

A short burst. That's what he would do. Squeeze off a short burst and watch as the little red flowers blossomed all over Dekka's—

"Ahhh!" Howard yelled.

Drake jerked back. So did Howard.

Howard was right in front of him, right at the hole, peering in like some kind of tourist.

Their eyes met.

Drake yanked the gun to the left and fired. The gun bucked in his hands. But Howard had flattened himself against the wall.

Dekka jerked awake.

Drake cursed and aimed the gun at her.

He squeezed the trigger. But Dekka was ten feet in the air and rising swiftly. The lawn chair twirled upward with her.

Drake aimed. Like shooting at skeet, he thought. Lead the target just a little and—

Belatedly Dekka stretched her hands out toward Drake. A suddenly weightless gun barrel rose too much. The burst tore the air over Dekka's head and she fell as her own personal gravity returned.

She slammed into the concrete. The chair landed on her. She didn't move.

Then slowly, slowly, she raised her head.

Drake took his time. He looked at her. Saw that she was

looking at him. Saw that she knew he had won. Saw the fear and resignation in her dark eyes.

"Scratch one freak," Drake whispered, and slowly squeezed the trigger.

"We've got to sneak up on him," Hank said. "Get him before he can do anything."

Zil was not happy about Hank giving the orders. Not happy at all. "The important thing is to knock him out fast before he can fry one of us. Then we tie him up and use the tinfoil."

"He'll bake his own hands," Turk said with grim contentment. "Like a turkey."

They made their way on foot, not wanting to be heard driving up. They raced across the highway, like they were being watched. Although they had no idea who might be doing that. It was fun. Like playing soldier when you were a little kid.

There was no sign of Edilio's soldiers. Or of any of Sam's posse.

They could smell the deer as soon as they crossed the road. It was amazing, Zil reflected, how well your sense of smell worked when you were really, really hungry.

Zil motioned Hank and Turk and Lisa to stay put, hide behind the garage. He and Lance crept forward, edged around the side of the garage, crouched to peer through the slats of the fence.

Hunter was wielding a big butcher knife. He was trying, very inexpertly, to slice off the deer's hide. He was making a mess of it. Portions of the animal were cooked almost black.

Other parts were bloody. Hunter stopped and hacked out a chunk of meat and stuck it in his greedy mouth.

Zil's own mouth watered, almost uncontrollably. His stomach hurt.

Zil and Lance crept back to the others.

"Greedy chud is eating it all up," Zil reported. "I swear, he's going to eat the whole thing himself."

"Yeah," Lance agreed.

"Okay, here's what we do," Zil said, laying out his plan.

Turk, Hank, Lisa, and Zil took the long way around the house to come up from the other side. Lance had been given a crucial role to play because Hunter didn't know him and had no reason to fear him.

When all was in readiness, Lance stood up behind the fence. "Hey, dude."

Hunter spun, guilty and scared. "What are you doing sneaking up on me? Who are you?"

"Dude, chill. I just smelled the meat. I'm hungry."

Hunter looked deeply suspicious. "I was going to sell it to Albert. Everyone can have some. I just fell asleep, is all, after I got some food. But I was getting it ready now."

Lance climbed over the fence, careful to look nonthreatening. "How about I help you skin that animal? In exchange for a little taste? Plus, you know you have to cut out its guts, right?"

"Of course I know that," Hunter said defensively. "I was getting ready to do that."

Zil thought it was obvious his old roommate knew no

such thing. He watched, nervous and impatient, while Lance moved smoothly, confidently toward Hunter.

Hunter's whole attention seemed to be focused on the big, good-looking boy. But he wasn't attacking. He wasn't even threatening.

"Now," Zil whispered.

He and Hank were first through the gate. They moved quickly, but quietly, not quite running.

The mistake came when Lance glanced at them. Hunter saw the flicker in the boy's eyes, looked over his shoulder, spotted Zil, turned too late, and caught Hank's crowbar in the forehead.

He dropped like a sack of rocks.

Hank raised it up to hit him again. "That's enough," Zil said, staying Hank's hand. "Tie him up. Foil his hands." Then when Turk started tying Hunter's hands in front of him, he said, "No, you moron, tie them in back."

Turk grinned sheepishly. "That's why you're the leader."

They bound Hunter tightly. Then Lisa came forward with a roll of Reynolds aluminum foil and wrapped it again and again around Hunter's hands.

Turk then wound a roll of duct tape around Hunter's hands, imprisoning the fingers.

Hunter did not move.

Zil took two steps, snatched up Hunter's dropped knife, and cut a hunk of meat from the deer's hindquarters. The chunk of meat was half cooked, half near raw. He attacked the meat like a hungry wolf. The others laughed and did likewise. Turk ate too much and vomited into a corner of the fence. Then came back to reload.

They fed and laughed with joy at their conquest.

Hunter began to stir. He moaned.

"Too bad we don't have cement around," Zil said. "Drake knew what he was doing when he plastered the freaks."

"Drake's a freak, though, isn't he?" Lisa asked innocently.

The question gave Zil pause. Was Drake a freak? His whip hand had, according to legend, grown to replace the arm Sam had burned off in a fight.

"I guess he is. I don't know for sure," Zil said thoughtfully, chewing the venison.

"We need, like, some way of figuring out," Turk said.

Hunter moaned louder.

"The freak's waking up," Lance said. "He's going to have a headache."

That struck Zil as funny. He laughed. And when he laughed, the others joined in. "See, guys: stick with me and we get nice, fresh meat."

"Got that right," Turk said.

"So, leader, is it time to deal with this chud?" Hank asked, respectful but impatient.

Zil laughed again. The food in his belly filled him with a sense of well-being. He felt almost giddy. And a little sleepy now, with the sun going down.

And he liked the use of "leader" as a title for him. It fit. It felt fine.

Zil Sperry. Leader of the Human Crew.

"Sure," Zil said. "Let's have ourselves a trial." He glanced around the yard. "Turk and Hank, drag him over to the back steps, prop him up."

Hunter could not seem to sit all the way up. He was conscious, but not fully. One of his eyeballs looked funny, and Zil realized it was because the pupil was twice as big as the other. It gave Hunter a stupid look that made Zil laugh.

"You should have just admitted you stole my jerky," he scolded Hunter.

Hank knelt down to get right in Hunter's face. "Do you confess that you stole the leader's jerky?"

Hunter's head lolled to one side. He seemed to be trying to speak, but all that came out was a slurred sound.

"Blrrrr gllll pluh," Turk mimicked.

"I think he said, 'Yeah, I did it,'" Hank mocked.

"I'll interpret for him," Turk said.

Hank asked, "Hunter, do you admit you killed Harry?"

Hunter said nothing, but Turk supplied the answer. "I sure do. I am a freak, nonhuman, chud scum who killed Harry."

Zil laughed happily. "What can we do? He confessed." He adopted a severe tone. "Hunter, I pronounce you guilty. Guilty as charged."

"Now what?" Lisa wondered. "He's hurt. Maybe we should let him go."

Zil was about to agree. His rage against Hunter was mostly burned out, the flames smothered by his sense of joy at having a full belly.

"Going soft on a freak, Lisa?" Hank taunted.

"No," Lisa said quickly.

Hank looked hard at her. "You think if we let him go he'll just forget about this? No. He'll get together with the other freaks and come after us. You think Sam will be gentle with us?"

Zil looked at Lance. "What do you think, big guy?"

"Me?" Lance looked troubled. "Hey, I do what you say, Zil."

So, Zil realized, it was on him. The thought soured the happy buzz. Up until now he had known he could more or less justify his actions. He could say, 'Look, Hunter killed Harry. I was bringing him to justice.' Kids would accept that. Sam might not accept it, but he probably would have no choice but to let it go.

But if they actually executed Hunter, like Hank obviously wanted, then Sam and all his kids would come after Zil. And the reality was, the five of them wouldn't last a minute in a fight with Sam.

If they killed Hunter, it would be open war with Sam. Sam would win.

Zil could not admit that, though. It would make him look pathetic.

He was trapped. If he looked soft, Hank would turn against him. And Hunter was sure to come after them if they let him go. But killing Hunter would doom Zil.

"We need more kids than just us five," Zil said. "I mean, we need other kids to be in on this."

Hank looked wary.

But Zil had an idea now. It was blooming like a flower in

his mind. "Sam can fight the five of us, but he can't take on the whole town, right? Who is he going to boss around if the whole town is against him?"

"How we going to get a bunch of kids to be on our side?" Hank demanded.

Zil grinned. "We have all this meat, right? Kids are really hungry. What do you think they would do for a deer steak?"

Edilio drove faster than he ever had before. Seventy miles an hour down the highway, weaving through the abandoned or crashed trucks and cars. The wind whipped words away as soon as they were spoken, so they drove in silence.

Turning onto the coast road that led to the power plant, Edilio had no choice but to slow down. There were hairpin turns, and a moment's inattention would send them all hurtling down the slope through brush and boulders into the sea.

Suddenly Edilio screeched to a halt.

"What?" Sam said.

Edilio held up a finger. He strained to hear. And there it was. "Gunfire," he said.

"Drive," Sam said.

Orc was peeing when he heard Howard yell, "Ahhh!"

He didn't care. Howard yelled more than was necessary. He was small and weak and scared easily.

He turned around just as Drake fired. He could see the muzzle flash coming from a hole in the wall.

Dekka was floating. Then falling. And Howard was

pressed flat against the wall.

"Orc!" Howard shouted.

Dekka hit the ground. Not really a problem for Orc. He didn't like Dekka much. She just ignored him, mostly, and looked away whenever he was close to her. Disgusted by the sight of him.

Well, who wasn't? Orc disgusted himself.

Then he saw the face behind the gun. Drake. Drake had gone after Orc with his tentacle and whipped him. It hadn't hurt much, but Orc still hadn't liked it. Drake had been trying to kill him.

Orc didn't like Drake. That didn't mean he liked Dekka. But Sam did, and Sam had been fair with Orc. Sam had gotten him beer.

Orc wished he had a beer right now.

Save Dekka, and Sam would probably reward Orc. Saving Dekka—that had to be worth at least a case. Maybe something from a foreign country. Orc hadn't tried any of that beer yet.

Drake was a hundred yards away. Dekka was half that distance. A motorcycle was parked just five feet away.

Orc grabbed the motorcycle. He held the front wheel in one hand, the handlebars in the other. He twisted hard and the wheel came off easily.

"Someone's shooting!" one of Drake's soldiers yelled, rushing in.

"Yeah, guess who?" Diana said.

"Too soon," Caine snarled. "I told him to wait. Jack. Do it."

"I don't want to rush and—"

Caine raised both hands, lifted Jack up in the air, and threw him into the instrument panel.

"Now!" Caine yelled.

They were out of the control room, at a separate monitor that showed the inside of the reactor itself.

Jack punched a sequence of numbers into a keypad.

The electromagnets switched off.

The cadmium control rods plunged like daggers.

It was all silent on the black-and-white monitor. But the effect was immediate. The vibration of the turbines, the steady hum that had been part of the background, suddenly dropped in pitch.

Lights flickered. The monitor picture wobbled then stabilized.

"Is it safe to go in?" Caine demanded.

"Sure, what could be dangerous about a nuclear—"

"Shut up!" Caine shouted. "Open it up, Jack."

Jack obeyed.

They stepped into a vast room that seemed to be made almost entirely of stainless steel. Stainless-steel floor. Stainless-steel catwalks. Cranes. Caine had the impression of a gigantic restaurant kitchen.

What wasn't stainless steel was safety yellow. Safety railings. The risers on steps. Signs in yellow and black warning of what surely no one who had made it here needed to be reminded of: radiation hazard.

The dome overhead was like something out of a cathedral. But there were no frescoes decorating the painted concrete.

Caine felt abashed by the scale of the place.

At the center of it all, a circular pit, like some ghastly blue-glowing swimming pool. Not that any sane person would ever be tempted to jump in.

A catwalk went all the way around. And a robotic crane hovered over it. Down there, below, in the sinister depths, were the fuel rods. Each filled with gray pellets that looked like nothing much. Stubby gray cylinders of what might as easily be lead.

A massive forklift held a steel barrel in midair, poised. Right where the driver left it when he poofed.

"I'm starting the sequence," Jack said, typing furiously, rattled, terrified, but giddy, too.

The robot moved faster than Caine had expected. It perched like a predatory insect above the too-blue water.

It was hot in the room. The emergency generators didn't keep the air-conditioning running and the temperature began rising almost instantly.

"How long?" Caine demanded.

"To extract it, make it relatively safe, transport it to the used-fuel cooling facility and—"

"We aren't going to have time for all that," Caine said. "Drake's already shooting. We need to get out of here."

"Caine, there's no way to—" Jack began.

"Just grab the fuel rod. Yank it up out of that pool. I'll take care of the rest," Caine said.

"Caine, we have to follow procedure just to get the rod out of here. The only way out is through—"

Caine raised both hands. He focused on the convex dome over their heads, the containment vessel that would hold the radiation in if there was ever an accident.

He blasted the concrete with all his power. There was a wallop of sound that hurt Caine's eardrums.

"What are you doing?" Jack cried.

"Caine!" Diana shouted.

The concrete would not give. Not at this distance. Not with nothing to use as a projectile.

Caine aimed his power at the forklift.

"Be ready, Jack," Caine grated.

The forklift flew. Like an invisible god had kicked it. It hurtled in a straight line. So fast, it broke the sound barrier with a loud bang that was immediately swallowed up in the far louder crash of steel and iron blowing a hole through concrete.

"How strong you think that fuel rod is?" Caine asked.

"Are you insane?" Diana cried.

"Just in a hurry," Caine said.

Drake squeezed the trigger.

A line of bullets chewed concrete just in front of Dekka.

Drake fought the recoil and raised the weapon just slightly, and the impacts advanced toward Dekka, who just stared at onrushing death.

Suddenly Drake was on his back. The gun, still in his hands, was blazing away at the ceiling.

A wheel bounced crazily around the room then fell onto a desk with a loud crash.

Drake let go of the trigger. He scrambled to his feet. He looked at the wheel, unable to make sense of it. How had a wheel gone flying through the air, through the hole?

Orc.

Drake ejected the magazine and racked in a replacement. He was bruised and shaken but not badly hurt. He crept back to the hole, cautious lest something else came flying in.

Dekka was no longer on the ground.

Orc was . . .

A massive gravel hand reached in and missed Drake's head by inches.

Drake fired blindly at the hole.

Then he turned and ran.

THIRTY-SEVEN

01 HOUR, 6 MINUTES

THE JEEP BLEW through the gate. Edilio drove straight to where a shaken, bruised, and seriously angry Dekka was picking herself up off the concrete.

"What happened?" Sam demanded, leaping from the front seat.

The adrenaline was finally kicking in. But even now he felt strangely disconnected. Even now, rushing toward trouble. Like it wasn't really his trouble. Like it was some other part of him that was doing this.

"I tried to fly," Dekka said in a low growl. She shook her head and bent over to squeeze her knee. "Ow."

"We heard something louder than gunfire," Edilio said. "Like thunder. Or like an explosion."

"Sorry, I wasn't noticing thunder," Dekka said.

Orc came loping over from one direction and Howard from the other.

"Orc, man, that was a seriously cool move," Howard

enthused. He ran to his friend and slapped the monster on the shoulder repeatedly.

"I owe you, Orc," Dekka said.

"What just happened?" Sam repeated.

Howard answered. "Drake, man. He took a shot at Dekka. Dekka goes zooming up. Then, bam, comes down hard. Orc, man, Orc snatches up this motorcycle, right? He yanks the wheel off it and throws it at Drake. Like a Frisbee." Howard actually clapped his hands in glee. "Right through the hole you burned in the wall, Sammy. Like sinking a full-court shot."

"Gonna cost you," Orc grumbled.

"Oh yeah," Howard seconded. "Gonna cost. Orc doesn't save the day for free."

"No one else heard a really big sound?" Edilio pressed.

"We kind of had guns going off, Edilio," Dekka snapped.

"You okay, Dekka?" Sam asked.

"I'll live," she said.

"Dekka: what do you think would happen to a cave or a mine shaft if you turned off gravity?" Sam asked.

"Is this a quiz?"

"No."

Dekka nodded. "Okay. I guess if I hit it a few times, on-off, on-off, like that, I guess it would start to crumble. Probably collapse."

"Yeah." Sam put his hand on her shoulder. "I have to ask you to do something."

"I'm going to guess that you want me to crash a cave or a mine shaft. So?"

"So it's not just some mine shaft," Edilio said darkly.

"There's a thing inside it. It's . . . I don't know how to explain it. It gets inside you. It makes you scared."

"I need you to go with Edilio. Seal this thing in," Sam said. "Howard? I need you and Orc to get back to town. I can't believe I'm even saying this, but I need you two to keep an eye on things in town."

"That's going to cost—"

"Yeah. I know," Sam interrupted Howard. "How about we negotiate later?"

Howard shrugged. "Okay, but I'm trusting you." He pointed at his own eyes, then at Sam, making an "I'm watching you" gesture.

"What are you going to do?" Dekka asked Sam.

"I'm going to deal with Caine. I have to stop him here."

"You don't want to go at Caine and Drake by yourself," Edilio objected. "No way. I'm not letting you kill yourself."

Sam forced a laugh. "I wouldn't dream of it. Howard, as soon as you get to town, find Breeze if you don't pass her on the way. If you don't find Brianna, find Taylor. Tell them to send help. And tell them I need someone to let me know what's going on with you guys at the mine."

"Maybe should have turned on the phones, huh?" Edilio said. He winced, realizing too late that it sounded like sniping.

Sam said, "Yeah. Add that to the list of mistakes I've made lately."

"Yeah, here's one not to make, Sam: don't go in there by yourself."

"Didn't I just say I wouldn't?" Sam said evenly.

Edilio looked him in the eyes. Sam looked down and said, "But in case anything happens to me, you all take orders from Edilio."

Dekka nodded solemnly.

"Do not do that to me," Edilio said. "Do not die on me, Sam."

The fuel rod. Twelve feet long. Sheathed in lead now, but still so dangerous, so deadly.

Jack held what looked like an oversized remote control. His eyes bulged. He swallowed convulsively. He tapped a button on the remote, and the rod stopped moving. He let go a shaky sigh.

The fuel rod hung from the crane, swinging just slightly. Caine found himself drawn to it, wanting to touch it. But it was hot. From twenty feet away it brought beads of sweat out on Caine's forehead.

Caine heard footsteps coming up from behind. Without turning to look, he said, "You jumped the gun, Drake."

"Not me," Drake said, panting. "Howard spotted me."

"And Sam?" Caine asked, mesmerized by the dull gray fuel rod, by the contrast between its devastating killing power and its featureless exterior.

"He just pulled up with the Mexican."

Caine glanced at the hole he'd made in the dome. A loose chunk of concrete came loose, fell a long way, and clattered noisily down on some unseen equipment. Through the hole he could see the hillside, purple in the dying light of the sun.

It would take Jack another ten, fifteen minutes, to maneuver the fuel rod to the loading dock. In ten minutes Sam could be here.

"We can't have Sam on our butts as we move," Caine said. An idea occurred to him. Beautiful in its simplicity. Kill two birds with one stone.

"Time for you to prove you're as tough and mean as you think you are, Drake," Caine said.

"I don't have to prove anything," Drake snapped.

Caine met his lieutenant's furious gaze. He moved close to Drake. Close enough to whisper if he wanted to, but no, he wanted this to be very public. "Drake, when I sent Diana to get Jack, you know what? She got me Jack. Now, someone needs to stop Sam, or at least slow him down. Should I ask Diana to take care of that? Because she might just find a way. Sam is a guy, after all."

Diana, bless her twisted heart, immediately saw what Caine was doing.

"Oh, Sam?" She laughed in her knowing way. "You know he's got to be frustrated with his ice princess. It shouldn't be too hard for me to . . . slow him down."

The line would have worked better before Diana had shaved her head and dressed to look like a boy, but Caine saw that Drake immediately took the bait.

"That's what you want?" Drake asked. "You want me to take Sam down? Either he kills me or I kill him, right? Either way, that's good for you and this witch here."

"You're stalling, Drake," Caine said.

Caine could practically read the psychopath's mind as the gears in his head turned over the possibilities. No way Drake could refuse.

No way. Not if he wanted to go on being Whip Hand. Not if he ever hoped to replace Caine.

"I'll take Sam down," Drake said in a voice he intended to be menacing but that came out sounding just a little wobbly.

He must have been less than satisfied with the effect. So with a low growl he repeated, "I'll stop Sam right here."

Caine nodded, offering just the slightest acknowledgment. He turned away from Drake and winked at Diana, who kept her expression carefully blank.

Poor Drake. It wasn't enough to be ambitious. A leader had to be smart. A leader had to be ruthless and manipulative, not just a thug.

Great leaders had to know when to manipulate and when to confront.

Most of all, a great leader had to know when to take great risks.

"Let's hope they built that fuel rod strong," Caine said.

He raised his hands and the fuel rod rose, floated in the air, tethered at one end to the crane.

"Hit the release," Caine ordered.

Jack said, "Caine, if it breaks open—"

"Do it!" Caine roared.

Even Drake took a step back. And Jack hit the button that released the robot crane's hold.

Caine thrust his arms forward, palms out. The cylinder

flew like the bolt from a crossbow.

His aim was good. But not perfect. The cylinder scraped the concrete as it shot through the hole.

"That's the quick way to do it," Caine said.

"If we find it and it's broken open, we're all dead," Jack moaned.

Caine ignored him. He turned to Drake. He saw shrewd calculation in his lieutenant's eyes.

"I'll take care of Sam," Drake said.

Caine laughed. "Or he'll take care of you."

"I'll catch up with you, Caine," Drake said.

It was a warning. He left little doubt that if he survived the encounter with Sam, he'd be ready to take Caine down next.

"Tell you what," Drake said. "I'll bring you your brother's hand. He took mine: it's time I paid him back."

Sam watched Edilio and the others drive off. He felt strangely peaceful. The first time in days.

The only life he was risking here was his own. And in his mind, he had a plan: If he did this, he was done. Done.

He'd made too many mistakes. He'd overlooked too many things. It wasn't him who'd thought to try fishing, it was Quinn. And it wasn't Sam who'd thought of using SUVs to keep harvesters safe from the zekes. It was Astrid.

Sam had been too late, too slow, too distracted, too unsure. He hadn't moved in time to ration food. He hadn't motivated enough people to help out. He'd let the resentment between freaks and normals get ugly. He hadn't protected Ralph's from Drake, or the power plant from Caine.

Kids were sitting in the dark in Perdido Beach, thinking thoughts of cannibalism. And he was in charge, so it was on him.

Even now, Sam had the nagging feeling that he had missed something vital. Something. A resource.

A weapon.

Well, if he survived this day, he was finished. Let Astrid be in charge. Or Albert. Or Dekka. Best of all, probably, Edilio.

If he won this day, if he stopped Caine, and if Dekka closed the mine shaft, then that was enough. More than enough.

And if one of them failed? If Caine got through and Dekka did not kill the gaiaphage? It had Lana. It had been inside Caine's mind. It knew what Lana knew, what Caine knew. Drake as well, no doubt. It knew all their strengths and all their limits. And if it became what it wanted to become, then what?

He was missing something.

But what else was new? Soon, it would be someone else's problem. He was going surfing.

He didn't need waves, not really. He could just paddle his board out and lie there. Just lie there. That would be fine.

But first . . .

Sam crossed the parking lot to the door of the turbine room. He expected to be challenged. He expected to be shot. But he reached the door and found it unguarded.

A relief. But not a good thing. Caine would have someone watching the door. If he was still inside.

He stepped through into the eerie and unexpected silence. The plant was shut down. The turbines were no longer turning. Normally you couldn't hear anything. Now he could hear his own footsteps.

He found the passageway to the control room with the door forced inward. It took him a moment to make sense of the tools driven into the floor and bent back.

The control room itself was empty and darker than usual. Emergency lights glowed. The instruments and computer screens were all still on. But there was no sign of life.

A puddle of sticky, drying blood had been tracked all over. Red footprints.

It was not what he expected, this silence. Where was Caine? Where was Drake?

The power plant was a vast complex and they might be anywhere. They could wait for him in a hundred different locations, wait in ambush until he stumbled onto them. Caine could hit him before he had a chance to react.

Sam stood poised, uncertain. What was going on? He wished he had asked Edilio to send Brianna here. She could search the entire plant in two minutes.

Think it through, he ordered himself. They were here to steal uranium. They were going to take their prize to the mine. So how would they do it? Where would they be?

The reactor, of course. That's where the deadly metal was.

"Not a happy thought," Sam said to the empty room.

He headed down the hallway, following the helpful wall signs.

A massive steel door guarded the entry to the reactor. Caine had not bothered to close it behind him.

Down a long, echoing, dimly lit, long hallway. A second massive steel door, this one open as well, though there was a security keypad beside it and surely it must normally be kept closed and locked.

It had been deliberately left open, Sam realized. For him. Was it because Caine had released radioactivity into the area? Was that it? Was his body already absorbing a fatal dose?

No. Caine wouldn't be shortsighted enough to contaminate the whole place so that the power could never be turned back on. The one thing he was sure of was that Caine would want the electricity back on someday, if only so that he could control it.

That made sense. It did not, however, put an end to Sam's fears. If Caine had contaminated the place, then Sam was a dead kid walking.

He stepped into the reactor room. It was hot and airless despite the vast, arching dome overhead. It was impossible not to be frightened by the reactor core itself, that too-blue swimming hole full of pent-up power. Impossible not to know what it represented.

He walked around it, poised, ready, alert. He came around the far side of the reactor, and there, waiting, was Drake Merwin, his whip hand waving lazily at his side. He was leaning calmly against an instrument panel.

"Hey, Sam," Drake said.

"Drake," Sam said.

"You know what's cool, Sam? I never paid that much attention in school, but that's because I never saw how I was going to use any of that stuff." Drake pulled what looked like an oversized remote control from his pocket. He tapped a button.

An urgent alarm blared.

"Walk away, Drake," Sam yelled over the sound of the klaxon.

"I'm going to hurt you, Sam. And you're going to take it."

"What are you doing, Drake?"

"Well, the way I understand it, Sam, there are these control rods. Stick them in, and the reactor goes dead. Pull a few out, and it starts up. Pull them all out at once, and you get a meltdown."

Something was rising from the ominous blue of the pool. Dozens of narrow poles that hung from a glowing circular collar.

"You're bluffing, Drake."

Drake grinned. "Keep thinking that, Sam. What do you think pretty Astrid will look like after her hair starts falling out in clumps?"

He turned the remote around so that Sam could see. "This button right here? It drops the control rods back in. And everyone lives. If no one hits the button . . . well. According to Jack, we'll die pretty quick. Everyone else in the FAYZ dies slow."

"You'd die, too," Sam said, knowing he was just stalling, mind whirring crazily, trying to figure out a way to stop this.

Was Drake crazy enough to . . . Yes. Of course he was.

The alarm redoubled in volume and intensity. It was an electronic scream now.

"I'm not worried, Sam, because you won't let it happen," Drake shrieked to be heard over the alarm.

"Drake . . ." Sam raised his hands, palms facing Drake.

Drake held his hand out over the glowing, throbbing pool. Held the remote now with just two fingers.

"If I drop it . . . ," Drake warned.

Slowly Sam lowered his arms to his side.

The alarm filled his brain. How many minutes? How many seconds? The control rods rose with majestic inevitability. How long until it was too late?

One more failure, Sam thought dully.

"Don't you want to know what I want, Sam?" Drake cried.

"Me," Sam said dully. "You want me."

"That's the idea, Sam. And you're going to stand there and take it. Because if you don't . . ."

Astrid was with Little Pete, doing one of the long-neglected exercises. This one involved separating balls by color. There was a blue box, and a yellow box; blue balls, yellow balls. Any normal five-year-old could do it. But Little Pete was not any normal five-year-old.

"Can you put the ball where it belongs?" Astrid asked.

Little Pete stared at the ball. Then his eyes wandered.

Astrid took his hand and placed it on a yellow ball. Too hard. She was hurting him.

"Can you put this where it belongs?" Her voice was shrill, impatient.

They were on the floor in Little Pete's room, sitting in a corner on the carpet. Little Pete was gone in his head, not there, indifferent.

Sometimes she hated him.

"Try again, Petey," Astrid said. She stopped herself from twisting her fingers together. She was sending signals of being tense. Not helpful.

She should be running exercises like this every day. Several times a day. But she didn't. She was only doing it now because she couldn't stand waiting. She needed something to take her mind off Sam.

"Sorry," she said to Little Pete, who was as indifferent to her apology as to everything else.

Someone knocked at the bedroom door, and she jumped.

The door swung in; it wasn't closed.

"It's me, John."

Astrid climbed to her feet, relieved it was just John. Disappointed it was just John.

"John, what is it?" They wouldn't send John with bad news. Would they?

"I can't find Mary."

A flood of relief, instantly replaced by more worry. "She's not at the day care?"

He shook his head. His red curls went everywhere, a counterpoint to his serious expression. "She was supposed to come in hours ago. She's almost never late. I couldn't leave to look for her because we're shorthanded and we have so many kids sick. I came as soon as I could. I looked in her room. I didn't find her there."

Astrid glanced at Little Pete. He had stalled with his hand on a yellow ball, and seemingly no interest in doing anything with it.

"Let me look," Astrid said.

They entered Mary's room. It was as neat and organized as ever. But the bed was unmade.

"She always makes her bed," Astrid said.

"Yeah," John agreed.

"What's that sound?" There was a steady hum. Coming from the bathroom. The fan. Astrid tried to open the bathroom door, but it was blocked. She leaned into it and pushed it open enough to see inside.

Mary was on the floor, unconscious. She was wearing a robe that exposed her calves.

"Oh, my God," Astrid cried. "Mary!"

"Help me push," Astrid said. Together they forced the door open enough to let them slip inside. Astrid immediately noticed the smell of vomit.

"She must be sick," John said.

The toilet water was slightly discolored. There was a thin trail of vomit running from Mary's mouth.

"She's breathing," Astrid said quickly. "She's alive."

"I didn't even know she was sick."

Then Astrid saw the little zipper bag, a little Clinique cosmetics bag lying with its contents half spilled onto the bathroom tile.

She picked it up. She dumped the contents out on the floor. A mostly empty bottle of ipecac. And several different types of laxatives.

"John, close your eyes for a minute."

"Why?"

"Because I'm going to open Mary's robe." She pulled the knot on the robe's tie and, feeling vaguely squeamish, opened the robe.

Mary was wearing only panties. Pink. Strange, Astrid thought, that she even noticed. Because the thing most noticeable about Mary was her ribs. They could be easily counted. Her stomach was hollow.

"Oh, poor Mary." Astrid breathed, and closed the robe again.

John opened his eyes. They were wet with tears. "What's wrong with her?"

Astrid leaned over to reach Mary's face. She gently pushed her lips back to see her teeth. She tugged at a lock of Mary's hair. Strands came loose.

"She's starving," Astrid said.

"She's getting as much food as the rest of us," John protested.

"She's not eating. Or when she does eat, she vomits it back up. That's what the ipecac is for."

"Why would she do that?" John wailed.

"It's a sickness, John. Anorexia. Bulimia. Both, I guess."

"We have to get her some food."

"Yes." Astrid didn't explain that just getting Mary food might not be enough. She'd read about eating disorders.

Sometimes, if kids didn't get treatment, they died.

"Nestor, Nestor, Nestor, Nestor." It was Little Pete, chanting at the top of his lungs. "Nestor, Nestor, Nestor, Nestor."

A wave of hopelessness swept through her. Astrid closed her eyes, not wanting to let it get the better of her. She did not need this. Did not need Mary passed out, maybe near death. She already had the autistic brother, and the depressed boyfriend in the middle of some battle. "God forgive me for that," she chastised herself. "Come on, John, we have to get Mary to Dahra."

"Dahra just has a medical book. She's not an expert."

"I know. Look, I don't know how to take care of someone with anorexia. At least Dahra's been reading about medicine."

"We have to get her some of that deer meat," John said. "We have to feed her."

"What deer meat?"

"Zil has a deer," John said. "He's going to share it this evening. At dinnertime."

Despite everything, Astrid's stomach rumbled. The idea of meat was more compelling than anything else. But even hunger couldn't quiet the warning bells in her head. "Zil? Zil's got a deer?"

"Everyone is talking about it," John said. "Turk is telling everyone that Zil caught Hunter. Hunter had this deer and was keeping it all for himself. Anyone who wants some meat just has to come and help them punish Hunter."

"At least," he added, "any normal. No freaks allowed."

Astrid stared at him. John showed no sign of really understanding what he had just said.

"Is Mary going to be okay?" John asked. "I mean, if we get
her to eat some deer meat? Will she be okay?"

"Ahhhhh!" Sam yelled as Drake struck again.

Again and again.

Sam on his knees now. Crying.

Crying like a baby. His shrieks of pain melding with the
harsh lunatic blare of the siren.

If only there was some way to record this, Drake thought.
If only he could tape this moment so he could watch it again
and again.

The great Sam Temple, bleeding and cringing and screaming out in pain as Drake brought his whip hand down again
and again.

"Does it hurt, Sam?" Drake gloated. "It kind of hurt when
you burned my arm off. Do you think it hurts like that?"

Again. Slash!

And the reward of a terrible groan.

"They said I wet myself while they were cutting off the
stump," Drake said. "Have you done that, yet, Sam? Have you
peed yourself, Sam?"

Sam was on his side now, arms over his face, covering
himself. The last blow hadn't even brought a scream. Just a
shudder. Just a spasm.

"Time to mess up that face of yours," Drake snarled, and
drew back to bring all his force to bear.

Down came the whip hand.

There was a blur. Drake wasn't even sure he had seen anything.

And then it was his own voice crying out in shock and horror. It didn't even hurt at first, didn't hurt, just . . .

Eighteen inches of his tentacle arm lay quivering, jerking spasmodically on the floor like a dying snake.

Blood sprayed from the severed end. He drew it back to stare at the stump.

The wire had appeared from nowhere. Wrapped around one of the catwalk ladders at one end. And at the other end, Brianna, holding the wire tight.

"Hey, Drake," Brianna said. "I heard about your idea for cutting me up with wire. Clever."

Drake's mouth gaped open, but no sound came.

The suddenness of it left him dazed, unable to respond. Frozen.

The severed end still jerked and writhed. Like it had a life of its own.

"The remote!" Sam cried out.

Drake spread his fingers.

The remote fell.

"Breeze!" Sam shouted.

Drake spun away and ran.

Brianna's body moved faster than humanly possible.

Her brain moved at normal speed. So it took her several split seconds to see the remote falling, to realize that if Sam was yelling about it in his condition, it was very, very important.

Another split second to guess that the glowing blue was not a swimming pool.

The remote fell.

Brianna dove.

Her hand gripped the remote just nine inches above the surface of the water.

If she plunged into that water . . .

She tucked her feet, spun around in midair, and hit the rising control rods as hard as she could.

It wasn't elegant. She cleared the lip of the pool and skidded across the floor.

But she had the remote. She stared at it.

Now what?

"Sam? Sam?"

Sam said nothing. She leapt to him, rolled him over, and only then saw to her horror the mess that Drake had made of him.

"Sam?" It came out as a sob.

"Red button," Sam managed to gasp.

THIRTY-EIGHT
53 MINUTES

EDILIO'S HANDS WERE gripping the wheel so tightly, his fingers were white. Dekka noticed.

He was gritting his teeth and then forcing himself to unclench in an unsuccessful effort to relax. Dekka noticed that, too.

She didn't say anything about it. Dekka was not a talkative girl. Dekka's world was inside her, not locked up but kept private. Her hopes were her own. Her emotions were her business, no one else's. Her fears . . . Well, nothing good ever came of showing fear.

The kids in Perdido Beach, like the kids at Coates before that, tended to read Dekka's self-contained attitude as hostile. She wasn't hostile. But at Coates, that dumping ground for problem children, being just a little scary was a good thing.

At Coates, Dekka had belonged to no clique. She'd had no friends. She didn't make trouble, kept her grades up, followed most of the rules, kept her nose out of other people's business.

But she noticed what went on around her. She had known longer than most that some of the kids at Coates were changing in ways that could not logically be possible. She had known that Caine had gained some strange new power. She'd seen Drake Merwin for the dangerously sick creature he was. And Diana, of course, beautiful, seductive, knowing Diana.

Dekka had felt the attraction of the girl. Diana had played her, teased her, mocked her, and left Dekka feeling more vulnerable than she had in a long time. But Diana had told no one Dekka's secret. In the environment of Coates, that fact would have come back to Dekka very quickly.

Diana knew how to keep secrets. For her own purposes.

In those early days at Coates, Dekka had barely noticed Brianna. That attraction had come later, after Caine and Drake had made their move and imprisoned all the budding freaks at Coates.

Dekka had been stuck beside Brianna, the two of them weighed down by the cement blocks encasing their hands. Side by side they'd eaten from a trough. Like animals. That's when Dekka had started to admire Brianna's unbroken spirit.

You could knock Brianna down. But she didn't stay down. Dekka loved that.

Of course, nothing would ever come of it. Brianna was probably totally straight. And with lousy taste in guys, in Dekka's opinion.

"Not far," Edilio said. "The ghost town's just ahead. Be ready."

"Ready for what?" Dekka grumbled. "No one's explained

any of this to me. All Sam said is, I'm supposed to crush some cave."

Edilio had his machine gun on his lap. He clicked the safety to the off position. He had a pistol wedged under his leg. He pulled this out, clicked the safety to off, and handed it to Dekka.

"You're starting to worry me just a little bit, Edilio."

"Coyotes," Edilio said. "And worse, maybe."

"What's the 'worse'?"

They slowed as they drove down the main street of what Dekka realized must have once been a town. All fallen down now. Sticks and dust and faded smears of cracked, ancient paint.

"Don't you feel it?" Edilio asked.

And she did. Had for several minutes already, without knowing what it was, what to call it.

"How close do you have to be to do your thing?" Edilio asked.

When Dekka tried to answer, she found her mouth was too dry, her throat too tight. She swallowed dust and tried again. "Close."

The Jeep reached the bottom of the trail. Edilio pulled the car around so that it was facing away. He left the keys in the ignition. "I don't want to have to fumble for the keys," he said. "Hopefully the coyotes haven't learned to steal cars."

Dekka found she was strangely reluctant to get out of the Jeep. She saw sympathy and understanding in Edilio's eyes.

"Yeah," he said.

"I don't even know what I'm scared of," Dekka said.

"Whatever it is," Edilio said, "let's go kill it."

They started up the trail. They soon came upon the fly-covered corpse of a coyote.

"We got one at least," Edilio said.

They stepped carefully past the dead animal. Edilio kept his machine gun at the ready, sweeping the barrel slowly, side to side. The pistol was heavy in Dekka's hand. She searched each rock, each crevice, waiting, tense, clenching muscles she didn't know she had.

Slowly they climbed.

And there, at last, the entrance to the mine.

"Can you do it from here?" Edilio whispered.

"No," Dekka said. "Closer."

Dragging feet through the dirt and gravel. Like they were walking through molasses. Every molecule of air seemed to drag at them. Slow-mo. Edilio's finger flexing spasmodically on the trigger. Dekka's heart thudding.

Closer.

Close enough.

Dekka stopped. Edilio, with exquisite slowness, turned to point his gun at the two coyotes that had appeared almost by magic just above the mine shaft.

Dekka tucked her pistol into the back of her belt. She had some vague, distant memory of someone telling her, "Better if it goes off to shoot a hole in your butt than in your . . ."

A million years ago. A million miles away. Another planet. Another life.

Dekka raised her hands, spread them wide and . . .

Movement from within the cave.

Slow, steady. A hint of pale flesh in the shadow.

Lana moved like a sleepwalker. She came to a stop just within the cave, under the overhang.

She looked right at Dekka.

"Don't," Lana said in a voice not her own.

When Sam came to some time later, Brianna was kneeling beside him, a first-aid kit open on the floor. She was spraying cold liquid bandage onto his worst whip marks.

"Drake," Sam managed to gasp.

"I'll take care of him later," Brianna said. "You first."

The alarm had stopped blaring.

He tried to sit up, but she pushed him back down. "Dude, you are hurt bad."

"Yeah," Sam admitted. "Hurts. Like fire."

"There's this," she said doubtfully. She held up an ocher-colored blister pack. The label read "Morphine Sulfate Injection USP. 10 mg."

Sam squeezed his eyes shut and gritted his teeth. The pain made him want to scream. It was beyond anything he could endure. Like his flesh was burning, like someone was pressing a red-hot iron against his skin.

"I don't know," Sam said through his teeth.

"We need Lana," Brianna said.

"Yeah," Sam said. "Too bad I sent Dekka to kill her."

He lay there feeling waves of pain so great, they made him

want to throw up. The morphine would dull the pain. But it would also probably take him out of the battle. No one else could stop Caine. No one else . . .

He had to function . . . had to . . .

He cried out in agony, unable to hold it in, unable to stop himself.

Brianna tore open the blister pack and jabbed the syringe into his leg.

A wave of relief swept through him. But with it, weariness, weirdness, and a dreamy indifference. He was sinking down and down and down into a dark place. Letting himself fall away, leaving Brianna staring down at him as he fell toward the center of the earth.

A resource, some wisp of his remaining consciousness was thinking.

A weapon.

"Breeze," Sam managed to say.

"What, Sam?"

"Breeze . . ."

"I'm here, Sam."

It would be ready. The creature knew their powers. Knew their limits. Knew everything Lana knew. Probably everything Caine and Drake knew.

But not everything there was to know.

With a sudden, spasmodic lurch, Sam managed to grab her arm and squeeze it tight. "Breeze. Breeze . . . get Duck."

"I'm not leaving you, boss," Brianna argued.

"Breeze. The radiation. You were exposed."

He couldn't see the expression on her face. But he heard the sharp intake of breath.

"Am I going to die?" Brianna asked. She made an unconvincing laugh. "No way."

She was so far away now. Miles away from Sam. In another world. But he still had to reach her.

"Oh, God," Brianna cried.

"Breeze. Get Duck. The mine. Lana."

He let go then, and fell into the pit and drifted from reality.

Brianna hit town like Paul Revere riding a rocket. She zoomed down streets, banging on doors, yelling, "Duck! Duck, get your butt out here!"

No Duck. Plenty of kids heard her yelling and ducked. Which on another day she might have found funny.

She ran as fast as she could. Not fast enough to outrun her own fear. Radiation. She had touched the reactor pool.

Was she already doomed?

She ran into Astrid with Brother John and her own little weird brother pulling a red wagon toward town hall. At first she couldn't believe what she was seeing. Mary Terrafino was in the wagon, curled up and covered with a blanket that dragged on the pavement.

Brianna hit the brakes and skidded to a stop in front of Astrid. Little Pete was chanting something at the top of his lungs. "Nestor! Nestor! Nestor!" Crazy. Like a crazy street person. Brianna didn't know how Astrid could stand it.

When Little Pete spotted Brianna, he stopped. His eyes glazed over, and he slowly pulled a handheld game from his pocket.

"Brianna! Is Sam okay?" Astrid cried.

"No. Drake tore him up." She wanted to sound tough, but the sobs came bubbling up and overtook her. "Oh, God, Astrid, he's hurt so bad."

Astrid gasped and covered her hand with her mouth. Brianna put her arms around Astrid and sobbed into her hair.

"Is he going to die?" Astrid asked, voice wobbly.

"No, I don't think so," Brianna said. She stood back and wiped her tears. "I gave him something for the pain. But he's messed up, Astrid."

Astrid grabbed her arm hard, squeezing enough to cause Brianna pain.

"Nestor," Little Pete said.

"Hey," Astrid snapped at Brianna. "Get it together."

It shocked Brianna. She'd never thought of Astrid as weak and girly, really, but she hadn't thought of her as tough, either. But Astrid's jaw was clenched, her eyes cold and steely.

"Nestor," Little Pete repeated.

"I'm supposed to get Duck," Brianna said.

"Duck?" Astrid frowned. "Sam was probably out of his mind."

"Duck," Little Pete said.

Astrid stared at him. Brianna saw the look, could almost hear the wheels spinning in Astrid's brain.

At that moment there was a commotion. Two dozen kids,

some cavorting like they were at Mardi Gras, came around the corner into the town plaza. Creeping slowly behind them was a convertible with its top down and its lights flashing. The car's CD player was blaring a song Brianna didn't know.

Splayed across the hood of the car was the half-mangled body of a deer.

Walking behind the car, stumbling, dragging one leg like it wasn't working right, face bloody, came Hunter. His hands were covered with something metallic, and wrapped in duct tape. A rope was around his neck. Holding the rope and sitting atop the backseat, like he was a politician at a parade, was Zil. Lance was driving. Antoine, whom Brianna knew to be a druggie jerk, was riding shotgun. Two other kids she didn't really know were in the other seats. One of them was holding up a small, hand-lettered sign that read, "Free Food for Normals."

"What the . . . ," Brianna said.

"Stay out of it, Brianna," Astrid said. "Go help Sam."

"They can't do this!" Brianna cried.

Astrid grabbed her arm. "Listen to me, Brianna. Your job is to help Sam. Do what he said: get Duck."

"This is major trouble coming, Astrid."

"Bad things," Astrid said. "Very bad things are going on. Listen to me, Breeze. Are you listening?"

Someone must have spotted Brianna because suddenly there were kids rushing toward her from the procession, kids waving baseball bats and tire irons and at least one long-handled ax.

"It's a freak! Get her!"

"She's spying on us!"

"Get out of here, Breeze," Astrid said urgently "Find a way to help Sam. If we lose him, we're done."

"These creeps don't scare me!" Brianna yelled. "Bring it on, you punks!"

To shock her, Astrid grabbed her face. She squeezed it hard, like a very angry mother with a very bad little child. "It's not about you, Brianna! Now get out of here!"

Brianna pulled back. Her face was flushed from anger. The mob was racing toward her. But "racing" meant one thing to them, and a whole different thing to her.

Astrid was probably right. They didn't call her Astrid the Genius for nothing. But Brianna knew if the mob lost her, they'd likely take it out on Astrid.

"Take care of yourself, Astrid," Brianna said.

Brianna zoomed fifty feet away from Astrid and came to a stop. "Hey. Morons. I'm right here. You want a piece? You want a piece of the Breeze?"

The crowd spotted her, turned, and went after her, veering away from Astrid.

"Get her!"

"Get that mutant freak!"

"Yeah, right," Brianna sneered. "Come and get me."

She waited, a coldly furious grin on her face, until the first of her pursuers was within ten feet.

Then she gave the mob a middle-finger salute and zoomed away at a speed even a car couldn't match.

THIRTY-NINE | 47 MINUTES

DUCK ZHANG WAS having a fine time if you set aside the fact that no one seemed to be distributing food anymore and he was so hungry, he couldn't see straight.

He'd reached the point where he bitterly regretted the lost hot dog relish he'd intended to give to Hunter.

But on the plus side he was no longer worried about falling through the earth all the way to its molten core. He had begun to figure out how to control this absurd power he had.

Duck was no genius, but it had finally occurred to him that his was the power of density. He could control the density of his body, without growing larger or smaller. If he went one way, he became so dense, he could fall straight into the ground. Like dropping a marble into a bowl of pudding.

Which, as he had discovered, was a bad thing.

But if he went the other way, as he was learning to do, he could float. Not fly, but float. Like a helium balloon. He could do it now even without having to experience violent mood swings. He could simply decide to sink. Or he could decide to float.

Floating was much better. It turned the whole world into a sort of giant swimming pool. And this time around, no one was going to crash his party.

He was floating now about fifty feet above the plaza. He'd started off over by the school. He'd lifted off and then just . . . drifted. The only concern being that he not drift too far from town and end up having a long walk home. Worse still would be drifting out to sea. That could be bad. He could imagine, say, dozing off up here and waking up to find himself two miles out to sea. In the dark. That was a long, long swim.

"What I need," he said to the rooftop below him, "is, like, wings or something. Or like a rocket pack. Then I could fly for real."

"Like Superman."

It was a happy thought. That did make it a little easier to stay comfortably aloft.

One of the other problems was that, unlike water, air was hard to move around in. Going up or down was easy. Going forward or backward was impossible. And even twisting around, for example, if you were lying on your back, well, that was not an easy thing to do, either.

As he was discovering.

He was, in effect, lying on his side at the moment, trying to come all the way around to face the ground. You couldn't really push against air.

But that was okay. He'd figure it out.

One thing he was considering was picking some cabbages or melons. Not now, not with the sun going down. But maybe in the morning. All that lovely, lovely food right out there in the fields. And he would be able to float just above the ground, out of range of the zekes, but able to reach down and snag a nice, juicy cantaloupe.

Only problem was, how to get out over the field to begin with. And then, how to get back. If there was no breeze, he might stay hovering above a deadly zeke field forever.

That was not a happy thought. Not at all. To make his power really useful he would have to learn how to move once he was in the air.

Right now he was having a hard enough time just keeping his eye on the ground below.

Something was definitely going on down below. There was some big thing going on in the plaza. Someone had driven a convertible right onto the grass. Sam was not going to be happy about that. And now there were maybe fifty kids down there, all milling around like they were having a party.

Duck smelled the meat before he saw it.

He had to squint hard in the failing light. There it was, across the hood of the car. A deer.

Now someone was building a fire in the dry bed of the fountain. The smoke was rising toward Duck, just a whiff, really, although he supposed it could get to be irritating eventually.

He was drifting on the slight breeze, so he wasn't too worried. What he was, was ravenous. The smell of meat was overwhelming. No wonder kids were freaking out.

He couldn't see who the kids were, just the tops of their heads, which didn't tell you much. But then he saw that one boy was tied by a rope to the bumper of the car.

Suddenly Duck had a very bad feeling about this gathering.

He spotted a face he knew, Mike Farmer, one of Edilio's soldiers. He was staring straight up at Duck.

Duck gave a little wave. He smiled. He was about to say, "Hey, what's going on down there?"

Then Mike yelled, "There's one up there! Look! It's one of them!"

One of who? Duck wondered.

Face after face looked up at him. Even the boy who was tied up. Hunter. It was Hunter, and not looking good, either. Looking like he'd been beaten up.

Others in the crowd looked up at Duck. And then, Zil.

Duck found himself staring down at Zil. Meeting his eyes. Realizing in one terrible moment what was happening below. Sam, gone. Edilio, gone. No one in charge. All of the leaders off. And Zil with Hunter as his prisoner and fresh meat on the menu.

"A chud spy!" Turk shouted.

"Get him!" Zil shouted.

Someone threw a rock. Duck saw it rise toward him, arc gracefully, and fall away.

Another rock, closer, but still too low.

Then Mike raised his rifle to his shoulder and took aim.

.   .   .

Sam was on the bus. Sun shining so bright through the windows.

It was bouncing along. Quinn there beside him. But something was wrong with Quinn, something Sam didn't want to look at.

Sam felt people staring at him. Eyes on the back of his head. Music playing from far away. Against Me! singing "Borne on the FM Waves of the Heart."

Something was happening at the front of the bus. The driver. He was clutching at his heart.

I've been here, Sam thought. *This happened.*

This happened.

Only it would be different this time. Last time, so long ago, he had taken the wheel as the driver slumped over from his heart attack.

But had the driver had a tentacle around his throat?

And had Sam been screaming?

Sam lurched to his feet, startled to find himself doing it. He hadn't intended to. But he was up and lurching from side to side, grabbing seatbacks for support, eyes staring at him.

The driver turned and grinned at him with teeth dripping blood.

The guardrail swung open like a big gate, and the bus roared through and plunged over the cliff. Falling, falling, the rocks and the sea rushing up at him, the whole bus full of kids not really reacting, not caring, just staring and the driver grinning, and now the worms . . .

Sam tried to cry out, but his voice didn't work. He was

choked by the driver's snake arm, choked and spinning.

Sam knew it was a dream, yes, had to be because the bus just kept falling forever and nothing could fall forever. Could it?

The dreamscape changed suddenly and he was no longer on the bus. He was coming around the corner into his kitchen and Astrid, not his mother, whom he expected to see, but Astrid, was yelling at someone he couldn't see.

No time for this, Sam told himself. *No time for dreaming. No time to waste here.*

Wake up, Sam.

But no part of his body worked anymore. He was glued down. Tied with a thousand tiny ropes that squirmed and writhed like snakes or worms.

And yet now, now, somehow he was moving.

He opened his eyes. Was he seeing this? Was he seeing the room, the floor, the dome ceiling a million miles away?

Was any of it real?

On the floor lay what looked like something washed up from the bottom of the deepest ocean. Pale and fleshy, moist. No more than eighteen inches long. It was pulsating slightly, just a ripple that moved it very slightly. Like a slug might move.

Sam felt sure he should know what the thing was. But he wasn't even sure it was real. And he had to go now. Now or never. Up out of the dark pit and out into the world while the morphine lasted.

Not real, he thought as he moved past the slug.

Maybe, he said to himself, as he shifted one foot forward. Maybe none of it is real. Except for this foot. And that foot. One then the other.

Duck felt the breeze of the first bullet.

He zoomed upward as fast he could. Which was not very fast.

The second bullet was farther from its target.

Duck yelled, "Hey! Stop it!"

"Freak! Freak!" voices cried up at him.

"I didn't hurt anyone!" Duck yelled back.

"So why not come on down here?" Turk shouted. Then, like he had said something brilliant, he accepted a high five from some chubby kid with a bottle of booze in one fist.

Maybe fifty faces were gaping up at Duck, orange highlights and black shadows in the light of the bonfire. Halloween colors. They looked strange. Little ovals with staring eyeballs and open mouths. He could barely even recognize them because this wasn't how you looked at people, from way up high, them with their necks craning.

He saw the barrel of the gun, and the face behind it, one eye open, the other squinted shut. Aiming. At him.

"Get him!" Zil encouraged. "You get the first steak if you can hit him."

"Mike!" Duck yelled. "You're a soldier, dude. You're not supposed to—"

Duck saw the muzzle flash. He heard the bang.

"Why are you shooting at me?" Duck cried.

Careful aim. A muzzle flash. A loud crack.

"Stop, man, stop!"

"You're missing him," Zil yelled.

"Let me have that stupid gun," Hank demanded. He jumped out of the convertible and ran toward Mike.

It may have been Hank's jostling that saved Duck's life. The third bullet whizzed by.

Hank grabbed the gun away.

Meanwhile, Duck had risen another thirty or forty feet, higher than he'd gone before. He was up to a giddy height now. He could see the roof of town hall. He was higher than the steeple of the church had been. He could see the school in one direction, Clifftop in the other. He could see far out to sea.

He was probably a hundred feet up now, ten stories. And up here was just a bit more of a breeze blowing off the water, pushing him gently, like a loose helium balloon, back inland.

Too slow.

Hank fired. A miss. But a close one.

It was insane. He was rising, rising, but too slow, too slow, and Hank had all the time in the world to take careful aim, to line up the back sights with the front, to settle them just below his target, and squeeze off a round.

Duck tensed, awaiting the bullet. Wondering if it would hit his leg, his arm, and merely cause horrible pain. Or strike his heart or head, and finish him.

Hank squeezed the trigger. Nothing happened.

Hank threw the gun at Mike in disgust.

Mike frantically reloaded, but in the time it took him to slide in more bullets, Duck had floated and drifted higher and farther.

Hank fired. By the time the bullet had come close to Duck, gravity had slowed it. Duck could see it fly past his head. He saw the moment it reached its apogee. And then he watched it drop back toward the ground.

Duck threw up as he drifted over the church. Sacrilege, probably. But his stomach was empty, so not much rained down on the shattered building below.

Duck floated on. Away from the horror unfolding in the plaza. They were going to kill Hunter. Hunter, who had begged for his help.

Nothing he could do: he went where the wind blew. And nothing he could have done—except get shot—if the wind blew him the other way.

"Superpowers," he said to himself, "don't always make you a superhero."

She had lost herself again.

She kept coming and going. One minute there, the next gone.

Sometimes she was inside herself. Inside her own brain. Other times she was somewhere else, looking at herself from a distance.

It was so sad seeing what had become of Lana Arwen Lazar.

Then she would be there, right inside her own lolling head,

looking out through her own red-rimmed eyes.

She walked now. Two feet. Walking.

Seeing the stone walls beside her.

Danger ahead—the gaiaphage felt it, and so did she. So did she. Had to be stopped.

Something Lana was supposed to get. Something she had dropped.

She stopped. The gaiaphage didn't know what to call it. And for a moment Lana couldn't make sense of the images in her head. The flat-steel surfaces. The cross-hatched grip.

"No," she begged the creature.

"No, I don't want to," she cried as she knelt.

Her hand groped for it. Fingers touched it. It was cold. Her index finger curled around the trigger. If she could just raise it to her own head, if she could . . .

But now she was walking, and the weight was in her hand, so heavy. So terribly heavy.

She reached the truck, still locking the mine shaft entrance. She crawled onto the hood, sobbing. Slid through the shattered window, indifferent to the glass as it cut her palms and knees.

Why couldn't she stop herself? Why couldn't she stop this hand, that foot?

The light of the stars overhead was blinding as she stepped into the mouth of the mine shaft.

The enemy there, the danger.

Lana knew the enemy's name. She knew what the enemy would do. When the gaiaphage had fed, he would be ready for Dekka. More than ready.

But not yet.

"Don't," Lana said to Dekka. "Don't."

Dekka froze. There was a look of horror on her face.

The other one stood to one side. He carried a gun. Lana knew his name, too. Edilio. But he was not the danger.

"It's Lana," Dekka said.

"Lana, run to us," Edilio said. He held out his hand.

Lana felt an overwhelming feeling of sadness. A sob that filled the world. It was as if that outstretched hand was all she could see, all she could feel.

She wanted so badly to reach for it.

"Come on, Lana," Edilio urged.

Tears filled Lana's eyes. Her head moved slowly, side to side. "I don't want to," her voice said.

Lana lifted the gun.

"I don't . . . ," Lana whispered.

She took aim. Inside her head a scream a scream a scream.

"Lana, no!" Dekka cried.

Lana didn't hear the shot. But she felt the gun buck in her hand. She saw the jet of flame.

And she saw Edilio fall straight back.

She saw him land on his back.

His head bounced as he hit.

Lana shifted her aim. Sights lined up on Dekka who seemed paralyzed in shock.

Lana squeezed the trigger.

Click.

Click.

Dekka raised her hands. Her expression was furious, determined. But she did not use her power. Her eyes flickered. She lowered her hands and rushed to Edilio.

Dekka knelt over Edilio. She gasped. Pressed her hand against the wound in his chest. Trying to hold the blood in.

"Lana. Lana," Dekka pleaded with tears running down her cheeks. "Help him."

Lana stood confused. The gun wasn't working. Why wasn't it working? The question was not hers, the thought not her thought.

The gaiaphage was confused. Why did the weapon not kill? It did not understand. So much it knew. But not everything.

The gun slipped from Lana's fingers. She heard it clatter on stone.

"Lana, you can save him," Dekka pleaded.

I can save no one, Lana thought. Least of all myself.

Lana took two steps back.

The last thing she saw was Dekka rushing to Edilio.

Lana returned to her master.

FORTY

THE SUN WAS sinking into the sea. Shadows were lengthening in Perdido Beach. The plaza was full of kids, far more kids than Zil could possibly feed with one deer.

It worried him at first. But then he realized the simple solution: Those who would take part in the sacrificing of Hunter would eat. Those who would only watch, would not.

Those who laid hands on Hunter would be a part of Zil's group. They would have demonstrated their loyalty beyond all doubt. Their bridges would be burned. He would own them, body and soul after that.

They would be lifetime members of the Human Crew.

A big fire had been built in the dried-out fountain. Someone clever had raided the hardware store and had rigged a spit onto which big hunks of the deer, chopped into slabs with an ax, were roasting.

The smell was amazing.

Turk had grabbed spray cans and tagged the fountain and

some of the sidewalks with Lisa's stylized "HC" logo.

"How we doing this, man?" Antoine asked.

"Doing what?" Zil answered.

"Hunter. How we doing it?"

Hunter had recovered a little from the hit to the head. He had tried to free his hands, but Hank had smacked him good. Cheers had risen from some of the crowd. Others had looked queasy.

"Yank," Turk said, and made a comic hanging motion.

"Where? Is what I mean, man," Antoine said. He was slurring badly, almost to the point of not being intelligible. Drunk.

"There." Lance pointed to the tumbled-down church.

"Where the door used to be? It makes an arch. You can pass a rope up through that hole. One end around Hunter's neck, right? The other end can be really long. You can extend it all the way down through the square, so you could have, like, a hundred kids pulling on it."

He frowned and glanced back and forth. "Pull him up, then you can tie the rope off to one of the trees, around the base."

Zil considered Lance curiously. It seemed strange to find this popular kid getting involved, actually coming up with a plan for an execution. Weird. Lance had none of Hank's seething, crazy rage. None of Turk's desperate toadying. He wasn't a pathetic burn-out like Antoine.

"That's a good plan, Lance," Zil said.

Hank's eyes glittered dangerously.

"If we're going to do this, we better get on with it," Turk

said. "Astrid's a freak-lover. And that Brianna. She could be bringing Sam."

"Sam's busy. Besides, I'm not afraid of Sam. We have all these kids with us," Zil said, sounding far more confident than he felt. "But yeah, let's get this thing going. Hank. Lance. Start stringing the rope."

Zil climbed up onto the trunk of the convertible. "Everybody! Everybody!"

He had everyone's attention almost instantly. The crowd was hungry, desperate, and very impatient. Several kids had tried to rush at the meat and grab some right from the flames. They'd had to be beaten back by Hank and a group of kids he'd enlisted as bodyguards.

"The food is ready," Zil announced to loud cheers.

"But we have something more important to do, first, before we can eat."

Groans.

"We have to carry out some justice."

That earned a silent stare until Turk and Hank started raising their hands and yelling, showing the crowd how to act.

"This mutant, this nonhuman scum here, this freak Hunter . . ." Zil pointed, arm stretched out, at his captive. "This chud deliberately murdered my best friend, Harry."

"Na troo," Hunter said. His mouth still didn't work right. Brain damage, Zil supposed, from the little knock on his head. Half of Hunter's face drooped like it wasn't quite attached right. It made it easier for the crowd of kids to sneer at him, and Hunter, yelling in his drooling retard voice, wasn't helping his case.

"He's a killer!" Zil cried suddenly, smacking his fist into his palm.

"A freak! A mutant!" he cried. "And we know what they're like, right? They always have enough food. They run everything. They're in charge and we're all starving. Is that some kind of coincidence? No way."

"Na troo," Hunter moaned again.

"Take him!" Zil cried to Antoine and Hank. "Take him, the murdering mutant scum!"

They seized Hunter by the arms. He could walk, but only by dragging one leg. They half carried, half marched him across the plaza. They dragged him up the church steps.

"Now," Zil said, "here is how we're going to do this." He waved his hand toward the rope that Lance was unspooling back through the plaza.

An expectant pause. A dangerous, giddy feeling. The smell of the meat had them all crazy. Zil could feel it.

"You all want some of this delicious venison?"

They roared their assent.

"Then you'll all grab on to the rope."

A dozen or more kids leaped forward to seize the rope. Others hesitated. Glanced toward the church. Glanced toward Hunter being held by Zil's crew.

Lance had tied a noose.

Hank now pushed it down over Hunter's head and tightened it around his neck.

But there was a disturbance in the crowd. Someone was

pushing through. Kids were yelling at the intruder. There was shoving. But finally Astrid appeared, disheveled, flushed, furious. She wasn't hauling a wagon anymore. And she didn't have John with her, which was good, Zil thought: Mary and John were popular. A lot of these kids had little brothers and sisters at the day care.

Astrid was a different story. She was tied to Sam, and a lot of kids thought she was too full of her own self. Plus, she had her creepy little brother with her. And no one liked him. Rumor had it that he was some kind of powerful freak himself. But was too retarded to do anything much about it.

Waste of time keeping a retard alive when humans were starving.

"Stop this!" Astrid cried. "Stop this now!"

Zil looked down at her. He was almost surprised to realize that he was not intimidated by her. Astrid the Genius. Sam's girlfriend. One of the three or four most important people in the FAYZ.

But Zil had the power of the crowd behind him. He felt it in his heart and soul, like a drug that made him all-powerful. Invincible and unafraid.

"Go away, Astrid," he said. "We don't like traitors here."

"Oh? And how do we feel about thugs? How do we feel about murder?" She was really very pretty, Zil noticed. Much hotter than Lisa. And now that he was taking over . . .

"We're here to execute a murderer," Zil said, pointing at Hunter. "We are bringing justice in the name of all normals."

"There's no justice without a trial," Astrid said.

Zil grinned. He spread his hands. "We had a trial, Astrid. And this chud scum was found guilty of murdering a normal.

"The penalty," he added, "is death."

Astrid turned to face the mob. "If you do this, you'll never forgive yourselves."

"We're hungry," a voice cried, and was immediately echoed by others.

"You're going to murder a boy in a church?" Astrid demanded, pointing toward the church. "A church? In God's house?"

Zil could see that those words had an effect. There were some nervous looks.

"You will never wash the stain of this off your hands," Astrid cried. "If you do this, you will never be able to forget it. What do you think your parents would say?"

"There are no parents in the FAYZ. No God, either," Zil said. "There's just humans trying to stay alive, and freaks taking everything for themselves. And you, Astrid, are all about helping the freaks. Why? I really wonder why?"

He was starting to genuinely enjoy this. It was great fun to see pretty, smart Astrid looking helpless.

"You know what I think, people?" Zil said. "I think maybe Astrid has some powers she hasn't told anyone about. Or else . . ." He paused for dramatic effect. "Or else it's the little retard who has the powers."

He saw the fear dawn on her face. Righteous anger surrendering to fear.

So smart, so quick, Astrid was. So dumb, too, Zil thought.

"I think," Zil said, "we may have another couple of freaks at our little picnic."

"No," Astrid whispered.

"Hank," Zil said, and nodded.

Astrid turned too late to see Hank behind her. He swung. Astrid felt the blow as if it had hit her.

It hit Little Pete.

He fell like a marionette with the strings cut.

"Now!" Zil said. "Grab her."

Diana could hardly believe it. They had moved quickly, easily up the side of the hill overlooking the power plant and had found the fuel rod.

It had not been hard to find. A fire had started in the dry brush where it hit. Just a low, scurrying fire. Caine was able to pluck the fuel rod up with ease and hold it high in the air.

Jack stood beneath the fuel rod, sweating from the heat, sweating too from fear, Diana guessed. The only light came from the fire.

"I don't see anything popped or broken," Jack said. He pulled something that looked like a yellow remote control out of his pocket and stared at it.

"What's that?"

"It's a dosimeter," Jack said. He thumbed a switch. Diana heard an irregular clicking sound. Click. Clickclick. Click. Clickclickclick.

"We're okay," Jack said, and breathed a relieved sigh. "So far."

"What's that clicking?"

"Whenever it detects a radioactive particle, it clicks. If it starts clicking constantly, we'll have a problem. There's a tone when it gets to dangerous levels."

Even now, Jack loved showing off his geek knowledge. Even knowing what was happening, what had happened. Guessing, at least, what was ahead.

"What you hear now is just background radiation."

"Let's get out of here," Caine said. "Fire climbs. We need to stay ahead of it."

They climbed the hill. The fire did not catch them. It didn't seem to be spreading. Maybe because there was no wind.

Down the other side to the highway.

No one had come after them. Sam was nowhere to be seen.

They rested—collapsed was more like it—inside an Enterprise Rent-a-Car office. The two soldiers went on a search through dusty desks and file cabinets, looking for food.

One triumphantly produced a small tin of hard peppermints. There were nine mints. Enough for everyone to have one, and then to salivate over the remaining four.

"Time to get a car," Caine announced. He had "parked" the fuel rod outside, leaning it against the exterior wall. "We need something with an open top."

He held up one of the peppermints for the two soldiers to see. "This goes to whoever finds me the best vehicle, with keys."

The two thugs raced for the door. Diana's stomach cramped, wringing a cry from her. A small piece of candy did not cure hunger, it sharpened it.

There were no lights in the office. None on the highway outside. Darkness in every direction except for the pale light of non-stars and a non-moon.

They slumped on sagging office chairs and propped weary feet on the desks.

Diana began laughing.

"Something funny?' Caine asked.

"We're sitting in the dark, willing to sell our souls for another peppermint, with enough uranium to give a terrorist a wet dream." She wiped tears from her eyes. "No, nothing's funny about that."

"Shut up, Diana," Caine said wearily.

Diana wondered if using his telekinetic power to "carry" the fuel rod was tiring him out. Maybe.

Diana forced herself to stand up. She went to Caine and put her hand on his shoulder. "Caine."

"Don't start," Caine said.

"You don't have to do this," Diana said.

Caine didn't answer.

One of the soldiers stuck his head in. "I found an Escalade. Keys are inside, but it's locked."

"Jack? Go open the car for him," Caine ordered. "While you're at it, rip the roof off."

"Do I get a mint?" Jack asked.

Diana laughed out loud, a borderline hysterical sound.

"What do you think your little friend in the desert will do once you've given it what it wants?" When Caine didn't answer, Diana said, in a puzzled tone, "By the way, should I be saying 'it,' or is it a 'he'?"

Caine covered his face with his hands.

"Does he have a nickname?" Diana went on remorselessly. "I mean, 'gaiaphage' is so long. Can we call him phage? Or maybe just 'G'?"

From outside came the sound of metal ripping, glass shattering. Jack converting an SUV into a convertible.

"The 'G' monster," Diana said.

Seconds later, the door burst inward. Jack.

"Someone's coming," Jack said urgently. "Coming right down the road."

"Driving?" Caine demanded, leaping up.

"No. We just heard footsteps, like someone running."

Diana's heart leaped. Sam. It had to be Sam.

But at the same time, she felt dread. She wanted Caine stopped. She did not want him killed.

Caine ran outside, Diana right behind him, and gunfire erupted. The two soldiers firing blindly down the highway. Bright yellow fire from the muzzles, a deafening noise, and off in the impenetrable gloom the sound of a voice cursing, yelling at them to stop it, followed by furious cursing.

"Stop shooting, you stupid idiots!" Caine roared.

The firing stopped.

"Is that you, Drake?" one of the soldiers called out, shaky and scared.

"I'm going to whip the skin off you!" Drake bellowed.

The gaunt psychopath appeared, eyes glittering in moonlight, hair wild. He was moving strangely, cradling his whip hand with his other hand.

There was something odd about it. Diana couldn't figure out what.

"What kept you?" Caine asked.

"What kept me? Sam. I took him down," Drake said. "Me. I whipped him and tore him up and he will never recover, never, not after what—"

"Whoa," Jack said, so shocked, he dared to interrupt Drake in mid-rant. "Your . . . your thing."

Diana saw then the way Drake's tentacle ended in a flat surface, a stump.

And then, to Diana's astonishment, Drake sobbed. Just once. Just one stifled sob. He is human, after all, Diana thought. Barely. But capable of fear, capable of feeling pain.

"You didn't kill him?" Caine asked Drake.

"I told you," Drake yelled. "He's done for!"

Caine shook his head. "If you didn't kill him, he's not done for. In fact, it looks kind of like the last time you fought Sam: you with part of you missing."

"It wasn't Sam," Drake said through clenched teeth. "I'm telling you, I took Sammy Boy down. Me! I took him down!"

"Then why are you looking suddenly . . . stumpy?" Diana asked, unable to resist the urge to take a shot at her nemesis.

"Brianna," Drake said.

Out of the corner of her eye, Diana noticed the way Jack's head lifted and his chest puffed out.

"She showed up. Too late to save Sam. You won't see Sam again."

"When I see his body, I'll believe that," Caine said dryly.

Diana agreed. Drake was too insistent. Too shrill. Too determined to convince them all.

"Let's move out," Caine said.

One of the soldiers turned the key on the mutilated Escalade. The battery was weak. It seemed at first it wouldn't start. But then the engine caught and roared to life. Lights came on inside the car. Headlights were painfully bright.

"Everyone in," Caine ordered. "If Drake's right and Sam is down—even temporarily—we're done sneaking. It's ten miles to the mine. Twenty minutes and we're there."

"Where's my peppermint?" Jack asked.

Caine raised the fuel rod and held it poised in the air above their heads. Close enough that the heat was like a bright, noon sun.

Little Pete lay unconscious.

Astrid was hauled, kicked, and shoved as Antoine tied her wrists and breathed alcohol into her face.

Her brain was spinning. What to do? What to say to stop the insanity?

Nothing. There was nothing she could say now, not with hunger ruling the mob. She could do nothing but witness.

Astrid looked into each face, searching for the humanity that should speak to them, stop them, even now. What she saw was madness. Desperation.

They were too hungry. They were too scared.

They were going to kill Hunter, and then Zil would come for Little Pete and for Astrid herself. He would have no choice.

The instant Hunter died, Zil and his mob would have drawn a line in blood down the middle of the FAYZ.

"Dear Jesus, I know you're watching," Astrid prayed. "Don't let them do this."

"Are you ready?" Zil shrieked.

The mob roared.

"Dear Lord . . . ," Astrid prayed.

"It's time for justice!"

". . . no."

"Edilio, don't die," Dekka begged.

"Don't die."

Edilio made a gurgling sound that might have been an attempt to speak.

Dekka had his shirt open. The hole was in his chest, just above his left nipple. When she held her hands against it, the blood seeped from beneath her palm. When she took her hand away, for even a second, the blood pumped out.

"Oh, God," Dekka sobbed.

Another gurgle, and Edilio tried to raise his head.

"Don't try to move," Dekka ordered. "Don't try to talk."

But Edilio's right hand jerked upward suddenly. He seemed to be trying to grab her collar, but the hand wouldn't connect, the fingers wouldn't grasp. Edilio dropped his hand and seemed for a moment to pass out.

But then, with what had to be almost superhuman effort, he said two words. "Do it."

Dekka knew what he was asking her to do.

"I can't, Edilio, I can't," Dekka said. "Lana's the only one who can save you now."

"Do . . ."

"If I do, she'll die," Dekka said. She was bathed in sweat, sweat dripping from her forehead, dripping onto his bloody chest. "If I do it, Lana can't save you."

"Do . . . uh . . ."

Dekka shook her head violently. "You're not going to die, Edilio."

She grabbed him around his chest from behind. Like she was doing the Heimlich maneuver on him. Using his own weight against her slippery hands to seal the wound.

She dragged him away from the mine shaft. Dragged him down the trail, his heels making tracks in the dirt. She wept and sobbed as she went, staggered under the weight, fell into boulders, but put distance between herself and the mine shaft.

Because he was right. He was right, poor Edilio, he was right, she had to do it. She had to collapse that mine. But Edilio wasn't going to be buried there, no way. No, Edilio would have a place of honor in the plaza.

The honored dead. Another grave. The first one that Edilio had not dug himself.

"Hang in there, Edilio, you're going to make it," Dekka lied.

She collapsed at the bottom of the trail, at the edge of the ghost town. Dekka sat on Edilio and pressed down on the wound. The force of the blood was weaker now. She could almost hold the blood back now, not a good thing, no, because it meant he was almost finished, his brave heart almost done beating.

Dekka looked up straight into the glittering eyes of a coyote. She could sense the others around her, closing in. Wary, but sensing that a fresh meal was close at hand.

FORTY-ONE

DUCK WAS SO high up, he could see smoke rising from the distant power plant.

He was still shaking from being shot at. Shot at! He had never hurt anyone.

Now it was like he had been drafted into a war he didn't even know was going on. It was nuts. He could have been killed. He might still be killed.

Instead, he had floated away, unharmed.

While others fought to survive. While others stood up against the evil that was being done.

Fortunately the slight breeze was wafting him away from the town square, where all the madness was going on. In a few more minutes he would raise his density and drop gently back to earth. Then, hopefully, he would find some food. The smell of cooking meat had left him crazy with hunger.

"Nothing you could have done, Duck," he told himself.

"That's true," he agreed. "Nothing."

"Not our fault."

He made a weak grab at a seagull that hovered just out of reach, floating on its boomerang-shaped wings. He was hungry enough that he would have eaten the bird raw. In midair.

Out of the corner of his eye he noticed a blur on the ground below. The blur stopped suddenly. He couldn't see her face, but it could only be Brianna. In her hand she held a pigeon.

Brianna could do what Duck could not. Brianna could catch and eat birds. Maybe she would share. After all, they were both freaks. Both on the same side. Right?

"Hey!" he yelled down.

Brianna stared up at him. "You!" she yelled. "I've been looking everywhere for you!"

"I'm so hungry," Duck moaned.

"How did you get up there?"

He was slowly increasing his density, sinking down to earth.

"It goes both ways," Duck said. "It's all about density. I weigh whatever I want to weigh. I can weigh so much, I sink through the ground, or I can float so—"

"Yeah, I don't care. Sam said get you."

"Me?"

"You. Get down here."

She ripped a wing off the pigeon and handed a dripping, gelatinous piece of flesh to Duck, who didn't even hesitate.

He looked up guiltily after a minute of slavering and grunting. "Don't you want some?"

"Nah," she said. "My appetite . . . I don't know. I'm feeling a little sick."

Brianna was looking at him in a way that made him distinctly nervous.

"There'll be some wind resistance," Brianna said.

"Some what?"

"Say you can control your weight? About ten pounds ought to do."

"Do for what?"

"Jump on my back, Duck. You are going for a ride."

The morphine did not eliminate the pain. It merely threw a veil over it. It was still there, a terrible, ravening lion, roaring, awesome, overpowering. But held barely at bay.

Barely.

His wounds were shocking to see. Bright red stripes across his back, shoulders, neck, and face. In places the skin had been taken off.

The morphine nightmare had faded and reality had begun to take on some of its usual definition. The ground was down and the sky was up. The stars were bright, the sound of his shoes on the concrete was familiar, as was the sound of his own breath, rasping in his throat.

He had a while. How long, he couldn't guess. A short while, maybe, to stop Caine.

And kill Drake. Because now, for the first time in his life, Sam wanted to take a life.

Drake. He was going to kill Drake. More than any high-minded concern for what Caine might do, it was the thought of Drake that kept Sam moving forward. Destroy Drake before the morphine wore off and the awful pain returned and left him crying and screaming and . . .

Should have done it the first time he'd had the chance.

Should have . . .

The scene appeared around him, shimmering, unreal. The battle on the steps of town hall. Orc and Drake, the hammering fist of the gravel boy, and the slashing whip of the true monster.

Sam had been busy with Caine. He'd barely survived. But he could have, should have, destroyed the psychopath Drake then and there. Put him down like the rabid animal he was.

Reality was wobbly as Sam crossed the parking lot. No one there, now. Dekka gone to . . . gone to do what? His mind was foggy.

Gone to destroy the mine shaft. Her and Edilio.

Lana. If Lana was in there . . . If she . . .

Sam's step faltered. Lana was his only hope. Without her, he would not survive. She could heal him. She could end the pain. Renew him.

So that he could . . .

He sagged into a car. For a while, he couldn't know how long, his mind went away. Consciousness failed. Not quite sleep, though, just a waking nightmare of memories and images and always the pain in his belly, the pain of his scarred flesh.

Keep moving, he told himself. Which way? The town was

ten miles away. But that's not where Caine was heading.

The side of the hill behind the power plant was glowing. Like it was burning in patches. A hallucination.

He would never be able to walk that far. The drug would never last that long. Faster. He needed to move faster.

He needed help. Someone . . .

"Someone help me," he whispered.

He began the long, wearying walk up the sloping road toward the security gate. No way he could move overland. Not a chance. And even . . .

Even . . .

Sam's head was playing tricks on him now. He saw a light. Like a flashlight. But coming from the ocean.

He sat down hard. The light swept slowly over the parking lot, like someone out at sea was car shopping.

The light crawled over the side of the power plant. It climbed the hill, then came back down. Someone was searching.

But he was just a crumpled form on a road, too small to be spotted. The light would never land on him. It was like some sick game. The light would come his way and then veer off.

He was invisible.

"No, Sam," he told himself as the realization dawned with ridiculous slowness on his addled brain. "Stupid moron. The one thing you have is light."

Sam raised his hands high. A pillar of pure green light pierced the night sky.

The searchlight zoomed instantly toward him.

"Yeah, here I am," Sam said.

It took Quinn a few minutes to beach the boat and climb up the rocks to reach Sam.

"Brah," Quinn said.

Sam nodded. "Yeah. I look pretty bad. How . . ."

"I was fishing. I saw the fire." Quinn knelt beside him, obviously unsure what he could do to ease his friend's suffering.

"I look bad, and my head isn't exactly on straight," Sam slurred.

"I'll get you back to town," Quinn said.

"No, brah. Get a car."

"Sam, you can't . . ."

"Quinn." Sam took Quinn's arm and gripped it tight. "Get a car."

"Back off, doggies," Dekka growled.

The coyotes moved closer, circling, always circling. Each circuit just a little closer.

"Which one of you is Pack Leader?" Dekka demanded. Desperate. How could she stop them circling closer and closer? "I have an offer. I . . . I can help you. I want to talk to Pack Leader."

One of the coyotes stopped moving and turned his intelligent face to her. "Pack Leader me."

The voice was high-pitched, strained, as though the act of attempting speech was painful.

Dekka had only seen Pack Leader from a distance, but she

knew this wasn't him. Pack Leader had a nasty-looking face, a scar on his muzzle. He was old and mangy. This coyote was obviously younger.

"You're not Pack Leader," Dekka said.

The coyote tilted his head quizzically. "Pack Leader die. Pack Leader now."

Pack Leader dead? Maybe this was an opportunity. "If you hurt me," Dekka warned, "my people will kill coyotes."

Pack Leader—the new Pack Leader—seemed to consider this. His eyes were bright and focused, but almost seemed to contain a trace of humor.

"Pack eat dead human," Pack Leader said in the eerie, grating voice of the mutated coyotes.

"He's not dead," Dekka said.

"Pack eat," Pack Leader said.

"No," Dekka said. "If you try, we will—"

There was a flash of tan and gray fur and something bowled Dekka over. She rolled and came up into a squat. Three coyotes were on Edilio. Blood was pumping freely from his chest.

"No!" Dekka cried.

She raised her hands and suddenly Edilio was floating up off the ground, along with three panicked, scrabbling, yip yip yipping coyotes.

Pack Leader bounded away to a safe distance.

And there came the sound of a car approaching at high speed.

. . .

"Almost there!" Drake cried, ecstatic.

The night wind whipped their faces as the torn-open Escalade bounced and flew. Overhead the fuel rod was like a cruise missile, keeping pace. Caine stood braced against the seatback, hands held high.

Diana could only see the side of his face, but his was not an expression of wild joy like Drake's. Caine's eyes stared from beneath low brows. His mouth was drawn back in a grimace. It was the only time Diana had ever looked at him and found him ugly. No trace of the easy charm. The movie star bone structure was there, but now he looked like a shrouded corpse, a mockery, a fading echo.

"Look! Hah hah hah! It's growing back!" Drake shrieked, and waved the end of his hideous tentacle in her face. He was right. Within the blunt-cut disk a bump was forming, a new growth. Like a salamander's tail, the whip could be cut, but would regenerate.

"There! It's the town," Drake yelled. "There! Now you'll see. Now you'll all see!"

"What is this place?" Jack wondered aloud. He glared at Diana, accusing, blaming her.

Not my fault, Diana argued silently. Not my fault, Jack, not my fault you were weak and followed me, you stupid fool, you needy, stupid fool. Not my fault any of this.

I'm just trying to survive. I'm just trying to get by, like always, like always.

It's what she did, Diana, survive. And always with style. Her own terms, no matter what anyone thought. It was her special genius: being used, but always using back. Being abused, but then returning the abuse, with interest. And remaining, always, Diana, cool Diana.

Not her fault, any of this.

"Look!" one of the soldiers yelled.

Something was happening in the road ahead. Like a small tornado, like a whirlwind made of coyotes, and there, at the center of the madness, a human body.

"Dekka," Drake said with special relish.

Dekka dropped the coyotes. Dropped Edilio, too. No choice. Nothing she could do to help him now.

"Good-bye, Edilio," she whispered.

Now there was only the mine shaft. She ran.

The Escalade skidded to a stop. Drake was out and running after her before the car had even stopped.

She had a head start of no more than thirty feet. And Drake was faster than she was.

The air cracked from the sound of his whip hand. She felt the breeze on the back of her neck. No way she'd make it back up the trail. No way.

Dekka spun and raised her hands.

Suddenly Drake's legs were pumping in air. He rose off the ground in a vortex of dirt and rock. Like a slow-motion explosion had gone off under him. His whip hand twirled crazily.

"I'll kill you, Dekka!" he yelled.

Dekka turned gravity back on, and Drake fell from ten feet up.

She turned and ran again, and now the coyotes were around her, bounding along on both sides of the trail, moving ahead of her. They would easily cut her off.

She powered up the hill, breath rasping in her throat. She turned a corner, and there was the new Pack Leader. She raised her hands. Too slow. They came from right and left. Leaped at her from all directions at once.

Dekka went down beneath a snarling, yelping, slashing pile of coyotes.

She screamed and tried to use her power, but iron jaws clamped her wrists.

The powerful made powerless.

The coyotes would have her.

FORTY-TWO

27 MINUTES

DRAKE WAS FIRST up the trail. He was limping, one leg badly bruised by his fall.

Jack was just behind him.

Drake limped up to the snarling coyote pack gathered around their intended kill. One of the coyotes, a creature with bright eyes and an almost human expression of detached interest, snarled a warning.

Dekka was pinioned, helpless. If she was conscious, she showed no sign of it. But she was still alive. Jack could see that she was still alive. And that in a few seconds, less, she wouldn't be.

"Don't worry, my coyote brothers," Drake said with a laugh. "I'm not here to stop you."

Drake looked down and shook his head mockingly at Dekka. "You don't look so good. I don't think this is going to end well for you." Then he looked back at Jack and said, "So much for mutant powers. Right, Jack?"

It was a warning. A threat. But Jack didn't care. He was sick. So sick, so sick deep down inside. He wanted to throw up, but there was nothing in his stomach. He wanted to run away into the night. But Drake or Caine or the coyotes would come for him.

Why was he here?

Because you're a stupid fool, Jack told himself. Smart stupid. Stupid smart.

"Just a little farther," Drake cried from up ahead. "Come meet him, Jack."

Jack stopped and looked back. He saw the fuel rod first. Floating along. Then Caine beneath it. Caine seemed almost bowed over, like he was carrying the weight on his shoulders. Like it was almost too much for him.

Jack felt as if a weight were pressing down on him, a weight that wanted to squeeze the blood from him, crush him like a piece of ripe fruit. Tears were running down his face, although he didn't remember when he had started crying.

For all his supernatural strength, Jack felt as if his arms and legs were stone. Each step took all his strength as he fought against his own paralyzing fear and horror.

Too much. All of it. Brittney, poor Brittney. And now Dekka. How many more would end up like them? And what about Jack himself?

Jack didn't think about what he was doing when he grabbed the nearest coyote by the scruff of its neck. The coyote yelped and tried to twist around to bite him. Jack threw the animal. It flew out of sight.

He grabbed a second coyote and hurled it into the night. A distant thump.

Two coyotes came straight at him, jaws open, teeth bared. Jack drew back and kicked the first. His foot connected with the animal's snout. The coyote's head ripped from its shoulders and went rolling down the trail a crazy bowling ball. The coyote's body stood for a few seconds, even seemed to take a step. Then it fell over.

The other coyotes stared. Then they stuck their tails between their legs and hurried away.

"What's the matter, Jack? Squeamish?"

Drake seemed to grow stronger with each step while Jack felt watery and weak despite his display of superhuman strength. It wasn't part of him, that strength. It wasn't him.

Drake stood over him at the top of the rise. He was outlined in moonlight, his whip hand twitching in the air.

"I just didn't like seeing it," Jack said. His stomach was in his throat.

Drake's whip reached for Jack and wrapped almost gently around Jack's throat. Drake pulled him close. Drake's mouth tickled his ear as he said voicelessly, "Back my play, Computer Jack."

"What?" Jack said desperately.

"Back my play," Drake said. "And I'll let you live. I'll even let you have Brianna."

Jack placed his hand on Drake's whip. He pried it off his neck. It was almost easy. It would be easy now to yank that hideous arm right off.

Drake laughed uneasily. "Don't start down that path, Jack. You're not the type for rough stuff."

Drake turned away and bounded ahead.

Caine labored up from below. Diana, the witch who had brought all this horror to Jack, was beside Caine. He could almost swear that she was helping Caine walk.

Lana had dropped the gun in the cave. Useless now.

Tried to explain. . . tried to form images that explained . . . But the gaiaphage didn't care, really, it had moved on, not concerned any more by the girl with the power of gravity.

Someone shot Edilio, Lana thought, marveling at the idea. Someone. Edilio.

She had a flash of sensation, the feeling of the gun bucking in her hand.

Someone . . .

She gasped as the gaiaphage split open her mind and poured the images into her brain. Images of monstrosities.

The largest was a shaggy thing like a grizzly bear with eighteen-inch spikes at the ends of its paws. . . creatures that were all sharp edges, as if they'd been assembled out of razor blades and kitchen knives. . . creatures of glowing inner fire. Things that flew. Things that slithered.

But when she saw them, she didn't just see the surface. She saw them inside and out at once. Saw their construction. Saw the way they were folded into one another, one inside another, monster within monster. Like a Russian nesting doll.

Destroy one and liberate the next.

Regeneration. Adaptation. Each new incarnation as dangerous and as deadly as the one before.

The gaiaphage had conceived of the perfect biological machine.

No, not his conception. He had reached into a mind, an imagination infinitely more visionary than his own.

Nemesis. That was the gaiaphage's name for him: Nemesis.

Nemesis with infinite power held in check only by the twists and turns, the blind alleys and sudden high walls inside his own damaged brain.

Nemesis and Healer, used and brought together here, in this way, to make the gaiaphage unstoppable, unkillable.

Only one piece was missing. The food. The fuel.

It is coming, the gaiaphage said.

Soon.

Someone had shot Edilio. And had tried to shoot Dekka.

Lana's shattered, overwhelmed mind, flooded with the gaiaphage's plans, held on to that single fact.

Someone had . . .

From far, so far away, she felt the gun buck in her hand as she squeezed the trigger.

No. No.

Edilio falling.

No.

Lana's mind exploded in a wave of fury so powerful that the gaiaphage's imagery faltered. The fire hose flow of plans and details faded.

I hate you! Lana screamed wordlessly.

The gaiaphage pushed back, forced her down inside her own brain.

But more slowly than it had before.

"He's going to go after you, Caine," Diana whispered in his ear.

Caine's arms ached. He could no longer feel his hands. Holding them up. Using the power. Using it to carry . . .

"Drake will try to kill you," Diana said urgently. "You know it's true."

Caine heard her. But her voice was so tiny, her warning so insignificant compared to the steady throbbing pressure inside his chest.

The gaiaphage's hunger was his hunger now. Feeding it would be feeding himself.

Not true, Caine told himself.

A lie.

"Do this, and you will die, Caine," Diana pleaded. "Do it, and I'll die.

"Stop, Caine.

"Don't do it."

Caine tried to answer, but his mouth was dry and clenched.

Step by step. Up the trail. To it. To him.

Jack was up there. And Drake. Drake talking to Jack. There was a dead coyote lying in the path, headless.

And Dekka, maybe alive, maybe not. Not his concern. Her problem. Shouldn't have backed Sam. Shouldn't have fought against Caine.

Not his problem.

He reached the top of the trail. There was the mine shaft entrance.

The fuel rod hovered in the air.

Feed me.

Caine moved closer.

"Do it!" Drake cried.

"Caine, stop!" Diana said.

Caine moved more easily now on level ground. Closer. Close enough. He could hurl the rod from here. Like a javelin. Right into the shaft.

Like a spear.

Easy.

"Don't," Diana said. Then, "Jack. Jack, you have to stop this."

"No way," Drake snarled.

"Shut up, you psychotic!" Diana shouted in sudden rage, all subtlety abandoned. "Go die, you filthy, stupid thug!"

Drake's eyes went dead. The dangerous, giddy light went out in them. He stared at her with black hatred.

"Enough," Drake said. "I was going to wait. But if it has to be now, let's do it."

His whip lashed out.

FORTY-THREE

13 MINUTES

DRAKE'S WHIP HAND spun Diana like a top.

She cried out. That sound, her cry, pierced Caine like an arrow.

Diana staggered and almost righted herself, but Drake was too quick, too ready.

His second strike yanked her through the air. She flew and then fell.

"Catch her!" Caine was yelling to himself. Seeing her arc as she fell. Seeing where she would hit. His hands came up, he could use his power, he could catch her, save her. But too slow.

Diana fell. Her head smashed against a jutting point of rock. She made a sound like a dropped pumpkin.

Caine froze.

The fuel rod, forgotten, fell from the air with a shattering crash.

It fell within ten feet of the mine shaft opening. It landed atop a boulder shaped like the prow of a ship.

It bent, cracked, rolled off the boulder, and crashed heavily in the dirt.

Drake ran straight at Caine, his whip snapping. But Jack stumbled in between them, yelling, "The uranium! The uranium!"

The radiation meter in his pocket was counting clicks so fast, it became a scream.

Drake piled into Jack, and the two of them went tumbling.

Caine stood, staring in horror at Diana. Diana did not move. Did not move. No snarky remark. No smart-ass joke.

"No!" Caine cried.

"No!"

Drake was up, disentangling himself with an angry curse from Jack.

"Diana," Caine sobbed.

Drake didn't rely on his whip hand now, too far away to use it before Caine could take him down. He raised his gun. The barrel shot flame and slugs, BAM BAM BAM BAM BAM.

Inaccurate, but on full automatic, Drake had time. He swung the gun to his right and the bullets swooped toward where Caine stood like he was made of stone.

Then the muzzle flash disappeared in an explosion of green-white light that turned night into day. The shaft of light missed its target. But it was close enough that the muzzle of Drake's gun wilted and drooped and the rocks behind Drake cracked from the blast of heat.

Drake dropped the gun. And now it was Drake's turn to stare in stark amazement. "You!"

Sam wobbled atop the rise. Quinn caught him as he staggered.

Now Caine snapped back to the present, seeing his brother, seeing the killing light.

"No," Caine said. "No, Sam: He's mine."

He raised a hand, and Sam went flying backward along with Quinn.

"The fuel rod!" Jack was yelling, over and over. "It's going to kill us all. Oh, God, we may already be dead!"

Drake rushed at Caine. His eyes were wide with fear. Knowing he wouldn't make it. Knowing he was not fast enough.

Caine raised his hand, and the fuel rod seemed to jump off the ground.

A javelin.

A spear. He held it poised. Pointed straight at Drake.

Caine reached with his other hand, extending the telekinetic power to hold Drake immobilized.

Drake held up his human hand, a placating gesture. "Caine . . . you don't want to . . . not over some girl. She was a witch, she was . . ."

Drake, unable to run, a human target. The fuel rod aimed at him like a Spartan's spear.

Caine threw the fuel rod. Tons of steel and lead and uranium.

Straight at Drake.

Drake, quick as a snake, twisted his shoulder and neck to the side. The fuel rod did not hit him full in the chest, but struck his shoulder and sent him flying down the dark shaft.

The fuel rod disappeared with him.

There came a loud crash. Dust billowed out of the hole.

Silence.

No sound, but the skitter of falling pebbles inside the shaft.

"Oh, God, did it break open?" Jack moaned. "Oh, my God, I don't want to die."

Caine raised his hands and stood, arms outstretched, right before the mouth of the mine.

The ground began to rumble.

Rock snapped and creaked.

No! the hated voice cried in Caine's mind.

"I'm no one's slave," Caine grated.

No! You will not!

Caine faltered. There were knives in his brain, knives stabbing and stabbing, and the agony was beyond imagining.

"Won't I?" Caine said.

Caine raised his hands high. He reached with his power into the cave and yanked his arms back.

Tons of loose rock, wooden support beams, the shattered fuel rod, a battered old pickup truck, the body of Hermit Jim, and the writhing, cursing figure of a wounded but still living Drake Merwin, came flying out of the cave. Like the cave had vomited up its contents.

The mass of it froze in midair. And then, as Caine formed his hands into a bowl, the suspended mass began to twirl. It swirled like a tornado.

And then, with Drake's cries lost in the howling madness,

Caine swept his arms forward and threw the entire spinning mass down the mine shaft entrance.

The noise was so great that Jack clapped his hands over his ears.

Then, a slow-motion rumble and crack and a sudden, overwhelming, earthquake jolt as the mine shaft collapsed. Millions of pounds of rock closed the shaft forever.

Caine walked on wobbly legs to Diana. He knelt beside her. She wasn't moving. He put his ear next to her lovely mouth. He heard no sounds of breathing.

But when he laid his palm on her back, he felt the slightest rise and fall.

Gently he rolled her over. The damage to the side of her head was awful to the touch. He couldn't see clearly, tears filled his eyes, but he could feel a warm slipperiness where her temple should be smooth.

A sob escaped from him.

He heard heavy footsteps. Sam, moving like he was drunk, staggering.

"Sam," Caine said calmly, not taking his eyes off the dark form of Diana, "if you're going to kill me, go ahead. Now would be a good time."

Sam said nothing.

Finally Caine looked at him. Through his tears Caine saw the way Sam wobbled, barely able, it seemed, to stay on his feet. He had been cut up badly. The pain must be excruciating.

Drake's work. Drake had not killed Sam. But he had come

close. And it seemed impossible that Sam would survive for long.

Quinn was struggling under the burden of the body he cradled in his arms. The Mexican kid, Caine guessed, or maybe Dekka.

"So. This is the end," Caine said dully. He stroked Diana's cropped hair. "I love her. Did you know that, Sam?"

"It's not over yet," Sam said. His voice shocked Caine. He'd never heard more pain in a voice. He heard a barely suppressed scream beneath the words.

"She can't live," Caine said.

"Edilio's hurt. Almost gone," Quinn said. "They shot him. And Dekka . . ."

"Not me," Caine said. "Not us. They were both like that when we got here."

He was not interested in Edilio or Dekka. Not even interested in Sam. So sad that Diana would die this way, all her beautiful hair gone. She looked younger this way. Innocent. Not a word he or anyone else had ever applied to Diana.

"Lana," Sam said.

Caine felt the faintest flicker. Lana. But where was the Healer?

As if he had heard the question, Quinn said, "She's in there. She's in there, with . . . it."

Caine looked at the mine shaft. He had been down there before. He knew what lay inside. And now, the fuel rod, too.

"We need to . . . ," Sam whimpered, unable to finish.

Caine nodded. "She must be dead after that."

"Maybe not," Sam managed to say. "Maybe not."

"There's no way to get in there now, anyway. It's a wall of rock. It's a lot harder to move rock back out. I'd have to move the whole mountain," Caine said. "Hours. Days."

Sam shook his head and bit his lip as though he would bite it off. Caine saw him hold on barely as the pain passed through him.

"May have another way," Sam said finally, staring back down the trail.

"Another way?" Caine asked.

"Duck," Sam said.

And Caine did, instinctively. There was a rush of wind and a cloud of dust and all at once, there was Brianna.

And towing along behind her, like some crazy balloon on a rope, a kid floating in midair and looking like someone had just taken him on a roller-coaster ride from hell.

"Are we there?" Duck, asked, his eyes squeezed shut. "Am I done now?"

"You want to eat?" Zil roared from atop his convertible perch.

The crowd roared its assent. Though not every voice. Astrid clung to that fact: there was grumbling and uncertainty as well as acquiescence.

"Then grab on to the rope!" Zil cried.

The rope stretched across the plaza. It ended around Hunter's neck. It would take no more than half a dozen willing executioners to do the foul deed.

Astrid began to pray. She prayed in a loud voice, hoping it would shame them, hoping that somehow it would reach through the madness.

"Grab on!" Zil cried, and he jumped down and seized the rope himself. The rest of his crew did the same.

Then four . . . five . . . ten . . .

Kids Astrid knew by name took hold of the rope.

"Pull!" Zil screamed. "Pull!"

The rope tightened. More came forward and took hold. But others, just a couple, changed their minds and let go.

It was a confusion of hands. A mess that turned suddenly to a shoving match.

The rope still tightened. It became a straight line.

And Astrid, to her eternal horror, saw Hunter lifted off his feet.

But the fight over the rope had turned nastier. Kids were pummeling one another, shouting, swinging wild fists.

The rope slackened. Hunter's kicking feet touched the ground.

Kids rushed to pull on the rope. Others blocked their way. It was becoming a kind of full-scale riot. And then a couple of kids rushed at the meat, pushing past Antoine and Hank and Turk, literally walking over them in their desperation.

Astrid took advantage of the melee to climb to her feet.

Zil, enraged at losing control, at seeing the venison snatched away by desperate hands, shoved her hard.

"Down on the ground, you freak-lover!"

Astrid spit at him. She could see the color drain from Zil's furious face. He grabbed a baseball bat, raised it over her. And then he flew into the air.

In his place stood Orc.

Zil was dangling from his fist. Orc drew Zil to within an inch of his own frightening face. "No one hurts Astrid," Orc bellowed so loud, Zil's hair was blown back.

Orc took a slow spin. Then a second, faster one, and launched Zil through the air.

"You okay?" Orc asked Astrid.

"I guess so," she managed to say. She knelt beside Little Pete and touched the egg-sized lump on his head. He moved slightly, then opened his eyes.

"Petey. Petey. Are you okay?" There was no answer, but for Little Pete, that wasn't abnormal. Astrid looked up at Orc. "Thanks, Charles."

Orc grunted. "Yeah."

Howard appeared, threading his way through the scattering mob. "My man, Orc," he said, and slapped Orc on his massive granite shoulder. Then, to the fleeing crowd, many loaded down with chunks of venison, he yelled, "Yeah, you better run away. You are some sorry fools messing with Sam's girl. If Orc doesn't get you, Sammy will."

He winked at Astrid. "Your boy so owes us."

"Yeah," Orc agreed. "Someone better beer me pretty soon."

"What happened to Edilio?" Brianna demanded. He was lying on the ground. Silent. Not even the sound of breathing.

Quinn answered. "Edilio's been shot. I don't think he has long."

"I can't believe Dekka let him get hurt," Brianna said. "Where is she?"

Quinn's involuntary glance was all Brianna needed. She flew to where Dekka lay, crumpled like a doll someone had tossed aside.

Brianna breathed hard. Stared. There was a rushing water-fall in her ears. A roar. Then a blur as the world around her screamed past and she hit Caine with all the speed and fury at her command. Caine went sprawling.

Brianna was on him before he could draw breath, and now a rock was in her hand.

"Breeze! No!" Sam yelled.

Brianna froze. Caine was on his back. He did nothing. He did not raise his hands. Barely seemed to notice her as she squatted, poised to hit him with the rock, poised to hit him a hundred times before he could flinch.

"No, Breeze," Sam said. "We need him."

"I don't need him," Brianna hissed.

"Breeze. Dekka's gone. Edilio will be dead in a few minutes. If he isn't already," Quinn said, speaking for Sam, who was clenching his teeth with such force that Brianna thought his molars might splinter. "And Sam . . ."

"What can this piece of filth do?" Brianna demanded.

"We need Lana," Sam managed to say.

Caine picked himself up and brushed the dirt from his shirt. "Diana is dying. The Mexican kid is dying. Dekka, well, you saw her. And Sam doesn't look too good," Caine said. "Lana's in there." He jerked his head toward the collapsed mine shaft.

"What I don't get," Caine continued, "is how we're getting in there to find her. The whole mine collapsed. It will take me a lot longer to dig out than it did to collapse it. I pull stuff out, more falls in."

"Duck," Sam said. "He's going to drill a tunnel."

"Um . . . what?" Duck said.

"Like when they rescue miners," Sam said. "They drill a shaft down to the original shaft."

"Um . . . what?" Duck repeated.

Quinn explained to an obviously baffled Caine, "It seems Duck has the power to sink right down through the ground."

"I don't really think I'm . . . ," Duck said.

"He can control his density," Brianna confirmed. "That's why I could carry him here. It was like carrying a backpack. But with more wind resistance."

"He drills," Sam said. "We go in. You've been down there, haven't you, Caine? Is there a place where—" A spasm of pain rocked him so hard, he seemed to lose consciousness for a minute.

"Guys, I don't really . . . ," Duck said.

"Don't you want to be a hero?" Quinn asked.

"No," Duck said honestly.

"Yeah, me neither," Quinn admitted. "But, Edilio, he's a hero. He's the real thing. And, Sam . . . well, I don't have to tell you what Sam has done for all of us." Quinn took Duck's arm and said, "We need you, Duck. Only you. Only you can do this."

"Dude, I mean, I want to help, but . . ."

"You get the next fish I catch," Quinn said.

"Not if I'm buried alive," Duck argued.

"Fried. Fried up so tender and flavorful."

"You can't buy me with food," Duck huffed. "I . . . I want a swimming pool, too."

FORTY-FOUR
7 MINUTES

THE MINE SHAFT was collapsed.

Lana stood facing a wall of debris. And for a fleeting moment, she felt hope that this, at last, spelled the end of the monster that had enslaved her.

But from that wall, the battered, blunted end of the fuel rod protruded.

The billions of crystals that were all the body the gaiaphage had swarmed over the spilled uranium pellets.

Lana felt the gaiaphage's anticipation, its rush of bliss. The fear of destruction drained from the creature. And for a while, Lana's mind was almost her own as the gaiaphage reveled in its dark joy.

It was no blessing recovering her senses. Lana knew now beyond any doubt that it had been she who had pulled the trigger and shot Edilio. She who had failed to blow up the cave. She who had allowed this to happen.

Too weak.

A fool, easily manipulated into delivering herself into the

service of the monster. Too weak to resist it.

And as it grew stronger, as its fear ebbed, it would reach into her mind again and use her power to build the body that would emerge from this lair. Burying the creature would not stop it. It would create the body that could tunnel its way out, the cunningly designed monster-within-monster nesting doll that could never be killed.

She was the key now. Lana knew that. The tunnel had been shut with a tremendous crash that would seal the gaiaphage in unless she gave it the key to escape.

Only her own death could stop it.

Her will was too weak. Her only hope was delay. The uranium, surely it would kill her. Surely it would destroy her if she did nothing to heal herself.

But would it happen quickly enough?

And would the gaiaphage know what was happening to her and force her to save herself? Did the creature understand that its food was her death?

Duck stood on the hillside. He was a hundred feet or so above the mine shaft. They had made a guess, hoping that this would position him above what Caine said was a wide subterranean chamber.

All guesswork, of course. If Duck didn't eventually fall into an open chamber, he would have to do it again. And again.

Quinn was all but carrying Sam, holding him up with his arms as Sam endured wave after wave of pain.

"The morphine is wearing off," Sam said. "Hurry."

Caine stood ready. Brianna had run off to fetch rope. But

when she returned she had fallen to her knees and vomited violently, heaving up nothing.

"Have to do this now," Sam said. He was panting. Holding on by his fingernails.

"Do it, Duck," Quinn urged.

They were all waiting for him. Looking to him. So many lives on the line, and they were looking to him. To Duck Zhang.

"Oh, man. It better be really good fish," Duck said.

And then he was falling through the ground. Falling and falling, and waving his arms as he went, tunneling through rock as if it were no thicker than pudding.

Falling and flailing, falling and flailing. Knowing he would be able to float back up and out into the air, but not 100 percent sure. Mostly. Not totally sure. Maybe this time—

Duck slipped suddenly as he fell through the ceiling of the mine shaft. He stopped his fall only after sinking two feet into the mine shaft's floor.

Duck breathed a sigh of relief. He was not in a wide, open chamber, just in a narrow mine shaft. A miracle he'd hit it.

He wondered if there were bats in here. Well, judging by the scared looks of all the others up above, there was something much worse down here. So maybe bats wouldn't be a bad thing. Maybe bats would be a good sign.

"Okay!" he yelled up.

No answer.

"Okay! I'm down!" he shouted as loud as he could.

A rope uncoiled and dropped.

Caine was first. He landed gently, using his own

power to cushion the drop.

"Dark down here," Caine said. He yelled up the shaft. "Okay, brother: jump."

Light shone blindingly bright down the shaft Duck had made. Like eerie sunlight coming through a chink in a shutter.

Caine raised his hands and Sam dropped slowly down the shaft.

Sam seemed to be holding a ball of brilliant light in his hands. Only not holding it, really, Duck realized when his eyes had adjusted. The light just glowed from Sam's palms.

"I know this place," Caine said. "We're just a few dozen feet from the cavern."

"Duck, we may need you," Sam said.

"But I was just going to—"

Sam's legs buckled, and Duck grabbed him just before he hit the ground.

"I'll stay," Duck heard himself say.

What? You'll what? he demanded silently.

Come on, Duck, he told himself. You can't just run away.

Sure, I can! Duck's other voice protested.

But just the same, he supported Sam's weight as they walked deeper into the cave.

Don't you want to be a hero? Duck mocked himself.

I guess I kind of do, he answered.

"Keep the light on," Caine said.

Sam could keep the light burning. That he could do. Could do that. Light.

His heart was a rusty, dying engine, hammering like it would fly apart. His body was scalded iron, hot, stiff, impossible to move.

The pain . . .

It was at him now, a roaring tiger that ripped him with every step, tore at his mind, shredded his self-control. He couldn't live with it. Too terrible.

"Come on, Sam," Duck said in his ear.

"Aahhhh!" Sam cried out.

"So much for sneaking up on it," Caine said.

It knows we're here, Sam thought. No sneaking. No tricking. It knew. Sam could feel it. Like cold fingers prodding his mind, poking, looking for an opening.

This is hell, Sam thought. This is hell.

Keep the light on, Sam told himself, whatever else, keep the light on.

There was a skittering sound as Caine's feet kicked some loose pebbles that on closer examination were identical, short, cylinders of dark metal.

"The fuel pellets," Caine said dully. "Well. I hope Lana does radiation poisoning. Otherwise we are all dead."

"What?" Duck asked.

"That's uranium scattered all around. The way it was explained to me, it's blowing billions of tiny holes in our bodies."

"*What?*"

"Come on, Goose," Caine said. "You're doing great."

"Duck," Duck corrected.

"Can you feel the Darkness, Goose?" Caine asked in an awed whisper.

"Yeah," Duck said. His voice wavered. Like a little kid about to cry. "It feels bad."

"Very bad," Caine agreed. "It's been in my head for a long time, Goose. Once it's there, it never goes away."

"What do you mean?" Duck asked.

"It's touching your mind right now, isn't it? Leaving its mark. Finding a way in. Once it gets in, you can never shut it out."

"We have to get out of here," Duck said.

"You can go, Goose," Caine said. "I can drag Sam along."

Sam heard it all from far away. A conversation between distant ghosts. Shadows in his mind. But he knew Duck could not leave.

"No," Sam rasped. "We need Duck."

"Do we?" Caine asked.

"The one weapon it doesn't know we have," Sam said.

"Weapon?" Duck echoed.

"It opens up just ahead," Caine said. "The cavern."

"What is it? What's it look like?" Duck asked.

Caine didn't answer.

Sam rode through a spasm of pain. It seemed to come in waves, each worse than the one before. Surfing the pain, he thought. But in the trough between waves, he sometimes had a few seconds of clarity.

He opened his eyes. He turned up the light.

As Caine had said, they were emerging into a space that

was no longer a mine shaft but a vast cavern.

But no natural geological event had created this vast, silent hole beneath the ground. No stalactites hung from the arched roof. No stalagmites grew from the floor.

Instead, the stone walls seemed to have been melted and then solidified. There was still a faint smell of burning, though no smoke and no heat except what radiated from the fuel rod behind them in the shaft.

"Figured out where we are yet, Sam?" Caine asked.

Sam groaned.

"Yeah, kind of have other things on your mind right now, huh? You know about the meteor that hit the power plant all those years back, right, Sam? Sure. You're a townie."

Sam rode the next wave. He didn't want to scream. Didn't want to scream.

"Meteor plows right through the power plant, right into the ground. Like our boy Goose, here: so heavy, moving so fast, it's like shooting an arrow into butter. Tears a massive hole. Stops here, what's left of it."

They had advanced fifty feet into the cathedral space of the cavern.

Sam nodded, not capable at that particular moment of speech. He tried to lift his hands, but their weight was too great.

Caine took his wrists and lifted up his hands, a motion that caused Sam to roar in agony.

But the light shone brighter.

And there, revealed, the thing being born. It was more lump than any definite shape. A seething hive of rushing, twisting, greenish crystals.

But as they watched, the surfaces facing their way took on a perfect, mirrored surface.

"Looks like he's ready for you, Sam," Caine said.

Then, a different voice. Eerie and awful.

"I am the gaiaphage," Lana said.

The transformation had begun when the gaiaphage touched the first of the scattered uranium pellets. Lana felt the surge of power, like grabbing an electrical wire, like grabbing every electrical wire in the world.

She had cried out in the shared ecstasy of that moment.

Food!

The gaiaphage's terrible hunger was gone. In its place a rush of power. Rage unleashed.

Now! Now it would become!

The billions of crystals that formed the gaiaphage's shapeless, random form began to rush like ants. Rivulets became streams, streams became rushing rivers. What had been little more than scum on the surface of rocks formed into mounds and peaks. Here and there, sharp points. Here flat and there peaked, here pliable and there stiff.

Crystals folded in endless dimensions, layers within layers. Even at this wild speed it would take days to finish, but already the barest outlines were beginning to reveal themselves.

The gaiaphage that had been spread through a thousand feet of the subterranean cavern now condensed, came together, like stars drawn into a black hole.

Lana could feel it all, as though her own nerves were part of the gaiaphage. And maybe they were, she thought. Maybe there was no longer a line between them. Maybe she was part of it now.

It was all around her. In her ears and nose, in her mouth and hair. Swarming insects covering every square inch of her.

And yet, she had begun to feel a sickness inside her. A feeling that was her own and not the monster's.

What fed the gaiaphage was blasting her apart, cell by cell.

She had to hide it. Couldn't let it see. She had to die to stop it, had to die of the radiation that churned her stomach.

Around her the crystals were hardening, forming a thick shield. And the surface of that shield began to shine, like steel. No, like a mirror.

A tremor of fear shook the gaiaphage.

Lana opened her eyes and saw the reason. Three dark shapes. Frail, afraid, but standing before the gaiaphage.

Too late, Caine. Your power will not shatter the gaiaphage.

Too late, Sam, she thought. Your burning light will not work.

The third . . . who was that? She felt the question in her own mind take on terrible urgency in the gaiaphage.

The gaiaphage held her like a fly in amber. It revealed her now to the gasps of the humans.

"I am the gaiaphage," Lana's mouth said.

Caine stared in horror. Lana's face floated, suspended within a seething mass of what might have been mirrored insects.

"Sam! More light!"

Sam had slipped. He was on his knees. Glowing hands down on the stone floor as he moaned.

Duck was staring, awestruck, at the glittering, shifting monstrosity with the face of a girl in torment.

Caine could not see the extent of the creature, but it felt huge, like it might go on forever.

He reached his hands over his shoulders. Reached back behind him. The bent fuel rod slid from the jumble of rock and debris.

Caine threw his hands forward with all his might. The fuel rod smashed into the monstrous glittering mass. It bounced off and clattered to the ground, spilling more pellets.

Nothing. No effect. Like hitting the gaiaphage with a Q-tip.

"Sam? If you've got anything left, now is the time," Caine cried.

"No," Sam whispered. "It's ready for me. Duck."

"What about him?"

"Duck . . . ," Sam said, and fell, facedown. He did not move.

"You got something besides falling into the ground?" Caine shrilled at Duck. "You got some nuclear bomb in your pocket?"

Duck did not answer.

"Sam?" Caine cried, and now the gaiaphage was moving,

shifting its weight, undulating toward Caine, with Lana's weeping, twisted face, her mouth speaking but Caine unable to hear from the sound of blood rushing in his ears, knowing it was over, knowing . . .

The gaiaphage poured liquid fire into Caine's brain, overwhelming every sense, crushing consciousness with pain.

You defy me?

Caine rocked back, barely kept his feet.

"Throw me!" Duck cried.

I am the gaiaphage!

"Throw me, throw me!" a voice kept shouting.

"What?" Caine cried.

"Hard as you can!"

The gaiaphage thought nothing of the soft, human body that flew toward him.

Up into the air the human flew. Toward the roof of the cavern.

Down he came.

The gaiaphage would never even feel the slight weight as it . . .

. . . hit with the force of a mountain dropped from the edge of space.

Duck hit the gaiaphage and drilled straight through its crystalline mass.

And straight through the cave floor beneath it.

Into the vortex, like grains of sand in an hourglass, fell the gaiaphage.

FORTY-FIVE
0 MINUTES

KIND OF LIKE the first time, Duck thought.

At the pool that day. Like that. Falling and the water rushing down with him.

Only this water was more like sand. A billion tiny crystals all sucked down the drain that Duck had made in the earth.

He could see nothing as he fell. The crystals filled his eyes and ears and mouth.

He couldn't breathe, and this panicked him and he fell even faster, trying to outrun the monster that fell with him.

No air.

Mind swirling, crazy, not even afraid now, just . . .

Memories flashed like a jerky video. That day when he fell off a pony at his fifth birthday party.

That time he ate the whole pie . . .

His mom. So pretty. Her face . . .

Dad . . .

The pool . . .

He stopped falling. Something had stopped him at last.

Too late, he thought.

Can't fall through to China, Duck thought.

Well, Duck thought, I guess I did want to be a hero.

And then Duck stopped thinking anything at all.

FORTY-SIX

CAINE STOOD IN darkness.

Sam's light was gone.

There was a soft, slurry sound. Like rushing water but without water's music.

Caine stood in darkness as the sound died slowly away.

And now, silence as well as darkness.

Diana. He would never save her now. He might survive, but for the first time in his life, Caine knew that his life, without Diana, would be unbearable.

She had teased him. Abused him. Lied to him. Manipulated him. Betrayed him. Laughed at him.

But she had stuck by him. Even when he had threatened her.

Could what they had really be described as love? He'd blurted it, that word. But were either of them capable of that particular emotion?

Maybe.

But no longer. Not now. Up above, up on the surface, she

was dead or close to it. Her blood seeping into the ground.

"Diana," he whispered.

"Am I still alive?"

At first Caine thought it might be her voice. Impossible.

"Light," Caine said. "I need light."

There was no light. For what seemed like an eternity, no light. The voice did not speak again.

Caine sat in the dark, too beaten to move. His brother curled in a ball. Dead, or wishing he was. And Diana. . .

Quinn fought panic as he descended the irregular shaft Duck had cut. The rope felt thin in his hands. The walls of the vertical shaft scraped his back and sides as he descended. Rocks kept falling on his head.

Quinn knew he was not brave. But there was no one left. Something was wrong with Brianna. She was doubled up on the ground, clutching her stomach and crying.

Quinn didn't know what was happening down below. But he knew that if Sam and Caine didn't bring Lana back up out of there, there would be too many deaths for Quinn to even think about.

Had to do this.

Had to.

He reached the bottom of the shaft and felt his legs swing freely. He lost his grip and fell the final few feet.

He landed hard, but without breaking anything.

"Sam?" Quinn whispered, a sound that died within inches of his mouth.

He fumbled for the flashlight in his pocket. He snapped the

light on. His eyes had adjusted to the dark. The light seemed blinding. He blinked. He aimed the beam ahead.

There, not a hundred feet away, a human figure in silhouette. Moving.

"Caine?"

Caine turned slowly. His face was stark and white. His eyes rimmed red.

Caine rose slowly, like an arthritic old man.

Quinn rushed to him and shone his light around, sweeping the area. He saw Sam facedown.

And there, standing with her arms at her side, stood Lana.

"Lana," Quinn said.

"Am I alive?" Lana asked.

"You're alive, Lana," Quinn said. "You're free of it."

A dark shadow passed over Lana's face. Her mouth twisted downward. She turned and began to walk away.

Quinn put his arm on her shoulder. "Don't leave us, Healer. We need you."

Lana stopped.

"I . . . ," she began.

"Lana," Quinn said. "We need you."

"I killed Edilio," she said.

"Not yet you didn't," Quinn said.

Mary Terrafino woke to the taste and smell of fish.

Instantly she twisted her face away. The smell was disgusting.

She looked around wildly. To her amazement she was tied

up. Tied to an easy chair in her day care office.

"What am I doing here?" she demanded, bewildered.

"You're having dinner," her little brother said.

"Stop it! I'm not hungry. Stop it!"

John held the spoon in front of her. His cherubic face was dark with anger. "You said you wouldn't leave me."

"What are you talking about?" Mary demanded.

"You said you wouldn't do it. You wouldn't leave me alone," John said. "But you tried, didn't you?"

"I don't know what you're babbling about." She noticed Astrid then, leaning against a filing cabinet. Astrid looked like she'd been dragged through the middle of a dog fight. Little Pete was sitting cross-legged, rocking back and forth. He was chanting, "Good-bye, Nestor. Good-bye, Nestor."

"Mary, you have an eating disorder," Astrid said. "The secret is out. So cut the crap."

"Eat," John ordered, and shoved a spoonful of food in her mouth. None too gently.

"Swallow," John ordered.

"Let me—"

"Shut up, Mary," John snapped.

Diana first. Caine would allow no other choice.

Then Edilio, who was so close to death that Lana thought he must have had his hand on the gate of Heaven.

Dekka. Horribly hurt. But not dead.

Brianna, with her hair falling out in clumps.

Last, Sam.

Quinn had hauled him up on the rope, helped greatly by Caine.

Lana sat in the dirt as the sun came up.

Quinn brought her water. "Are you okay?" he asked her.

She could say the words he wanted to hear, but Lana knew she could not make him believe. "No," Lana said.

Quinn sat next to her. "Caine and Diana, they took off. Sam is sleeping. Dekka . . . I don't think she's over it yet."

"I can't cure a person of memories," Lana said dully.

"No," Quinn agreed. "I guess if you could, you'd cure yourself."

He put his arm around her shoulders, and she started crying then. It felt like she could never stop. But it didn't feel bad, either. And Quinn did not leave her. Far off there was the sound of a car's engine.

Quinn said, "Hey, Brianna zipped back to town. Brought Astrid and someone else."

Lana didn't care. Lana didn't think she would ever care about anything again.

But then, there was the sound of a car door opening and closing. And suddenly, Patrick was there, his cold, wet nose thrust insistently against her neck.

Lana put her arms around him, hugged him close, and cried into his fur.

FORTY-SEVEN

IT WAS LATE the next day before Edilio could bring himself to the job at hand. But then he fired up the backhoe and dug two holes in the corner of the plaza.

Mickey Finch. A bullet hole in his back.

Brittney, mangled so badly, no one could look at her. Some sort of slug seemed to have attached itself to her, an eighteen-inch-long thing that could not be pried away from her.

In the end, they buried it with her. She was dead, after all: she wouldn't care.

There was no hole for Duck Zhang. But they put up a cross for him. They had searched the cavern as best they could. But all they'd found was a hole that went down and down seemingly forever.

The hole was collapsing in on itself as Sam shone his light down. It was already filling with tons of rock and dirt.

"No one knew Duck all that well," Sam said at the service. "I don't think anyone would have guessed he'd be a hero. But he saved our lives. He did it willingly. He made the choice to give his life for us."

They put a few wildflowers on the graves.

After the service Edilio took a can of black spray paint and began to paint over the "HC" tags that had appeared on too many storefronts.

THREE DAYS LATER

"**SO, HOW'S** IT going to work, Albert?" Sam asked. He wasn't as interested as he should be. Probably because he hadn't slept much yet. Too much to do. Too much to figure out.

He was done. He'd told them all: He was done. Done being *the* Sam Temple. From now on he was just a kid. Like any other. No longer *the* anything.

But not just yet. Right now there was still too much to do. Kids to feed. A terrible rift to be somehow patched up.

Memories of suffering that would have to be dealt with, somehow, absorbed, accepted.

They were at the edge of the cabbage field. Sam, Astrid, Albert, Edilio, and Quinn.

Quinn was standing in the bed of a pickup truck wearing tall rubber boots. In the truck were a dozen of Duck's famous blue bats. They kept being hauled in by Quinn and Albert's fishermen. Perfectly good protein, but so noxious, so foul that even the starving couldn't gag down the putrid meat.

"We disburse a given amount of gold to every kid," Albert was explaining. He at least was excited. "Then, if they want, they trade it for paper currency, the McDonald's game pieces. The gold is kept in a central deposit. They can come back and trade their paper currency for gold anytime they want. This is how they know the paper currency has lasting value."

"Uh-huh," Sam said for about the millionth time. He hid a yawn as well as he could.

In the three days since the horror in that cavern, Sam had been kept running. It was a game of whack-a-mole. One crisis after another.

They had found Zil. He had three broken ribs and was in terrible pain. No one felt very sorry for him. Astrid wanted him imprisoned. It might still happen. But Sam had too many other problems on his plate.

Fresh anti-freak graffiti continued to appear in Perdido Beach.

Mary was eating, but Astrid had warned him that that alone meant very little. Mary was a long way from being well.

The power plant was damaged, probably beyond repair. The lights were out everywhere now. Probably forever.

The FAYZ had gone dark.

But Jack was with them again, and maybe Jack could do penance by making things work again. He stood awkwardly near Brianna.

Dekka watched them and kept her silence.

"Let's do this," Sam said to Quinn. Then, to Astrid, "I'll bet you five 'Bertos this doesn't work."

Howard had dismissed Albert's list of names for the new currency and had dubbed them "Albertos." 'Bertos. The name had stuck. It was Howard's peculiar genius to invent names for things.

"I don't need money," Astrid said. "I need to cut your hair. I like seeing your face. Although I can't imagine why."

"Done." Sam shook her hand, sealing the bet.

"Ready?" Quinn called out.

"Orc, you ready?" Sam asked.

Orc nodded his head.

"Do it," Sam said.

Quinn lifted one of the blue bats and hurled it into the cabbage field. In a flash, the worms swarmed over it. In seconds it was just bones, like a turkey after a Thanksgiving feast.

"Okay, let's test this," Sam ordered.

Quinn tossed the second bat to Orc. Orc caught it and walked into the field. After a dozen steps, he tossed the blue bat ahead of him.

Again, the surge of worms. Again, the zekes reduced it to bones.

"Okay, Orc," Sam said.

Orc bent down and yanked up a cabbage.

He tossed it back to land at Sam's feet. A second and a third cabbage followed.

The zekes made no move toward Orc.

But they wouldn't be sure until the zekes were offered

something more easily digested than Orc's stone feet.

"Breeze?" Sam said.

Brianna hefted a bat and zipped into the field. Sam waited, tense, knowing she was faster than the worms, but still . . .

Brianna tossed the bat. The zekes hit it.

And Brianna ripped a cabbage from the ground.

"You know," Astrid said, "I seem to recall a certain condescending—one might even say contemptuous—response when I first suggested negotiating with the zekes."

"Huh," Sam said. "Who would ever be dumb enough to be condescending to you?"

"Oh, it was this bald guy I know."

Sam sighed. "Okay. Okay. Grab your scissors and do your worst."

"Actually," Astrid said, "there's something else you have to do first."

"Always something," Sam said gloomily.

Quinn joined them and apologized for stinking of fish.

"Brah, don't apologize. You're a very big part of keeping people from starving."

The other reason the danger of mass starvation had receded for a while, at least, was Hunter. He had recovered most of his function, although his speech seemed permanently slurred, and one eye drooped above a down-twisted mouth.

Hunter had been charged with killing Harry. He had been sentenced to exile from Perdido Beach. He would live apart from them, alone, but living up to the name his parents had given him.

So far, Hunter had killed a second deer and a number of smaller animals. He dropped them at the loading dock of Ralph's. He asked for nothing in return.

Dekka bent over and lifted one of the cabbages. "This would go great with some roasted pigeon."

Hunter's trial had been carried out by a jury of six kids, under rules set up by the Temporary Council: Sam, Astrid, Albert, Edilio, Dekka, Howard, and the youngest member, Brother John Terrafino.

"Well, back to work, huh?" Sam said.

"Get in the car," Astrid said.

"What are—"

"Let me rephrase. By order of the Temporary Council: get in the car."

She steadfastly refused to explain what was happening on the drive back to town. Edilio drove, and he was equally mum.

Edilio pulled up and parked in the town beach parking lot.

"Why are we going to the beach? I have to get back to town hall. I have, like, all this stuff—"

"Not now," Edilio said firmly.

Sam stopped walking. "What's up, Edilio?"

"I'm supposed to be the sheriff, right? That's my new title?" Edilio said. "Okay, then, you are under arrest."

"Under arrest? What are you talking about?"

"You are under arrest for trying to kill a kid named Sam Temple."

"Not funny."

But Edilio persisted. "Trying to kill a kid . . . just a *kid* . . .

named Sam Temple. By stressing him out with the whole load of the world on his back."

Sam didn't find it amusing. Angry, he turned back toward town. But there was Astrid, close on his heels. And Brianna. Quinn, too.

"What are you all up to?" Sam demanded.

"We voted," Astrid said. "It was unanimous. By order of the Perdido Beach Temporary Council, we sentence you, Sam Temple, to relax."

"Okay. I'm relaxed. Now can I get back to work?"

Astrid took his arm and all but hauled him across the beach. "You know what's interesting, Sam? I'll tell you what's interesting. A fairly small disturbance in deep water, creating a ripple, a surge, can become a pretty impressive wave as it nears shore."

Sam noticed that someone had set up a tent on the beach. It looked forlorn.

Out to sea, a boat putted by, its motor chugging in low gear.

"Is that Dekka out on the boat?" Sam asked.

They reached the tent. Lying in the sand there were two surfboards. Quinn's. And Sam's.

"Your wet suit's inside, brah," Quinn said.

Sam resisted. But not for long. After all, the council had authority now. And if they said he had to go surfing, well . . .

Ten minutes later Sam was facedown on his board. His feet were already tingling from the cold water. The sun was already baking his back through the wet suit. The taste of salt was in his mouth.

Out to sea, the boat had anchored. Dekka stood in the bow and raised her hands high. The water rose, rose, a big bulge of water temporarily released from the force of gravity.

Dekka let it drop, and the ripple fanned out.

"You even remember how to get up on that thing?" Quinn teased.

The ripple had become a wave. A fast-moving wave. It would break big. Not north shore Oahu big, maybe, but big enough for a ride.

Sam smiled at last. "You know, brah? I think it may just come back to me."

In a hole. Lightless. Soundless.

Not even the sound of a beating heart.

Nothing moved but the pale slug that shared this terrible place with her.

Pray for me, Tanner, Brittney begged.

Pray for me . . .

LIES

66 HOURS, **52** MINUTES

OBSCENE GRAFFITI.

Smashed windows.

Human Crew tags, their logo, along with warnings to freaks to get out.

In the distance, up the street, too far away for Sam to want to chase after, a couple of kids, maybe ten years old, maybe not even that. Barely visible in the false moonlight. Just outlines. The kids passing a bottle back and forth, taking swigs, staggering.

Grass growing everywhere. Weeds forcing their way up through cracks in the street. Trash: chip bags, six-pack rings, supermarket plastic bags, random sheets of paper, articles of clothing, single shoes, hamburger wrappers, broken toys, broken bottles, and crumpled cans—anything that wasn't actually edible—formed random, colorful collections. They were poignant reminders of better days.

Darkness so deep, you'd have had to walk off into the wilderness in the old days to experience anything like it.

Not a streetlight or a porch light. Electricity out. Maybe forever.

No one wasting batteries, not anymore. Those, too, were in very short supply.

And not many trying to burn candles or light trash fires. Not after the fire that burned down three homes and burned one kid so bad, it took Lana, the Healer, half a day to save him.

No water pressure. Nothing coming out of fire hydrants. Nothing to do about fire but watch it burn and get out of its way.

Perdido Beach, California.

At least it used to be California.

Now it was Perdido Beach, the FAYZ. Wherever, whatever, and whyever that was.

Sam had the power to make light. He could fire it in killing beams from his hands. Or he could form balls of persistent light that would hang in the air like a lantern. Like lightning in a bottle.

But not too many people wanted Sam's lights, what kids called Sammy Suns. Zil Sperry, leader of the Human Crew, had forbidden any of his people to take the lights. Most of the normals complied. And some freaks didn't want a bright advertisement of who and what they were.

The fear had spread. A disease. It leaped from person to person.

People sat in the dark, afraid. Always afraid.

Sam was in the east end, the dangerous part of town, the part Zil had declared off-limits to freaks. He had to show the flag, so to speak, demonstrate that he was still in charge. Show that he wouldn't be intimidated by Zil's campaign of fear.

Kids needed that. They needed to see that someone would still protect them. That someone was *him*.

He had resisted that role, but it had come to him, anyway. And he was determined to play it out. Whenever he let up, whenever he lost focus, tried to have a different life, something awful happened.

So he walked the streets at two in the morning, ready. Just in case.

Sam walked near the shore. There was no surf, of course. Not anymore. No weather. No vast swells crossing the Pacific to crash in magnificent showers of spray against Perdido's beaches.

The surf was just a soft whisper now. *Shhh. Shhh. Shhh.* Better than nothing. But not much better.

He was heading toward Clifftop, the hotel, Lana's current home. Zil had left her alone. Freak or not, no one messed with the Healer.

Clifftop was right up against the FAYZ wall, the end of Sam's area of responsibility, the last part of his walk-through.

Someone was walking down toward him. He tensed, fearing the worst. There was no question that Zil would like to see him dead. And out there—somewhere—Caine, his half brother. Caine had been helpful in destroying the gaiaphage and the psychopath Drake Merwin. But Sam didn't kid himself into believing that Caine had changed. If Caine was still alive, they would meet again.

And God knew what other horrors were out in that fading night—human or not. Out in the dark mountains, the black caves, the desert, the forest to the north. The too-calm ocean.

The FAYZ never let up.

But this just looked like a girl.

"It's just me, Sinder," a voice said, and Sam relaxed.

"T'sup, Sinder? Kind of late, huh?"

She was a sweet Goth girl who managed mostly to stay out of the various wars and factions raging within the FAYZ.

"I'm glad I ran into you," Sinder said. She had a steel pipe in one hand, the grip cushioned with duct tape. No one walked around without a weapon, especially at night.

"You okay? You eating?"

That had become the standard greeting. Not, "How are you?" But, "Are you eating?"

"Yeah, we're getting by," Sinder said. Her ghostly pale skin made her seem very young and vulnerable. Of course the pipe, the black fingernails, and the kitchen knife stuck in her belt made her seem not entirely gentle.

"Listen, Sam. I'm not someone who, like, you know, wants to tell on people, or whatever," Sinder said. Uncomfortable.

"I know that," he said. He waited.

"It's Orsay," Sinder said, and glanced over her shoulder, guilty. "You know, I talk to her sometimes. She's kind of cool, mostly. Kind of interesting."

"Yep."

"Mostly."

"Yeah."

"But, you know, weird maybe, too." Sinder made a wry grin. "Like I'm one to talk."

Sam waited. He heard the sound of a glass bottle shattering and high-pitched giggling from the distance behind him. The kids throwing their emptied bottle of booze. A boy named K. B. had been found dead with a bottle of vodka in his hand.

"Anyway, Orsay, she's at the wall."

"The wall?"

"On the beach, down by the wall. She's like, she thinks . . . Look, talk to her, okay? Just don't tell her I told you. Okay?"

"Is she down there now? It's, like, two A.M."

"That's when they do it. They don't want Zil or . . . or you, I guess, giving them a hard time. You know where the wall runs down from Clifftop to the beach? Those rocks out there? That's where she is. Not alone. Other kids are there, too."

Sam felt an unwelcome tingle running up his spine. He'd developed a pretty good instinct for trouble over the last few months. This felt like trouble.

"Okay, I'll check it out."

"Yah. Cool."

"'Night, Sinder. Take care."

He left her and continued walking, wondering what new craziness or danger lay ahead. He climbed the road up past

Clifftop. Glanced up at Lana's balcony.

Patrick, Lana's Labrador, must have heard him because he gave a short, sharp warning bark.

"Just me, Patrick," Sam said.

There were very few dogs or cats still alive in the FAYZ. The only reason Patrick had not ended up as dog stew was because he belonged to the Healer.

From the top of the cliff Sam looked down and thought he could make out several people on the rocks, right down in the surf that wasn't quite surf. They were big rocks, dangerous back in the days when Sam would take his board out there with Quinn and wait for a big one.

Sam didn't need light to scale down the cliff. He could have done it blind. In the old days he'd done it hauling all his gear.

As he reached the sand, he heard soft voices. One speaking. One crying.

The FAYZ wall, the impenetrable, impermeable, eye-baffling barrier that defined the boundaries of the FAYZ, glowed almost imperceptibly. Not even a glow, really, a suggestion of translucence. Gray and blank.

A small bonfire burned on the beach, casting a faint orange light over a small circle of sand and rock and water.

No one noticed Sam as he approached. So he had time to identify most of the half-dozen kids out there. Francis, Cigar, D-Con, a few others, and Orsay herself.

"I have seen something . . . ," Orsay began.